ONLY THIS SIN
WOULD SATISFY HER

Young Roger Haggard lay in bed enjoying the afterglow of the pleasure he had dreamed of for so long. His entire body throbbed with the memory of it, and his very soul swelled in gratitude to the woman beside him.

"Marry me," he whispered. "Say that you will."

He heard low, throaty laughter.

"I can't marry you, silly. But if you wish it, we can tumble like this whenever you are at home."

"At home?" he said uncomprehendingly.

"I spend all my time there. And it is a dismal place, with only your father for company . . ."

And now Roger knew who this woman was. Alison. The stepmother who had tormented his senses. And now his treacherous guide into hell. . . .

HAGGARD

SIGNET Books You'll Enjoy

HAGGARD

By

Christopher Nicole

A SIGNET BOOK

NEW AMERICAN LIBRARY

TIMES MIRROR

PUBLISHER'S NOTE

This novel is a work of fiction. Names, characters, places, and incidents are either the product of the author's imagination or are used fictitiously, and any resemblance to actual persons, living or dead, events, or locales is entirely coincidental.

Copyright © Christopher Nicole 1980

Ⓢ SIGNET TRADEMARK REG. U.S. PAT. OFF. AND FOREIGN COUNTRIES
REGISTERED TRADEMARK—MARCA REGISTRADA
HECHO EN CHICAGO, U.S.A.

SIGNET, SIGNET CLASSICS, MENTOR, PLUME, MERIDIAN AND NAL BOOKS are published by The New American Library, Inc., 1633 Broadway, New York, New York 10019

First Printing, August, 1980

1 2 3 4 5 6 7 8 9

PRINTED IN THE UNITED STATES OF AMERICA

HAGGARD

BOOK ONE

The Father

Chapter 1

The Planter

"Haggard," chanted the men. "Haggard, Haggard, Haggard."

They formed a circle in the center of the highly polished parquet which up to a few minutes ago had served as a dance floor. Even with the great French windows wide to allow the trade wind to sweep into the plantation house, the Barbadian evening was close, and the men's faces, reddened at once by the sun which was their daily enemy and the drink which poisoned them at night, gleamed with sweat; white cravats had been pulled loose and lay damply against dripping throats; black tailcoats clung to perspiring shoulders as if there was no layer of cambric between.

And now they clapped, as one of their number stepped into the center of the ring, a sword in his hand. He was in his middle twenties, his hair black and lank, his body tall and muscular. His face was aquiline, robbed of handsomeness by the long nose and the jutting chin, saved from ugliness by the high forehead and the wide mouth, rendered interesting and a little disturbing by the intensity of the pale blue eyes. He settled his dancing pumps as well as he could on the slippery floor, tilted his head back to gaze above him at the glowing chandelier that hung from the high ceiling. He felt in his pocket, found a silver coin, and carefully placed this on his chin. Then, with even more care, holding the sword in both hands, he raised it above his head and brought the point slowly down to rest on the coin.

"Haggard," chanted the onlookers.

"How absurd," commented one of the ladies seated against the wall.

"They're drunk," remarked another.

"But how stupid, to risk disfigurement over a wager," said a third.

"I wonder what the blacks think of it."

Adelaide Bolton glanced at the red-liveried menservants

3

standing impassively against the far wall, their trays of sangaree poised, waiting to circulate the moment the excitement was over, and beyond them, at the orchestra, free black men from the capital town of Bridgetown, still sweating from their last endeavors, also watching the white men at play, and waiting. She knew that in the darkness beyond the French windows, where the fireflies winked and the sandflies seethed, there would be several hundred more black people, peering into the lighted house, enjoying as vicariously as they could their masters' and mistresses' pleasures. What did they think of it all?

But then, what did *she* think of it all? She was a slight young woman, twenty-three years of age. Her pale brown hair was rendered almost white by the powder which clustered over the carefully dressed rolls that descended to either side of her ears. Despite the difficulties presented by the revolting American colonists, the Boltons were among the leading Barbadian planters—as they exemplified by throwing such a ball as this—and the daughter of the house must display the latest fashion. Thus her gown, ballooning over its hoop, was in pink silk, as was her bodice, tightly constricted by the corset beneath, and her underskirt; her embroidery, a sprig pattern, was in grass green, matched by her fan, and there was a gold necklace round her throat. Her clothes enhanced the essential plainness of her features, the sallowness of her creole complexion, just as the corset did little to enlarge the small white breasts thrust high enough almost to touch her throat. But she was the most attractive girl in the room. Looks had very little to do with it, as few girls born and bred in the heat and humidity of the West Indies could be described as beautiful. Here was wealth and breeding and confidence, and purpose, too, as she regarded Haggard, watched the sword point come to rest in the center of the coin, watched his hands slowly leave the blade.

"He has courage," she murmured. "No one can deny that."

The room was so silent her soft voice almost reached the slowly circling man.

"So does Malcolm," objected Annette Manning, beside her. "He did it first."

There was a gasp from the onlookers as the sword appeared about to slip, but Haggard, eyes wide, face rigid with concentration, regained its and his balance immediately.

"Two of a kind," Adelaide Bolton observed, watching her brother. Of course the idea of the madcap wager had been his. No one else had quite such a devilish mind, such a will to self-destruction, as Malcolm Bolton. But Haggard was the only man to have taken him up. Haggard! Two years a widower now, and not a prospective bride in sight. Not even a flirtation. Of course he would not be every woman's choice, save for his money. John Haggard was reputed to be the wealthiest planter in Barbados, and that made him the wealthiest planter in all the West Indies, and that in turn made him one of the wealthiest men in the entire world. And he was attractive, no denying that. And every inch a man. But he was not like her other friends. For one thing, he had not had a proper education. Old Roger Haggard had had peculiar ideas, and instead of sending his son to England, to Eton and then Oxford, had kept him in Barbados, and imported a governess and then a tutor.

This Adelaide did not consider only a social weakness, although, money or no, it would be a considerable sacrifice for any girl to tie herself for life to a man who had never been to Drury Lane or walked in Vauxhall Gardens, had never danced at Almack's or read the latest novel. More important was the insularity which clouded Haggard's outlook. He regarded Barbados as the richest island in the world—with some justification, in terms of wealth per head of property-owning gentlemen—and as he topped that mound of wealth was not even disposed to regard the king as greatly his superior.

And then he *was* a widower, and Susan Haggard had been one of those very rare birds, a beautiful West Indian. Nor as mistress of Haggard's. While all Barbados gossiped about could anyone who had seen them together doubt that genuineness of his love for her, which had often been displayed with an extravagance disturbing to the rigidly ruled propriety of the planting community. She would be difficult to follow what an odd fellow her husband had become, how the deaths, in rapid succession, of his father and his wife, which had pitchforked him into wealth and power at twenty-three, a dozen years before he should have been forced to accept such responsibility, had had an adverse effect on his personality. How he drank too much and was given to moods of black depression, when he would strike his best friend. How, at the same time, and quite incredibly, he was far too lenient a master—almost a Quaker, Papa Bolton called him—who used the lash sparingly and had been known to shake a slave by the hand. Such points of view only encouraged the blacks to ideas above their stations—again Papa Bolton. But a point of view which could be changed by a loving and forceful wife.

"Ten seconds," shouted fat Billy Ferguson, Haggard's head bookkeeper, who was timekeeper for this occasion. "Enough, John, enough."

Haggard jerked his head away from the gleaming sword point and caught the blade as the weapon came down. He smiled, an unholy widening of the gash of a mouth. "Well, Malcolm?"

"The horse is yours." Malcolm Bolton's mouth resembled a steel trap.

"Then give me your hand on it," Haggard said.

Bolton hesitated, glanced from left to right at the men around him, then extended his hand, had it tightly gripped.

"It was only a wager," Haggard said gently.

"And well won it was," said Papa Bolton. "Sangaree for these bold lads. By God, sir, but we lacked such temerity in my youth."

The men were lost to sight as their friends crowded round, to congratulate Haggard, to commiserate with Bolton. Adelaide Bolton raised her fan, and the Negro butler hurried over, to stoop beside her chair.

"Tell them to recommence playing," Adelaide said. "Now that the men have had their sport."

"Yes, ma'am, Miss Adelaide." He hurried off again.

"You have a gleam in your eye," Annette Manning suggested.

"I was but considering masculine stupidity."

"You were considering the sound of 'Adelaide Haggard.' "

Adelaide glanced at her, mentally cursing the flush she could feel in her cheeks. Sometimes best friends were worst enemies. But why, she wondered, take offense at the truth? It had been in prospect for some time, however little Haggard seemed aware of it. But only Haggard's was superior to Bolton's. Unite the two—supposing John Haggard and Malcolm Bolton could ever agree to work together. But the next generation, the generation of her children . . . Her flush deepend, and she got up to prevent Annette noticing. Adelaide Haggard. If he could ever be convinced that was what he really wanted, really needed. But all it required was courage, and opportunity. Both had been lacking until now. But surely opportunity would never be more available. As for courage . . . She squared her shoulders as the music started, moved toward the men, seized her brother by the arm as he would have left the throng.

"Visit me in the summerhouse in ten minutes." She spoke softly.

"Eh? Really, Addy, I am not in the mood for games."

"No game, Mal. But ten minutes. Not a second sooner." She released him, found herself surrounded by black-coated young men, like a swarm of bees, she supposed.

"My dance, Adelaide."

"No, mine, Miss Bolton."

"Miss Bolton, you promised . . ."

"To the victor the spoils, surely," she said, keeping her temper under control. The lout had not even looked at her, had continued drinking an entire tumbler of sangaree.

But he looked at her now, replacing the glass on the tray held at his elbow and immediately taking another.

"Do you not agree, John?" she asked, keeping her tone seductive.

"I'll tread on your toes," he pointed out. "I'm shaking like a babe." He drank half of the second glass.

"You, John Haggard? Afraid?"

"Of a sword through the throat? Oh, I was afraid, Addy. I'm just about to recover, with the help of this good fellow." The slave had three tumblers left on the tray.

"You'll fall down," she pointed out. "And I said nothing of dancing." She took the half-empty glass from his hand, placed it on the tray, linked her arm through his. "A walk in the cool will do you more good than all of that wine."

Haggard seemed about to scratch his head with his free hand, but changed his mind. "I had never suspected such *decision*, Addy," he said banteringly. But he allowed himself to be carried along toward the open door, while behind them the room filled with dancing couples.

"Don't you suppose a woman is capable of decision?"

"I'm sure she is. It is merely beyond my experience." He stood on the terrace, inhaled deeply, honeysuckle and night-blooming jasmine, gently disengaged himself. "You are right. Fresh air. There's the ticket. And I *was* afraid, you know."

"But you did it anyway. That is true courage."

He glanced at her and frowned. "Decision, and flattery. Whatever next?"

"Or did you only wish to get the better of Mal? Why must you two always rival each other?"

Haggard shrugged. "Because we are rivals, I suppose. At planting, at horse racing, at the mere business of being men."

"Men." She walked down the steps. She was placing her faith entirely in the fact that whatever his moods, however odd some of his attitudes, Haggard was a gentleman. Thus he would surely follow. And after a moment he did. She allowed herself a sigh of relief. "I think you did it because you do not really care whether you win or lose, live or die."

"Decision, and flattery, and perception. I feel as if, having regarded a closed book for several years, I have suddenly opened the first page."

Still she led him into the darkness, between the hibiscus hedges which bordered the lawn. "Now *you* are flattering *me*. It is merely that we are such good friends, have been such friends for so long, that I worry about you. I think of you, sitting all alone in that great house . . ."

"All alone?" Haggard gave a brief laugh. "There are forty-three house slaves . . ."

"Oh, bah. You cannot possibly count slaves as company."

". . . together with fifty-seven bookkeepers and their wives and children."

They had reached the door to the summerhouse. Adelaide went inside.

"I do believe you say things like that just to irritate me. How can a planter be friends with his bookkeepers?"

"Because most of them are very good fellows. As you must think, or you would not have them here tonight."

Adelaide seated herself on the bench which ran round the inner wall of the small wooden building. "One must have more men than women at a ball, John Haggard, and you know that as well as I. Will you not sit down?"

Haggard sat beside her. "I am feeling better already. And Flyaway is a fine stallion. Worth risking a scar for. Although I suspect poor Mal will never forgive me."

"I did not bring you out here to talk about Mal. John . . ." She chewed her lower lip in sudden nervousness. "I do think about you, a great deal of the time."

"Whatever for?"

"Oh, John . . . because I love you, you silly great lout. There." She peered into the gloom, but could not see his face. And he had not moved. "John," she said desperately, "I love you." She seized his hands, waited for the fingers to close on hers, and when they would not, brought them against the bodice of her gown. "John Haggard, you must have some feeling for me."

"Indeed I do." Haggard's knuckles rested against the pushed-up softness of her breasts. "I think you are a jolly good sport, Addy. But you are too serious to make a good mistress."

"Mistress?" she shouted, throwing his hands away. "I have no intention of being anyone's mistress."

"And I have no intention of marrying again. Ever. So I would say we had best end this farce right away and get back to the dancing."

"Why, you . . ." She glared at him in the darkness, her brain consumed by a raging fury. "You unutterable cad."

Haggard stood up and gave her a brief bow. "Your servant, Miss Bolton." He turned to the door, watched Malcolm Bolton hurrying along the path. "Ah," he commented. "A plot." His voice remained soft, gave no indication of his sudden anger.

"Plot?" Malcolm came up to the doorway. "I heard Addy cry out. Whatever has happened, Addy?"

"He . . ." Adelaide sucked air into her lungs noisily. "He assaulted me."

"He did *what?*"

"Your sister is a hysterical liar," Haggard said, speaking very evenly, although his mind had already seethed into the black rage which left him wishing to hurt, and hurt. These people had made it plain to him, often enough during their youth, that they regarded him as an ill-educated lout. While at his wedding, with Sue still on his arm, incredibly lovely, incredibly willing to love him, he had heard Adelaide Bolton whispering to her friend Annette Manning, "What a waste of a beautiful woman. She must love money even more than we, my dear Annette." And now *she* would fill those irreplaceable shoes? "With the instincts of a whore. I will bid you good night."

He stepped past the momentarily dumbfounded young man onto the path.

Malcolm caught his breath. "Stop right there," he commanded.

Haggard stopped, half-turned.

"You'll apologize, sir," Malcolm Bolton demanded. "On your knees, you'll apologize for those words."

"I have never apologized in my life," Haggard pointed out. "And certainly I shall never do so for speaking the truth."

"Then you'll answer to me, John Haggard."

"Don't be more of a fool than your sister, Mal. Go to bed and sleep it off."

Once again Haggard turned, and walked toward the house.

"Stop," Malcolm bawled. "Stop," he screamed.

Haggard ignored him, walked up the steps and into the suddenly overheated ballroom. He caught Willy Ferguson's eye, and the overseer hastily apologized to his dancing partner and hurried toward his employer.

"I shall be going home now, Willy," Haggard said. "But you and the others stay to the end."

Willy frowned at him. "Is something the matter?"

"Probably not." Haggard walked toward the head of the room, where the senior Boltons were sitting with the guests in their own age group. But he had not reached them when there was a shout from the doors to the terrace.

"Haggard."

The music had just stopped, the dancers were about to leave the floor. Now they paused, and looked toward the door, and gasped in unison. Malcolm Bolton stood there, the sword which had so recently been the cause of the wager held in his right hand, the arm itself extended to point at Haggard.

"You'll apologize." Malcolm's nostrils dilated. "Or I'll kill you."

"With that?" Haggard inquired softly. But the couple standing closest to him, and able to see something of the expression in his eyes, backed away.

"Malcolm." Papa Bolton was on his feet. "John. What nonsense is this?"

Malcolm Bolton came closer. "He has insulted Addy."

"John?" Bolton inquired, frowning.

"He called her a liar, and a . . . a whore," Malcolm said.

There was another gasp, and a woman pretended to faint.

"John?" Papa Bolton's voice was an octave higher.

"That is correct, sir," Haggard said. "I called your daughter a liar, because she had just told a lie, and accused her of having the instincts of a whore, because she had just revealed them." Once again he spoke very clearly and distinctly.

"My God," Papa Bolton said.

"You'll leave this house, John Haggard," cried his wife. "Do not ever come back."

Haggard bowed in her direction. "I had that in mind, Mrs. Bolton. I will bid you good night."

"You . . . you'll just let him go?" Malcolm Bolton shouted. "You'll answer to me, you lout."

"Don't be a fool," Haggard said. "I could blow out your left eye while you were still leveling your pistol."

"Ha," Malcolm said. "I doubt you are as good as you pretend, John Haggard. I'll have satisfaction or brand you a coward from here to Jamaica."

Haggard gazed at him for some seconds, then shrugged. "I will need a second," he said, glancing around his fellow planters, and hardening his expression as he saw them turning away. He knew he was hated as much as he was envied, as much as he was feared.

"If Mr. Bolton will permit me." Willy Ferguson gallantly stepped to the support of his master.

"I am sure he will be delighted," Haggard said. "You'll inform me of the arrangements in due course, I have no doubt. You . . ." His hand came up, the forefinger outstretched, to point at one of the Bolton slaves. "You've a horse in your stable called Flyaway. He belongs to me. Have him sent over to Haggard's in the morning. And have my mare saddled. Mrs. Bolton, I apologize to you for spoiling your ball. The fault was not mine."

He turned and walked from the room, while behind him the buzz of conversation suddenly boomed into the night.

Haggard walked Calliope along the beaten earth road, enjoying the cool of the evening, tricorne tilted back on his head. His brain was clear; he might have been drunk when he accepted Malcolm's foolish wager, but he was sober now. And angry. It was an anger he knew well, a deep-hearted resentment which he could neither understand nor combat. Nor expect anyone else to understand. He was John Haggard. He was enormously rich, utterly healthy, had normally no more cares in the world than which of the thousands of acres he planted should be inspected on the morrow. And yet, for three years now he had seemed pursued by a malevolent fate, as if nature or God—he belonged to that rationalizing group which doubted—had said that man has enough, make him suffer.

On his wedding night, five years ago, there could have been no happier man in all the world. His father had still been young and healthy, so that the burdens of plantation management lay a long way in his future, he held in his arms the loveliest girl in all the West Indies, and a girl who loved him, and the American problem, then, had seemed no more than a colonial quarrel which could affect the lives of no one in Barbados.

But that had been before Lexington and Bunker Hill, Burgoyne and Saratoga. It had been before the yellow-fever epidemic which had struck down Father in the prime of his life. It had been before Sue's pregnancy, and the resulting puerperal fever. All *that* had happened in a single year, at the end of which he had supposed himself damned. And yet, he had continued to be Haggard, to act the part to which he had been born, because he knew no other.

So now he must kill a man. Or be killed. The decision was his. But Malcolm Bolton was a good, if slow shot. If he was not brought down before he could aim, he would hit his target.

It might have been better to marry the whore. But Adelaide Bolton in Sue's bed, lying in his arms? Adelaide Bolton presiding over Haggard's dinner table? Adelaide Bolton at his side for the rest of his life? He could feel the anger building in his belly. Against all women, but against Adelaide Bolton as the representative of her sex. He hated them all. Illogically, as he recognized. But they were there, strutting the streets of Bridgetown, whirling across the Boltons' dance floor, engaging in their feminine conspiracies and flirtations. While Sue was dead, nothing but bones in the coffin which lay in the Haggard vault, on the hillock a mile from the great house.

And now, with their conspiracies, they had forced him to kill or be killed.

Dogs barked, and the mastiffs frisked about the mare, who ignored them, as she knew them so well. Haggard had in fact been riding across his own land for some time, but now he was approaching the town. For Haggard's Penn was a town. Beyond the wide wooden gateway through which the moonlight streamed there was a pleasant pasture, watered by a little stream, and providing grazing for a herd of cows. The estate buildings were half a mile farther on. To the right of the drive was first the circular, many-arched sugar house, and then the boiling house, dominated by the tall, square chimney, now silent like a monument, as the cane was not yet fully ripe, and beyond that the slave logies, arranged in orderly rows, each backed by its own carefully cultivated vegetable garden. To the left of the drive waited the houses of the European staff, and the chapel, every one whitewashed and with a substantial red shingled roof to keep off the annual rainstorms brought by the hurricane winds of the early autumn.

Farther off yet, set half a mile from the nearest other habitation, was the great house. The Haggards had planted in Barbados for over a hundred and fifty years, coming to the islands in the very early days of the colony when the Courteens and the Willoughbys had still been debating ownership. Thus the house retained traces of its less secure heritage in the massive stone cellars which formed its foundation, loopholed as a last refuge for the family and their retainers against revolting slave or marauding pirate. Above, the great windows and the wide-open doors gleamed with light, for Middlesex lit every candle every night for all that only the master and his infant son actually lived in the house. But every window and every door was also guarded by a thick shutter. Nowadays these acted as protection against hurricane winds, but they too suggested a stormy past.

The gamboling dogs had alerted the watchmen, and they hurried forward to escort their master, seven of them, big black men armed with nightsticks, and happy to see their favorite white man. Whatever Haggard's dark moods, he seldom directed them at his own people.

"Man, Mr. John, but you home early."

"Man, Mr. John, but it ain't midnight yet."

"Man, Mr. John, but them white people ain't still dancing?"

They reached the foot of the steps leading up to the veranda, and Haggard swung himself from the saddle.

"They're still dancing," he said. "Abraham, I wish you to saddle up and ride into Bridgetown. Fetch me Mr. Lucas."

"Eh-eh? But he going be happy to come out this time, Mr. John?"

"You tell him I want him here before dawn. Tell him it is an urgent matter." Haggard climbed the stairs, confronted James Middlesex, his butler. It had been his father's fancy to name all the house slaves after English counties.

"Mr. John?" Middlesex peered at him. "I going fetch the port."

"Not tonight, James. The boy asleep?"

"Oh, yes, man, Mr. John." But Middlesex frowned. Haggard seldom inquired after his son. Enough that the boy's life had been purchased at the expense of his mother's.

Haggard walked into the hallway. He had not bothered to

replace his pumps with boots, and his feet did no more than whisper on the polished mahogany floor. But even the whisper echoed. The hall was some thirty feet deep and rose twenty feet above his head. The walls were hung with pictures of past Haggards, the stands filled with walking sticks and sporting guns and hats; Haggard added his to the collection. To his right, archways gave into the withdrawing room, another vast area of polished floors and uncomfortable chairs and low incidental tables laden with brass ornaments. The smoking room, shrouded in netting to repel mosquitoes, lay beyond; here were the billiards table and the baize-topped card table, as well as the deep trays for cigar ash. On his left a similar archway allowed access to the dining room, equally large, but almost filled by the mahogany dining table and its accompanying sideboards, and sparkling with the array of silver trays and crystal glasses and decanters which filled the polished surfaces. Beyond the dining room were the pantries, and then the kitchen, built away from the house proper to lower the risk of a disastrous fire commencing in the huge wood-fed ranges, and connected with the main building by a covered corridor.

Immediately in front of Haggard waited the main staircase which led up to the galleries above his head, off which opened the dozen bedrooms. He walked toward this, pausing at the foot. "John Essex," he said.

"Yes, sir, Mr. John."

All of the footmen had gathered beyond the stairs, by the red velvet curtain which allowed access to the back of the house, the offices and the rear staircase, and the other entrance to the pantries. Now one of them came forward.

"Prime my pistols and set up a target, John Essex."

"Yes, sir, Mr. John."

Haggard continued his climb, turned to his left at the top, made his way toward the nursery. Here was unfamiliar territory; he seldom saw his son other than for a good-night kiss on the forehead. He opened the door, and immediately Amelia the nurse sat up from her bed against the wall.

"Who is there?" she demanded, blinking at the flickering candle.

"Hush. You'll wake the boy."

"Eh-eh, but is it the master?" Amelia inquired at large. She still counted her good fortune. Four years ago she had been a field slave, but she had been the only girl to have lost a child in the week Susan Haggard had died, and so had been brought into the house. She had ceased feeding the little boy two years ago, but her position as nurse was not in doubt; she was the only person on the entire plantation could quell Roger Haggard's bellowing when he chose to reveal the famous Haggard temper.

Now she threw back the coverlet, and hurried before her master to open the inner door. Conscious of her recent authority, she wore a white linen nightdress which undulated across her fat buttocks.

Haggard stood in the doorway, looked at the cot and the boy who lay there. In a few hours' time, he thought, there will be the last Haggard in all the world. Perhaps. I wonder what he will make of it all?

"You want for kiss he, Mr. John?"

"Tomorrow," Haggard said. Whenever tomorrow comes. He turned, left the room and a sorely puzzled Amelia, and went down the stairs. The footmen still waited, marshaled by Middlesex. They could sense that this was not as other nights. For one thing, their master had returned from a ball sober.

"Go to bed," he said. "All of you. But call me at five, James."

"Yes, sir, Mr. John."

But still they waited, while he went through the curtain and down the lower staircase to the cellars. Here a wide corridor allowed access to the storerooms, of meat and wine, of ice—brought in specially sawdust-packed containers all the way from the Labrador coast—of arms and ammunition. At the far end two cellars had been knocked together to make one large room, some twenty-five yards across. Here there was a counter immediately inside the door, on which there lay six pistols. The candles lining the wall had been lit, and at the far end there waited the wooden figure of a man. John Essex stood by the door.

Haggard took his position at the counter. He inhaled slowly, grasped the first pistol, raised and sighted, squeezed the trigger, laid it down and picked up the second, raised and sighted, and squeezed the trigger, and moved on to the third. The six explosions seemed to merge into one, the entire cellar became a rumbling echo shrouded in black smoke that left him coughing. As Haggard laid down the last pistol, John Essex hurried forward to examine the target.

"Four in the chest, Mr. John. One in the shoulder. And one gone."

Haggard nodded. There was no one in Barbados able to improve on that accuracy. He practiced every day. Not with any idea of dueling in mind. He had in fact but exchanged fire once in his life, five years ago, and then he had killed his man entirely by accident. That had been enough to give him a reputation. But practice was necessary, because for all the present tranquillity of Barbados, the obvious contentment of his own slaves, in a planting society one could never tell when the contagion of revolt would spring up and spread like a brushfire, involving all with the business of survival. Yet it was reassuring to discover that his hand was as steady as ever. Only his mind, his will, mattered now.

He left John Essex to set up another target, climbed the stairs, met Ferguson in the hall.

"Well?"

"You are challenged. I chose pistols, at six."

"There's an early hour. You'll call the morning briefing for five."

Ferguson frowned at him. "You'll brief today?"

"Today, is it? My God. Of course I'll brief today, Willy. It is a day like any other. Where is this exchange?"

"On the hill between the two plantations."

"Reasonable. All right, Willy. Get some sleep."

"And you?"

"Come to me at five."

Haggard went into the office, sat in his swivel chair before the enormous rolltop desk in which were kept the Haggard accounts going back to the very first shipment of sugar in 1671. He leaned back, closed his eyes. Only my will, he thought. To take a man's life, coldly and deliberately. And a man with whom I have drunk and played polo and gambled. A friend. No, he supposed that was wrong. He had never been a friend of Malcolm Bolton's. Malcolm was too consumed with jealous ambition.

He awoke with a start as the door opened, surprised that he had slept at all. But the air was cool with the promise of dawn.

"Mr. Lucas does be here, Mr. John," Middlesex said.

"Harry. Good of you to come." Haggard stood up, stretched his stiff arms.

The lawyer peered at him. "What's happened? It had better be important."

"It is important. I'm to fight a duel in a couple of hours."

"A duel? My God." Harry Lucas sat down in the one other chair in the room. "Who with?"

"Malcolm Bolton."

"Oh, my God. Whatever for?"

"A matter of honor."

"Which can surely be resolved?"

"I doubt it. Anyway, I cannot take the risk." Haggard sat down again. "You will be my executor."

"I had not anticipated the possibility so soon. The boy . . ."

"That's why you're here. You, and you alone, will control his upbringing."

"But . . . what of Susan's people?"

"Jamaicans. I'll not have it. You, Harry. A governess, here, until he is eight, then England and Eton. Make no mistake, now. Willy Ferguson will manage the plantation."

Lucas found a handkerchief to wipe sweat from his brow. "Yes, well, it may not happen. One exchange . . ."

"Is usually sufficient where two good shots are involved. Don't fail me in this, Harry, or by God, I'll haunt you."

"I'll not fail you, John. But—"

"Then let's get on with it." Haggard opened the door, went into the hall. Ferguson was just entering the front door. "Five o'clock?"

"The staff is waiting."

Haggard nodded, went on to the veranda. The faintest tinge of gray was diluting the black, and the air was now distinctly chill. At the foot of the steps the trestle table had been erected as usual, and the lanterns gleamed. The forty-odd bookkeepers stood around, waiting for their master.

"Good morning, John."

"Good morning, John."

These from the senior hands who had known him as a boy.

"Good morning, Mr. Haggard."

"Good morning, Mr. Haggard."

These the recent arrivals.

"Good morning." Haggard stood against the table, looked at the huge plan of the plantation extended there, held down by a lantern at each corner. He reflected for a moment, then tapped two of the grid squares into which the map was divided. "Northwest three and four. Weeding parties."

"Northwest three and four." Ferguson made notes.

"The parallel road, surfacing."

Ferguson wrote busily.

"The sugar house. Time to commence fumigation."

Ferguson nodded.

Haggard continued to study the map. His mind seemed unusually clear this morning, as if he could foresee the future, the way the war would go, the measures that would need to be taken.

"How many acres have we under cane?"

"Five thousand," Ferguson said.

"And under corn?"

"Two hundred and fifty."

"I want a further twelve hundred acres diverted to maize after next grinding."

"Twelve hundred acres under corn?" Ferguson was incredulous. "It'll halve your profit."

"My profit can stand it. Lay in the grain, Willy. Today. Thank you, gentlemen."

The overseers hesitated, exchanging glances. Then their senior, Arthur Prentice, stepped forward.

"Good fortune, John."

"Thank you. Thank you all." He turned to Ferguson. "Punishments?"

Ferguson snapped his fingers and the three black men hitherto waiting in the darkness were brought forward by six of the Negro drivers.

"Yes?"

"Jonah Seven, stealing from Peter Four."

It had long been Haggard practice to give numbers as well as names to their field slaves, for ease of indentification.

"This had been proved?"

"He was caught red-handed, Mr. Haggard."

"Six lashes."

"Yes, sir, Mr. Haggard." Ferguson made a note.

"I thank you, Mr. John," Jonah Seven said. He knew that on any other plantation his sentence would have been triple that.

"David Eight, fighting with Judas Three."

"Again, David Eight? A month's loss of privileges. Next."

"Cain Seven, troubling Martha Three."

"Troubling? Are you there, Martha?"

"I am here, Mr. Haggard. He jumping on me every time. I got man, Mr. Haggard. I got Abraham Three. And I happy. But this Cain, he does be bigger than Abraham."

"You're a lecherous rogue, Cain," Haggard said. "Bind up his cock for twenty-four hours so that he cannot pee. You'd best saddle up, Abraham Two."

"I got them here, Mr. John."

Haggard went back up the steps. Lucas still waited there.

"No nerves?"

"I'm shaking like a babe." He held out his hand. "Come and dine tonight. No matter what happens."

Lucas sighed, and nodded. James Middlesex waited with a tray and a glass.

"Brandy, Mr. John. It is the best."

"I'm sure you're right." Haggard drank deeply, replaced the glass. "Ready, Willy?"

"Will you not change?"

Haggard looked down at his evening suit. And shrugged. "It's dark. Tonight, Harry. You'll not forget that."

"I'll be here."

Haggard went down the steps, mounted, but waited as he heard hooves. Even in the gloom he could recognize the gray horse.

"Good morning to you, Reverend."

The Reverend Paley was still panting with the exertion of his ride. "John Haggard," he gasped. "You'll cease this madness."

"Are you from Bolton's?"

"Indirectly." He brought his horse close to Haggard's mare, and she backed off, giving a nervous whinny. "You are at fault."

"I'd argue that, if I had the time. You'll excuse me."

"You insulted Adelaide."

"I reminded her of what she was, Mr. Paley."

"And it will be murder."

"I pointed that out at the time, also."

"Then apologize, John. Surely to God you can do that. No one in Barbados is going to accuse *you* of cowardice."

"Mr. Paley," Haggard said, slowing his speech to those even tones which indicated his anger, "my father, before he died, made me promise him three things. One, always to remember that I am a Haggard. Two, always to tell the truth. Three, never to turn my back on any man. You are asking me to break each and every one of those oaths. Now, stand aside, sir, or I'll ride you down."

Paley pulled his mount out of the way. "They'll hate you," he shouted. "All Barbados will hate you, now and forever."

"They hate me already, Mr. Paley." Haggard touched his mare's side with his heel and walked away from the house.

● ● ●

Anger, bubbling deep in his belly. Never fight a duel while angry. Some more advice from Father, on the previous occasion. Then Roger Haggard Senior had himself acted as second. Then he had not been alone. Well, he was not alone now. Faithful Willy Ferguson rode at his heels. But he was the only Haggard. Save for a four-year-old boy.

They would hate him. As he hated them. Because he was Haggard, he was condemned, before a word could be spoken in his defense. But then, he reflected, they would have hated me had I surrendered to blackmail and married Adelaide Bolton.

To either side the nearly ripe cane stalks, standing ten feet tall, rustled in the dawn breeze, but now the ground was rising. Only half a mile farther on was the hillock which marked the end of his property, and the beginning of Bolton's, and there already were four men. Even in the half-light he recognized them: Malcolm Bolton; Jeremy Campkin, who would be his second; old Peter Woodbury, the senior planter on the island, who would be the umpire; and Dr. Meade, who looked after the health of both the Haggard and Bolton families.

"Gentlemen." Haggard made to raise his hat and discovered that he had forgotten to put one on.

"Haggard." Woodbury came up to him as he dismounted. "In the name of heaven, call an end to it."

"I am willing to accept an apology, Peter."

"You'll accept an apology. My God." Woodbury turned and walked back to the waiting men.

"John . . ." Tom Meade hesitated.

"We'd best be at it," Haggard said.

"You'll inspect these, if you please, Mr. Campkin." Willy opened the pistol case, and Campkin held the weapons up to the light, peered at the priming, one after the other. Haggard glanced at Malcolm Bolton, but his rival preferred to look away.

"For the last time, gentlemen," Woodbury said.

"No," Bolton said.

Woodbury sighed. "Then take your places. You know the rules. And so help me, should any man raise his arm before I give the word, I'll shoot him down." He took a fowling piece from his saddle holster to prove the truth of his words.

Haggard stepped forward into the center of the meadow. Willy handed him one of the pistols, and he let it hang at his side, at the end of his fingers. A moment later he felt a touch on his shoulder blades and knew that Bolton stood behind him.

"Commence," Woodbury said. "Even paces. One, two . . ."

The breeze played on Haggard's face, began to dry his sweat. Or was it, now that he actually held the pistol in his hand, he was no longer afraid?

"Three, four . . ."

His foot scuffed on a clod of earth, but he kept his balance. So, now, an act of will. He could aim and fire faster than Malcolm Bolton. If he wished.

"Five, six . . ."

But he must aim to kill, or Bolton would bring him down. He would be branded murderer. But the alternative was to die himself. To join Susan, the reverend would say. But he had no faith in a hereafter for a slave owner. And a Haggard.

"Seven, eight . . ."

So what would he do? What must he do?

"Nine, ten. Turn and fire."

Haggard turned quickly. His right arm was raising even as he did so. He gazed at Malcolm Bolton's face, just visible in the first light, pale and determined, and angry. Well, no doubt his own face looked no different.

His hand was extended; Bolton's was just starting to move. The pistol was absolutely steady as he looked down it, and his fingers were squeezing, instinctively, coldly, without even his will behind them. The explosion surprised him, and the powder smoke clouded into his face and made him cough. But he stood still, as he must, to receive fire. Supposing there would be any. Malcolm Bolton was on his knees, his face a picture of concern, his coat front an explosion of dripping red. For a moment longer he tried to raise his weapon, then fell on his face.

Campkin and the doctor ran forward. Willy Ferguson came to Haggard, took the pistol from his fingers. "There was never any doubt."

Never any doubt, Haggard thought. He gazed at the dead man. Because there could be no doubt about that either.

Slowly Dr. Meade stood up. "You've no nerves at all, John Haggard. And no pity either."

Haggard walked to his mare, mounted.

"There'll be an inquest." Woodbury's face was grim.

"I shall attend it." Haggard turned the mare away from the bridle path leading down to his land, made instead for the turnpike which led into Bridgetown. His throat was dry and his brain was swinging. But more than that, he was angry, with a vicious loathing which made his rage of the previous night and this morning no more than a sulk. This day would never end, for him. So should he have died?

He reached the turnpike, kicked his horse, and then dragged on the rein as another rider suddenly came from beneath the shelter of a tree.

"Murderer," Adelaide Bolton shrieked.

Haggard pulled Calliope away.

"Murderer," she shouted again. "Foul thing from the pit of hell." She swung her arm, and her riding whip uncoiled. Haggard looked up, caught the flailing lash as it scythed through the air. The young woman jerked, but released the whip in time to stop herself being dragged from the saddle. Slowly Haggard uncoiled the lash from around his hand, watching the flesh redden before turning blue. He dropped the whip on the ground, touched his mare with his heels, walked on.

The pain in his hand seemed to mingle with the pain in his mind and increase the anger in his belly. But suddenly it was a curious anger, embracing all womankind to be sure, but taking on a sexual slant. He wished to have Adelaide Bolton naked at his feet. To do what? He was not a vicious man. At least, he had never supposed so. Merely to jump on her belly would accomplish nothing for his spirit, at this moment. He wanted to hurt her while he loved her. He wanted to hear her moan in agony and ecstasy at the same time. And when he was finished, he wanted to throw her away like a rotten fruit.

Because, after all, he was what they said of him? A monster of arrogance and impatience and self-indulgence who merely concealed his true self beneath the facade of a gentleman? That could not be true. He had not taken a woman since Susan had died. Four years. No doubt that was the trouble. Because how badly did he want one now. But he had never been attracted by any of the black girls, however willing they might be. He possessed too great a sense of dignity. He could not be Haggard after a night tumbling one of his possessions. Father had not had to remind him of that.

But he was realizing that if he did not take a woman now, he might indeed do something foolish, or vicious.

He topped the last gentle hill—Barbados possessed no mountains—and Bridgetown lay below him, the town clinging to the edges of Carlisle Bay, the square church tower immediately in the foreground, the inlet of the careenage, where the ships were warped alongside to facilitate their loading and unloading, in the middle distance. Beyond, the bay itself was dotted with anchored vessels waiting their turns at the quay, and even as he watched, one was being drawn by her boats closer to the land. Lying as it did a hundred miles upwind of the main arc of the West Indian islands, Bridgetown was the safest harbor in the Americas, at this moment, for British ships.

He walked his horse down the hill. It was still early in the morning, and the town was just coming to life. Haggard turned down a narrow side street, pulled Calliope to a halt before the two-storied house with the high gable, dismounted, and tried the door.

"Who's there?"

He tilted his head back to look at the upper window. "John Haggard, Polly."

Polly Haynes peered at him. "Mr. Haggard? Well, glory be. We're all asleep."

"Then wake up. I want a girl, Polly."

"At seven in the morning? Oh, my, my. There was to be a duel."

"There's been a duel, Polly. Come down and open the door."

"And you're standing there. And you want a girl. No, no, Mr. Haggard. Not this morning."

"Now, don't be a fool, Polly. You'll not refuse John Haggard."

"I'll refuse any man what's just fought a duel. Last time I let one in, Margo had her arm broke. Go home and sleep it off, Mr. Haggard. Come back tonight." She saw Haggard considering the door. "And if you try to break down my door, Mr. Haggard, I've a blunderbuss up here, and it's loaded."

Haggard hesitated, fingers closing into fists and then opening again. Then he remounted and rode back up the street. Not even a whore would have him. He was John Haggard. With a snap of his fingers he could buy the whole lot of them.

He drew rein, and the mare obediently stopped moving. Then why did he not do so? Why did he not go back and offer Polly a hundred pounds—no, a thousand pounds—for the right to break one of her girl's arms? She'd not refuse that. But suddenly he didn't want to. He wanted a woman, but she had to be his, his to do what he liked with, his to abuse to his heart's content, not just for an hour. His to torment until in her agony she expiated Adelaide Bolton's crime.

So then, are you a bad man, John Haggard?

But whatever the answer to that, his best course was to return to Haggard's as quickly as possible, and discover the prettiest young girl he possessed, and take her and take her and take her until he felt utterly satiated.

He stood his horse on the trampled earth close to the careenage, watched the hustle and bustle in front of him, the gangs of slaves carrying bales of cloth and boxes of hats and manhandling great crates of machinery on to the dock, the anxious passengers waiting to take their turns on board for the long and hazardous journey to England, listened to the babble of conversation, inhaled the tang of dust which eddied upward. He was in no hurry to go home. He wanted to avoid thought.

He dismounted, walked into the throng, the mare obedient at his heels. People parted before him. Everyone in Barbados knew John Haggard, and most people in Barbados would also have heard of the duel; his presence would be sufficiently indicative of the result.

"Mr. Haggard, as I live and breathe."

Haggard paused before the sea captain. "Biddles. Had a good voyage?"

"Good enough, Mr. Haggard. Good enough." Biddles was short and stout; even standing still, he seemed to roll with the waves. "Saw a Yankee sail but once, but gave her a clean pair of heels. Oh, aye." He frowned at the planter; Haggard was one of his principal customers. "There was a rumor—"

"You don't want to listen to rumors, Biddles." Haggard looked past the seaman at the eleven people shambling down the gangplank; five women and six men. Their clothes were in rags, even at a distance of thirty feet he could smell them, and their faces wore at once the pallor and the misery of people without hope. "Indentures?"

"Cutpurses," Biddles said. "Well, there's no longer a welcome for them in the Virginias. Fancy a white servant, Mr. Haggard?"

"Not I," Haggard said. "We tried them once, and they were dead within the year. You'd get a better price for them if you turned a hose on them for five minutes before landing."

"Would make no difference at all, Mr. Haggard. They're

not for sale. Indenture. Ten pounds a piece for a ten-year term. What they smell like is immaterial."

Haggard frowned at the gangplank. The first group had come ashore and were standing sullenly together, blinking in the suddenly fierce sunlight of the morning, looking around them at the blacks and the sun-browned planters with suspicious fear. But now a twelfth convict came down the plank, pushed on her way by one of the seamen, and this girl's wrists were bound behind her. Because she was a girl, Haggard realized. A rather lovely girl, for all the grime and the stench. Her hair was a deep red, and waved on its way past her shoulders. Her face was gaminlike rather than classical, but the beauty was there in the rounded chin and the short, straight nose, the high forehead and the wide-set eyes; he could not tell their color. And she was young, certainly only in her mid-teens.

"What's with that one?" he asked, and was surprised to find his heart pounding.

"Aye, well, every so often we gets a bad one. She's for the rope."

"She's been sent to Barbados for hanging?"

"Oh, no, Mr. Haggard. Stealing from her mistress. But on the way out, oh, 'twere a bad business. Witchcraft." Biddles lowered his voice.

"Now, Biddles," Haggard said. "You'll not pretend to believe in that nonsense." He watched the girl reach the land. Her legs trembled and for a moment she nearly fell. But she regained her balance, gazed into the crowd, and looked away again with a little toss of her head, preferring to stare back out to sea. She wore what must have once been quite a decent blue gown. Now its rags exposed her shoulders and left her feet bare from the knees down; she had exquisite calves and ankles. Just looking at her made him wish to adjust his breeches.

"Well, Mr. Haggard, I'll tell you straight, I never did," Biddles confessed. "But when you see something happen with your own eyes . . ."

"Tell me." Haggard gazed at the girl, watched the wind take her gown and wrap it close on her body. Fifteen? Or just young for her age?

"Well, Mr. Haggard, they was in the hold, the women one end and the men the other. But this one always had ideas above her station, and the others soon took a dislike to her. Well, sir, there was a quarrel and a fight, and this one all but killed the other. Well, sir, my mate, Tom Hargreaves, and a good man he was too, well, sir, he decided the fault was the girl's, and he ordered her twelve lashes. You'll not do it, she said. So she was strung up, and the cat put across her. She took it without screaming, sir. Just a tear on her cheek. But when it was done, and they cut her down, she looked at Tom, and she said, I curse you, Tom Hargreaves. I curse you into your grave." He paused and wiped sweat from his neck.

"Well?" Haggard found he was interested despite himself.

"A week later, he was dead."

"Dead? She poisoned him? Knifed him?"

"He just took to his bed, Mr. Haggard. Took to his bunk and died."

"Coincidence."

"Witchcraft, Mr. Haggard."

"You'll get no court to convict her of that, Biddles. This is 1780, not 1680."

"I've an entire crew will swear to it, Mr. Haggard. So will those eleven over there."

Haggard watched the girl. Despite her determination, her legs would no longer support her. Slowly her knees gave way and she sank into a bundle on the ground. Dust eddied about her shoulders. Haggard walked toward her slowly. Are you a bad man, John Haggard? Are you everything they say of you?

He stood before her, but she did not seem to notice. Or had she noticed? Her head started to move, then slumped again. Haggard put out his riding crop, tucked the end of the bone handle under her chin, raised her head. Her eyes gloomed at him. They were pale blue, like his own.

"What's she called?" He walked back to Biddles.

"Emma, Mr. Haggard. Emma Dearborn is what her sheet says."

"Condemned for stealing from her mistress. You'll not convict her of more than that in Barbados, Biddles."

"Well, sir, I've a crew—"

"You've a magistrate standing here, Biddles. You may take my word for it. But you can make her over to me."

Oh, indeed, you are a bad man, John Haggard. Those who criticize you, who hate you, do not know the half of it. But how his heart swelled in tune with his penis at the sight of so much feminine beauty, sitting there, waiting to be destroyed.

"To you, Mr. Haggard?"

"Ten pounds, is it? I'll give you twenty."

Biddles frowned, and pulled his nose. "I'm not sure I understand you, Mr. Haggard."

"She'll wish she could hang, Biddles. Twenty pounds."

The girl knew they were discussing her even if she could not hear what they were saying. She glanced from one to the other of the men, and a frown was gathering between her eyes.

"Twenty pounds," Biddles murmured. Of which ten would be for his pocket. "She's yours, Mr. Haggard."

Haggard nodded, looked into the throng, snapped his fingers. "You. You belong to Mr. Crippen?"

The big black man hastily touched his forehead. "I does, Mr. Haggard, suh."

"Tell him I want the hire of a kittareen. Now. He'll have it back this afternoon."

"Yes, suh, Mr. Haggard." The Negro put down his bale of cloth and hurried up Broad Street.

"I thank you, Biddles. Remember, tear up her sheet. She's guilty of murder."

"Oh, aye, Mr. Haggard." But Biddles looked worried. "You'll be careful, Mr. Haggard. Tom just took to his bunk and died."

"I'll remember that," Haggard said. "Stand up, Emma."

The girl gazed at him.

"Stand up," Haggard said. "Or you'll be dragged."

She seemed to consider the threat; then she stood up.

"Walk in front of me," Haggard said. "Over there." He pointed with his crop at the more open space of Broad Street, where the kittareen—a small two-wheeled vehicle with two seats beside each other, and a single horse—was already waiting.

Emma Dearborn walked through the crowd. They parted before her, both because they saw Haggard behind her, and, he thought, because a second glance made them wish to look a third time.

"Are you a lord?" she asked. Haggard was surprised. Her voice was low, with just a trace of a North Country accent.

"I'm better than a lord," he said. "I'm John Haggard. Get up."

"I'm to ride beside you?"

Haggard nodded. The girl grasped the side of the equipage, put up one leg. Haggard watched the skirt fall away, watched the muscles ripple in the thigh, watched the veins suddenly stand out on her neck, realized that she was desperately weak with cramp and hunger. He gripped her thighs, lifted her effortlessly from the ground. Her head turned sharply, then looked away again, and she sat down. Haggard tied the mare's reins to the back of the kittareen, sat down himself, nodded to the Negro who held the bridle. The whip flicked, and the equipage bumped up the street toward the green hills beyond.

Haggard looked at the girl. She gazed around her with interest, the more so as windows were opening to allow people, mainly other women, to stare at her. She made several attempts to straighten her gown, to conceal her legs. There was breeding locked away in there, Haggard realized. But it was not a subject to be pursued. She was there to amuse him, to remove the canker gnawing at his mind. He could not permit her to exist, as a person.

The houses thinned, and they were in the open air. Ahead of them lay the sea of waving cane which was the wealth of the island.

"Captain said I'd be hanged," Emma said.

"I changed his mind for him," Haggard said.

They exchanged quick glances, and she looked away again. Haggard realized his entire body was a swollen mass of desire; he could not recall being in such a state before in his life, even on his wedding night. But it was almost a pleasure to feel that way, to feel the passion growing, to know that it was going to be assuaged, the very moment he was ready.

"Sugarcane," she said. "They told me about sugarcane." She looked up at the sun; it was nearly noon, and she wore no hat. But already Haggard's was in sight. Emma stared around her in wonderment as they rumbled down the drive, as the mastiffs came out to bark and frolic, as the black men hurried forward to hold the reins, and as she slowly realized the size of the great house rising above them.

"Mr. John." James Middlesex hurried down the steps. "Oh, Mr. John, but we is too glad to have you back." There were tears in his eyes.

"It's good to be back," Haggard said, and squeezed the black man's hand. "Where is Annie Kent?"

"She there, Mr. John. She there."

For all the house slaves were gathered on the veranda by the pantry.

"Annie," Haggard said. "This girl needs a bath. And then food. Take her upstairs and get her clean, then allow her to eat with me."

"Yes, sir, Mr. John." Annie Kent could size up the situation at a glance. "You coming, child?"

Emma hesitated, gave Haggard a quick glance, and received a nod. She climbed down, all but fell, then recovered her strength and went up the steps. Haggard got down more slowly, followed. He stood in the hallway, watched the two women disappearing on the gallery above his head, now surrounded by several other upstairs maids. He inhaled. He stood once again in his own house. Had there ever been any doubt? None at all in retrospect.

"Man, Mr. John, this suit finish," Middlesex observed.

"Burn it," Haggard said. He did not wish to be reminded of last night, in any event. He climbed the stairs, hesitated at the top. He could hear water being emptied into a tin tub, the scurrying of the maids as they ran down the back staircase with empty buckets. He turned to the left, went to the nursery. Amelia sat in a rocking chair, moving slowly to and fro.

"Mr. Haggard, suh." She hastened to her feet. "The boy sleeping, Mr. Haggard. He does be have he breakfast one hour ago, and he sleeping."

"You didn't tell him where I'd gone?"

"He ain't asking, Mr. Haggard."

Haggard nodded. He didn't suppose Roger really knew who his father was, or indeed if he had one. He went into his own room, where Henry Suffolk, his valet, waited for him. "Get rid of all of these, Henry," he said as he undressed.

"Yes, sir, Mr. John. Mr. John . . . we is too glad you didn't get hit."

"So am I, Henry. So am I." The last of his clothes fell to the floor, and Henry hastily gathered them up, averting his eyes from his master's erection. Now, how long was it since Henry had had to do that? And why was he waiting any longer? He was here, she was there . . . but she would be better after she had eaten.

Yet there was no reason not to look. He allowed Henry to wrap him in an undressing robe, left his feet bare, walked along the gallery, and opened the door to the spare bedroom where Emma had been taken. The four slave girls who had been scrubbing her hastily stood up. For a moment it seemed Emma did not realize what had happened; then she saw Haggard standing in the doorway, gave a startled half-scream, and leaped out of the tub, kneeling on the far side in an attempt to hide herself while her hands closed on her breasts.

Haggard realized that he had done better than he supposed

possible. The skin was creamy white, dotted with occasional freckles; the legs were long and slender; the belly was only slightly pouted; the breasts were bigger than he would have dared hope—they overflowed from the small hands attempting to conceal them. While the whole was made utterly entrancing by the wet red hair which seemed to stain her shoulders, by the dark forest at her groin, just visible above the lip of the tub.

He licked his lips. "Stand up, girl," he said. "I would look at you."

Her own tongue came out slowly, anxiously. "You're a man," she accused.

"You got a queer one here, Mr. John," Annie remarked.

Haggard gazed at her for a moment longer. Could she really be the innocent she pretended? Or even the half-lady she pretended? But to think about *her* would be to lose his own purpose. Remember only that she should be hanging, and dying. She had no existence, save in his mind and his presence. He walked into the room, stood behind her; she would not turn her head. There were only faint marks on her flesh where she had been flogged. "Give her something to wear and send her to me," he said, and was surprised to find his voice was thick.

He went down the stairs and on to the veranda, where Middlesex and his army of footmen had already arranged breakfast. Fresh flying fish, fried in butter, slices of ripe green avocado pear, a plate of soft-boiled eggs, and lashings of coffee, imported from England at prohibitive cost, but sweetened with Haggard's own sugar. Haggard sat down, watched the girl descending the stairs. She had been dressed in one of the shapeless gowns the house slaves wore, but her hair had been left loose instead of being bound up in a bandanna. It was still wet, and hardly moved as she came outside.

"Sit down," Haggard said. "Eat."

Emma swallowed, and he realized her mouth must have filled with saliva. She sat opposite him, stared at the food.

"Eat," Haggard said, and nodded to Middlesex, who hastily loaded the girl's plate. Still she stared at the food, and glanced at Haggard, rather like a kitten, he thought, who is being fed by strangers for the first time. She waited until he had taken his first mouthful before starting herself. Then not all her attempts at self-control could restrain her. She tore at the food, gulped it into her mouth, scarce seemed to swallow before seizing another handful of fish or fruit or another egg.

Haggard leaned back to drink coffee and watch her, and she flushed, and took some coffee herself.

"That will do," Haggard said. "If you eat too much now, you will be ill."

Her tongue came out, stroked egg from the corner of her mouth. Somerset came forward with a finger bowl and a napkin, but she did not seem to know what to do with it, waited for Haggard to show her.

The bowl was removed, and she drank the last of her coffee. They looked at each other for some seconds. Then she said, "Your wife is not here?"

"My wife is dead," Haggard said.

Her nostrils dilated as she breathed, and then closed again. "I am to work in the field?"

Haggard shook his head.

"I do not understand," she said. "Captain said I would hang."

"And I thought you too pretty to die," Haggard said. "So I bought you. For my bed."

Once again she did not immediately seem to understand. Then her head jerked and she rose to her feet in the same instant. "No," she said.

Haggard gave a quick nod, and Middlesex and Essex came forward, each to grip one of her arms. She turned her head wildly, at last dislodging her hair. "Hang me," she cried.

Haggard got up. "You'll not pretend never to have had a man?"

"Never," she said. "Never," she gasped, pulling on her arms, without success.

"Then it's time you did," Haggard said. "Take her upstairs."

"No," Emma screamed. She attempted to dig her heels into the wooden boards of the floor. "No. Please. No."

"Or will you curse me, as you cursed the mate?" Haggard asked.

She stopped struggling, gazed at him, panting.

"But I don't believe in curses," he pointed out. "So you'd best save your breath for screaming."

Her eyes gloomed at him, her mouth opened as she sought breath. He could see her nipples rising against the thin cotton as she inhaled.

"Take her upstairs," he said. "To my room."

Middlesex and Essex half-carried her through the door. She had stopped screaming, but instead he heard a sob. So, then,

John Haggard, you are not a bad man, you are a monster. Because he believed her. But if he was acting the monster, he was only becoming what all Barbados accused him of being, all the time. And however much he might hate himself when he was finished with this girl, he would hate himself more if he did not take her now. Besides, she was a condemned felon. She had no existence, save in him. Remember that, keep remembering that, and he need have no conscience.

He climbed the stairs. Middlesex and Essex stood just inside the bedroom door, still holding the girl. She had entirely stopped attempting to fight, seemed rather to have sagged between them.

But Middlesex was a cautious man. "You know what I thinking, Mr. John?" he said. "I thinking this one going scratch you."

As if, Haggard thought, I have done this sort of thing every day for the past four years.

"Then tie her up," he said. "Tie her to the bed."

"No," Emma whispered, and kicked Middlesex on the ankle.

"Annie Kent," Middlesex bawled. "You helping me." It was not a question. A moment later Annie bustled into the room together with two of her girls. "Hold she legs," Middlesex panted, having been kicked again.

The girls got hold of an ankle each, and Emma was carried across the room to the great four-poster.

"Henry Suffolk," Middlesex called, making the rafters ring. "Fetch some cord up here. Stout stuff."

"Let me go," Emma screamed. "Oh, please let me go." She gasped and panted, and kicked, and was placed on the bed—a tented four-poster, but with mosquito netting presently looped to the tester, instead of drapes—and held there while Annie Kent expertly stripped the gown from her body. By then Suffolk had arrived with the ropes. Haggard watched in fascination as she was spread-eagled, one ankle secured to each of the bottom bedposts, and one wrist to each of the upper. He felt like a man in a dream as he gazed at the heaving white flesh, the straining blue veins, the surging bush of pubic hair; she had ceased begging or crying now, and fought with a deadly determination, but without the slightest hope of success.

James Middlesex stood straight, wiped sweat from his forehead. "She ready, Mr. John."

The slaves backed away from the bed. How their minds

must be teeming with questions, Haggard thought. Nothing like this had ever happened before. They must wonder if they were not dreaming also.

He nodded. "Shut the door."

They filed from the room, and the door closed behind Middlesex. Haggard stood above the bed.

"I curse you," Emma Dearborn whispered. "I curse you all the way down to hell."

Haggard took off his undressing robe, and she gave a gasp and then shut her eyes.

"I curse you," she whispered. "I curse you, I curse you, I curse you."

There was so much beauty, he hardly knew where to begin. To kiss her would be too dangerous; her teeth were white and obviously in excellent condition. But he could finger the firm-textured flesh of her shoulders, slip down to cup and hold her breasts, and kiss the nipples, which came erect dispite her anger.

"I curse you," she whispered. "Curse you, curse you, curse you."

There was so much to be done to her, but suddenly he knew he could wait no longer. It seemed he had wanted this all of his life, certainly over the past four years, and her legs were pulled wide, waiting for him. He used his fingers first, sliding them into her slit the way Susan had always liked, waiting for her to come wet. Despite herself, her bottom moved on his hand, and her breathing quickened. He knelt between, holding himself in his hands, stroked with his penis where his fingers had gone before, slipped in and in and in, while she gave a gasp which became a cry, of mingled pain and anger and disgust, fell on her belly and crushed her breasts, but retained enough control of himself to lie away from her face, came and came and came as if it was the first ejaculation of his life, so that it was almost painful for him.

And lay still, gasping, and feeling the slow growth of distaste within himself, or self-hatred that he could have done such a thing. "Oh, Christ," he said. "Oh, Christ."

The girl had ceased moving and ceased speaking. He raised his head in alarm, but her eyes were open and staring at him. Slowly he pushed himself up, back onto his knees, looked down at her body, more red than white now, at the trickle of blood running down the inside of her thigh.

"I am not always so," he said. "Today is a bad day."

She made no reply, continued staring at him. He pushed

himself off the bed, went to his bureau, found the long-bladed knife he always wore on his belt, leaned across her to cut the ropes holding her wrists. "Free your legs," he said, and gave her the knife. He did not wish to look at her anymore, at this moment. He went to the stand in the corner, filled the basin, washed himself, dried himself with a towel, and heard a movement behind him. He turned in time to see her, face drawn and hard and pale, hair still moving from the speed with which she had crossed the room, knife-filled hand darting forward as she saw she had been discovered; he realized he had dealt only with slaves for too long—it had never occurred to him she might possibly have the courage to attack him.

He threw both hands down to deflect the blade, knew he had missed. There was a searing thrust of pain into his ribs, and he fell to his knees.

Apparently he had cried out in alarm, and equally apparently Middlesex had remained on the gallery outside the bedroom, just in case, for immediately the door was thrown inward and the butler and Suffolk both burst in. The girl was trying to withdraw the knife, either for another blow at Haggard or perhaps to kill herself, but he retained hold of her wrist and after a moment she released the weapon and pulled herself away. Her hand was covered in blood, and she looked at it in horror for a moment before turning toward the open windows.

But Suffolk already had his hands on her shoulders. The force of the pull threw her off balance, and she struck the floor with a crash and a gasp. Haggard remained on his knees. Between them they had withdrawn the knife, and blood was cascading down his side, but surprisingly he felt very little pain.

"Ow, me God," Middlesex said. "Ow, me God. Annie Kent," he shouted. "Fetch cloth and water. Fetch Mr. Ferguson. Fetch woman. Fetch."

"What about this one?" Suffolk inquired, holding Emma by the shoulders and laying her flat again as she attempted to rise.

"Hold she there," Middlesex commanded. "Just hold she. Come now, Mr. John, you got for lie down."

Haggard obeyed without meaning to. The floor seemed to come up to meet him. He gazed up at a ring of anxious black faces, soon to be joined by anxious white ones. He heard orders and instructions being given, he felt fingers probing at the wound in his side, and realized he was being wrapped in yards of white bandage. "Willy," he said. "Are you there, Willy?"

"I'm here, John. Now, just let's get you to bed. I've sent for the doctor. Easy, now."

Haggard was lifted from the floor and laid on his bed. He attempted to smile at them. "What a damned silly thing, Willy, to survive a duel and be brought down by a chit of a girl."

"She'll suffer, John. By God, I'll strip the skin from her bones before I burn her."

"No," Haggard said. "No. Don't mark her, Willy. Wait for me."

Now, why did I say that? he wondered. I meant, don't harm her. I don't want to harm her. I have already harmed her.

The bed was soft, and now the entire room was spinning about him. He closed his eyes, and the spinning increased, whirling about his head, sending him drifting away into unconsciousness, to return to earth with a bump at an unearthly sound, a wailing, anguished scream which seeped through his open windows.

His eyes opened, and he sat up, only to fall back again. He gazed at Middlesex and Annie Kent, faces drawn with anxiety.

"What is happening?" His mouth was dry.

"Is only Mr. Ferguson seeing to that murdering girl, Mr. John," Middlesex said reassuringly.

Another scream cut across the afternoon, more dreadful than the first. Haggard forced his eyes open again, all his strength, got his feet out of bed.

"Man, Mr. John, you got for stay here until the doctor does come," Annie remonstrated.

"Away with you," Haggard said, stumbling for the door.

"Man, Mr. Middlesex, but what we got for do?" Annie wailed.

"Go with him," Middlesex decided.

Haggard reached the stairs, clutched the banisters, nearly fell, and regained his balance as yet another scream tore through the morning, making him gasp with its terrible intensity. "Willy," he shouted as he half slid and half fell down the stairs. "Willy."

Servants bustled out of the pantries and the withdrawing

room and the dining room, stared at their master as, followed by Middlesex and Annie, he stumbled across the hall and onto the veranda, clutched the balustrade to look down on the half-dozen overseers who were clustered there round the naked body of Emma Dearborn. One held her ankles and another her wrists, stretched above her head. Between them her body writhed and twisted on the grass.

"In the name of God," Haggard shouted. "What are you doing to her?"

"Tickling her tits with red pepper, John," Ferguson said. "Oh, aye, we'll make her know she's alive. Now, lads, let's anoint her tail as well. That'll make her yelp, indeed it will."

Haggard fell down the outer stairs, landed on his hands and knees beside them. "Away," he shouted. "Away with you."

They stared at him, slowly released the girl. Emma's legs came up as if powered by a spring, her knees hugged against her belly, and her hands tore at her breasts.

"Water," Haggard shouted. "Fetch water. And butter." He crawled toward her.

"Let her suffer, John," Ferguson said. "And you should be in bed. You're bleeding again." He attempted to grasp Haggard under the armpits to help him to his feet.

"Let go of me," Haggard said, and Ferguson withdrew as if stung. Haggard reached the girl, and Middlesex was already beside him with a bucket, while Annie had a smaller bucket filled with home-churned butter. Haggard emptied the water over the girl's chest, bringing another moan, then gently parted her hands and rubbed the butter on the swollen nipples and aureoles. Tears were flooding from her eyes, and he did not know if she could see him or not.

"She's going to burn, anyway, Mr. Haggard," said one of the bookkeepers. "Pretty treason, it is, to take a knife to a master. She has to burn."

Haggard thrust one arm under Emma's knees, the other under her shoulders, reached his feet with a gigantic effort. He could feel the blood trickling down his naked leg.

"John . . ." Ferguson reached for him again. "This is madness."

"Away," Haggard said, and found himself at the foot of the steps, the entire afternoon revolving round and round his head. He gritted his teeth and commenced the ascent, foot in front of foot, step by step. The girl was making a peculiar moaning sound, and she was shivering as if frozen, for all the heat in the afternoon.

Amazingly he was at the top and crossing the hall. But in front of him loomed yet another flight, an endless accumulation of heights to be mounted. His teeth were clamped so tight he could almost feel the enamel wearing away. But up he went, again and again and again, aware that Middlesex was immediately behind him, waiting to catch him if he fell backward.

The gallery. And in front of him the open door to his bedroom. Now the afternoon had turned black, and he could hardly breathe. He fell forward, keeping his balance by an act of will, hit the bed with his thighs, and fell across it, the girl rolling out of his arms to come to rest against the pillows where she had so recently rested her head.

"Help me," Haggard snarled.

Middlesex held his legs and got him into the bed. He rolled on his back, stared at the canopy above his head, watched it turn black. And felt the girl beside him.

"Don't die, Mr. Haggard," she begged. "Please don't die."

Chapter 2

The Mistress

The flickering light of a candle caught Haggard's attention, and he found he could focus. On Tom Meade's face, examining his wound, bending over him. "You took your time," he said.

Meade's head turned. "Awake, are we? Well, that's something." He straightened. "You've lost enough blood to kill most men. There's a trail from here to the front steps and back again. What were you trying to do, commit suicide?"

Haggard tried to sit up, but found he could not move.

"Now, you listen to me," Meade said. "The wound itself isn't serious; the blade was deflected by a rib. But you're dangerously weak. A fever now and you wouldn't have a hope in hell of survival. So you just lie in that bed for two weeks. Not a minute less. I'll be out each day. Now, let go of that witch and I'll take her into town."

With an enormous effort Haggard turned his head. Emma Dearborn lay, or rather crouched, beside him; his left hand gripped her right wrist. She gazed at him with huge beseeching eyes.

"Come along, girl," Meade said.

"She stays here," Haggard said.

"For God's sake, John, have you forgotten? She stuck the knife into you. Don't you suppose she's just waiting for an opportunity to do it again? Hand her over and we'll have her hanging by morning."

Haggard continued to look at the girl. Her tongue came out and circled her lips. "She stays here," he said again. "But you lot can clear off. I need my sleep."

Meade drove both hands into his hair. "Have you lost your senses entirely? She was a condemned felon before you picked her up. Now she's a murderess, all but. What in the name of God has got into you?"

"Out," Haggard said. "Out. James, are you there?"

"I's here, Mr. Haggard."

"Is Mr. Lucas here?"

"I'm waiting, John."

"You're invited to dinner. Sorry I can't be with you. Serve Mr. Lucas the best wine, James. Dr. Meade as well, if he wishes to stay. Willy, are you there?"

"Yes, John." Another voice from the darkness.

"You're in charge for the next fortnight."

"Yes, John."

"But so help me God, no one is to attempt to lay a finger on this girl. James, fetch some food for her. Can I eat, Tom?"

"A broth. I've ordered it prepared."

"Then send it up." Haggard sighed and closed his eyes. He was exhausted. Nothing more than that. Just exhausted. It had been a long day.

"Mad," Meade remarked at large. "Stark, raving mad."

But people were filing out of the room. Haggard waited until he could no longer hear their footsteps. Then he released the girl's wrist. She rubbed it with her other hand. "You asked me not to die," he said. "After stabbing me. What changed your mind?"

He could just see her in the semidarkness; the candle was now in its holder on the far side of the room. "I don't want to be burned alive," she said. "Or to hang."

He smiled at her. "Honest enough."

"But I did stab you, Mr. Haggard. Why didn't you let them take me?"

Haggard raised his arm, and she came closer, allowed him to feel the texture of her hair, run his hand over her shoulder and down onto her breast, still slippery with butter. "You're mine," he said. "I want you here."

"Do you suppose I could have a bath, Mr. Haggard?" Emma propped herself on her elbow, looked down at him.

"You may have anything you wish," Haggard said. "There is a bell pull behind the bed. But have it here, where I can watch you."

She gazed at him for some seconds, in a peculiarly intense way she had. Then she leaned forward and licked the end of his nose. "You must not be excited."

She got out of the bed, pulled the silk cord. She had not left the bedchamber for ten days, had slept snuggled up against him. He had not tired of either watching her or feeling her. She moved with an unconscious grace, full of the most delightful little intimacies—the way she flicked her head to settle her hair on her back, the way her breasts just trembled, the way her belly fluttered, the way the slivers of muscles rippled down her legs. All of these things Susan had possessed, as indeed no doubt did all women, but for four years he had seen none of them. No doubt he had been foolish to turn his back on sex for that long. Or had he merely been fortunate, in that, had he sought it earlier, he would never have found it in Emma?

She sat beside him, held a glass of water for him to drink. He took her hand, guided it beneath the sheet to feel him harden.

"No," she said. "You are not well yet." But she left her hand there for a moment. To reassure him? That she would, eventually, give herself to him?

He wondered if he was not, indeed, being a fool. He was John Haggard. He snapped his fingers and people jumped. And he owned this girl. But he knew nothing about her, save that the seamen from Biddles' ship thought of her as a witch. Perhaps she was, and he was bewitched.

"Yes, sir, Mr. John." Annie Kent stood in the doorway.

"Miss Emma would like a tub, Annie. She'll have it here."

"Mr. Haggard—" Emma began, withdrawing her hand.

"You'll do as you're told," Haggard said.

"I going fetch the tub," Annie said.

"I wish you to be well and strong," Emma said. "And you are still very weak."

"Why?" Haggard asked. "I bought you for my bed. When I am well again, I shall want you twice in every day. Will you fight me twice in every day?"

"No," she said.

"Why not?"

"I have nothing left to fight for," she said. "And I understand more. Is it true you had just killed a man when you bought me?"

"Yes."

"I can understand your mood. And you saved me from those men."

"Those men are my bookkeepers. And my friends. You will have to see a lot of them, living here."

"As long as I am your mistress, Mr. Haggard, I do not have to fear them."

He held her arms, brought her down on to his chest so he could kiss her mouth; no strength required here, she seemed to enjoy kissing him. "You've a very cool and calculating head on those lovely shoulders."

"When I remember," she said enigmatically, and pushed herself away as Annie Kent bustled back into the room behind a bevy of girls carrying the tub and buckets of boiling water. Emma gathered her hair on the top of her head, secured it there with a ribbon, sank into the heat. She soaped, gazing at him, her mouth half-open and her cheeks pink. Too pink merely for heat. She still felt embarrassed at performing so intimate a function before him. Yet she had worn not a stitch of clothing for ten days, had used the pot beside him, for ten days, had assisted him in his own necessaries.

But everything about her was surprising. She did not speak like a servant girl, and certainly she did not act like one. Her past was worth investigating. But to do that would allow her a personality of her own, and he was not sure he wanted to risk that.

James Middlesex stood in the doorway. "Begging your pardon, Mr. Haggard, but some gentlemen are here."

"Ask them to come up," Haggard said.

"No," Emma said, hopping out of the bath.

"Fetch a robe for Miss Emma," Haggard commanded, "and come over here to prop me up." The girls fussed about him, thrusting pillows under his back, while one of their house gowns was found for the girl. Harry Lucas hesitated in the doorway. Behind him were Peter Woodbury and the Reverend Paley.

"Come in," Haggard said. "James, chairs for these gentlemen."

The visitors each glanced at Emma, who had taken up a position by the window, untangling her hair with Haggard's brush.

"The matters are confidential, John," Lucas said.

"She talks to no one save me, Harry, so there's no risk to your confidence."

Lucas licked his lips.

"Pull the bell, Emma," Haggard said. "Our guests will have a glass of sangaree. Come to think of it, so will I. And so may you."

"It may not be good for you," Emma said.

"Of course it will be good for me. I feel better today than I have all week. Well, Harry? The inquest?"

"Death by misadventure. The coroner added a corollary

deploring dueling in any form, but particularly between
gentlemen of unequal skills."

"Did you come out here to annoy me, Harry? Or on matters of business? Malcolm Bolton would have shot me down
had I not hit him first."

"Aye, well, the fact is, you did hit him first. I'm not here
to criticize, John. You asked."

"So I did," Haggard agreed. "Sangaree." He took the
goblet from Middlesex's tray, raised it. "I think we should
drink to my health."

Lucas sipped cautiously, exchanged glances with his two
companions. "John . . . I really would like a word in private."

"Off you go, James," Haggard told his butler.

"I did not mean . . ." Lucas bit his lip.

"I've made that position clear. For God's sake, man, un-
bend a little. Say what you will."

Lucas sighed. "Aye, well, you'll have heard the news?"

"What news?"

"That the French have taken Brimstone Hill," Woodbury
snapped. "St. Kitts is theirs. Last year it was Grenada and St.
Vincent. Man, things are getting serious."

"What was Rodney doing while this was happening?"

"Rodney is in England. Hood was in command. But it
matters naught. We just do not have the ships to be everywhere at once. It is up to each island to look to its own defense. Now, we—that is, the House—would like to know how
many people we can call on, from each plantation, and what
defensive measures each plantation has already taken."

"They'll not come here," Haggard said.

"Now, John . . ."

"Take my word for it," Haggard said. "What, beat a
hundred miles to Windward to sack a few sugar plantations?
The frogs have more important things to do. If we do not
have sufficient ships to guard everywhere, they have even less
to attack with, and protect. As you say, they have taken St.
Vincent and Grenada, and now St. Kitts. That is the limit of
their ability to hold. They'll not come here."

Lucas scratched his head. "You'll not cooperate?"

"There is no need. Volunteers? I've my own force."

"They talk of keeping all the sugar to send home in convoy."

"Stuff and nonsense," Haggard said. "I'm grinding next

month. My sugar will not rot here until you can accumulate twenty ships, if you ever can."

Woodbury looked through the windows at the fresh painted houses, the fat cattle in the meadow. "Your last crop got through, then?"

"I shipped in four bottoms," Haggard said. "Only one was taken."

"Not that it would have made much difference to you if all had been lost," Woodbury said.

"Indeed, Peter, it would have meant no profit for the year. I would not have liked that."

The Reverend Paley cleared his throat. Obviously he was afraid Woodbury would antagonize their host before the real purpose of the visit could be discussed. "The fact is, John," he said, "you'll agree things are going from bad to worse."

"I'll agree the Yankees are running wild," Haggard said.

"Aye. Meanwhile . . ." Paley glanced at Lucas.

"For God's sake, John," said the lawyer. "You must be aware of the situation. So three-fourths of your crop got through. Not every planter has been so fortunate. But 'tis the goods coming this way that are most hurt. There is no food reaching us. Bridgetown is on half rations. As for the blacks . . . Peter?"

"Forty of mine have died of starvation over the past year," Woodbury said. "And the rest are emaciated."

"You'll have some more sangaree, gentlemen," Haggard said. "And try some of cook's pasties. Home-ground flour, you understand. Oh, yes, my last shipment is no doubt now on sale in Boston."

"But you can grow your own?" Lucas inquired.

"I have two hundred and fifty acres under corn at present. I am intending to transfer another twelve hundred after my next grinding."

"Twelve . . ." Woodbury seemed to lose the power of speech.

"Where will you get the grain?" Lucas asked.

"Wherever I can. Wherever I have to."

"You'll be robbed."

"Times are hard, gentlemen. If I have to pay over the odds, then I shall do so. I have already laid in as large a store of imported foodstuffs as I could. Oh, I go short. I doubt my coffee will last. My only cheese is what we produce here on the plantation. But I still have a dozen cases of best claret left, and even a drop of port. I'll manage until the end of it."

"You'll manage, by God," Woodbury grumbled.

"The fact is, John," Lucas said, "we are well aware of your foresight and self-sufficiency. I only wish others had shown equal wisdom. Although, let's face it, there are not many planters so financially viable they can afford to do without a quarter of their acreage. But we are all in this. Barbados stands or falls together. I'm sure you agree with that principle." He paused, gazed at Haggard in the hopes of finding some support, then hurried on. "So it has been decided in the House yesterday, after a long and serious debate, that it is time to introduce an island-wide system of rationing our foodstuffs and indeed everything else that is normally imported. A pooling of resources is what we have in mind. And of course, we are looking to Haggard's as the fountainhead, so to speak. If you are indeed growing corn on that scale, you will be our granary."

Haggard's brows drew together. These were the people who hated him and everything he stood for, who had refused to second him, who had willed Malcolm Bolton to shoot him down. "I was not present at this debate—"

"You were here in bed," Woodbury pointed out.

"I was going to say, 'or I would have opposed it.' In effect, you are asking me to subsidize a number of planters who through either carelessness or imcompetence now find themselves in a difficult position."

"Subsidize . . . yes, well, I suppose that is right," Lucas agreed.

"I see no reason why I should do so."

"Eh?"

"I don't remember ever hearing that anyone lifted a finger to help Roger Haggard the first when he created this plantation. Rather do I remember hearing that he was opposed at every turn."

"That was a hundred and fifty years ago," Paley objected.

"We Haggards have long memories. I don't remember Father claiming any assistance when we had that smallpox epidemic here in fifty-eight. Half our slaves died. Did you give any assistance then, Peter?"

"Well . . . it was a difficult time for all of us. There was a war on then, too."

"There is always a war on, somewhere. No, no, gentlemen, it seems to me that wars, like plagues, are sent along by nature every so often to separate the weak from the strong. That is nature's way, gentlemen. Subsidize, supports, sharing, only prolong the existence of those unable to survive on their own, and what is the ultimate result of that? Why, the entire breed becomes weaker."

Lucas frowned at him. "You are refusing to help us, sir?"

"I am refusing to contemplate the death of one of my people through the carelessness of somebody else. As you say, Harry, foresight. I saw this coming, and I prepared for it. We shall manage, but I have close on two thousand people here on this plantation, and by God, not one of *them* is going to starve."

"And suppose," Paley said, "I told you that there is a risk of white people starving as well? It could well come to that, John Haggard. Would you feed your blacks knowing that was happening?"

"God give me patience," Haggard said. "And you a priest. Black or white, what's the difference?"

"The one is a slave and the other a freeman."

"Oh, balderdash. They weren't born slaves. At least their ancestors weren't. We went to Africa and got them. I'm no mealymouthed Quaker, Paley. I'm a planter. I need slave labor to work my plantation, and I work them hard. But by God, when I buy a black, I assume full responsibility for him or her, and they'll not starve, even if every goddamned layabout in Bridgetown drops dead."

"My God," Paley said. "My God. To hear such words spoken by a white man . . ."

"There is talk of requisitioning, where voluntary cooperation isn't forthcoming," Lucas said.

"Indeed?" Haggard allowed his mouth to widen in a smile. "Don't frighten me, gentlemen. You send a single redcoat up that driveway, and I'll turn out my slaves, and arm them. This is Haggard land. No one sets foot on it without my permission."

Lucas sighed, stood up, sat down again. "I'll speak plain, John Haggard. I was your father's attorney before yours, and I've a right. You must be the best-hated man in all Barbados, at this moment. There's those saying you murdered Malcolm Bolton. And there's others saying you've lost your senses since that."

"And what do you say, Harry?" Haggard's tone was soft.

"I . . ." Lucas went very red in the face as he pointed at the girl. "She's a condemned felon. Worse, there's those say she's a witch. You're bewitched, Haggard. Look at you, wounded half to death, but keeping her here with you, never letting her out of your sight, smiling and laughing . . .'tis not yourself."

"Now have I heard it all," Haggard said. "A man must be bewitched because he smiles. If I smile, Harry, it is because I am happy. And if I am happy for the first time in four years, it is because she makes me so. Go and report that to the gossiping ladies of Bridgetown, and come back out here when you are in a better humor."

The three men exchanged glances, then stood up.

"I had not supposed it would ever come to this," Lucas said.

"Mad," Woodbury said. "You are mad, John Haggard."

"Bewitched," Paley muttered. He stared at Emma.

"If you mean to insult my housekeeper, sir, I'll ask you to leave," Haggard said.

"Oh, we are leaving, Haggard," Lucas said. "And we'll not be back. But you, sir, will be condemned by every right-thinking person on this island."

"Oh, come now," Haggard said. "Am I not already? Have I not been, for four years? You should practice more honest thinking, gentlemen, then you wouldn't get yourselves in these scrapes."

"Mark my words, Haggard," Woodbury said, going to the door. "You'll be brought down. Oh, aye, you'll be brought down."

"Should I interpret that as a threat?" Haggard inquired, his voice sinking into that deceptively quiet and even tone which indicated his anger.

"You may interpret it in whatever way you wish, sir," Woodbury said, and went down the stairs.

"It is true that feelings against you are running high in town, John," Lucas said.

"And you agree with them."

"I endeavor not to take sides. I would suggest you are careful how you go."

"May God have mercy on your soul," the Reverend Paley said.

Emma came back to sit beside him. "Why do you not help them? They seemed to be talking sense."

"No doubt they were, from their point of view. I do not need their help."

"Nor their friendship?"

"I have never had their friendship. I have only been realiz-

ing that this last fortnight. 'Tis best it is out in the open at
last. Why, would you have their friendship?"

"Were you not here, they'd tear me limb from limb."

"Something for you to remember." He held her arms, slid
his hands up and down the silky flesh. By God, he thought.
Perhaps I *am* bewitched. "*Are* you a witch, Emma?"

"I never heard so."

"Then tell me who your father was."

"A rich man, Mr. Haggard. Squire of the village of Derleth, in Derbyshire. There's coal mines there, and a canal."

"And your mother?"

"Alice Dearborn was her name, Mr. Haggard. Upstairs
maid."

"Ah. Both in the past tense."

"Aye, well, while Papa lived . . . I can remember him,
Mr. Haggard, he was old, but jolly with it. Well, while he
lived, life was good. Then he died, and having no sons, the
estate passed to his brother. And Mama and me was out on
our ears. Well, she died soon after. Starved she did, Mr. Haggard."

"How old were you?"

Emma shrugged. "Twelve, maybe. It was four years ago.
But I had friends. I was sent to next village, and found a
position as skivvy. Then, because I'm pretty, I guess, and
with some knowledge of what a lady should do, they took me
upstairs."

"And you stole."

"I like pretty things, Mr. Haggard."

"Pretty things, by God. I'd forgotten what it's like to have
a woman about the house. Pull that bell rope, Emma."

"You'll not send me away?"

"Not I, Emma. But you're to have something to wear.
James. James. Come in here, man. Send to town, fetch
Mistress Bale out here."

"This time, Mr. Haggard? It going be dark in one hour."

"Fetch her out, James. Tell her to prepare to stay the
night. I want Miss Emma measured for clothes. Everything
she can think of. Send for her, James."

"Ayayay," Middlesex said, and hurried back down the
stairs.

"Mr. Haggard," Emma said, "I didn't kill that mate. I just
said what Mama used to say when she was angry."

"I believe you, Emma," Haggard said.

"If you're bewitched, Mr. Haggard, you done it yourself."

"Aye." He held her arms again, brought her down on to the bed beside him, slipped his hands down the cotton gown to massage her bottom. "I'm bewitched, Emma. But I don't want ever to be normal again."

"They're coming down." Willy Ferguson straightened his cravat, took his place beside the other five bookkeepers commanded to dinner. They waited, perspiring, casting anxious glances at the great staircase. Haggard came first, wearing a dinner suit, white cravat gleaming. Only the tightness of the flesh over his cheeks, the slight hesitancy with which he negotiated each step, indicated that he had left his bedchamber for the first time in a fortnight.

Emma followed, equally slowly, matching her time to Haggard's, to be sure, but the men could tell she was no less nervous than they. But having glanced at her once, they could not look away. She wore a pale blue satin gown, with a white underskirt, ballooning away from her hips on the panniers. Her fan was a matching blue and there was a carcanet of pearls at her neck. Only the powdered wig was missing from the ensemble of a lady of fashion; Emma's hair had been left loose to lie in a red stain on her neck and across her shoulders. She was the most beautiful sight any of them had ever seen.

"Gentlemen," Haggard said. "Good of you to come. I'd have you meet Miss Emma Dearborn."

Willy Ferguson took her hand, and she gave him a brief smile. The last time she had seen him, he had been rubbing pepper into her nipples. The last time she had seen Jonathan Gleason, immediately behind Ferguson, he had been holding her wrists above her head. But she allowed them each a smile and a squeeze of her hand.

"Champagne, gentlemen," Haggard said, gesturing James Middlesex forward. "I feel like a new man. Perhaps I am a new man." He raised his glass. "To Miss Dearborn, who has nursed me back to health."

The bookkeepers exchanged glances; After nearly killing you in the first place, their eyes said.

"I shall be resuming the morning briefings, as from tomorrow, Willy," Haggard said. "And I shall make a tour of inspection as well. I am sure there is much to be seen. Are we ready for grinding?"

"Indeed, John. You'll find everything as you left it."

"I never doubted that, Willy. Shall we go in?"

He gave Emma his arm, escorted her into the dining room. The overseers followed. Emma was seated at Haggard's right hand, with Willy Ferguson opposite. "I would also like to propose a toast," Willy said. "To our new mistress."

The other bookkeepers rose, glasses high. Emma watched Haggard, a faint frown marking the white flesh between her eyes. And for a moment Haggard hesitated. Then he too rose. "And very apt that is, Willy," he said. "To your new mistress, Emma Dearborn."

"They still hate me," she grumbled.

Haggard held her closer. At last. After a fortnight of watching her and smelling her and touching her, he was well enough to love her. And she was willing. Her naked body squirmed on his, his hands were allowed to wander where they chose. But after all, she was just humoring him.

"They will get used to you. Now, forget about them. The only person in the entire world for you to worry about is me, and I am here in your arms."

He peered at her face in the gloom. He wanted to shout with sheer joy, that all this should be his, should be here and now, toes and knees, thighs and cunt, belly and breast, and now lips, pressed against him, his to possess over and over and over again, if he chose, if he was able.

And able to love him back. Her tongue was as eager as his, and her hands sought his own buttocks. To have her touch him was as enjoyable as to touch her. Even Susan had been nothing like this. Susan. Roger. He had not thought of the boy for a fortnight.

Her head moved away. "What is wrong?"

He rolled on his back. "You've not yet met my son."

"I have," she said. "I went along there while you were asleep, two days ago. He is a fine boy. A fine Haggard."

"Oh, Emma, Emma." He brought her back on top of him. "For a moment I . . . No, there is nothing wrong. Could you love me, Emma? After a beginning such as we have had?"

"Could you love me, Mr. Haggard?"

"I do. I had thought I could never love again, but no man could ever have been more wrong. Oh, I love you, Emma. Love you, love you, love you."

"Because you have not had a woman for too long. Will you love me when you are sated with me. Mr. Haggard?"

"Will you not become sated with me, Emma?"

"You are my life," she said seriously.

"And you are mine, Emma. That will not change." His turn to frown at her as she rolled away from him. "Do you not believe that?"

"I do not believe it is possible for two people to love each other physically, the way we do, for a long period. Our fire is burning too brightly, Mr. Haggard. Too brightly to last."

"And when it is done, you will curse me to my grave?"

She smiled at him. "And when it is done, you will hand me to the hangman?"

He kissed her on the mouth. "So you see, my pet, as we can mutually destroy the other, we have no choice but to stay in love, for the rest of our lives."

"I would like that, Mr. Haggard," she said. "I would like that."

Black smoke belched from the chimney of Haggard's Penn, mingled with the rain clouds which, swept in from the Atlantic by the unchanging trade wind, gathered above Barbados every noonday. The plantation seethed, with laborers in the field, cutting the cane as fast as their machetes would swing, with creaking bullock-drawn carts into which the severed stalks were loaded, with curses and groans and sighs, punctuated by the cracking of the cartwhips, over humans and animals alike as they were driven to the edge of endurance and beyond. But those in the field still did better than those in the factory. Here the slaves were naked as they clung to the treadmill, as they sifted the fresh green stalks into the first massive rollers which crushed them to a pulp, as they added water—macerating, it was called—to the remnants of the first crushing to dilute the remaining sugar content and enable it too to be drawn, as they poked the huge vats of liquid, slowly cooling, slowly evaporating to leave the crystalline sugar clinging to the sieved bottoms, while the molasses dripped through into the hogsheads beneath, to be reprocessed and then to be converted into the plantation's principal by-product, rum; as they toiled in the pits beneath the rollers, gathering the bagasse, the shattered and pulped cane stalks from which all juice had been extracted, and which was now to be used as fuel to maintain the enormous fires beneath each of the separation vats—for a grinding sugar plantation was self-perpetuating. Other slaves hammered at the hogsheads in which the crystalline wealth would be stored. These were the lucky ones, as they were somewhat removed from the heat and the sickening stench of the factory. Yet even these sweated and panted and grew weak with exhaustion. Grinding was no time for backsliding. The slightest transgression was rewarded, even on Haggard's, with twenty lashes. On the success of the grinding depended the entire prosperity of the coming year.

It was a time when whites worked as hard as blacks. There was no time off for either. In the fields, the bookkeepers ranged their mules to and fro, whips at the ready for any sign of slackening effort. In the factory they were stripped to the waist, bodies gleaming with sweat, hair lank and matted to their scalps as they walked the catwalks and kept their slaves at the highest pitch of endeavor. And no man worked harder than the master. For seven days Haggard had not taken off his clothes, had slept in a chair on the veranda, cooled by the evening breeze, restored by copious quantities of ice-cold rum punch. After his wound, he swayed with fatigue, yet would not permit any man to take his place by the great vats, where he himself could test the quality as well as the quantity of the sugar as it came through. He reckoned on turning eight percent of the gross weight of cane into pure brown sugar, an improvement on his father's seven percent because of the greater maceration he permitted; induced with sufficient care, and with the cane subjected to an ever more intense crushing, there was no diminution in the quality of the sugar itself.

But now at last the fortnight of hell was all but over. The fields had been devastated, and the ratooning, the transplanting of the green shoots, had been completed. The filled hogsheads were already creaking their way down the road into Bridgetown, where the ships were waiting to load and be on their way to England, hopefully without sign from a Yankee privateer. The plantation chemists were already beginning their tasting and their mixing and their sweetening in the process of manufacturing the rum, much of which would also be finding its way across the sea, and the slaves and their overseers could at last begin to think of holidays and nights in their beds.

And Haggard could allow himself to relax. He walked from the factory, and blinked in the afternoon sunlight. "A good crop."

"The best ever, John," Willy agreed.

"You'll dine tonight. Bring up Mr. and Mrs. Prentice as well, and the Allisons."

Willy Ferguson chewed his lip and shifted from one foot to the other. In the past fortnight the crisis which loomed above the plantation had seemed less important; grinding was like a prolonged battle, in which only the good of the cane and personal survival mattered. But now the Penn would be settling into a long quiescent eight months. The ladies would have nothing to do but gossip and gaze up the hill at the great house.

"Seven o'clock," Haggard said. "I'm for bed early tonight."

He mounted his mule, rode up the slope. So Mistress Prentice and Mistress Allison had let it be known that they would not recognize their master's whore. He wondered if they would have the courage to refuse a dinner invitation. It would be amusing to find out. A thought, as usual followed by another. They were his friends. He had grown up with their husbands. And now he was prepared to throw them over for a chit of a girl, not yet seventeen, whose body excited him. Was he then so much of a fool?

His head raised, and he gazed at the veranda. Emma stood there, auburn hair fluttering in the afternoon breeze, wearing a loose pale green house gown. This was normal, and usual. But her demeanor was not normal. Absent was the habitual quiet suspicion of all those around her. As he came closer, she ran down the steps with a girlish energy he had not previously observed.

"Mr. Haggard," she cried. "Mr. Haggard."

He threw the reins to Absalom, stepped down, thrust the dogs out of the way. "What's amiss?"

"Amiss?" She laughed. "Naught's amiss, Mr. Haggard. I'm certain sure. I'm with child."

He frowned at her. "How can you be certain?"

"Because I have been on the plantation better than two months, Mr. Haggard, that's why. I knew, I was sure, four days ago, but I made myself wait until grinding was done. Until there could be no chance. Until you'd be free to understand." She put both arms round his neck. "Your child, Mr. Haggard. Your child."

He swept her from her feet, tucked his arm under her knees. He had lifted her like this on that first day, when she had twisted and moaned and blood had dripped down his side. He walked toward the veranda steps.

"Are you happy about it?"

"Happy. You'll love me now, Mr. Haggard. Now and always."

"I loved you already, now and always, Emma."

"Aye, maybe you did. But now I'm sure of it too. Love me, Mr. Haggard. Love me now. Please."

He hesitated at the foot of the steps. "What of the child?"

"It cannot be harmed, Mr. Haggard. I know it. Love me now, Mr. Haggard. I beg of you. And let me love you."

She had never said that before. She had never been so excited before. And he had had no time for her for over a week. He carried her up the stairs and across the hall. Gone was her modesty. She kissed his cheek and bit his ear as they climbed the stairs. She slipped from his arms before they were properly inside the bedroom, threw off her gown, helped him to undress. She knelt to kiss his penis and bring him hard, moaned as he gently kneaded her breasts, lifted her again and laid her on the bed, stooped to kiss her in turn. She spread her legs wide and cried out in delight. To her always consuming beauty there was added a throbbing passion he had never suspected her to possess.

"Slowly, Mr. Haggard, oh, slowly," she whispered, expelling her breath in a long gasp as he sank into her. Her nostrils dilated, her mouth sagged open, her hair scattered to either side of her head. It was how he liked to see her, the composed loveliness of her face, so watchful, so suspicious, disintegrating into pure womanhood, knowing nothing but desire and delight. But never had he seen it quite so possessed, never had he been so possessed himself. Her legs curled around his thighs, and he felt her nails scraping down his back, causing his head to jerk with pain even as he climaxed, and her own breath once again hissed into his ear.

"Oh, Mr. Haggard," she said. "Does a man feel like a woman?"

"I don't know how a woman feels," he said. "Or if she feels at all."

"She feels, Mr. Haggard. Sometimes. I felt then. I want to feel again, Mr. Haggard. I want to feel always." Her eyes gloomed at him. "Will I feel always?"

"If you're that passionate, always."

"I'm passionate now. I'm feeling now, Mr. Haggard. I want it again, now."

He smiled, and kissed her on the nose. "You'll have to wait until after dinner."

"You have hands, Mr. Haggard."

Bewitched, he thought. Oh, indeed, I am bewitched. That John Haggard should lie here and masturbate a woman, that a woman should wish masturbating, that a woman should be capable of physical feelings as deep as that. And there was no pretense. She came again and again, eyes dilating and mouth sagging, body vibrating with pleasure. He knew of no woman who could possibly behave like this. It was impossible to imagine any woman of his acquaintance, Adelaide Bolton or Annette Manning, knowing such feelings, or being able to express them in words. As for Susan . . . But there was no room for thoughts of Susan while in Emma's arms.

And incredibly, her passion communicated itself even through his own exhaustion, left him more aware than ever before in his life, had him beaming down the table at Clara Prentice and Lucy Allison. They had not, after all, been able to resist their curiosity, or their desire to sit at Haggard's dining table and drink expensive wine from Haggard's crystal goblets. And now too they could inspect Emma, and sneer at her plunging décolletage, and no doubt feel their milk curdling as they estimated the cost of her gown or the value of her pearls, as if they did not already know—Mistress Bale's visit to Haggard's was common gossip all over the island.

And they were helpless before her glowing sexuality, her sparkling wit. They might exchange glances whenever she made a grammatical slip, whenever her laugh was a trifle high for breeding, whenever she revealed her ignorance of literature or politics, but they could do nothing more than sit helpless as their husbands warmed before the fire of her beauty and her personality.

While Haggard sat at the top of the table, and sipped wine, and smiled at them all. He possessed so much, and yet he felt he had never possessed anything in his life before. Even Emma had only truly come into his possession this night. But she was his now, and he could not see that ever changing. And soon she would be the mother of his child. Emma, youthful, magnificent Emma, slowly swelling. Emma, with an infant at her breast. Emma, walking her son, with Roger at her side—for she made a great show, at the least, of loving the boy . . . Emma.

"You'll raise your glasses," he said, seizing his opportunity during a brief lull in the conversation. "And drink to Miss Dearborn and myself. Emma is to become a mother."

"To Emma," said Arthur Prentice.

"To Emma and John," Willy hastily added.

"And to the fortunate child," remarked Clara Prentice. "May I ask, John, if you and Miss Dearborn will now be married?"

There was a moment's silence; then Haggard stood up.

"You'll excuse us, I'm sure," he said. "But I for one am exhausted after a fortnight's grinding. I think I shall go to bed."

He left the room, climbed the stairs slowly. He *was* very tired. Behind him he heard the hasty scraping of chairs, the mutter of conversation. And Emma's voice.

"He really wasn't strong enough for it," she said.

Henry Suffolk waited for him in the bedchamber, helped him out of his clothes. Emma stood in the doorway.

"You'll not apologize for me again," Haggard said. "Not ever, under any circumstances."

"I'm sorry. They . . . they were so upset."

Haggard got into bed. Henry Suffolk released the mosquito netting, allowed it to cloud down outside the bed, shrouding the occupant behind a white gauze curtain.

"I saying good night, Mr. John," he said, and left, to be immediately replaced by Elizabeth Lancashire, Emma's maid.

"I'm sure Mistress Prentice meant no harm." Emma stood with her arms above her head as Elizabeth released the gown and began to remove the petticoats beneath.

"She's not a fool," Haggard said.

"Well, if she meant harm, it was directed at me. They hate me. All of them."

"Do you suppose they'd hate you any the less as my wife?"

"Why, no. But . . ." She bit her lip, turned away as Elizabeth began to unfasten her corset.

How lovely she was. How lovely she would become. Sixteen years old, and with all of her life crammed into the past two months. But there was so much more to come. He looked through the netting at the long, slender legs, the absolutely smooth curve of her buttocks, almost brushed by the long red hair, as she tilted her head back to have the carcanet taken from her throat. She faced the mirror on the far wall, and he could at the same time look at the swell of hair which thatched her groin, and the sudden thrust of breast; these she was gently massaging underneath, where the corset had cut her. And the face, so young, and yet so strong. She would make any man a superb wife.

He rolled away from her violently, stared out of the window at the night. But he'd not marry again. He had said that when they had sealed Susan's coffin. Well, no doubt many a man made a similar oath. It was not one he'd be expected to keep. But why should he marry again? It was not necessary. He owned this girl, far more than he ever could own a wife. And did John Haggard, *the* Haggard, give a tinker's damn for the opinions of anyone in Barbados, even his own employees? Or especially his own employees?

So, then, are you a bad man, John Haggard? It was not a question he had asked himself for two months. But it could not be begged. He knew in his heart that no slave owner could honestly be considered a *good* man. So why pretend? He was John Haggard. He owned, and he bought, and he ruled. This was best for him, and it was best for those with whom he came into contact. But for him, Emma Dearborn would have been a lump of putrefying flesh hanging from the end of a rope by now. He could not do more for her than that.

Or perhaps, he thought, I am afraid to share anything more than my body and my lust with any woman ever again. Because I shared with you, Susan, and the grief was more than I could bear.

And why had the question arisen at all? Because of those silly hags at dinner. They were married. They had to be, to secure their own futures. Overseers' wives. Did their opinions count? Did the opinions of anyone in Barbados count? He was John Haggard. He had turned his back upon Barbadian society, Barbadian opinion, even at the highest level. Because *he* was the highest level. It was only necessary for Emma always to remember that, to know that she had but to please him and her future was far more secure than it could ever be for a wife who sought to follow Susan.

A discovery she seemed to make for herself, soon enough. The child gave her a confidence she had never previously possessed. It was an easy pregnancy, a simple delivery. She wished to call the babe Alice, after her own mother, and Haggard was content to please her. Soon enough she was pregnant again and this time they named the boy Charles, after his father. Then Haggard called a halt, demanded she be careful. Three children were enough for any father, two for any mother. He did not suppose she could be lucky all her life.

Certainly she was busy enough. Apart from the children—and she insisted upon feeding them both herself, without conspicuous detriment to her hard-muscled body—she set to work in her own way to make herself a worthy Haggard woman. She already knew how to read, and now she made a study of every book in his library. She spent hours in the flower garden, to the delight of the yard boys, and other hours closeted with Cook in the kitchen, to no great purpose, as Haggard would no longer even entertain his own staff to dinner.

For in a strange way, as Emma appeared to grow more content with her lot, with a life built entirely around Haggard, so Haggard grew more discontented. Not with Emma. Far from it. But with Barbadian society, and even Barbados itself. The rejection had been mutual, and by the end of the American war, was complete. Barbadian society could never forgive him for having killed Malcolm Bolton, for having gone his own way in the crisis of that same year. And Haggard did not wish to be forgiven. But his gnawing distaste for Barbados itself did stem from Emma. From the tales she told of England, of snow on the Derbyshire hills, of long, cozy nights before the fire, of the immensity of London, an impression gained on her brief visit to the metropolis while awaiting transportation. She made England sound so much more interesting, even exciting, than Barbados could ever be. Slowly he began to realize that he wanted to leave, wanted to travel, wanted to remove himself of a society where he would not be hated, and where he would not have to hate, himself.

But what an incredible idea. A Haggard leaving Haggard's Penn? Father would turn in his grave. But Susan would understand. He stood before the white marble vault, his tricorne in his hand, the trade wind whipping at his hair. Over the last few years he had been able to do this again, where for too long he had shunned the cemetery as if it were haunted. But now it had a special place in his daily routine. It was incredible that Susan had been dead fourteen years, that it was ten years since he had shot down Malcolm Bolton. Ten years in which Haggard's Penn had become as socially isolated as if they all had leprosy, in which all his senior staff, driven by their wives, had gone, to be replaced by young men from England seeking their fortunes. But also ten years in which he had prospered while all others had struggled. Ten years in which Great Britain had lost a war. Ten grindings and ten ratoonings. Ten crops of maize. Ten years of exploring the delight that was Emma, of teaching her to read and write, of sharing the mystery that was her mind. Of making her his.

Ten years, he realized, which had passed before he was aware of it. He was thirty-seven years old. There was a suddenly disturbing thought. And tomorrow she would complete her term of indenture. He wondered if she remembered that. She had not spoken of it.

"Father. Father." At fourteen, Roger Haggard was already tall and strongly built, his features cast in the distinctive Haggard mold. He really should be at school in England, but Haggard had been reluctant to let him go, had preferred to obtain a tutor from Bridgetown, a clerk from the shipping company which handled his sugar and who possessed a smattering of Latin. Roger was all of Susan that was left, and if he possessed the Haggard nose and chin, he certainly had his mother's eyes, amber and sparkling. As well as his mother's innate gentleness of spirit, which went ill with the tales Haggard had heard of the hardship of life at Eton. And besides, he was already proving a useful and knowledgeable bookkeeper.

Then am I getting set to repeat the mistake of my own father? Haggard wondered. But why suppose it had necessarily been a mistake?

"There are visitors, Father." Roger paused for breath. "From Bridgetown."

Sufficient cause for excitement. Who from the outer world that was Barbadian society would visit Haggard's?

"Then I'd best attend them." He slapped his son on the shoulder, began the descent. Emma waited at the foot of the slope, Alice beside her, while Charlie seemed absorbed as ever in his own private thoughts. He was eight as his sister was nine. Two of the strangest Haggards of all, Haggard supposed, both with the red hair of their mother, both with the slightly suspicious expression which haunted her own face. But now suspicion was mixed with disappointment. No doubt in her heart she had hoped, with each child, that she might squeeze a little closer to the strange man who was her master. Now she was resigned.

But *had* she forgotten that this time tomorrow she would be legally free to leave him? If she wished.

Would he care? Could he possibly live, now, without those long legs and those heavy breasts, slightly drooping now because she had fed both of her children. Without that throbbing belly, with all its gentle stretch marks, without that wealth of straight auburn hair, without that sudden smile and that continuing shyness whenever he reached for her. Could he possibly?

"You have visitors, Mr. Haggard," she said as he came toward her.

"So the boy is saying. Now, there's a strange circumstance. Can we be at war again?"

"I hope not, Mr. Haggard. I wish you had more visitors. I wish you would get off the plantation more often. It cannot be good for you to lock yourself away here."

"I have everything I wish, right here, sweetheart," he said, and put his arm around her shoulder to kiss her on the cheek. Leave the plantation? Whatever for? To be booed or hissed at? Or just regarded with silent fear and hatred? Haggard the murderer. Haggard the bluebeard. Haggard the man who would not help his fellows. Even, so he had been told by Willy Ferguson, Haggard the madman. Names given him by people who understood none of his strengths or his weaknesses, or his fortune, or his happiness.

Then what of the object who provided that happiness? He looked down at her, and she gave a quick smile. Undoubtedly she would stay, were he to propose marriage. But he did not want to share. He wanted to own, as he did own. It was a way of life now. There was no one in all the world could question any decision he cared to make. That could not be so, were she to be his wife.

But what, then, did that make him? Why, he supposed, just Haggard. At least he was honest about what made him happy.

But what *did* she think of it all? She never complained, and that he found disturbing. Was she patiently waiting, believing that she must, in the end, achieve her goal? Or was she as bewildered as he, knowing only the mutual satisfaction of each other's bodies, but in her case accentuate ¹ by the sudden wealth and power with which she was surrounded, and to which she had access, provided only she remember to call him "Mr. Haggard"? He had suggested, often enough, that she try "John," but she had refused.

Or was that her own way of punishing him? She would call him "John" when he put a ring on her finger.

"I'd best discover what they have on their minds," he said, and strode away from her toward the house. He could see the horses waiting there, each held by one of the Haggard grooms. Two horses, and two men on the veranda being served sangaree by James Middlesex. Peter Campkin and the Reverend Paley. Peter Campkin had married Adelaide Bolton, and since the death of old Papa Bolton, was now a planter in his own right.

"Gentlemen." He climbed the stairs. "You'll sit down." He did not offer his hand, nor did they offer theirs in return.

He smiled at them, and waited, while they exchanged glances.

"You'll be acquainted with the news from England," Campkin said at last.

"What news from England, Peter? Or are the French tearing down more bastilles?"

"I am not the slightest bit interested in what the French may do or not do, Mr. Haggard," Campkin said. "I am talking of this." He held out a paper.

Haggard glanced at it, made out the names Wilberforce and Clarkson.

"Ah," he said. "The do-gooders. What are they at now?"

"A motion, Haggard, to abolish the trade," Paley said.

Haggard frowned at him. "A motion? Where?"

"Before Parliament," Campkin said. "To abolish the trade. What do you think of that?"

Haggard stroked his chin. He was well aware that over the past half-dozen years a small party of British reformers had been steadily sniping away at the entire institution of slavery, that there was actually a parliamentary commission sitting to hear evidence regarding the worst excesses of the slave owners and their overseers, but he had not given it much thought. Waves of humanitarian sentiment swept Britain from time to time, like epidemics of the plague. The reformers knew very little about the realities of life on a West Indian plantation. If there were slave owners who were monsters of cruelty, he had no doubt there were squires and shipmasters and industrialists in Bristol and Liverpool and London who were also monsters of cruelty to those in their power. But not very many of them, just as most of the planters, certainly those in Barbados, realizing the amount of capital they had tied up in each black man or woman, were unlikely willingly to harm them any more than they would willingly harm one of their horses.

"Well?" Paley demanded.

"It poses several interesting conundrums," Haggard admitted. "Supposing the bill is made law, which is doubtful to say the least."

"I would not be too sanguine about that," Campkin said. "This French business has set everyone by the ears. What with all the old nobility renouncing their titles and their rights to serfdom, well . . ."

"I had supposed you were not interested in the French."

"Only insofar as they affect us."

"What interesting conundrums?" Paley asked.

"Well, just for example, should the trade be outlawed, the value of every slave we own must be immediately doubled, as they will become a very scarce commodity."

"By God," Paley remarked. "Trust you to think of that." He snorted. "And of course you have sufficient births among your thousands to take care of wastage."

"Of course," Haggard agreed.

"I told you," Paley said. "I told you we were wasting our time, Peter. This man is a selfish monster. I have never met anyone like him."

"Mr. Haggard," Campkin said. "I know we have not seen eye to eye over the past ten years, and I further know that you have opted for staying out of Barbadian politics. But ten years is too long to have a feud dividing the very heart of our society, especially when there is a crisis at hand. It is our intention, sir, to place our case before the British Parliament. We have already opened negotiations with certain M.P.'s who are prepared to speak for us on the floor of the Commons. But they must represent a united island. Every planter must subscribe his name to the brief we send them—"

"And subscribe his share of the cost, no doubt."

Campkin flushed. "Well, sir, I will not deny that there is a cost. But nothing the master of Haggard's Penn would find the slightest heavy, and not a fraction of what we stand to lose should the trade truly be outlawed."

Haggard pointed his finger at the young man. "Peter, you are a liar and a hypocrite."

"Sir?" Campkin sat up very straight.

"Strong words, Haggard," Paley protested.

"But true enough. You know very well that the last time you attempted to present a remonstrance to the House of Commons, when that fellow Coke was hunting around these islands seeking evidence of mistreatment of slaves, your petition was thrown out because it did not contain my name. You can do nothing without Haggard's support, and you know it. Why not come out and say so?"

Campkin glanced at the parson.

"And suppose we admitted that?" Paley inquired.

"I'd still have no truck with you."

"You . . ."

"Because as usual you are creating fantasies which will probably never come to pass. You are actually encouraging these fellows. Can't you see that? So there are reformers and

Quakers and abolitionists in England. Do you seriously suppose that the English Parliament is going to take any steps, any at all, to ruin Britain's most prosperous and wealthiest colonies? Would you seriously cut off your own hand. Paley, because it occasionally touches something of which you disapprove? Absolute nonsense. Unless, as I have said, we planters ourselves leap up in protest, thereby suggesting that we *know* we are in the wrong, at least morally."

"There," Paley said. "As I said. You'll get no help from John Haggard."

He got up, and after a moment Campkin also rose. "You will regret that attitude, sir. I am sure of it. Just as you will regret your continued antagonism to your fellow planters. There will come a time, sir, when you will need us and we shall not need you. Just as there will come a time when you will know how shallow and useless has been your life, locked away on this plantation as if it were the entire world." He paused, and gasped, as if amazed at his own temerity. "And you may take offense if you wish."

Haggard waved his hand. "Take him away, Paley," he said. "I shall entirely stop receiving delegations from town if their sole purpose is to read me lectures. Take him away."

The men stamped down the steps, stopped to stare at Emma, who was approaching the house with the children. Then they mounted their horses and galloped down the drive.

"Another quarrel?" she asked as she came closer.

"The quarrel was ten years ago, sweetheart. This is but a further installment of it."

"And I am the cause." She allowed Amelia to replace her, ascended the steps.

"You? No, no. The cause was there before I knew you existed. You are perhaps a continued irritant to the good people of Bridgetown. They are too *good*—there is their trouble." He sat down, took a fresh glass of sangaree, gave it to her, drank from his own.

She sat beside him. "I can feel their hatred, on every puff of breeze."

He glanced at her, frowning. "And it frightens you?"

"Yes," she said fiercely. "Yes, it frightens me. Should something happen to you, Mr. Haggard . . ."

"Now, what is going to happen to me?" But his frown deepened. There were enough layabouts around the Bridgetown docks for an assassin to be found, should one be needed. It had never occurred to him before. Certainly it had never been something to cause him concern. He was John Haggard. Haggards lived, to the limit of their capacity, until they died, whether from old age, or yellow fever, or a bullet, sure always that there were other Haggards waiting to continue the family, the amassing of wealth, the prosperity of the plantation. Even when he had set out to fight Malcolm Bolton, he had not feared the future, for his son, had only sought to improve its security.

But now . . . It occured to him that the hatred he had incurred and was incurring would not easily be assuaged. They would hate Roger Haggard as much as they hated his father. While Emma and her children . . . Undoubtedly she was right. They would tear her limb from limb. Nor would Willy Ferguson be any protector. However much he pretended, and she pretended, he was the man who had rubbed pepper on her nipples. She must hate and fear him, and he must hate and fear her.

Then why not cooperate with them? If the idealistic machinations of the British Parliament could not harm him, it was just possible that they could, in the course of time, harm Roger. He had spoken the truth when he had told Campkin and Paley that he thought they were going about defending themselves in the wrong way. That did not mean that the planters *should* not defend themselves, under his leadership.

Did he still hate them that much?

Or was it more likely that he was afraid of his own reactions, afraid that if he set out to defend slavery, he would find that it was indefensible?

The understanding had been growing on him for ten years. Emma's doing, although she did not know it. He had always been inclined to ask himself questions, always vaguely afraid, and equally uncertain, although he would never admit that to anyone. He wondered about too much. He wondered who, or what, had made the decision which had caused him to be born in the great house and James Middlesex, for example, to be born in a slave logie. He wondered who had made the decision that Father and Susan should die, and he should live. And why. And he wondered why someone like Emma Dearborn had been sent to him, so strangely, and at so strange a time. Even more, who had sent him to her, when she had been about to die.

"Mr. Haggard?" She rested her hand on his arm.

"Aye," he said. "What would you have me do?"

"Me, Mr. Haggard?" Her surprise was utter.

"Supposing, of this moment, I told you you could have anything you desired in the world, go anywhere, be anything, what would you choose?"

She flushed. "I have everything I could wish, right here, Mr. Haggard."

"Save security."

"I am secure in your love, and . . ." She bit her lip.

"And while I live. But think, Emma. Let your imagination run riot. What would you have, what would you do? Suppose you are the mistress of Haggard's. Not my wife. My daughter, inheriting the plantation and everything that goes with it."

"Oh, Mr. Haggard . . ."

"Think, Emma, and tell me. You have an imagination. Use it."

"Well . . ." She licked her lips, drank some sangaree, leaned forward, her face suddenly intense, and the more lovely for that. Too much of the time it revealed only suspicion and a smattering of fear. But now she was animated in her thoughts, in her imagination. "I'd go to England, for a start."

"Sell Haggard's?" Haggard pulled his nose. " 'Tis the ultimate source of our wealth, even if you could find someone to pay the price."

"I'd not sell Haggard's, Mr. Haggard. Never. But it can be managed by an attorney, surely."

"Mm. What would you do with your life?"

"I'd go to Derbyshire, Mr. Haggard. I'd buy a manor house there, and live a civilized life."

"Derleth Hall, I'll wager."

She leaned back in her chair. "That's something personal."

"And what do you call a civilized life? Balls and hunts and fetes and gossip?"

"They help you to understand you're alive."

"And if you were a man?"

"Well, Mr. Haggard . . . Derleth is a county borough. It carries its own seat, and there are only a few electors. You'd not lack for something to do."

"Parliament, by God." He got up, walked to and fro, paused at the veranda rail to stare at his plantation. *His* plantation. He had never known anything else. But was the girl not right, however much of a private dream she was indulging? Had he not been thinking that very thought, with increasing force, every day for ten years, and rejecting it only because it was too great a step to contemplate? To be born, and live, and die, on Haggard's, surrounded by hatred and by criticism—could he really say, as he breathed his last, that he had lived? He was a slave owner. He had been born a slave owner, and he would die one, but could marshaling gangs of black men and women, ordering their floggings, granting them holidays, really be the beginning and end of his life? Because he hated it. The realization came to him with a sense of shock. What heresy. But could he not do more for Haggard's, for all the West Indies, by taking his seat in the Commons, then he could ever do by stalking this veranda and defying all of Barbados? It would be an adventure, a great and glorious adventure, and he had never truly adventured. Certainly Willy Ferguson was capable of managing the plantation. And his children would grow up away from the atmosphere of hate. And it would also be a magnificent way of settling his own conscience, of helping those people he despised. Let them prepare remonstrances and petitions. He would stand on the floor of the House itself to make the cause for slavery.

"I have angered you," Emma said softly.

"You have made me think," Haggard said. "I have not thought, except about you or the plantation, for too long."

"You told me to imagine whatever I chose."

"So I did. How soon can you undertake a sea voyage?"

"Mr. Haggard . . . ?" She scrambled to her feet. "You wouldn't. Would you?"

"I asked you a question."

"Tomorrow. But Mr. Haggard . . ." She panted with excitement.

"They'll call me a coward," he said, half to himself. "Who ran away because he could no longer face up to them."

"Oh, Mr. Haggard."

"Would you call me a coward, Emma?"

"How could I, Mr. Haggard? You are the boldest man I have ever known."

He put his arm round her shoulders. Suddenly he was as excited as she. It occurred to him that, even with Emma to love every night, he had been becoming bored.

"You aren't really going to do it, Mr. Haggard?" Her voice had sunk to a whisper.

Haggard kissed her on the ear. "What do they call colonists who make a lot of money and return to England to live a life of ease?"

"Why . . . nabobs, Mr. Haggard."

"Aye," he said. "Nabobs. Well, then, Emma Dearborn, stand back and look at your first nabob."

Chapter 3

The Nabob

"Man, but you ever see such houses?" demanded James Middlesex.

"Man, but there ain't no sun," complained John Essex.

"Man, but what is that thing?" cried Annie Kent.

"Man, that does be a castle," explained Henry Suffolk.

"Man, but you ever see church like that?" Elizabeth Lancashire inquired, pointing at the dome of St. Paul's.

"Man, but it too cold," Abraham grumbled, pulling his cloak tighter around his massive chest.

They stood together in the waist of the *Yarmouth Lass* as she ghosted up the Thames on the rising tide; there was just enough wind to keep her steerage way. They were excited, and happy. In the beginning they had been terrified. Although none of them had ever made the Middle Passage from Africa, they had heard sufficient tales about it from their parents and grandparents. They had been unable to convince themselves that an ocean voyage, even in the company of the master, could be any different. They had been afraid of the sea and terrified of the howl of the wind. They had been unable to estimate the length of time required to travel from Barbados, up the arc of islands, using the current and the trade wind, to the Bahama Passage, where the westerlies could be found which would drive them across to Europe. But three days ago, when land had finally come in sight through the autumnal mists, their spirits had begun to rise.

And what of my spirits? Haggard wondered. He stood on the poop deck, Emma at his side, her two children hugged against her.

Roger preferred to stand by himself; leaning on the gunwale. He was a silent, introverted boy. On the voyage, for the first time ever, Haggard had attempted to befriend him, as well as he was able—in leaving Barbados, he had turned his back on Susan and all resentment against the child who had caused her death. Besides, the experience had been new to both of them—the handling of the ship, the care of the rigging, Captain Biddles' daily exercise in navigation, as much as the wind and the sea, had been equally fascinating. Yet Roger smiled seldom, regarded his father with watchful suspicion. It would take time. But there would be time, once they got to England.

And at least Emma was happy; no doubt when she had left here, in the hold of this selfsame vessel more than ten years ago, she had supposed she would not see England again. But *I* have never seen it before, Haggard reminded himself. And he was not impressed at this moment. The sky was gray, as it had been unfailingly gray for the past week, and the city which was opening in front of him, if far larger than anything he had imagined possible, was huddled close together and suggested dirt and disease, while the air, even on the river, was tainted with the nostril-choking stench of coal smoke and woodsmoke. Yet, like his slaves, he was happy enough to come to land. It had been his first ocean voyage as well, and John Haggard could not be allowed to show fear, of apprehension, or even concern at the odd wave slapping the hull.

But at least the heaving sea had precluded thought. Now it returned with redoubled intensity. Barbados had been amazed at the news that he was going. Thus Willy. No one had come to say good-bye, nor had anyone in the crowd gathered on the shore of the careenage done more than stare. No doubt they thought him a coward, running away from them. Well, was he not a coward? Emma had made him so. Emma and her children and his fears for them. Or was that just male pride bubbling over? On every count this move was at once desirable and sensible. He alone of all the Barbadian planters had never been to England; his father's foolish love had robbed him of that essential youthful broadening of the mind. Certainly, as he was thirty-seven years old, it was time to put right that mistake. And again, he was Haggard. Was it not right that he should take his place upon a larger stage than the Barbadian House of Assembly? Why, who could tell what future lay before him? At the least he did not doubt his brains or his ability. So perhaps Haggard's Penn would not be quite so prosperous under an attorney as under himself. He had every confidence in Willy Ferguson, but the fact was that it was no longer essential to his well-being; to continue to regard the plantation as the fount of his wealth, he recognized, was merely to pander to family pride. The Haggard fortune was too diverse to be confined to sugar. His great-grandfather, happening to be in England at the time, had delved into the murky depths of the South Sea adventure and had had the sense to take his profit before that bubble had burst so alarmingly. On such a foundation, added to the growing profits from sugar, had the Haggard millions been based. And they *were* millions. He kept a million pounds at interest with the bank, and another million in consols. His plantation pulled in a yearly profit of a hundred thousand, and itself was worth another million, at the least. He had naught to fear from the future. He could be what he was, what he had always been, Haggard, do what he liked, live as he chose, for the rest of his life, and still bequeath to Roger a handsome fortune. Fear and uncertainty were really childish emotions.

And Emma? He had not raised the subject of her indenture, still could not believe she was unaware that she was free to walk away from him whenever she chose. He could not help but wonder whether the whole idea of coming to England was not some plot on her part to facilitate her escape. Except that she did not *need* to escape.

He looked down at her, found her looking up at him. "Happy?"

"Oh, yes, Mr. Haggard."

"Does it get much colder than this?"

"Oh, yes, Mr. Haggard. Why, it's just October. Come January, there will be snow everywhere. Especially in Derbyshire."

"Then we must obtain some warmer clothing." He wore a cloak, as did she, but only cotton underneath. But now even he began to feel some excitement as the last sail was brought in, and the *Yarmouth Lass* came alongside the quay, where a crowd of men, and even some women, were waiting.

"There we are, Mr. Haggard," Biddles said. "Safe and sound."

"Indeed, Biddles, and I am grateful for it. Would my agent be here, do you suppose?"

"He is, sir. The tall gentleman in the tailcoat. He'll be first aboard, you may lay to that."

Haggard inspected Cummings. How odd, he thought, that I should have corresponded with this man for thirteen years, allowed him the investment of my capital, and yet now be seeing him for the first time. George Cummings was about fifty, he estimated, both tall and thin, with a large nose and a square chin. He wore dark brown, tailcoat, waistcoat, breeches, and even boots, and looked every inch a solid merchant. But he also wore a small wig tied in a bow on the nape of his neck, Haggard observed as he raised his hat to the people on the poop deck. "John Haggard, I'll be bound," he shouted. "I'd have known you anywhere."

He did not wait for the gangplank to be run out, but leaped over the bulwarks and came up the ladder, hand outstretched. Haggard squeezed the strong fingers, and felt reassured.

"It's good to be here, Mr. Cummings."

"A safe voyage?"

"Aye. Not a hurricane in sight."

"And this is Mistress Haggard? Faith, sir, I had no idea you had wed again."

Emma flushed.

"I have not wed again, Mr. Cummings," Haggard explained. "This young lady is my housekeeper."

"Housekeeper? Ah. And this . . ."

"My son Roger. My daughter, Alice. My younger son, Charles."

Cummings shook hands with Roger, patted the children on the head while he clearly endeavored to collect his thoughts. "And those blackamoors on the deck . . ."

"Are my domestic slaves."

"Ah." A frown flitted across Cummings' features, but disappeared quickly enough. "I'll arrange transport for them. You'll want to get ashore, Mr. Haggard. I've a hotel rented for you—"

"We're for Derbyshire," Haggard said. "You did obtain that property?"

"Oh, indeed, Mr. Haggard. Well, there was no sale in the beginning. It was necessary to buy up the mortgage and threaten to foreclose. And that cost a pretty penny. I doubt you'll see an adequate return."

"I'm not concerned with a return on that outlay, Mr. Cummings. It is where I will live. And where I wish to commence living as soon as possible. Is it far?"

"Two days by coach, Mr. Haggard. And will you not like to see something of London Town?"

"Not if all of it stinks like the river."

Cummings smiled deprecatingly. "Your hotel is well removed from the river, Mr. Haggard. And if you do not wish to look at London Town, be sure that London Town wishes to look at you. I will arrange transport to Derleth as soon as can be done, sir, I do promise you that. But you will need time to rest, and establish your gear ashore, and there's business to be attended, oh, indeed, sir, you'll not be bored." He glanced at Emma, and his ready smile almost faded. "No, indeed, sir."

"Isn't it wonderful?" Emma cried, peering out of the window of her carriage. They had left the stench and the grime and the crowds of the docks behind, and after winding their way through narrow and unprepossessing streets, had emerged into a broader thoroughfare, with a great park looming on their right, while the buildings to their left each seemed to be as large as Haggard great house.

"Hyde Park, Miss Dearborn." Cummings was seated opposite them, Roger beside him. "Oh, 'tis a lovely spot. And the last of all sights for a great number. Over there is Tyburn Brook, and if you look through the trees, you'll see the gallows."

"Ugh," Emma said, and leaned back in her seat.

Haggard gazed at the houses, at the great trees, at the ordered gardens. He was, after all, impressed, despite himself. Just as, although he would scarce admit it to himself, he had been impressed by the sheer size of the city, by the number of vessels loading or unloading in the pool, by the hustle and bustle of the streets through which they had passed, the vast numbers of people, sufficient of them clearly poor and half-starving, to be sure, but equally many of them prosperous and busy, by the endless shops and emporiums, by the eager street hawkers, from young girls selling flowers or shellfish to gnarled old men offering to perform any service from catching rats to sharpening knives. The place was *alive*, in a way Barbados had never been. And not a black face to be seen. He wondered what the slaves, following behind in another equipage, would think of it all, just as he wondered what they must be thinking at traveling in a coach.

He glanced at Emma; had she ever traveled in a coach and four before? But she was staring out of the other window, as the berlin left the road and rumbled through a pair of wrought-iron gates before proceeding down a short winding driveway bordered with oaks, and coming to a halt before a mansion with a high portico and a display of great mullioned windows. Here there were yard boys and grooms waiting to take the horses' bridles, and footmen lined up to see to the baggage, the whole marshaled by a very dignified gentleman in a black tailcoat. And everyone with a white face.

"We're to stay *here?*" Emma whispered.

" 'Tis not very large, I agree," Cummings apologized. "But as it is only for a few days . . . Will it suffice, Mr. Haggard?"

The door was swinging open and the steps were being unfolded. "I'm sure it will do very well," Haggard said, and stepped down.

"Good afternoon, sir," said the dignified gentleman.

Haggard glanced at Cummings, unsure of his response.

"Hardy will be your butler, Mr. Haggard."

"Ah," Haggard said. "And good afternoon to you, Hardy. But I have brought my own people."

"For Derleth, sir. You may be sure it will take them some time to find their feet."

Haggard supposed he was right. It would take some time for any of them to find their feet. He walked through the open door and stopped at the sight of the half-dozen maids, all starched white aprons and caps, hastily bowing to their master. White girls, who in the West Indies would not lift a finger to help themselves. Marshaling them was an elderly woman in blue, every bit as dignified as Hardy.

"Mistress Broughton, Mr. Haggard," Cummings explained. "She will be your . . . ah, housekeeper."

Haggard half-turned, to look over his shoulder at Emma.

"The word has a different connotation, in England, sir," Cummings whispered, somewhat urgently, for Mistress Broughton was commencing to frown.

"My pleasure, Mistress Broughton," Haggard said, and stared at the marble floor, the oak-paneled walls, the paintings, mainly of racehorses and their riders; through the door to his right at a small withdrawing room, down the hall to another doorway, and up the curving stairway in front of him to the second-floor gallery.

"I'm sure 'tis not so elegant as your own house, Mr. Haggard," Mistress Broughton said. "But we do our best. Ma'am." She gave Emma a brief curtsy, at the same time glancing at Cummings in turn for information.

"Ah, yes," Cummings said, suddenly very businesslike. "You'll wish to inspect upstairs, Mr. Haggard, and decide upon bedrooms."

Haggard nodded, and climbed the stairs, Mistress Broughton at his elbow, Emma and Cummings behind.

"Come along, children," Emma said.

"My dear Mistress Haggard," Mistress Broughton said. "One of the girls will see to them. Margery," she commanded, "show the children the garden."

"Oh," Emma said. "I'm not . . ." She bit her lip.

Mistress Broughton turned her frown on Cummings, who gazed at Haggard in a helpless fashion and waggled his eyebrows.

Clearly it was time to take charge. "Miss Dearborn is my companion," Haggard said.

Mistress Broughton's mouth opened and then shut again.

"But I am sure one of the girls *can* see to the children, at least until Amelia arrives, Emma," Haggard said. "Now, Mistress Broughton, you were to show me the bedchambers."

"Of course, Mr. Haggard." Mistress Broughton hurried in front of him, up another flight of stairs, along another gallery, and opened a pair of double doors. "This is the master suite."

Haggard stepped into a small withdrawing room furnished with well-upholstered chairs and settees in a generally rose-pink motif, which also applied to the walls; beyond, another pair of double doors led to the bedchamber itself, where the great tester as well as the hangings were once again in rose pink.

"The previous tenant was a lady," Mistress Broughton explained. "Through here, sir, you will find the privy and bath chamber . . ."

"Bath chamber?"

"Of course, sir, her grace insists upon them in all of her houses."

Haggard stood in the smaller doorway, gazed at the large tin tub. "Her grace?"

"The house is part of the property of the Duchess of Devonshire, sir. Now, then, sir, if this is suitable, we shall find a room for the, ah . . . the young lady."

"The young lady will share this room," Haggard said.

Mistress Broughton again commenced to frown. "Oh, well, sir, I am afraid that her grace—"

"Have I, or have I not, paid rent for this building, Cummings?" Haggard demanded.

"Well, of course you have, Mr. Haggard. For one month."

"Therefore, for one month, Mistress Broughton, the building belongs to me, saving only I do not attempt to burn it down or damage the furnishings. I have no intention of doing either of those things. For the rest, you will be pleased to humor me."

Mistress Broughton's mouth opened and closed again. She looked at Cummings.

"Yes, well, a nursery. That is what we need," Cummings decided. "A room to use as a nursery. Close by. Come along, young fellow, let us find you a nice room." He grasped Roger's hand and hurried off.

Mistress Broughton remained standing in the center of the floor for a few moments longer; then she also turned and left.

Emma licked her lips. "Mr. Haggard . . ."

"Would you have a room of your own?"

"By no means, sir. But I'd not antagonize the servants, either. Mistress Broughton, now . . . she is very angry."

"But she *is* a servant, Emma. I am really not going to be put out by her anger."

Emma bit her lip, but thought better of whatever she had been going to say. Haggard threw back the curtains at the windows, looked down at the lawn and the rose garden, where Alice and Charlie were already running up and down in delight at having been let off the ship.

"This is actually a very pleasant place," he said. "Is Derleth Hall anything like it?"

"Well . . . it is a little older," Emma said cautiously.

"And larger?"

"Oh, yes, Mr. Haggard, much larger."

"I look forward to seeing it." He drew the draperies from around the bed, sat on it. "Soft enough. Come here."

She crossed the floor hesitantly.

"Are you happy to be here?"

She sat beside him. "Oh, yes, Mr. Haggard."

"Then undress and love me."

"But, Mr. Haggard, the doors are open."

"We never closed any doors at Haggard's Penn."

"Yes. But, Mr. Haggard . . ."

"Come along, sweetheart. Don't change on me. Or we'll catch the next packet back to Bridgetown."

Emma stood up, took off her hat and cloak, turned at a soft sound. Someone had closed the outer door.

The dining table was no more than a quarter of the size of that at Haggard's, and their places had been set, one at each end. Hardy, the butler, took up his position by the doorway, the footmen brought in the consommé and the saddle of lamb, the pork chops and the apple tarts, the roasted venison and the mulled red wine.

"Are we supposed to eat all of this?" Haggard demanded.

"Only what you feel like, Mr. Haggard," Emma explained.

"And what will happen to the rest?"

"It will go to the servants."

Haggard drank some wine. Hardy had been scandalized when he had ordered supper for eight o'clock. "The more normal hour, Mr. Haggard," he had explained, "is ten."

"I had a light dinner," Haggard told him. "And, Hardy, I like to eat when I am hungry."

"Of course, sir," Hardy had agreed, suppressing a sigh. No doubt he and Mistress Broughton had spent a profitable afternoon gossiping, but in any event they had had enough on their plate finding rooms for the slaves, and indeed in gazing at the black people with mingled distaste and alarm.

"Slaves, indeed," Mistress Broughton had commented. "We don't hold with such things in England, that we don't."

The Negroes had gazed around themselves in amazement and huddled close to the great fire blazing in the pantry.

"They'll get used to it," Haggard said. "As no doubt will I." He raised his glass. "A toast, my darling. To us. I can hardly believe we are here. And I will tell you this, it is a deal stranger than I had suspected."

He was feeling pleasantly relaxed after a long afternoon closeted with Cummings, who had been anxious to discuss the state of consols, the average price per ton of sugar, the details of the property transaction in Derbyshire, and the fitting out of Roger for attendance at Eton—he was due there in the new year. There was a far greater feeling of control over his money here in England than there had ever been in the West Indies. Now he just wanted to enjoy his evening. Emma had never looked more lovely, as she had never been more loving—there could be absolutely no doubt now that she had *not* realized her term of indenture was completed.

She wore her best gown and her pearls, because he had asked her to, as he had himself put on his black tail suit with the white piqué waistcoat. "For as we are here," he said, "we may as well see something of the place. Hardy, what can a man do with his evenings in London Town?"

"Well, sir . . ." Hardy stood stiffly to attention. "An unattached gentleman might go to White's or Boodle's."

"What in the name of God are those?"

"They are gentlemen's clubs, Mr. Haggard. But you would have to be a member."

"And I am not yet one," Haggard pointed out.

"Indeed, sir. Not yet," Hardy said, his tone suggesting he would be very surprised if Haggard ever achieved such eminence.

"Nor am I unattached," Haggard pointed out.

"Indeed, sir. Well, of course, the season is over, and most of the gentlemen are away shooting, to be sure, with their ladies."

"Shooting? There are wild beasts in England?"

"Birds, Mr. Haggard. Game birds. Pheasant and, ah . . . partridge. But for those confined to town, sir, by the calls of business or political matters, well, there is the theater."

"Oh, Mr. Haggard," Emma said. "I have never been to a theater."

"Neither have I," Haggard said. "And I did not travel four thousand miles to be bored."

"Well, sir," Hardy ventured, "there is always Almack's."

"Which is?"

"Reception rooms, sir. But . . ."

"Yes?"

"Well, sir, you would have to be introduced. By another gentleman, you understand, or a lady."

"What nonsense. I am John Haggard. Have my carriage prepared. Miss Dearborn and I will have a look at this place. Shall we not, Emma?"

"That would be splendid, Mr. Haggard. I have heard of Almack's. It is the place to be seen."

"And that can be no bad thing. Well, Hardy?"

Hardy raised his eyes in despair. "If I may advise, Mr. Haggard . . ."

"Hardy, one of my rules is, never to take advice, certainly not from my butler. Prepare the carriage."

"Yes, sir, Mr. Haggard." Hardy snapped his fingers, and a footman sprang forward. "I had merely supposed Miss Dearborn might be tired," he said, changing his tactics.

"Miss Dearborn has spent the past two months cooped up on board a small vessel, like myself, and is as anxious as I am for some exercise."

Hardy looked scandalized. "Of course, sir," he said, and withdrew.

"I can't dance," Emma said. "I don't know how."

"I'll teach you," Haggard said. "And we'll let the nobs have a look at us."

"Your card, sir?" requested the majordomo. He wore a green jacket decorated with gold braid and made a very splendid figure. Behind him were a dozen footmen, similarly dressed, with white wigs and highly polished leather shoes, knee breeches, and white stockings. The lobby in which they stood was floored in marble on which their heels clicked disconcertingly, while the ceiling rose a good thirty feet above their heads; it served also as a ceiling for the second floor, which loomed above them behind marble balustrades and was reached by a ceremonial staircase.

"I have no card," Haggard said, refusing to allow himself to be overawed. "You may announce me. John Haggard, of Barbados, and Miss Emma Dearborn."

"No card, sir?" The majordomo's face froze. "Have you attended Almack's before, sir?"

"Of course I have not," Haggard said. "I only landed in this confounded country this afternoon. Nor am I used to being kept waiting in antechambers. You'll step aside."

He moved toward the great staircase, but the majordomo stepped in front of him. "I am afraid, sir, that it is impossible to admit you."

"Eh?"

"I have my instructions, sir, from the Duchess of Devonshire."

"The Duchess of Devonshire? Why, you dolt, I am a tenant of hers. If you will be good enough to inform her that I am here . . ."

"Her grace is not attending this evening, sir. No doubt, when you return, you will bring an invitation from her, and then I may admit you. I should also point out, sir, that you are improperly dressed. Gentlemen are not admitted unless they are wearing wigs."

"By God," Haggard shouted. "You impudent rogue. I've a mind to slit your nose for you, sir. By God, sir . . ."

"Mr. Haggard, I beg of you," Emma whispered, clutching his arm. "Let us begone."

"Begone?" Haggard demanded. "Begone. Why, I'll . . ." He stared at the young man just descending the stairs toward them.

"My cloak, Martin," said the man. "Is my gig waiting?"

"Of course, Mr. Addison." Martin gave a shallow bow and accepted a folded piece of paper.

Mr. Addison gave Haggard and Emma a brief glance, went to the door.

"Mr. Haggard," Emma begged, still dragging on his arm.

"You, sir," Haggard said, pointing with his stick.

Addison half-turned, looked at the stick rather than the man. "Are you addressing me, sir?"

"There is no one else present," Haggard pointed out. "I have just been refused admittance to this rout."

"Indeed, sir? Now, there is a surprise."

The sarcasm was lost on Haggard's anger. "And I am about to pull this fellow's ears for him. Can you give me a reason why I should not?"

"Because he would very likely break your head for you, sir," Addison suggested.

"By God," Haggard said. "Does all London seek to provoke me?"

Addison allowed himself a smile, and this time he inspected Emma, to his obvious satisfaction. "Indeed, sir, I am sure the city does not. Especially as I can perceive, both from your complexion and your speech, that you are a stranger to our fair land. You'll take a glass, sir, with your charming companion."

"A glass? Upstairs?"

"Ah, no. I'm afraid that will not be possible. At my rooms, perhaps." He held out his hand. "Henry Addison, at your service."

"John Haggard. And this is—"

"Haggard?" Addison's brows drew together in a frown, and then as hastily cleared, while his smile broadened. "Of Barbados."

"That is so, sir. I have not had the pleasure, I am sure."

"The pleasure is all mine, Mr. Haggard." Addison seized Haggard's hand between both of his. "We had heard, sir, oh indeed, Cummings spread it about, that you were returning to take your place in the forefront of affairs. Derleth, is it?"

"I have purchased the manor, yes," Haggard said. "But I am not sure I understand . . ."

"Forgive me," Addison said. "Madam?"

"Miss Dearborn."

"Dear Miss Dearborn." He seized Emma's hand in turn and kissed it. "You will sup with me. I insist. We have much to discuss. Much."

"Sup?" Haggard inquired. "But we have already——"

Emma pinched his arm. "We should very much like to sup with you, Mr. Addison."

"You'll excuse old Martin, of course." Henry Addison leaned back and lit a cheroot, smiling at Emma. "The fact is, he is completely under the thumb of dear Georgiana."

"Georgiana?" Haggard inquired.

"The Duchess of Devonshire, don't you know?"

"My landlady."

"Indeed? We shall have to obtain you an invitation to one of her soirees, as soon as she returns to town, and then all doors will be open to you."

"Yet you say everyone knew of my coming."

"Well, perhaps not everyone. But to anyone with a political bent it was important. Why, John Haggard, of Haggard's Penn, we'll have had no more illustrious West Indian, if you'll pardon the expression, in recent times. The fact is, Haggard, 'tis the color of your politics that interest me. You'll know Derleth carries a seat?"

"That is why I chose it."

"Aha. We had supposed as much. And you'll know further that Billy Pitt plans to go to the country before the end of the year?"

"You will have to instruct me in English politics."

"Aye, well, it is necessary to increase our majority. There are great things afoot. Oh, aye, great things." Addison leaned forward. "So how now, Haggard? Do you vote Whig or Tory?"

"I doubt I understand the difference," Haggard confessed. "But I will tell you this, Addison. I am a slave owner. I do not hold with ill treatment of the unhappy devils. But I understand that my prosperity is based upon them. Now, you tell me straight, with all this talk in the air, with the names of Wilberforce and Clarkson echoing from one end of the West Indies to the next, how stands the Tory party?"

"That is simple. To us a man's property is inviolable, and slavery, however undesirable in the principle, is, as you say, an essential part of the economy of the wealthiest part of the British Empire, sir, to wit your own sunlit islands. Nor can we believe that such prosperity can be other than impaired by outlawing the trade."

"Well said, sir," Haggard agreed. "Then I am your man."

"Then, sir, as time is pressing, as I have said, the sooner

you are to Derbyshire and in possession of your seat, the better. For depend upon it, there will have to be an election, and by Christmas. We wish you to be returned for Derleth, sir. None other."

"Here is my hand and my promise," Haggard said.

"And I will see to the matter of some proper introductions for yourself and Miss Dearborn. Oh, dear me, the poor young lady appears to be asleep."

"It has been an exhausting day," Haggard agreed. "And for me also. I must away to my bed."

"Perhaps you'll permit me to escort Miss Dearborn to her lodging?"

Haggard gave a short laugh. "Away with you. She lodges with me."

Addison frowned at him. "Here? In London?"

"Until we can move ourselves to Derby."

"But . . ." His frown deepened. "Dearborn. Dearborn. There is a family of that name in Devon."

"She has no family, Addison. She was—and I will tell you this in confidence—indentured labor. But the mother of my younger children. I am a lucky man."

Addison slowly subsided back into his chair, produced a silk handkerchief, and wiped his brow. "Indentured labor? And you sought to introduce her to Almack's?"

Haggard's turn to frown. " 'Tis but a dance hall, is it not?"

"A dance hall. Ye gods. It is the very center of London society. What Georgiana would say . . ." He leaned forward again, lowered his voice. "You have no intention of marrying the young woman?"

"None at all."

"Thank God for that. But you are deeply enamored of her."

"I'm damned if I see where you have the right to ask me such impertinent questions."

"Believe me, Haggard, I'd not give offense. But 'tis important. London is not Barbados. No, indeed. I perceive in you a man of talent, sir. I already know you to be a man of wealth. And I can also discern in you a man of character, a man of determination, a man of decision. Why, sir, to such a paragon the world itself is almost too small a field for conquest. I would wager all London will lie at your feet, sir. But not if you insult the sensibilities of the ladies who rule us."

"By God, sir, I've a mind to take offense, at that," Haggard said. "Will you pretend to me that no man in London keeps a mistress?"

"Then they would hardly be men," Addison pointed out. "But they are discreet, sir. Discreet. And *should* they desire to make a display of it, they choose their mistresses from their own society. Now, sir, hear me out. We of the Tory party need you, and we will honor you, and promote you, should you only make it possible for us to do so. Love your delightful indenture, by all means. But do so at Derleth, I beg of you. And leave her there when you come to town." He threw himself back in his chair and mopped his brow.

"Do you know," Haggard confessed, "I had thought to have left such backbiting behind me? I had supposed London society as free as air."

"I wish it were, Haggard. I wish it were."

"Aye, well, no doubt you have given me good advice. And to say the truth, I have not been greatly impressed by what I have seen of this city of yours. It was Cummings' idea that I should spend sometime here. I will leave for Derleth in the morning."

"And when you come back, you will be one of us."

"Oh, indeed," Haggard said. "When I come back, I will know more of this land, you may be sure of that."

"There," Emma said, rolling down the window of the berlin to point. If she had guessed the reason for their abrupt departure from town, she had not revealed it, had bubbled with enthusiastic gaiety all the two days they had spent on the road, despite the fact that the previous morning she had begun sneezing and was now suffering from a streaming cold.

"A pretty picture, Mr. Haggard," Cummings said. And if he had certainly guessed the reasons behind Haggard's decision to abandon the city, he had been wise enough to keep it to himself.

Haggard decided he could not be referring to the gallows, fortunately vacant, which loomed beside his window. The berlin had halted on a shallow hill, and below him the valley was delineated. The road led down and through a small village, rather reminiscent of the bookkeepers' village on Haggard's, save that there was more than one street, and the houses were not quite so orderly and by no means similar in size or shape; vines grew up the walls, smoke drifted from the chimneys, and at the far end waited an inn, fronting onto the village green beyond which there was a sizable pond, the home, it appeared, of a flock of ducks.

Behind the village, to either side, there was open pasture, grazed by sheep, and at a distance of perhaps a half-mile, reached by a winding lane between the gravestones, was the gray stone church; close by were the vicarage and then the village school.

"Old, that is," Cummings said, indicating the church. "Twelfth-century. There are some houses in the village date back that far too."

"And the manor," Emma said. "Do you like the look of it, Mr. Haggard?"

The somewhat rambling building was in the far distance, and the afternoon was well advanced. "I shall reserve judgment until we get closer. I was told there are coal mines."

"In those hills beyond the manor house, Mr. Haggard," Cummings said. "Oh, a goodly return is to be obtained from them."

"But no farms?"

"Seven farms, sir. Also beyond the hills, but all paying rent to the manor, to be sure."

"Then what do the people of the village work at?"

"Why, sir, they are mainly miners. But there's a deal of home work, as well. They spin cotton in those cottages. Or they did before the American colonies revolted. But the cotton trade is picking up again, sir. You've a prosperous community down there, Mr. Haggard. No backslidings on the rent roll. I'll promise you that."

"There's no water."

"Indeed there is, sir. The Derleth River comes down from the hills over there, and runs hard by the manor house. Good fishing, too. You'll not see it from here. But it traverses your park."

"Then let's to it," Haggard said, and rubbed Roger's head.

The cavalcade, for there were two other carriages behind, containing the slaves and the baggage, rumbled down the hill and along the main street. Doors and windows opened, people looked out to oversee the arrival of their new squire. Many waved, and Emma waved enthusiastically back.

"Do you recognize any of them?" Haggard asked.

"One or two. But they'll not know me." She was wearing her new deep crimson pelisse, lined with ermine, and a matching velvet hat.

Haggard watched the manor house approaching. It formed

one arm of a U-shaped series of buildings, outhouses, stables. It was three stories high, with somewhat small windows and a sloping roof. Unpainted, the stone was weathered a deep green where it could be seen beneath the ever-present ivy.

Waiting in the courtyard was a score of people. But he had anticipated this, after his London experience. And at least here, he reflected as he climbed down, there was no Hardy and no Mistress Broughton. The butler was a very old fellow who found it hard to stand straight.

"Welcome to you, Mr. Haggard, sir," he said. "Pretty is the name."

"Good evening to you, Pretty."

"John MacGuinness, at your service, Mr. Haggard." This was a big bluff fellow with a red face.

"Mr. MacGuinness is your bailiff, Mr. Haggard," Cummings explained. "Anything you desire, just mention it to him."

"Oh, aye, Mr. Haggard, anything you desire."

Haggard nodded, walked down the row of gamekeepers and grooms and yardboys and footmen and women. Once again all the housemaids were young girls, all white, and one at least definitely pretty. And if they were not slaves, they were most definitely his servants, and as they lived in his village, his tenants as well. He was aware of a most peculiar sensation, which he could not identify.

And was distracted by a shout behind him. "Tom Pretty. Well, glory be. I'd have thought you dead by now."

Haggard turned, watched Emma embracing the butler, who was blinking at her uncertainly. "Miss . . . not Emmy Dearborn?"

"The same Tom. The same."

"But . . ." He scratched his head and displaced his wig. "We heard . . ." He glanced at Haggard.

"What did you hear, Pretty?"

"That . . . well, sir, that she'd been sent overseas."

"Which is where I have come from, Pretty. Shall we go inside, Emma?"

She flushed. "Of course, Mr. Haggard." She hurried in front of him into the somewhat low hallway.

Haggard sniffed as he climbed the stairs. "Damp."

"Aye, well, 'tis an old building," MacGuinness explained. "But we've a fire in here." He opened the door to the winter parlor, which was certainly cozy enough.

Haggard nodded. "You've made arrangements for my people?"

"Indeed, sir, their rooms are all prepared. Will you come upstairs?"

He climbed the next flight, and Haggard waited for Emma to precede him. "I'm sorry, Mr. Haggard," she whispered. "Truly I am. It was just that, well, I knew him as a girl."

"There'll be many people here you knew as a girl," Haggard pointed out. "But you'll bear in mind that you have risen above them."

"Of course, Mr. Haggard." She paused on the landing, blew her nose. "This house is just as I remember it."

MacGuinness had opened the door of the main bedroom. Here too a fire blazed in the grate, but nothing could expel the lingering smell of damp.

"This house, Mr. MacGuinness, is a recipe for rheumatism," Haggard said.

" 'Tis a damp neighborhood, sir, what with the river and the canal. But no one ever died of rheumatism." His attempted smile died as he saw Haggard was not amused.

"There's a housekeeper?"

"Oh, indeed, sir. Margaret. Come along, girl."

She had followed them up the stairs, and Haggard saw to his surprise that she was the pretty one. Indeed, now he could look closer, he could see that she was somewhat older than the other girls, although clearly still in her early twenties. She was tall and solidly built, with a mass of curly dark hair, presently carefully pinned beneath her cap, but yet attempting to escape in every direction. Her features were regular, and dominated by her large brown eyes. Now she gave a brief curtsy.

"Margaret, is it?" Haggard said. "You'll have fires on, day and night, in the bedrooms."

"Of course, sir."

"Show me," Emma decided.

"Yes . . . mum," Margaret agreed. The two women left the room, but did not close the door behind them. Haggard heard Margaret's voice: "Are you really Emmy Dearborn? Well, what a . . ." They were beyond earshot.

"Well, sir," MacGuinness said. "I hope you are satisfied?"

"Hum," Haggard said. "You'll stay to dine."

"Thank you, sir."

"And tomorrow you can show me the coal mines."

● ● ●

Haggard stood on the raised platform and gazed at the entrance to the mineshaft. It was a dull day with a smattering of drizzle in the air; his tricorne was pulled low over his forehead and his cloak was gathered tightly around his shoulders. But the entire scene would have been gloomy even had the sun been shining, he thought. The greenness of the hills behind—and they were far more green than in Barbados—was quite offset by the huge mound of slag on the far side of the pit itself, by the discoloration of the grass, and even of the water; the canal which ran straight as a rule into the distance was muddy brown in color.

And even these evidences of the contamination caused by the coal were pleasant to look upon compared with the yawning black pit in front of him.

"Men work down there?"

"Oh, indeed, Mr. Haggard," said the manager. "Well, we employ all sorts. Men to do the hard work, you understand. But we have the kiddies doing the drawing."

"Kiddies?"

"Well, they're small, see, and able to get through the passages easier than grown men, who have to crawl. And we don't have to pay them no more than a quarter of a man's wage. They'll be up, now."

A bell was gonging, and the office staff were issuing from the building to his left, pulling on cloaks and hats.

"Friday, you see Mr. Haggard," MacGuinness explained. "We only work half-day on Friday."

Haggard watched the entrance to the shaft. The men came up first. It was hard to decide they weren't Negroes, stripped to the waist, with coal dust clinging to their sweating skins. But they were *not* Negroes; each splash of rain revealed a trace of pink flesh beneath. And they were not slaves, although their backs were in many cases permanently bent, and they blinked at the daylight as if half-blind. But then, what was he to make of the children who straggled behind, and to his horror he saw that these were girls as well as boys; indeed, there were more girls than boys. And these were naked, plastered, like the men, in coal dust, long golden hair stuck to their shoulders and streaked with black. Most of the children were clearly very young, but several were well past puberty, and apparently cared little for that; if they immediately sought threadbare cloaks to wrap around themselves, it was because of the rain, not the watching men. In Barbados every field slave had worn at least a pair of drawers.

"Now, wait a moment and listen to me," MacGuinness shouted.

Heads turned uninterestedly.

"This here is the new owner, Mr. John Haggard, of Barbados."

They touched their hats or their foreheads.

"I don't have to speak with them, do I?" Haggard asked, suddenly nervous for the first time in years.

"No, sir, you do not. But it does them good to see the owner once in a while." MacGuinness raised his voice again. "That will be all, good people. Mr. Haggard is very pleased with you."

They touched their foreheads again and shambled off. Some of the children broke into a run, and began to laugh and play, bare feet splashing through the icy puddles. Haggard shivered.

"They seem jolly enough."

"Oh, indeed, Mr. Haggard, especially on a Friday afternoon."

"But . . ." He chose his words with care. "Do they not suffer? I was thinking of the girls . . . and the boys, of course. Naked, down there."

"Well, sir, coal dust is not the healthiest of beverages, to be sure. We've a high incidence of lung complaints here in Derleth." He dropped his voice and gave a portentous wink. "There's a saying you can have any girl in the village by offering her a domestic post at the manor instead of sending her down the mine." He sighed, as once again his attempt at humor seemed to have missed its target. "You'd like to go down the shaft, sir?"

"Down there? Good heavens, no." Haggard walked to the edge of the canal, studied the empty barges; the horses had been removed from the traces for the weekend. "Where do these go?"

"This branch canal joins the main one three miles off, Mr. Haggard. Then it's on to the northwest. Liverpool and Manchester."

"And there is truly a demand for coal on this scale?"

"Oh, indeed, Mr. Haggard. Especially with winter coming on. Living in cities, you'll understand, there is not sufficient wood to keep the fires burning. People must have coal, sir."

Haggard nodded, returned to his horse, mounted, walked it up the slope to the cut through the hills. Here he paused, watched the miners and the children ahead of him, trooping along the road past the manor house and toward the village. He had no desire to overtake them.

"Anywhere else you'd like to visit, Mr. Haggard? The village?"

"Is it customary?"

"Only on special occasions, sir, like the church fete. But you'd always be welcome at the inn, sir. You'd be buying."

"Yes," Haggard said. "Maybe Sunday."

"Now, there is a happy thought, sir. After service."

"Service?"

"Morning service, sir."

"Hum," Haggard said, and walked his horse down the slope. Water gathered on the brim of his tricorne and dropped past his nose. In Barbados it either rained angrily and violently for several hours, and then stopped altogether, or the sun shone from a cloudless sky. He had never known anything like this perpetual drip; it had begun the previous evening, and it had not once ceased. "Who are the electors of this borough?"

"Ah, well, sir, there's Parson Litteridge, and there's Hatchard the publican, and there's the farmers, and Coleman the merchant and Plaidy the blacksmith, and Johnson the schoolmaster, and, well, sir, there's me. Fourteen in all."

"That's all?"

"And yourself, sir, of course."

Haggard drew rein, gazed at the manor house. It seemed to have grown darker and more gloomy in the lowering clouds and splashing drizzle. "I see what you mean about visiting the inn," he said. "MacGuinness, I don't like the house."

"Sir?" The bailiff hastily rode alongside.

"It is damp, and smells. Can you find me an architect? The best in the country."

"Oh, well, sir, they do say Mr. Nash—"

"Fetch him to Derleth."

"Very good, Mr. Haggard. A new manor house. Well, glory be."

Haggard could almost see his brain working. There'd be perquisites for the bailiff in that. No problem with his vote, to be sure.

Haggard and Emma dined alone. The room was small, as was the table. And it was gloomy; even for the midday meal the candles were burning. The silver was well worn, and the plates were similarly old, while the roast beef was tough and tasteless.

"Did you see the mine?" Emma asked.

"Aye. By God, what a place to have to work." He frowned at her. "How is it you were never sent down?"

"I told you, I was squire's bastard."

"Aye." She had certainly been a virgin when he had taken her, and anxious to preserve her maidenhead into the bargain. "And your day?"

"I didn't know where to begin. Oh, and we had a visitor. The Reverend Litteridge."

"Does he remember you too?"

"No, sir. He has only had the living two years. I asked him to wait, but he said he'd call back this afternoon."

"Ah," Haggard said, and drank some mulled wine. He was very tired, and pleasantly inebriated; this was his third glass. It was a good afternoon to go to bed with Emma. Save that Emma's sniff was off-putting.

He tried to imagine a twelve-year-old Emma, naked and stained with coal dust, and found it disturbingly simple to do. The mental picture made him quite hot; he had had nothing of her during the journey from London or last night—her cold had made her at once easily tired and generally peevish. But suddenly he wanted, more than at any previous time in his life since the day he had brought Emma herself home. All his life he had been surrounded by willing womanhood. But they had been black women, slaves. Here they were white, and free. And yet, if MacGuinness was to be believed, everyone was as willing to please the squire as any slave her master. Did that go for the house servants as well? Margaret, the housekeeper? There was a fine-looking woman. "And have the servants become used to you?"

"I would like to talk about that, Mr. Haggard," she said seriously. She looked at the footmen, motionless by the sideboard, at old Pretty, hovering in the doorway.

"We'd best go into the parlor." He walked in front of her, sat down in a comfortable chair, stretched out his legs toward the fire; his boots were wet, and began to steam. Pretty hurried forward with a pipe.

"You'll take some port wine, sir?"

"Yes," Haggard said. "Bring the decanter, and then leave us."

"If course, sir."

"Well?" Haggard asked.

Emma sat beside him, blew her nose. "With the slaves, we do not need all of these servants."

Haggard nodded. "We'll still require the maids, but the sooner Annie Kent gets in the kitchen, the better."

"Pretty can go," Emma said. "You have Middlesex as your butler. And I will take over the housekeeping duties." She flushed. "So we can let Margaret go. And then . . ."

Haggard stroked his chin. "All those who may remember you."

"Well . . ." Again the flush.

"I had supposed, from the way you greeted Pretty, that you were glad to see him."

"I acted without thinking. I *was* glad to see him. But it is embarrassing. You *do* want me to manage the house for you?"

"Do you wish to?" She had never shown the slightest inclination to manage Haggard's.

"Yes. Really I would."

"Aye, well, it will give you something to do. When you are feeling better."

"I am feeling perfectly well, Mr. Haggard."

"You do not look perfectly well. It is the damp. And you'll have enough to do, settling the children." He finished his port, got up. "I'm for my bed."

She pushed herself to her feet.

"I've been thinking," he said. "It would be best if we had different rooms, for the next few days."

"Different rooms?" Her expression was utterly bewildered.

"I'd not catch your cold, Emma." He ran his hand into her hair, disturbing her cap, kissed her on the forehead. "Have Margaret see to it."

"Mr. Haggard . . ."

Haggard, already at the door, paused and turned.

"I'd like Margaret, at the least, to go. Annie Kent can be housekeeper until I am able."

"I doubt the maids would take to Annie. And I told you, I want her in the kitchen."

"I would like Margaret to go, Mr. Haggard." Never had he seen her face so set.

"Why? Because she recognized you?"

"She's familiar, Mr. Haggard."

"She's confused, you mean. I'll have a word with her."

"Mr. Haggard . . ." Emma bit her lip. Haggard smiled at her and went into the hall, snapped his fingers. A footman hurried forward. "Send Margaret to me," he said, and climbed the stairs. His heart was commencing to pound; the wine had taken hold of his senses as well as his belly; he could hear the rain dripping from the eaves, and as he passed an open window, he saw that the entire valley was shrouded in wet mist. A good afternoon to be in bed.

"Sir?"

She stood in the doorway.

"I wish you to have your girls make up a bed for Mistress Emma in the next room. Now. Be sure there is a fire and a warming pan."

"Yes, sir." She waited. She knew he was not finished.

"When you have done that, come back to me here. I wish to have a word with you."

"Yes, sir."

She was replaced in the doorway by Henry Suffolk. "Man, this is a place, Mr. John. You ever seen such rain? It going stop?"

"I suppose so," Haggard said. "I'll undress myself, Henry. Are you settled in?"

"Oh, yes, sir, Mr. John. I got room and all. But is true these white people does be servants just like we?"

"Just like you, Henry. Tell James I want a word with all of you later on."

Suffolk looked vaguely distressed. "I going to tell he, Mr. John, when I does see he."

The door closed. Haggard undressed slowly and thoughtfully, then stood in front of the fire, allowing the heat to chase some of the damp from his bones.

The warmth sent the blood pumping through his veins, brought him up in a massive erection. This time, he knew, there would be no need for ropes or force. So, then, after all, John Haggard, you are a monster. Or merely a retarded human being; in all his life, to this moment, save for the odd boyhood fling with Polly Haynes's girls in Bridgetown, he had taken but two women to his bed.

A gentle knock.

"Come," Haggard said.

The door opened. "Oh," Margaret said. "I'm sorry, sir."

"I said come." He turned to face her.

She hesitated for a moment, then stepped into the room, closed the door behind her. Her gaze dropped to his penis for a moment, then returned to his face. Blood filled her cheeks.

"Have you not seen a man before?" Haggard asked.

Margaret licked her lips. "Yes, sir."

"Are you a virgin?"

Again the quick flick of the tongue. "No, sir."

"Betrothed?"

"No, sir."

"Come, here," he said.

She gave a glance to right and left, almost as if she wished to reassure herself that she was actually alone with him, then crossed the room slowly. He took her face betwen his hands and kissed her on the mouth. It opened readily for him, and her tongue pressed against his; her breath was clean. And immediately he felt her hands closing on him. He wanted to shout for joy. Here was pure desire.

He took his mouth away. Her eyes had been shut. Now they opened anxiously; her fingers released him.

"Undress," he said.

She frowned at him. "My clothes?"

"I wish to see *you* naked," he said.

She gave a quick glance to either side. He realized with a start of surprise that while she would allow him her body without a thought, to be naked in front of him embarrassed her.

But she was his servant. "Come along," he said.

A last hesitation, then she tore at her clothes, almost desperately. Her gown and her cap and her shift fell to the floor. Her eyes were shut as she stepped out of her shoes.

"The stockings also," he said.

She opened her eyes, looked around her; her cheeks were red.

"You may sit on the bed."

She sat down, and he stood in front of her. Here was beauty on a scale he had not previously observed. Susan, like Emma, had rather been slender. But this girl was big—five feet, six inches in height, he estimated, with square shoulders and large, high breasts. Her belly was flat—she had clearly never been a mother—and gave into wide thighs and long powerful legs. Her pubic hair was surprisingly scanty, where Emma's was a magnificent bush, but even this difference was exciting, because he could see more of her, know more of what he was about.

The stockings lay on the floor, and she gazed at him. She did not seem to know what to do with her hands.

He knelt between her legs. He wanted to explore, to kiss and to suck, as once he had wanted from Emma. Margaret seized his head to hug it against her belly, and moved her bottom on the sheet at his touch. Then she fell back, strong legs closing on his neck, so that he almost lost consciousness, and had to part them with his hands. He rose himself, came up the bed, kissed her, holding her face again and feeling her breasts surging against his chest, stroking her with his penis before thrusting it in; she closed on him and held him there for a moment, and when he moved his head, surprised at once by her intention and her strength, he found her smiling, her face alive with an expression of incredible lewdness.

"You're hurrying," she whispered.

She relaxed, and he moved more slowly, withdrawing when he felt about to burst, to give himself a fresh lease of life. But the second time there could be no stopping. He surged into her again and again, and she moaned and twisted and snapped at his ear with her teeth, before throwing her arms wide and expelling the breath from her lungs in a long gasp.

Haggard remained lying on her. There was no question that she could bear his weight. There was no need to move. There was no need ever to move again.

"Miss Dearborn said I would have to go," Margaret said against his ear.

"Did she, now?"

"Will I have to go, Mr. Haggard?"

"We shall have to see, Margaret," Haggard said. "We shall have to see."

The Reverend Thomas Litteridge was a tall, thin man with aquiline features and a perpetual frown which indicated that he was shortsighted. He stood uneasily by the fire as Haggard entered the room, carefully arranged his mouth into a smile.

"Mr. Haggard. This is indeed a pleasure."

Haggard shook hands, glanced at Emma, who had remained seated on the far side of the fireplace.

"You've met Miss Dearborn?"

"Oh, yes, sir. Miss Dearborn has very kindly been entertaining me while you dressed."

Another glance. Emma was not smiling, and her cheeks were pink. No doubt it had been simple enough for her to discover where Margaret Lacey had spent the afternoon.

Now she stood up. "I am sure the reverend wishes to converse with you in private, Mr. Haggard," she said. "You'll excuse me, Mr. Litteridge."

He gave her a brief bow. She went to the door without looking at Haggard, closed it behind her.

"A charming young woman," Litteridge remarked.

"I find her so, Mr. Litteridge. Sit down, man, sit down. You'll take a glass of wine?"

"Wine, Mr. Haggard? At so early an hour?"

Haggard listened to the clock striking six. It was already dark outside. "Late enough for me, Mr. Litteridge." He pulled the bell rope. "It is good of you to call."

Litteridge sat down, as carefully as he did every other thing. "It is a privilege as well as a pleasure, Mr. Haggard. From Barbados, I have heard."

"Correctly. Ah, Pretty. Where the devil is Middlesex?"

"I do not know where he is, Mr. Haggard. He is not in the pantry."

"Well, find him for me. And bring in some of that mulled wine of yours." Haggard lit a cheroot.

"And is the young lady also from Barbados?" Litteridge inquired.

"Oh, come now, Litteridge. No dissembling. She is from here, and you know it. You will also have been told she was transported for stealing."

"Well, sir . . ." Litteridge sneezed into his kerchief to hide his embarrassment, remained hidden while Pretty placed the jug of mulled wine on the table next to his master; he, at the least, was learning fast.

"You were saying, Litteridge? Have a drink, man, have a drink."

"Thank you." The parson regarded the glowing red liquid with some suspicion. "There has been talk, of course."

"I have no doubt of it. Well, you may as well know the facts. I bought the girl on indenture. She's a pretty child, you'll agree. And I am well suited by her. She's the mother of my younger children."

Litteridge drank some wine and seemed to feel better. "You've no plans for marriage?"

"To Emma? I have no plans for marriage to anyone, Litteridge. I had a wife, and she died. I'll not repeat the experience."

"Oh, dear," said Litteridge. "Oh dear, dear me."

"But I want it clearly understood that Miss Dearborn is no serving girl, and no criminal either, in my eyes."

"Oh, dear," said Mr. Litteridge.

"Once that fact is accepted, well, then, I should think I will get on famously with everyone in Derleth. And I think we had best start being social, don't you? I'd like you and Mrs. Litteridge . . . There is a Mrs. Litteridge?"

"Oh, indeed," the parson agreed, wiping his brow with his handkerchief.

"Well, I'd like you to come to supper on Monday night. I shall have MacGuinness as well, and we can all have a chat about the future of Derleth."

"Oh, dear," Litteridge said. "Oh, dear, dear me. I'm afraid that won't be possible, Mr. Haggard."

"Why not? Ah, you have some church function. Then Tuesday will do."

"Not Tuesday, Mr. Haggard. The fact is . . ."

"You won't sit down to supper with Miss Dearborn."

"Why, sir, I personally . . . well, sir, the fact is, Mrs. Litteridge is a Cobham. Oh, a distant cousin to be sure, but none the less . . ."

"The decision is yours, of course," Haggard said, keeping his temper under control with an effort; this man was one of his electors. "I assume you have no objection to my bringing Miss Dearborn to church with me?"

"Of course not, Mr. Haggard. It will be our great pleasure."

"Good. Well, then . . ." Haggard rose, and the parson followed. "I am sure you have a great deal to do. I would like to have a closer look at your church, after Sunday's service, if I may."

"Why, Mr. Haggard, it would be a privilege to show you the church."

Haggard walked with him to the door. "I understand it is several hundred years old."

"Oh, indeed, sir, indeed. It was built by the Normans."

"And must require a great deal of upkeep, I should think."

"Ah, well, sir, old buildings, they do cost money to maintain. But your predecessor here was very generous. Oh, indeed, very generous."

"As shall I be. Would five hundred pounds be of any use to you, Mr. Litteridge?"

"Five hundred pounds? Why, Mr. Haggard, I don't know what to say. Five hundred pounds? Why, it is a princely sum."

"I'd not have your church, *our* church, Mr. Litteridge, falling down," Haggard said. "My agent will give you a check on Monday morning." They had reached the stairs leading down to the lower hall, and a footman was waiting for them. "Where is Middlesex?"

"I do not know, Mr. Haggard."

"Well, you go and find him as soon as you have shown Mr. Litteridge out. And tell him I wish a word with him."

"Yes, sir, Mr. Haggard."

"I will say good-bye, Mr. Haggard," Litteridge said. "And again, many thanks."

Haggard nodded, watched him go down the stairs, turned, and saw Emma at the top of the second flight. Slowly she came down. Her face was still frozen.

"Well, Mr. Haggard?"

"They'll not come to supper. It seems that Mistress Litteridge would not approve. She is a Cobham. What is a Cobham?"

Emma led him into the withdrawing room. "Worcestershire gentry. Are you angry?"

"I am amused by their little prejudices. Although I had thought to leave those things behind in Barbados."

Emma stood before the fire. "Perhaps we should have stayed there."

"Now, sweetheart, it was your idea that we come home. Your triumph." He sat down, poured two glasses of mulled wine, leaned back, and crossed his legs. "No doubt I shall get used to England, and English weather."

"And English ways?"

"They will have to get used to me."

Emma remained standing, nor did she take her glass. "I disagree, Mr. Haggard. It is you must get used to them. To having white servants instead of black, for example. Have you come to a decision on Margaret Lacey?"

"Ah . . . no. I do not want to burden you with housekeeping duties, Emma. I wish you to get well as soon as possible. I really think we should have a doctor in to see to you. And Annie Kent, well, it will take time for her to understand the supervision of a house like this."

"While you can sleep with that girl to your heart's content." Emma produced a large handkerchief and blew her nose loudly and vehemently.

"My dear Emma, surely who I sleep with is no concern of yours? Provided I also sleep with you, regularly. And this I shall do the moment you get rid of that cold. But I'll confess I'm mortally afraid of catching it from you, with the climate so dismal."

She sat down. Her knees seemed to give way, and she collapsed into a chair. "You'd not treat me so if I were your wife."

"I'd certainly sleep with more serving girls if you were my wife."

She sniffed. "But they'd not be able to sneer at me and suggest they'd be taking my place next."

"Now, who would do something like that?"

"Margaret."

"Oh, come now."

"It's true."

"I'll speak with her."

"And fuck her while doing it. I won't have it, Mr. Haggard." Her chin came up; there were tears in her eyes, but her mouth was set in a determined line. "I won't have it."

"Oh, really, Emma. No crisis tonight, I beg of you. I have had a wearing day, with everyone doing their damnedest to irritate me. Middlesex, now, was not even in the hall to show Mr. Litteridge out."

"He wasn't there when the parson arrived, either," Emma remarked.

"Wasn't he, by God. I shall have to have a word with him. Now, Emma, sweetheart, why don't you go and have a rest, and then change your clothes. MacGuinness is certainly coming to supper."

Emma stood up. "But I shall not, Mr. Haggard."

He raised his head. "Oh, really, Emma, whatever is the matter?"

"I shall not sit down at your table while that girl remains in the house. If we are to be treated as equals, then we are both servants. I will take my meals downstairs."

"In the name of God," Haggard shouted, the anger which had been simmering in his belly since the visit to the coal mine suddenly bursting forth. "Do what the devil you like. Get out. Get out of my sight." He glared at the door. "What do you want?"

Henry Suffolk stood there, shifting nervously from foot to foot.

"Well, Mr. Haggard, sir, it is a fact that James can't be found nowhere."

Haggard frowned at him. "What the devil are you talking about?"

"Well, sir, Mr. Haggard, he gone. And he take his things

with him. And that boy John Essex say he see he riding a horse down the road this time in the morning."

"Gone? To the village?"

"Well, that I ain't knowing, Mr. Haggard, sir. But he take all he belonging with he."

What he was being told only slowly penetrated Haggard's understanding. Emma gave a little gasp as he slowly rose to his feet.

"You are saying that Middlesex has absconded?"

"Well, sir, Mr. Haggard . . ."

"This morning?"

"Well, sir, Mr. John . . ."

"And nobody told me up to now?"

"Well, sir, Mr. John . . ."

"I'll have you whipped. By God, I'll flog the lot of you myself. Now, you get out of here, and saddle me a horse. Emma, my coat and boots. Henry. Tell John Essex to prime my pistols."

"Yes, sir, Mr. John." Suffolk ran from the room.

"What are you going to do?" Emma asked.

"Do?" Haggard said. "I'm going to bring him back. By God, I'm going to bring him back, tied to my horse's tail."

Chapter 4

The Runaway

"Mr. Haggard," Emma begged. "John."

It was the first time she had ever used his name.

"Middlesex will come back," she said. "I'm sure of it."

Haggard frowned at her, at the same time wondering why he was so angry. But he *was* angry. It was a combination of many things, the boys and girls at the pit head, the attitude of the parson, his self-contempt at the course of bribery on which he was engaged—but most of all the sudden realization that he was in the center of a country which consisted entirely of Emmas, that however much he might love her, or might have loved her once, she was no longer the uniquely beautiful and sexual creature she had been in Barbados. And could not all those new Emmas be similarly bent to his will, similarly rendered his and only his?

But he loved *her*. Did he, still? She was the mother of two of his children.

"He's a runaway," he said. "I'll fetch him back. By God, I will."

"The horse done saddle, Mr. John." Essex stood in the doorway with the pistol case. Suffolk was behind him, with Haggard's hat and cloak.

"You want me to come with you, Mr. John?"

"No," Haggard said. A white posse would be more appropriate, he thought, in a white man's country.

"Can I come, Father?" Roger already had on his hat and coat.

"No. You'll be soaked to the skin. But you can help me with these boots."

Suffolk knelt before one leg, Roger before the other. Emma recovered from a fit of sneezing.

"And won't you be soaked to the skin, Mr. Haggard? You'll catch a cold just like me."

"Oh, go to bed," Haggard snapped, standing up and stamping his feet to make sure they were comfortable. "If I'm not back by Sunday morning, mind you attend church. With the children." He went outside, pulled his hat lower over his eyes, adjusted the weight of the pistols in his pocket. The rain settled around him like a wet blanket. Whatever had possessed Middlesex to abscond? No Haggard slave had ever absconded. Perhaps it was, after all, only an explicable mistake. But what mistake could take a slave away from his proper situation?

He mounted, walked his horse down the drive. He did not look over his shoulder, although he knew that every window in the house was filled, from Emma in the withdrawing room to the servants on the ground floor to Charlie and Alice in the nursery upstairs. This was something entirely out of their ken. The remarkable thing was that it was out of his as well.

He rode down the main street of the village. It was Friday night, and Derleth was a glow of candlelight. A prosperous community, MacGuinness had said, even if their lungs were filled with coal dust. But it was the thought of all those other places which were also filled with coal dust which kept ranging through his mind. He had not been so affected in years. He could not ever remember having been so affected.

He drew rein outside the inn, from whence there came the sound of voices and laughter. He dismounted, opened the door of the pot room, went in, gazed at the men, and women, and children, gathered there, some sitting at a long table to one side, most standing, drinking ale from pint pots, gossiping and giggling. Certainly they looked happy enough.

Hatchard, the publican, saw the squire in the doorway and touched his forehead. Slowly the understanding that they were in the presence of a superior being spread away from the bar counter. Conversation ceased, and smiles died, and everyone in the room turned.

"Good evening to you all," Haggard said.

"Good evening, Mr. Haggard," they chorused.

"I need some help," Haggard said. "One of my people has absconded."

They stared at him, not apparently understanding his meaning.

"Mr. Haggard?" MacGuinness emerged from a table at the far side of the room, his face red, his mug of beer still in his hand.

"Ah, MacGuinness. I would like you to organize a posse for me. One of my blacks has run off."

MacGuinness came closer, a fixed smile on his mouth. "Let me buy you a mug of ale, Mr. Haggard."

"I've no time for ale, MacGuinness. Nor any inclination."

"Please, Mr. Haggard." MacGuinness lowered his voice.

Haggard remembered what he'd been told that morning. And an extra half-hour would not matter very greatly. "All right, MacGuinness. I'll take a mug with you. But I shall buy. I shall buy for everyone." He shouldered his way through the crowd. "Mr. Hatchard, you'll serve everyone in the room, and render the tally to me."

"Indeed I will, Mr. Haggard. The squire's buying, lads and lasses. Who'll give a cheer for the squire?"

The noise echoed, and the room burst into a babble of conversation. People squeezed Haggard's fingers, and one or two even slapped him on the shoulder. A full tankard of ale was thrust into his hand, and he found himself against the counter, with MacGuinness beside him.

"Your health, Mr. Haggard. That was a masterly stroke, it was." He lowered his voice again. "Now, what's the trouble?"

"My man, Middlesex, has run off. I'm damned if I know why. But I'll have him back."

MacGuinness commenced to frown. "Run off," he muttered. Then his expression brightened. "He stole, of course. Took some money."

"Why, I have no idea. I doubt it."

"He stole, Mr. Haggard. That's what you must tell these people if you'd obtain their help."

Haggard's turn to frown. "I'm not sure I understand you."

'Well, Mr. Haggard . . ." MacGuinness drank some beer. "English people, and especially people up here, well, sir, they don't much hold with slavery. I doubt they'd come with you to return a man to bondage. No, sir."

"But he's my property."

"No doubt, sir, no doubt. According to law. But, well, sir, living out here, there is no law, really, saving what we makes our own. They'll not have it, sir. Believe me. I know them well. And you want to remember, almost your entire electorate is in here, saving the parson."

"You mean I must just let him go, unless I ride after him myself?"

"No, sir. You tell them not that he's an absconding slave, but that he's a thief and a robber, sir, who took money from the kindest master who ever lived. And one of your horses,

I'll be bound. They'll ride with you then, sir. They don't hold with thieving."

Haggard scratched his head; he had never told a lie in his life. But he had never had to deal with a runaway, either. He straightened his tricorne. "Very well, Mr. MacGuinness. If I must stoop to subterfuge. Let's get it done."

"Leave it to me, sir." MacGuinness banged on the counter with his empty mug. "Now, you listen to me, lads," he cried. "As you know, this gentleman who has just bought you all a pint is the new squire, Mr. Haggard. And you can take it from me, lads, that he's the best and kindest gentleman any of you will ever have known, or ever will know. So what do you think has happened to him? His very own butler has run off with the family silver. Every last piece of valuable from the manor dining room. Can you believe it, lads? This scoundrel, who has lived and worked with Mr. Haggard all of his life, and been looked after by Mr. Haggard all of his life, has now turned on the hand that has fed him all of his life. What time did he leave, Mr. Haggard?"

"Early this morning."

"Would he have been a black man, Mr. Haggard?" someone asked.

"Aye."

"I saw a black man riding down the street, on way to pit," the man said.

"And so did I," said another.

"Where was he heading?" MacGuinness asked.

"For the London road."

"Aye," Haggard said. "I made the mistake of letting them have a look at London during the couple of days we were there." Middlesex was intelligent enough to suppose that in so big a city he would easily disappear.

"But he weren't carrying no bag of silver," said the first man. "Leastways, I didn't see none."

"He had saddlebags, didn't he?" MacGuinness asked. "He wouldn't have been stupid enough to carry it in his arms. I need three volunteers to ride after him with Mr. Haggard and me."

There was a moment's silence while glances were exchanged.

"You'll be well paid," Haggard said.

"I'll come with you, Mr. Haggard," a young man said. "Peter Wring is the name."

"Thank you Wring. Anyone else?"

"Me, sir. Jemmy Lacey."

Very obviously Margaret's brother, alike in size and in his handsome looks. Haggard wondered he hadn't noticed him before. "Thank you Jem."

"And me, Mr. Haggard. Toby Doon."

"Then let's be at it. There are horses in my stables." Haggard finished his ale, went to the door. "I thank you. I thank you all."

" 'Tis us to be thanking you, Mr. Haggard," Hatchard said. "We'll back you, sir."

"At least there'll be no problems with your election, Mr. Haggard," MacGuinness said. The two men rode down the London road, jolting in the saddle, as even the horses could not avoid occasionally stumbling in the deep ruts carved in the rain-softened earth by the stagecoaches. Their three companions rode behind.

"Would there have been in any event?"

"Independent people, Derleth folk," MacGuinness said. "Why, Squire Redmond, that was here before you, sir, he didn't get on too well with them, was always cursing at them for lazy dirty scum. He never drank with them."

"And he took his seat in the Commons just the same," Haggard said.

"Ah, but there was some question of it, sir. There was talk of an opposition candidate, but they couldn't raise the deposit money. But eleven of them abstained. Mr. Redmond was elected by five votes."

"Yet he was elected," Haggard pointd out. "Nor is there the slightest prospect of a community of farmers and coal miners raising the money to finance a parliamentary deposit."

"Still, sir, it's best to be a popular squire, if it can be managed," MacGuinness said.

"No doubt," Haggard agreed, and gazed down the turnpike in front of them. The rain was falling harder than ever, and the road had remained empty, save for the stage, which had rumbled by them several hours before. But now he could see lights.

" 'Tis a village, sir," MacGuinness said. "And a good place to stop, if you'll pardon the liberty."

"Stop?" Haggard inquired.

"Well, sir, it must be nearly dawn, and we've ridden all night. The horses need fodder, and if you'll pardon me, sir, so do we. And a warm fire for an hour."

"And what of Middlesex? Will he have stopped, do you suppose?"

"He must eat as well, Mr. Haggard."

"Oh, very well." Haggard pulled his horse into the gateway of the inn, dismounted, stretched. He was very tired. And hungry. He stamped up the steps to the door, banged his fist on the paneling.

It was some minutes before a window opened over his head. "Who's there?"

"Five men, seeking breakfast."

"It's four o'clock in the morning."

"We're on urgent business, man. Come down and open up."

"You'll be highwaymen," the landlord complained.

"I am John Haggard, squire of Derleth Hall, with four companions. I've silver coin in my pocket. Now, come down or I'll break the door."

The window closed, and a few minutes later there was the scraping of a bolt. "You hold that blunderbuss ready, mistress," the landlord said, and cautiously opened the door. "Urgent business, you say? What urgent business?"

Haggard pushed the door wider and stepped inside. The fire had burned down but the room was still warmer than the open air. He raised his hat to the large, stout woman, clad in an undressing robe and with her hair concealed beneath a mobcap, who leveled the blunderbuss at his chest. "John Haggard, ma'am. We seek a . . . a servant of mine who has absconded with my silver."

"A thief, you say." The landlord peered at the other four men as they came in and shook water from their hats.

"A black man," MacGuinness explained.

"A blackamoor. Why . . ." He glanced at his wife.

"He's been here?"

"Oh, aye, sir, he's been here. Last evening it was. Stopped to have a bite of supper. I didn't see no silver, though."

"But you served him supper," MacGuinness pointed out. "Therefore he had coin."

"Why, sir, so he did. Food for these gentlemen, Rebecca. Eggs. Bacon. Bread."

"Now, that sounds attractive." MacGuinness led the way to the table. "And some ale."

"Right away, sir. Right away."

Haggard remained standing. "Did he stay the night?"

"Well, no, sir. He left with Mr. Sharp?"

"Who the devil is Mr. Sharp?"

"Well, sir, I don't rightly know. Save that he is a wealthy gentleman." The landlord set five foaming tankards of ale on the table, while a most delicious smell started to drift in from the kitchen. "Lives up north, he does, sir, but has businesses in London, and travels this way regularly. Well, sir, he was here last night with his berlin, on the way to town, and he got talking with this man, sir. I don't know what was said, but Mr. Sharp offered the black man a seat in his carriage, sir, and away they went. About eleven of the clock it was."

"And the horse?" demanded MacGuinness. "It was Mr. Haggard's."

"They left the horse here, sir. If it is yours, Mr. Haggard, if you are really Mr. Haggard, you are welcome to it."

"The devil," Haggard said. "What do you suppose has happened?"

"Now, that I couldn't say, sir," MacGuinness confessed. "But if this Mr. Sharp is so well known on the road, you may be certain he is known in town also. We shall find him, sir, have no fear."

"Then let's be at it." Haggard drank his beer.

"There's time for a bite to eat, Mr. Haggard," Lacey protested. "Why, sir, my belly wouldn't let me leave such a smell without filling."

"The lad's right, Mr. Haggard," MacGuinness agreed. "If Middlesex has gone with this Mr. Sharp, we'll find him, like I said."

"Only if he stays with Sharp," Haggard pointed out. "He could be away in a different direction by now."

"No, sir," MacGuinness said. "Then he'd have taken the horse with him. My opinion is that we'll find him when we find Mr. Sharp."

Haggard sighed and sat down. But the food, which was now being brought out of the kitchen, great steaming platters of eggs and bacons, was really irresistible. And why should he ride himself to death in pursuit of a slave? So long as they caught up with him in the end. But MacGuinness was a shade too definite in his opinion.

"You've heard of the fellow?" he asked, as eggs were piled before him. "Sharp?"

"Aye, well, I have, sir."

"Well?"

"Well, sir, he's a wealthy gentleman . . . nothing like so

wealthy as yourself, of course, but with money to spare, who spends his time supporting our weaker brethren."

"A Quaker, you mean?"

"Now, that I couldn't say, sir, but I doubt it. No, sir, what is the word I am thinking of? 'Tis a long one, to be sure."

"Philanthropist?"

"The very thing, Mr. Haggard. Education is a wonderful thing. Aye, sir, that's what he is, a philanthropist." He rolled the syllables around his tongue.

"Who has taken up the cause of Middlesex, has he?" Haggard said. "How old would this gentleman be?"

MacGuinness shrugged. "Older than you, sir, to be sure. Past fifty."

"Then he should know better. You find him for me, MacGuinness."

"Soon as I've had my breakfast, sir. You may count on that."

They rode down Piccadilly two days after leaving Derleth. By then Haggard has sent the three tenants home with the horse Middlesex had stolen, and retained only MacGuinness. He did not anticipate any trouble with Granville Sharp, and if MacGuinness was wrong, and Middlesex had taken off in some other direction, well, then he was lost anyway, and the only answer would be to take out an advertisement in the *Times*. But MacGuinness remained confident enough. He made a few inquiries from street vendors and at a coffee shop, and led Haggard down one of the broad, pleasant thoroughfares which stretched away from the open fields where the great May Fair was held every spring.

"There we are, sir," he said, pointing to a three-storied house set in its own grounds. "The town residence of Mr. Granville Sharp."

"I'll do the talking," Haggard said. MacGuinness was far too fond of taking over a conversation.

"Of course, Mr. Haggard."

They walked their weary horses through the gate and under the trees. A dog barked, and immediately grooms ran from the stables, while the front door of the house opened to reveal a butler.

Haggard dismounted. They had stopped for a night's sleep in St. Albans, and the rain had at least ceased, but he still felt chilled and damp and very tired.

"Good morning, sir," said the butler. "Is Mr. Sharp expecting you?"

"No," Haggard said. "But I'll see him just the same."

The butler frowned at him. "Your name, sir?"

"John Haggard. I should think he knows it by now."

"Ah. Yes, sir. If you'll come this way, sir." The door was held open, and Haggard and MacGuinness were allowed into the hall, and thence into a small withdrawing room on the ground floor, where a footman relieved them of their hats and coats.

"A hot bath," MacGuiness said. "That is what I feel like, Mr. Haggard. A large tub filled with boiling water. Does that not appeal, sir?"

"When we get back to Derleth, MacGuinness." Haggard turned to face the door as it opened, and was disturbingly surprised. He had prepared himself to loathe Sharp on sight, had built up his antagonism to combat any suggestion of exhaustion or pity for Middlesex. But he found it hard to hate the short, slight, well-dressed, and open-faced man who entered the room. Granville Sharp wore a Cadogan wig and carried a pair of gold-rimmed spectacles. He blinked at his visitors, gave them a benign smile.

"John Haggard," he said. "Welcome, sir. Granville Sharp."

He extended his hand; Haggard had to refuse to take it with a conscious effort of will.

"You have knowledge of some property of mine, sir."

Sharp gazed at him for a moment. "Property of yours," he said at last. "My God, how easily the words roll off the tongue of a nabob. We are speaking of a human being, sir."

"Where is he?" Haggard demanded.

"That, sir, I am not prepared to tell you."

Haggard frowned at him. "You are condoning larceny, sir, at the very least. I would be within my rights to take him by force."

"What, Mr. Haggard, will you assault me in my own home? Be sure that I have six stout fellows waiting outside just in case your West Indian temper gets the better of your good sense." He opened the door as he spoke; there were indeed six footmen waiting, expressions suitably determined.

"By God," Haggard said. "I had supposed you a gentleman."

"I hope I am, Mr. Haggard. An *English* gentleman. Now, answer me this conundrum, sir. Can there be such a thing as a gentleman who is also a slave owner?"

Haggard glanced at MacGuinness, who raised his eyebrows helplessly. "They are too many for us, Mr. Haggard."

"Tell me where he is," Haggard said.

"I shall not do that, sir," Sharp said.

"But you'll not deny that you assisted him to abscond?"

"I shall do more than that, Mr. Haggard. He is my responsibility, as of now."

"I have a witness," Haggard said.

"Then shall I repeat it, for the benefit of your witness?"

"Sir," Haggard said, "I respect your motives, as you wish to spend your life in aiding our less fortunate brethren. However, you have put yourself beyond the law, and in addition, believe me, done Middlesex no good at all by this madcap venture. Now, let me see him. I promise you, no violence shall be done in your house. I merely wish to speak with my servant."

"And I, sir, forbid it in my house," Sharp said. "Oh, you are a big man, Mr. Haggard, a wealthy man, a rich man, and a most forceful personality. I doubt Middlesex would retain his courage were he to come face to face with you."

"You leave me no option but to take you to law," Haggard said.

Sharp gave a brief bow. "Then, sir, I look forward to seeing you in court."

Haggard stared at him for some seconds. He had never been so angry in his life; his every instinct called out for him to smash his way through this house until he found the Negro. But it was a strange anger. He did not want to flog Middlesex. He had always supposed himself a friend to his blacks, and more especially his house slaves. He did not even want to harm Sharp. He just felt like committing an act of violence upon someone or something, it did not matter who or what.

But his instincts were also warning him that this was not Barbados. John Haggard was not omnipotent here, beyond the reach of the law just because he owned the largest plantation in the land. And if he was to achieve his seat in Parliament, then he must not be seen to break the law.

"Be sure, sir, you *shall* see me in court."

"How long will it take?" he asked Cummings, when the three men met over dinner in a private chamber off the tap room of the inn where MacGuinness had found him a room.

"I will begin this afternoon, Mr. Haggard," the agent said.

"You may leave it to me. I'll talk to a magistrate, he is a friend of mine, and have a writ made out, and deliver it before nightfall. Oh, we'll have Mr. Sharp, and the man Middlesex, in court by the end of this week, you may be sure of that."

"The end of this week?" Haggard demanded. "I had not meant to remain this long."

"Ah, well, sir, the wheels of justice grind slowly. But they do grind."

"The devil." Haggard gazed at MacGuinness. "Then you'd best return to Derleth, MacGuinness. Report to Mistress Dearborn on what has happened, and tell her I will be back as soon as possible."

"Of course, Mr. Haggard. But I cannot leave you here, without a manservant. And you've not even a change of linen."

"I will procure a manservant for Mr. Haggard, and some clothing," Cummings said. "Indeed, sir, I would take it as a privilege if you would care to move in with me. Mistress Cummings would be more than pleased to see to your requirements."

Haggard was not sorry to move. But the Cummingses lived in the City itself, a small, cramped house set on the edge of a narrow thoroughfare leading away from Threadneedle Street. The windows were small and the interior gloomy; the furniture was well worn and the smell was musty. To cap Haggard's depression, Mistress Cummings turned out to be very nearly as old as her husband, and however attractive she might once have been, she was now tall, thin, angular, and a trifle brusque.

"Mr. Haggard," she said, her mouth widening into a wintry smile. "This *is* a privilege."

But her gaze was suspicious; no doubt Cummings had regaled her with tales of Emma. Haggard could only console himself with the thought that it was for only a few days, while Mrs. Cummings was at least an excellent cook.

But, he reflected as he accompanied Cummings to court three days later, wearing a new broadcloth suit hastily run up by the agent's tailor, he could not for a moment pretend that England was in any way like his expectation of it. So what had he expected? That they would provide a guard of honor as he left the ship, that the sun would shine, that all the nobility of London would come flocking to see him, that the villagers of Derleth would line the street and wave flags as he rode through them, that Derleth Hall would turn out to be a palace, that his coal mines . . . But he did not know what to think about the coal mines. He did not know what he dared think of them. For some reason, whenever he remembered those naked, coal-stained girls, his breeches seemed to halve in size. And he had spent his entire life surrounded by naked humanity.

He reasoned that it was just the transition which was confusing and upsetting him. And his precipitate flight from London. While now he had come back without notice, simply in pursuit of a runaway. It would be different once he was an M.P., when he visited the city to take his place in the Commons, when his voice would be heard pronouncing on all the great issues of the day, when his new manor house was built, when Emma . . . But strangely he did not wish to think about Emma, either, at this moment. There were too many others.

He must merely keep on his course, completing each step in his plan as it came upon him. And the first step was the regaining of James Middlesex, the understanding of all who came into contact with him that he was Haggard, and not to be trifled with. He gazed across the small courtroom at the black man, no longer wearing his Haggard livery, but in a suit of gray no doubt provided by Sharp, who sat beside him. "Who is the third man?" he asked Cummings.

The agent was frowning. " 'Tis Barcroft, the solicitor."

"Do we need a solicitor?"

"I would not have supposed so. You have but to lay claim. Now."

For the magistrate was peering at them. "Will the plaintiff stand up?"

Haggard stood up.

"State your name and occupation and address."

"I am John Haggard, late of Haggard's Penn on the island of Barbados, but now resident at Derleth Hall in Derbyshire."

"State the charge you propose to bring."

He found himself becoming irritated by the monotonous disinterest of the voice.

"My charge is very simple," Haggard said.

"Your Honor."

"Eh?"

"You will address the bench as 'your Honor,' Mr. Haggard."

Definitely he should have had a solicitor. Cummings was

incompetent. "My charge, your Honor," he said, his voice slowing to that even tone which betrayed his anger, "is that that black man over there, whose name is James Middlesex, is my slave, whom I brought from Barbados as my butler, and who ran away from Derleth Hall six days ago. He was aided in his escape by Mr. Granville Sharp, whom you see sitting next to him. I pursued my slave, but was prevented from regaining him by Mr. Sharp. I am here today, your Honor, to obtain restitution of my lawful property."

The magistrate peered at him for a while longer, then nodded. "You may sit down, Mr. Haggard. Mr. Sharp?"

Barcroft stood up. "I represent the defendant, your Honor."

"Yes, Mr. Barcroft."

"Your Honor . . ." Barcroft grasped the lapels of his coat. "My client contends that there is no charge for him to answer, by the very simple reason that slavery is not recognized in this country, therefore the man Middlesex cannot be a slave, therefore he cannot be accused of having run away from anyone. My client is prepared to admit that the man Middlesex borrowed a horse belonging to Mr. Haggard, but the animal has since been returned, and Mr. Sharp is prepared to pay a reasonable sum as rental for the animal during the two days it was away from Derleth Hall."

"One moment, Mr. Barcroft," the magistrate interrupted. "Do I understand, from what you have said, that your client does not deny assisting the man Middlesex to abscond?"

"My client does not deny befriending the man Middlesex and assisting him, your Honor. Certainly he denies assisting him to abscond, because how may a free man abscond?"

"Hum," said the magistrate. "Hum. Mr. Haggard?"

"I am amazed that you listen to such rubbish," Haggard said.

"Mr. Haggard? This is a court of law."

"And I expect it to uphold the law, your Honor. I am an Englishman, and I own certain property. That man is mine, just as the horse he took is mine, just as Derleth Hall is mine. No one can deny these things. A man's property is inviolable. There is the oldest of all English common laws. I must insist upon the return of Middlesex to my care."

"Hum," said the magistrate. "Hum. Mr. Barcroft?"

"Your Honor," said the solicitor, "this great nation of ours has ever led the entire world in the efficacy of our laws, the transparent goodness, humanity, lawfulness of our laws. Your

Honor, in common with many other nations, centuries ago we recognized the pernicious institution of serfdom. We allowed certain men to rise above themselves and seek to own others less fortunate than themselves. Your Honor, for two centuries my ancestors and yours fought for that terrible injustice to be abolished. Your Honor, a hundred years ago we won that fight. When King William came to the throne, uplifted and protected, but also constrained, by the Bill of Rights, the possibility of one man enslaving another was gone from this great land our ours. Your Honor, I know not, and I care not, what barbarous practices obtain in remote colonies such as Barbados. You know, and I know, that the West Indies have ever been a breeding ground for piracy and every ill known to mankind. Possibly conditions in those savage climes necessitate different men who project different attitudes. But this is not Barbadian soil on which I am standing. I am standing on English soil, your Honor, and regardless of what I have done, no man has the right to enslave me. If I am in debt and cannot pay, my creditor has the recourse of sending me to prison. If I have committed murder or treason, the law has the recourse of taking my life. But so long as I am alive and English, no man can put fetters on my wrists and say 'You belong to me.' Your Honor, to grant the claim that this man Middlesex be returned to Mr. Haggard's custody, to the whip and the chain and the insults of serfdom, would be to lower our great country once again to the level of Russian autocracy. It cannot, it will not, happen here, sir."

"By God," Haggard said.

"Hum," said the magistrate. "I must ask you to control your temper, Mr. Haggard."

"Then return me my property," Haggard said.

"Hum," said the magistrate. "I really feel that this entire matter is beyond my jurisdiction and should be referred to a higher authority."

Haggard frowned at him. He could not believe his ears. "You are confessing your incompetence to pronounce on a matter of law?"

"Be careful, Mr. Haggard," the magistrate said, "or I will hold you in contempt. I can understand your situation. But I must also take note of Mr. Barcroft's arguments. There *is* no slavery in England. That is the law. Why, sir, I shudder to think of the consequences were any judgment of mine to suggest a restoration of so uncivilized a possibility. At the same time, the man was not enslaved here, but was brought from overseas. Now, there is a complicated matter."

"And as there must be many other gentlemen who, like myself, have black servants, your Honor," Haggard pointed out, "can you not shudder to consider the consequences of a judgment which would set all of them free?"

"It is not proven that such other black servants are slaves, your Honor," Barcroft said.

"Gentlemen, gentlemen, these cross-arguments are both irregular and confusing. And I repeat, it seems to me that the issues at stake here are too great to be decided in this brief discussion. Should you wish to pursue your claim, Mr. Haggard . . ." He paused, peered at Haggard once again, this time more hopefully. "You do wish to pursue your claim to this man's person?"

"He belongs to me," Haggard said. "Why do you suppose I should not wish to pursue my claim?"

"Then you will have to take the matter to a superior court. I would suggest, Mr. Haggard, that you employ a solicitor to see to your interests, and that you instruct him to brief a barrister for the presentation of your case. Thank you, gentlemen."

"Wait just a minute," Haggard said. "How long will this reference to a higher court take?"

"It will be expedited as soon as your solicitor prepares your case, Mr. Haggard. Certainly not more than a year."

"A year?" Haggard shouted.

"You will address me as 'your Honor,' Mr. Haggard."

"A year," Haggard repeated. "And what of the custody of Middlesex?"

"Ah," said the magistrate.

"Your Honor," Barcroft said. "The defendant will of course be happy to cooperate with your Honor's decision to refer the matter to a higher court. But you must see that such a decision is meaningless should the man Middlesex be returned to the custody of Mr. Haggard. He will be immediately treated as a slave. Why, my lord, we cannot even be sure he will be here to appear in a year's time."

"Are you suggesting Mr. Haggard would . . . ah . . . do him an injury?"

"That I cannot say," Barcroft said, casting Haggard a contemptuous glance. "But we do know that Mr. Haggard owns a sugar plantation in Barbados. Once given inalienable rights over the body of Middlesex, he might well decide to return him to that bondage from which he has so fortunately escaped."

"Hum," said the magistrate. "There's a point, Mr. Haggard."

"You will have to take my assurance on the matter," Haggard said.

"Hum," said the magistrate.

"Your Honor, I must protest," Barcroft said. "It would be quite intolerable to expose Middlesex to Mr. Haggard's whims and angers and cajoleries, without hope of redress, until the case is decided one way or the other."

"And what proof have we that Mr. Sharp will not send Middlesex from the country during the year?"

"Gentlemen," said the magistrate. "You will address the bench and not each other. Mr. Sharp will give financial assurance that Middlesex will appear before the Supreme Court as and when he is required to do so. In the meanwhile, he is remanded in the custody of Mr. Sharp."

"By God," Haggard said. "I have never heard just a travesty of justice."

"I will overlook that remark, Mr. Haggard, as I am about to adjourn this court." The magistrate stood up. "Court adjourned."

"Congratulations, Barcroft. " Sharp shook hands with his solicitor, as did Middlesex. "You did us proud."

Haggard glared at them. He could not recall ever being so angry in his life. British justice. Why, he might as well have stayed in Barbados. At least there he had known exactly where he stood.

"We'd best leave, Mr. Haggard," Cummings muttered. "There is a gentleman—"

"The devil with it," Haggard growled. He left his seat and crossed the floor. Sharp saw him coming and stepped away from the other two.

"My day, Mr. Haggard. But you'll have another chance."

Haggard stared at him, brows drawing together. "Do you suppose this is some game, sir?"

"I regard it as a contest, certainly, Mr. Haggard, between at best two different interpretations of the law, at worst between the forces of repression and the forces of liberty. It is a contest I propose to win, if it is possible to do so, but I can respect a formidable adversary."

"By God," Haggard said. He looked at Middlesex. "Have you nothing to say to me?"

Middlesex chewed his lip. "Well, I must be sorry to have caused you this trouble, Mr. John."

"Why?" Haggard demanded. "In the name of God, why? Have I ever ill-treated you? Have I ever shown you anything but kindness? Come now, man, speak the truth."

"Well, Mr. John, is a fact you have always been good to me."

Haggard scratched his head in sheer frustration. "Yet you have run away."

"Well, Mr. John, sir, is a fact a man got for be free, if he can. All the people I am meeting, they are free, Mr. John. And they asking me, why you are not free? How are you a slave? They asking, Mr. John, and I am thinking. How am I a slave?"

"And there you have it in a nutshell, Mr. Haggard," Barcroft said.

Haggard looked from one to the other, then turned back to Sharp. He was aware of a feeling of total humiliation. Sharp had made a fool of him, in the most public fashion. There was only one course of action left to a gentleman, and a Haggard. "You, sir, are nothing more than an agitator. And, through the mouth of your attorney here, you have seen fit to cast the gravest aspersions upon my honesty and indeed my humanity. I regard that as an insult, sir. My second will call upon you."

Sharp gathered up his papers. "And he will be shown the door, sir. I am not afraid to be a coward. Go and fight with your fellow planters, and leave honest men in peace." He walked past Haggard to the door. Middlesex and Barcroft followed.

For the first time in his life Haggard was speechless. It had never occurred to him that it was possible for a gentleman to refuse a challenge. He stared after the disappearing men, his fists opening and shutting.

"Mr. Haggard," Cummings said.

"I doubt this country is truly for me," Haggard said. "It is composed of lawyers and cowards so far as I can see."

"Not entirely, Mr. Haggard. There is a gentleman most anxious to have a word with you."

"And I have no desire to speak with anyone at this moment," Haggard said.

"Please, sir. It will certainly be to your advantage."

Haggard sighed, allowed himself to be escorted to the back

of the courtroom, where he found a very elegant man, older than himself, and only of medium height with a stocky build, but dressed in the height of fashion in a dark green heavy cloth garrick overcoat, white buckskin breeches, and black leather hessian boots with braided tops and a gold tassel hanging from each. His coat was pale green, worn over a piqué waistcoat; his hat was a gray felt with a silk cord, which he now proceeded to raise. His face was uncommonly fine, having small, perfectly etched features, small nose and mouth and chin all fitting smoothly into the other. He made Haggard feel like a tramp.

"John Haggard." He held out his hand. "Thomas Brand, at your service."

Haggard shook hands. "You find me at a difficult moment, sir."

"Indeed, that man Wallace is a confounded Whig. Not to be trusted. You are staying on in town?"

Haggard shrugged. "There seems little point. Cummings here can find me a solicitor. It seems I must crawl back to Derleth with my tail between my legs."

"Stuff and nonsense," Brand said. "You'll not let a trifling setback like this disconcert you? Not John Haggard, I'll be bound. You'll dine with me, sir. I insist upon it."

"You are very kind," Haggard said. "Perhaps you'd explain your interest in me."

"I had heard you were a plain-spoken man as well. It will be my pleasure. You'll excuse us, Cummings."

The agent did not seem offended. "Of course, Colonel Brand. I'll see to the matter right away, Mr. Haggard."

"Aye," Haggard said, and followed Brand outside into the drizzle. Here a phaeton was waiting, and a moment later they were seated side by side, the gate closed and a rug thrown across their knees. Brand drove himself, handling reins and whip with considerable skill.

"I was told of your arrival in England by Harry Addison," he explained.

"Ah," Haggard said. "Then you'll be a political gentleman."

"Indeed I am. I am one of the Tory whips."

"You'll have to explain that to me."

"It is my business to marshal sufficient support for Mr. Pitt in the Commons, whenever he feels the need of it. I may say he is most anxious to meet you. Will you not stay over for another few days?"

"To meet Pitt?"

"Amongst others."

"Aye, well, with this business over Middlesex dragging its feet, I doubt I will be much use to you."

"But you must, Mr. Haggard. These are tumultuous times approaching. We shall need every vote we can find to carry through Mr. Pitt's program. No, no, sir. You have suffered a setback. Believe me, every right-thinking man will sympathize with you. But nothing more can be done, at least by you personally, until the case comes again to court. Now you must concentrate on your election. Of course it is a simple matter, owning Derleth Hall as you do, yet must you campaign forcefully, allow your views to be heard, bring yourself before the public. I may say we were disappointed at the haste with which you abandoned London."

"I received little welcome here," Haggard pointed out. "And I wished to see my new home."

"You would have been welcomed, had you but spared the time," Brand insisted. "But that is an ommission on our part for which I humbly apologize, and which I personally shall see is remedied. But first, dinner." He turned the phaeton through the driveway of a house situated in a close off Bond Street. Yardboys hurried forward to take the bridle, while others opened the gate to allow their master down. Brand waited for Haggard, escorted him into the entry hall. "I'd have you meet my daughters," he said. "Alison and Emily."

For the second time that morning Haggard found himself bereft of speech as well as breath. For Alison Brand *was* breathtakingly lovely. About the same height of her father, she possessed similar features, but on her refined to such an extent that save for the delicious flare of her nostrils she might have been carved from marble. Her complexion was pale, with just a touch of color at her cheeks, and the whole was shrouded in a halo of magnificently fine pale gold hair which descended past her shoulders in a dead-straight shawl. Her figure had the slenderness of youth, but that it would match up to the promise of the face and the hair Haggard did not doubt for an instant.

Her sister was but slightly less perfect, and had the more ready smile; Haggard observed that although they were not twins, Alison being clearly the elder, they dressed alike, each wearing a simple blue gown, with a high waist and a low bodice, bosom modestly hidden by a white fichu, and their movements and gestures were remarkably similar, as were their voices, low and caressing.

"Mr. Haggard," Alison said, extending her hand and leaving him uncertain whether to shake it or kiss it. "Papa has told us so much about you."

"Mr. Haggard," Emily said, her actions duplicating her sister's, "it is a pleasure to have you in our house."

"They look after me," Brand said, "now that my dear wife has passed on. Ah, me, I must prepare myself to lose them, would you not say, Haggard? Next summer Alison will be eighteen, and for presentation at court. If she does not run off and elope before then."

Alison flushed prettily. "Papa listens to the sound of ladders against my bedroom window, every night," she said. "You'll take a glass of punch, Mr. Haggard." She led him into the withdrawing room, her sister at her side, while Haggard realized he had not spoken since entering the room. He was John Haggard. He was not the sort of man to be struck dumb by feminine beauty or feminine poise like some mooning youth. Yet he could think of absolutely nothing to say.

"Papa tells us you will be spending a few days with us," Emily said, sitting beside him on the settee.

"Why, I—"

"Of course you will, Haggard. What, a man of your caliber staying with an agent? I'll send my man for your things."

It was time to assert himself. "You are too kind," he said. "But really it would be an imposition on your household. You will have heard, I am sure, Brand, that I am an uncouth colonial, who does not wear a wig, as you can see, and whose habits are truly appalling. Why, I was refused admission to Almack's on my last visit to town."

"Everyone who is anyone has been refused admittance to Almack's, at some time or other, Mr. Haggard." Alison Brand had seated herself on a straight chair opposite him. "It really is a mark of distinction. But if it would suit you to return there, we shall see to it that you are admitted. As for being a colonial, I consider you as a breath of fresh air blown in the front door to scatter away the cobwebs of this stuffy city."

She paused, and looked almost surprised at the temerity of her speech, which only added to her attraction. Haggard glanced at Brand to see if he had taken offense, but the colonel continued to smile.

"As I said, Haggard, they rule me with a rod of iron. And

mighty pleasant it is, too. I'd take deep offense, man, were
you to refuse my invitation. How else could I have you meet
the more important members of our party?"

He sat at Brand's right hand, opposite the tall, spare figure
of Mr. Pitt. On his right, consuming port in great quantities,
was the huge, jolly frame of Henry Dundas, while opposite
Dundas in turn was his earlier acquaintance Henry Addison.
Completing the party, at the foot of the table, was a very
young man named Canning, like Haggard not yet an M.P.
but who was apparently a protégé of the prime minister's.

The six of them had dined alone, the young ladies being
dispatched to have supper in their own quarters. In fact it
had occurred to Haggard, during the three days he had spent
in this house, that for all Brand's pretense of being subject to
petticoat government, *he* ruled his household, and his daughters, with an iron will. Certainly there could be no doubt that
he was the center of the conspiracy which had as its object
the ensnarement of one John Haggard. To what end? Merely
to ensure he became a staunch supporter of the Tory cause?
Or something far deeper, far more sinister, perhaps, looked at
in the cold light of day, but impossible to regard as other
than a delightful prospect when continually subject to the
sight and the scent and the rustle and the gentle voices of the
two sisters. With his senses in a continual state of inflamma-
tion in any event, he found it difficult to keep his hands off
them whenever he saw them, and he saw them all day, for
they had been deputed by their father to show him something
of London, and each morning they had taken him sightsee-
ing, to the Tower, and the park, down the river by ferry to
Greenwich and into the City to view the Bank of England.
They had clustered close as the rain had dripped from their
bonnets and soaked their pelisses, and when he had said,
"Now, there is a remarkable thing," as he had gazed up at
the great colonnades of the bank, "I keep more than a million inside those vaults, and this is the first time I have ever
seen the place," Allison had given an almost hysterical laugh
and clung to his arm for a moment.

So, then, a plot. A Brand beauty in exchange for the Haggard money. An absurd idea, with Emma waiting for him in
Derleth. And besides, as Alison was only seventeen and her
sister a year younger, the difference in ages was a shade too
great to contemplate. But a plot which could make no
progress, as he was aware of what was intended. And mean-

while it was almost the limit of pleasure to be so blantantly wooed by two such gorgeous creatures. *Almost* the limit of pleasure. And the limit remained, if the opportunity presented itself. If he dared. For these were ladies, not serving girls.

But he was John Haggard. It was only necessary to establish himself among these Tory barons instead of depending upon the support of someone like Brand, and that should not take long.

So, then, are you a bad man, John Haggard? Or are your ambitions too great to be contained by manners or convention? It was not a question he wished to answer at this moment.

"Ireland," Pitt was saying. "There is our prime concern, gentlemen."

"You choose a thorny path," Dundas grumbled.

"The path of justice," Pitt insisted. "Oh, they are mostly savages. I am under no false impressions about that. They rob and they steal and they murder each other without compunction. But the fault is surely ours. It was the ambition of Strongbow took us across the sea. Now, how long ago was that? Nearly six hundred years. And in all that time successive English governments have treated the Irish as a conquered, and more, an inferior species. In the last two hundred years the quarrels have been deepened by the difference between Catholic and Protestant. It must end someday, and the sooner it does, the better. I would regard my entire parliamentary career as a failure should I not eradicate the penalties of worshiping the Catholic faith, bury the Test Act, and have Irishmen, Protestant or Catholic, sitting at Westminster before I die."

He paused to drink some port, and the table was for a moment silent.

"Have you any strong views on the matter, Haggard?" Brand asked.

"I agree with Mr. Pitt," Haggard said. "There are few barriers to Catholic advancement in the colonies, save of course in the government service. And I cannot persuade myself that the pope poses any threat to England in this day and age."

"Well said," Pitt agreed.

"Aye, well, as I said, you choose a hard road," Dundas repeated. "And we'd best hope that we are granted the peace to pursue such ideals. What is your opinion of events in Paris, Haggard?"

"Faith, Sir Henry, I have had little time to consider them. But it appears the French are pursuing, in their own fashion, the goal of constitutional monarchy, which has been a considerable blessing to Great Britain, surely. I would say, if we could see the last of French ambitions, we may well be in for a period of peace in Western Europe."

"My own thoughts entirely," Pitt said enthusiastically.

"You do not suppose a French cabinet, even if free from the jurisdiction of a Louis XVI, might be similarly ambitious?"

Pitt gave a wintry smile. "A French cabinet headed by whom, Harry? Jacques Necker?"

The men laughed.

"No, no, there is a complete absence of warlike intent in France at this moment, to my way of thinking. Indeed, whatever the outcome of the constitutional quarrel, we have little to fear. Louis XVI, God bless him, is less warlike even than Necker. Besides, they have no money with which to go to war. Which does not mean we shall not have occasion to defend ourselves. I fear the Russians, gentlemen. Their appetite is wet with Poland, and they start to dream of Mediterranean expansion. You'll agree there is naught to stop them in Turkey. As a matter of fact, as Dundas will agree, one of the first acts of the new Parliament must be to double the navy appropriations."

"I'll say amen to that," Dundas said.

"So will I," Haggard said. "I'm a West Indian, gentlemen. Any scheme for improving and enlarging the navy will meet with my approval."

Pitt finished his port. "I must be on my way. Tomorrow is a busy one." He stood up, came round the table, held out his hand. "This has been a pleasure, Mr. Haggard. You are going to be a source of strength, sir, I can see that. Be sure you are there when the new Parliament convenes."

"You have my word on it," Haggard said.

Pitt gazed into his eyes for a moment, then nodded and left the room, and the other guests went with him.

"I knew you'd appeal to Pitt," Brand said. "This night has seen you properly launched, Haggard. Another?" He had had a great deal to drink himself; his speech was very slightly slurred, and he swayed.

"I suspect bed is indicated," Haggard said.

"Bed," Brand said. "I've no notion for it." He poured himself a glass. "Come wi' me, Haggard. I'll show you the most beautiful sight you've ever seen."

"Not tonight, Brand. Besides, it's raining. I've had just about all of this dismal weather I can stand."

"Ah, be off wi' you," Brand snorted. "I'm not proposing to go out. I'm proposing to go upstairs and look at my darlings. You'll come with me, Haggard. They're fond of you. Oh, yes, I could tell that at a glance. Fond of you." He picked up the decanter with his other hand, swayed toward the door, waved away the footman who would have opened it for him, splashing port.

Haggard followed him into the hall. "I'm not sure I understand you," he said. But his heart was pounding like a bass drum.

"Have you no eyes for a pretty girl?" Brand commenced to climb the stairs. "There's a rumor you keep one in Derleth. She'd have to go, of course."

"Indeed?" Haggard climbed behind him. "Go where, and when?"

Brand had reached the upper landing; now he poured some more port, set the decanter on an incidental table. "I'm thinking it would be the match of the century, Haggard. You may take your pick. Then you'd really be one of us. There's talk, you know." He attempted to wag his finger, and spilled some more wine. "You'll not do well, socially, with a thief in your bed."

"Addison," Haggard said. "I ought to wring his neck."

"Ah, bah, 'tis true. But you're a colonial. People forgive easily. And with a wife on your arm, out of the top drawer, why, you'd be presented at court. I'd see to that." He waved his arm, and this time port splashed onto Haggard's waistcoat. "They're along here."

Haggard knew where the sisters' bedroom was. Now he was hard as a rod; he had drunk enough himself to have lost just a little control of his wits. Presented at court? Why, of course he had to be presented at court. He was John Haggard.

Drunk as he was, Brand appeared to be a mind-reader. "Because they're a damnably stuffy lot," he grumbled, fumbling at the doorknob. "It's the queen, God bless her. All of her sons are lechers. Every one. Why, that Frederick tried to make advances to my Alison. Spurned him, she did. Nothing but debts and worries, she said. She has an old head, she has.

But her majesty, now, she'll receive no one with the slightest blemish on his affairs. No, indeed."

The room was dark, and filled with the scent which the girls each used. Haggard waited while Brand reached up and took a candle from a holder on the wall, held it above his head as he went inside.

"Aren't they splendid?" He drew the side drape from around the bed.

Haggard tiptoed forward, stood beside him. The girls wore white linen nightgowns, and as the fire still glowed in the grate and the room was warm, they had half kicked off their covers. They lay facing each other, Alison on the outside, with her back to him, Emily facing him. Their arms were stretched toward each other, and their fingers were inter-twined; the position pushed their breasts together and thrust them out of the tops of their gowns. Their legs were clearly to be delineated beneath the soft material. Haggard licked his lips and found that his throat was dry. How strange, he thought, that they should share a room, and a bed. Or is Brand even more strapped than I had imagined?

Ladies. It was remarkable how inadequate that one word made him feel. But since Susan he had only ever bedded serving girls and thieves. And even Susan had possessed none of Alison Brand's beauty.

"Take your pick, Haggard," Brand said, turning toward him.

"Really, Brand, this is somewhat unseemly. I am a widower, and old enough to be Alison's father."

"Alison, is it? Thought as much."

"I'd not considered marrying again."

"Stuff and nonsense. A man must have a wife. Come along and we'll talk about it." He turned away, and the girls fell back into shadow. Haggard followed reluctantly, watched his host appear to subside forward, losing the candle and hitting the floor with a most tremendous crash.

"For God's sake," Haggard cried, almost falling over him in turn. But Brand did not reply, and the candle had fallen from his hand and rolled against the wall, going out in the process.

"Papa?" Alison scrambled out of bed.

Haggard stepped over the unconscious man into the gal-lery, found another candle, held it above his head. Both girls were out of bed now, and kneeling beside their father.

"He just fell over," Haggard said helplessly.

"I don't think he's hurt himself," Alison opined, "except perhaps a bruise. We must get him to bed." She looked up, gave a brief smile. "He will be all right, Mr. Haggard. Truly."

"He always is," Emily explained.

Haggard knelt beside them, got his hands into Brand's armpits. His shoulder brushed Alison's, and her hair flopped against his face. "You mean this has happened before?"

"Mmm," Alison said, straining. Slowly they pulled Brand to his feet, and Haggard got one of his arms over his shoulders. Alison went round the other side, took the other arm, and Emily came behind. "Just along here," Alison panted.

"Can I assist you, Miss Alison?" asked the butler, coming up the stairs with a footman at his heels.

"No, thank you, Partridge," Alison said. "I'm sure we can manage. You may retire."

Partridge disappeared, and Emily was opening the door to Brand's bedroom. Haggard and Alison dragged him across the floor and laid him on the bed.

"You may go back to bed, Emily," Alison said.

"But . . ."

"Go back to bed." Alison climbed onto the bed to kneel beside her father, began to loosen his cravat. Haggard stood above her, holding the candle at her shoulder, listened to the soft sound of the door closing as the younger sister withdrew. He looked down on the gentle curving sweep of back beneath him, on the upturned bare feet—she was sitting on her heels as she tugged at the cloth—on the golden hair which had fallen forward to each side of her ears to expose her neck. He inhaled her perfume, and felt quite dizzy with desire. She was seventeen years old. Another Emma had come into his life, but this one had no drawbacks at all. So he would have to marry her. The thought was suddenly extremely pleasant.

But how could he even think like that, with Emma waiting, warm and loving, for him at Derleth. And sniffing and sneezing? But that could only be a brief misfortune.

"Now his boots," Alison panted, sliding down the bed. She undid the laces and began to pull.

"Can I help you?" Haggard asked.

She shook her head, got the first boot off, cheeks pink with effort, turned her attention to the other.

"I should apologize for being in your room," Haggard said. "The fact is, your father—"

"Wished you to see us sleeping," she said without raising her head. "I hope we were decent."

"You were entrancing," Haggard said without meaning to.

The second boot fell on to the floor, and Alison's head at last came up to allow her to look at him. Was she smiling? He could not be sure in the flickering candlelight.

"Well, you were," he said defensively.

"I think we can leave him like this," Alison decided. "He'll be all right." She uncoiled herself, got off the bed, waited.

For him to do what? He stood beside her, and with sudden decision put his arm round her shoulders, at the same time moving forward as if escorting her to the door. She half-turned, in to him, then gave a little sigh and rested her head on his shoulder.

"Alison." He snuffed the candle with his free hand, dropped it to the floor, lifted her into his arms, kissed her on the mouth. Her tongue was shy, and almost attempted to escape his, before she hugged him as tightly, and as passionately. His arms were round her shoulders, and the nightdress was slipping. He drove his hands downward, found her buttocks, gave them a squeeze, and attempted to move between, carrying the cloth with him, but she gave a little wriggle and slipped away altogether.

"Alison." He reached for her, and she stepped back and opened the door.

"You must speak with Papa," she said. "Tomorrow."

"But you." She left her hand on the doorknob, and he caught it, allowed himself to be drawn outside into the comparative light of the gallery.

"I will do whatever Papa tells me to do," she said. "But I know he likes you, Mr. Haggard."

"Do *you* like me, Alison?"

"I will like you, Mr. Haggard."

He brought her closer, but she was shaking her head slowly. "You must speak with Papa."

"Before I can kiss you? I have already kissed you."

"Do you just wish to kiss me, Mr. Haggard?"

His fingers relaxed in surprise at the directness of her question, and she freed her hand. "After you've spoken with Papa."

After I have spoken to Papa. Haggard pulled rein, sat his horse on the hilltop looking down into Derleth Valley. For a moment there he had nearly lost his senses. He was John

Haggard. He had no need, and certainly no desire, ever to marry again. He had his son and heir, and two other children besides. He had Emma. Pray to God she had got over her cold by now. And besides, the Brands were clearly after his wealth as much as his obvious ability to rise in the ranks of the Tory hierarchy. It was a trap well avoided.

But how splendid it would be if Alison could be at his side, looking down at his valley. His to possess, with none of the drawbacks of marriage. There was a dream.

And had he not acted too hastily? He had fled the Brand house as if it had contained the devil, whereas it might well have contained his future social standing. However much Pitt appeared to like him, he was only of interest as a parliamentary candidate. Friendship and political advancement would depend upon his acceptance by the great London hostesses. That had been made painfully clear. And he had fled the most beautiful girl he had ever seen, who wanted only to be his wife.

Because of Emma? She was his conscience. But more than that he knew. She was his halter, the one face on earth which restrained him from descending into the pit of angry profligacy which was so much more attractive in England than ever in Barbados. Are you a bad man, John Haggard? Oh, indeed. But here, at the least, acting an honorable role.

He walked his horse down the road and into the village street. It was late afternoon, and the miners were already home. Several were outside the inn, and Haggard nodded to them as he passed. They hastily raised their hats, but there were no smiles and no greetings. The last time he had seen them they had been drinking at his expense, and had been happy enough to smile then. Surly lot. They compared very badly with the happy black people of Haggard's Penn.

The village fell behind and he passed the church and the vicarage, where candles already glowed at the windows, before approaching the manor house, and a much warmer welcome. There were no dogs to gallop out and greet him—he must put that right, immediately—but the grooms waited to take his bridle, and John Essex opened the door for him.

"Man, Mr. John, sir, but is good to have you back." John Essex took his hat and cloak. "But you didn't catch that stupid black man?"

Haggard frowned at him. Was it possible that Essex did not sympathize with Middlesex? "If I had, he'd be with me now," he said, and went to the foot of the stairs.

"Father." Roger came out of the pantry, arms outstretched. Haggard gave him a hug. Even in ten days he seemed to have grown some more.

"Papa." Charlie was tugging at his hand, with Alice jumping up and down behind him.

"Here I am, safe and sound," he said, squeezing them each in turn. How febrile the world of London seemed beside this domestic bliss.

"Mr. Haggard."

Emma stood at the top of the stairs, looking down at him. She wore a blue gown, high-necked and prim. Her hair was loose and was the auburn stain he had always loved. And the glowing red was gone from her nose, as the thickness had disappeared from her voice. Haggard released the children, ran up the stairs. "Emma. Oh, my darling Emma."

She was in his arms, and he was kissing her mouth. Here was no shyness, only desire. Here was what he had always wanted, and it was the only thing he would ever want. He swept her from her feet, hurried along the corridor, the children running behind. Annie Kent and Amelia emerged to clap their hands at the fun. The door of the bedchamber was open, and he carried Emma through. Her arms were tight around his neck, her cheek pressed against his. But her scent was absent from the room.

He set her on her feet and frowned at her.

"You commanded me to move out," she said.

"I command you to move back in."

"And I must obey your commands, sir," she said with a smile. "Off you go, children," she said. "Your father and I have things to discuss."

"Come along, come along," Amelia shouted, clapping her hands. "You all can' see yo' mother and father got business?"

The door closed. Haggard unfastened Emma's buttons, slid the gown away from her shoulders, thrust his hand inside to find and caress her breasts. She lay back against his chest and sighed. "Did you miss me, Mr. Haggard?"

"I missed you, Emma. My God, how I missed you." Gently he pulled her nipples hard, as he knew she liked, and she wriggled her bottom against the front of his breeches.

"What must the children think?"

"That we love each other." He released her to undress himself, watched her tall, slender beauty unveiling itself in front of him, leaped forward and caught her again. She gave a gasp, then she was in the bed and he was lying on her belly, pushing the hair from her forehead, kissing each eye and her nose and her chin.

"Mr. Haggard," she said into his ear, "I have let Margaret Lacey go."

Haggard kissed her on the mouth, raised his head to smile at her. "The devil with Margaret Lacey, Emma. You are my housekeeper."

Chapter 5

The Tyrant

Mr. Johnson, the schoolmaster, stood in front of the fire, shifting uneasily from foot to foot. He was a short, heavyset man with pugnacious features, presently somewhat embarrassed. It was as usual raining outside, and his boots left damp imprints on the hearth rug.

"Mr. Johnson." Haggard held out his hand. Never had he felt in such a bubbling good humor. Even the climate was nothing more than an irritation. "I'm sorry I've not yet been down to the school, but you'll have heard I was in London."

"Oh, indeed, Mr. Haggard. A bad business."

"You may say that again. Sit down, man, sit down. A bad business. I'll have the scoundrel back, I promise you. I was merely hoodwinked by the intricacies of English law. I'll have him back." He frowned. "Aren't you going to sit down?"

"I would prefer to stand, Mr. Haggard."

"Suit yourself. At least have a glass of wine."

"Thank you, sir, but no."

"Well, you'll excuse me if I have one." Haggard drank deeply. "I've been inspecting my orchards and the wood. Now, there is a pleasant spot. Or it would be if this confounded rain would ever stop. I think I will erect the new manor house closer to that wood. You know I'm going to build?"

"Well, sir, Mr. Haggard . . ."

"I've a man called Nash coming out to see me. Oh, aye, we'll replace this gloomy ruin with something more suitable. But not to fear, Johnson, not to fear. There will be ample funds for improving your school. Now, then, I assume this isn't just a social visit?"

"No, sir, Mr. Haggard. The fact is . . ."

"But I'm glad you're here in any event. I have it in mind to call an election meeting. I'd like to explain to my people just what I propose, when I am elected. Never does any harm to communicate, eh?"

Johnson licked his lips. "It is about the election that I wish to speak, sir."

Haggard leaned back. "Well, go ahead."

"May I first of all ask some questions, sir?"

"Anything you like."

"Well, sir, is it true that all of the black servants you have here are slaves?"

Haggard frowned at him. "They are slaves, Mr. Johnson, if it is any concern of yours." His frown deepened. "You disapprove of slavery?"

Johnson's face was slowly turning crimson with embarrassment. "Every right-thinking man must disapprove of slavery, Mr. Haggard."

Haggard allowed his finger to point. "Are you accusing me, Mr. Johnson, of being a wrong-thinking man?"

"By no means, Mr. Haggard." Johnson forgot his earlier resolution and sat down. "I understand your background, sir. You were born to a certain station in life, and the higher that station, the less likely are we to question the perquisites that accompany it. I would hope, sir, that when the facts are put to you, you would appreciate them, and be swayed by them."

"The facts?" Haggard sat up. "Don't come to me with any balderdash, Johnson." The anger was back, bubbling in his belly, quite dispelling his mood of contentment. Why, it seemed that this entire country was engaged in a vast conspiracy against him. "I'll give you some facts. Have you ever seen happier or healthier people than my blacks?"

"No, sir. But——"

"Do you know the sort of existence their forefathers had in Africa? A continual round of murder and mayhem, an unending sequence of disease, a total absence of literature or any refinement, and, I may add, the worship of the most vicious and heathen gods you may care to name. Compare that existence with the lives they now live."

"Yet are they subject to the whim of a single man, sir."

"Do you not suppose they were subject to the whim of their king, in Guinea?"

Johnson sighed, and stood up again. "Mr. Haggard, if indeed your ancestors removed these people from Africa in order to elevate their standard of living, they are to be honored. But, sir, they did not apparently consider the matter in its entirety. To take a man from one bondage, and clap him in another, is hardly Christian, even if the second bondage is less severe than the first. And I may say, sir, that on the evidence presented before the royal commission, in many cases this second bondage is far *more* severe than the first. Of course I excuse *you* from such a stricture, Mr. Haggard. Every report says that you have ever been a humane man. Yet, sir, are you but one amongst hundreds, perhaps thousands. And in addition, sir, I am bound to say, that by belonging to such a community, you place yourself in the dock of human opinion along with them."

Haggard scratched his head. "I really am totally confounded, Mr. Johnson. But I will tell you this: I do not propose to be lectured in my own house and by my own schoolmaster. You have said your piece, and I am perfectly willing to allow you your own point of view. But I regard the matter as now closed."

"That decision must be yours, Mr. Haggard. But I will not be silenced," Johnson said.

"In the name of God, man, have you come here to quarrel with me?"

Johnson's flush, which had faded during his lecture, now began to gather again. "No, sir, and I apologize for my heat. I came here, sir, to make certain inquiries, resulting from rumors I have heard and information I have received. I now feel it is only proper for me to tell you that I have decided to stand as parliamentary candidate for Derleth."

Haggard stared at him for a moment in total bewilderment. Then he laughed. "You must have lost your senses."

Johnson got up.

Haggard kept his temper with an effort. "And the deposit?"

"That has been made available."

"Sharp, by God." Haggard got up. "Granville Sharp. He seeks to bring me down. Well, we shall see about that. Do you seriously suppose the electors of this borough will vote for their schoolmaster instead of their squire?"

"We shall have to find out, sir. But they are Englishmen, Mr. Haggard. And to any right-thinking Englishman, slavery is an abhorrence. I will bid you good day."

MacGuinness panted, rolled his tricorne between his hands. " 'Tis a meeting. Hard by the church."

Haggard nodded. "You've some lads?"

"Oh, aye. Ten of them. But costly, Mr. Haggard. A guinea apiece."

"Well, hopefully it won't come to violence." He put on his hat, fastened his coat. Emma stood in the doorway to watch him, Roger at her side. "You'd not assault the schoolmaster, Mr. Haggard?"

"I'd not assault anyone, sweetheart. But I cannot have my people suborned." He looked up at the ten mounted men. "Peter Wring, is that you?"

"It is me, Mr. Haggard, sir. And I've Toby with me as well."

"Good man. And Lacey?"

The men exchanged glances. "Well, sir, no. Lacey wouldn't join us."

Haggard mounted. Because of his sister? he wondered.

"Will you take the dog, Mr. John?" John Essex asked.

Haggard pulled the mastiff's ears. But he was only a pup. "I don't think we'll need him."

"Please let me come, Father," Roger begged. "If there's to be a fight, I can swing a stick as well as anyone."

"Your business is to look after Emma," Haggard said. "Anyway, there isn't going to be a fight. We're going to attend a meeting, that's all. We'll be back by ten o'clock." He turned his horse and rode into the darkness, followed by his men.

Emma looked down at the boy who stood beside her, put her arm round his shoulder, and gave him a squeeze; Rufus rubbed against his leg—he had immediately adopted Roger as his master. "Time enough, Roger."

He made no reply, and after a moment she released him. He was a strange boy. She was the only mother he had ever known, and she believed he was genuinely fond of her. Certainly no one, watching him play with Charlie and Alice, could doubt that he loved them. But equally no one could doubt that he worshiped John Haggard, wanted only to be included in his father's plans and ambitions.

"Does he really go to assault Mr. Johnson?" Roger asked.

"Of course not. It is just his way. And Mr. Johnson is really being very wrong in bringing discord to Derleth. His business is teaching, not quarreling with his squire."

Roger went into the house, and Emma closed the door. "Is what he said true, Emma? Is it wrong to have slaves?"

Emma sighed. "Some people say it is wrong to drink strong liquors or eat rich foods. Some people say it is wrong to be ambitious, and certainly wrong to be rich. When you are a man, you will have to decide for yourself what is right and what is wrong."

He gave her a curious glance. "Emma? Is it true that Papa owns you too?"

At last, she thought. For how many years had she waited for that simple question to be asked? "Your father and I are lovers," she said.

"But did he buy you?" Roger persisted.

Emma put her arm back around his shoulders as they climbed the stairs. "Why, yes, he did. He saved me from being hanged, because of a lot of superstitious men. I will tell you about it someday."

"And he owns you?" Roger asked.

"Not anymore." She smiled. "I doubt he knows."

"And yet you stay with him?"

She gave him a squeeze. "I told you, I love him. I'm not going anywhere. I'm going to be here for the rest of his life."

"For the rest of *my* life, Emma. I don't want you ever to go."

She rubbed his head. "For that kind thought, you can sit at the table with me for supper."

"But, Emma, *is* Papa a good man? Do you think he is a good man?"

"He's a good enough man for me, Roger Haggard," she said. "Now, off you go and wash your hands."

Haggard drew rein in the shelter of the willows which grew around the little cemetery. By the side of the schoolhouse a platform had been erected, and on it there stood the Reverend Litteridge. Litteridge, Haggard thought bitterly. He might have known he would be involved. Seated to either side of him were half a dozen other men, none of whom Haggard recognized, save for the schoolmaster and the very obvious slight figure of Granville Sharp himself. In front of the rostrum, breaths clouding into the still November air, was a considerable number of men and some women; Haggard estimated that most of the village must have turned out to hear what their vicar had to say, as they turned out most Sunday mornings for the same purpose.

He dismounted, handed his reins to Peter Wring, and made his way through the trees and into earshot.

"A blight," Litteridge was saying. "A blight across our fair land, and more especially, our fair village. Now, my friends, Mr. Haggard is not a bad man. Indeed, there is sufficient evidence that he is a good and generous one, according to his lights. But are his lights in accord with our way of thinking?

We have this man, born and bred a planter, and therefore, my friends, by definition belonging to the most stiff-necked and arrogant group of men in the world. And do not his actions indicate his attitude? He wishes to return to England, to enjoy the proceeds of his slave-created wealth. So he commands his agent to buy Derleth Hall. No matter that the Redmonds have lived here for four generations. They were not slave owners. Thus they were not wealthy people. There were debts. As we all have debts. So Mr. Haggard's agent buys up the mortgage, and forecloses. There is an end to the Redmonds. And what do we next see? Mr. Haggard takes up residence, with his entourage of slaves, black and white, my friends. For living in the hall is a woman who was convicted as a thief, and deported from this village across the seas, where she could suffer her sentence in justice. But she was a pretty girl, so Mr. Haggard, with another snap of his arrogant fingers, buys her and takes her to his bed, and now brings her back to Derleth as lady of the manor. Can you believe that, my friends? A convicted thief, sentenced to transportation, returned to us as our better. Is this the sort of man you would have represent you in Parliament, my friends, make the laws that will govern this country, stand on our behalf in matters of national import? But I have not yet finished. This man, this Haggard, is also a slave owner, as I have said. And when one of his people, unable any longer to bear the heavy burden of bondage, sought succor away from Derleth, what does Haggard do? He calls for a posse, saddles up, and rides in pursuit, for all the world as if James Middlesex had been a convicted criminal, like his own paramour. A man whose only crime, if it can possibly be a crime, was to seek his freedom, an act any one of you would be honored for attempting, should you ever find yourself in so iniquitous a position. Is *this* the man you would choose to represent you?"

The parson paused, straightened, listened to the murmurs of agreement which came from in front of him. Haggard left the trees and walked toward the platform. For a moment he did not appear to be noticed; then heads began to turn and a muttering began.

"You'll excuse me, Mr. Litteridge," Haggard said. "But you'll not refuse a man the right to speak for himself?"

Litteridge blinked at him. Even in the darkness he seemed to turn pale.

"Do you give others that right, Mr. Haggard?" Sharp demanded.

"I've never stopped a man airing his opinions yet," Haggard said, and mounted the steps to the platform. "Well, now," he said, raising his voice. "Do I have the right to speak?"

"Nah," someone shouted. " 'Tis the parson's platform."

"Be gone wi' you," bawled someone else, apparently addressing the last speaker. " 'Tis the squire's right."

"Aye," said someone else. "Let the squire speak."

Haggard grinned at them, the widening of his mouth hiding the surging anger in his belly. "My right," he said. My right, he thought, to have to wait on the whim of a bunch of stinking coal miners. "Well, then, listen to me," he said, speaking loudly and clearly, but not shouting. " 'Tis true I am a slave owner. And there is the sole reason these men have elected to oppose my taking a seat in the Commons. A slave owner. They have filled your heads with notions about my brutality, about the iniquity of the trade, about the degradation of being a slave. You know my people at the hall. Are they degraded? Do they have stripes on their backs? Are they starving? Are they naked? Answer me that, my friends. Those are slaves. My slaves. Haggard slaves."

"One ran away from you," a voice said.

"Aye, so he did," Haggard said. "As the prodigal son ran away. But, by God, the prodigal was glad to get back, eh?"

There was a roar of approval.

Haggard raised his hands. "You want to be represented in Parliament. You want the best for this great country of ours just as you want the best for this village. Now, let me ask you this. Who is better qualified to achieve that best, a schoolmaster, or your very own squire? Now, Parson Litteridge has just accused me of every vice he can think of. But I accuse him of the greatest vice of all. The vice of being uncharitable. For what is another of the charges he has brought against me? That I keep, as my mistress, a girl from this very village, convicted of theft. Let me tell you about Emma Dearborn, my friends. She was transported, as the vicar says, sold into bondage for ten years. Had I not purchased her, someone else would have done so, and used her hardly, I can promise you that. But in addition, falsely accused of a crime on board the vessel in which she was imprisoned, she would have been sentenced to hang. I could not permit that, my friends. I bought her. And having done that, I fell in love with her. She is a beautiful girl. So I love her.

Have none of you fellows ever fallen in love with a beautiful girl?"

There was a bellow of laughter and a chorus of ayes.

"But you ain't married her," shouted someone from the back.

"No, I have not married her," Haggard said. "I have no intention of ever marrying again. I am a widower, and will remain so. And I'd expect every man to respect that decision."

Another chorus of ayes. But the voice at the back, a vaguely familiar voice, was not to be silenced.

"Fine words, Mr. Haggard. You ain't marrying again because you can't keep your hands off nothing in skirts. That's why he wants us to send him to Westminster, lads. So he can fuck every wench in London."

Haggard peered into the darkness, could only make out a blur of faces. "You'll come forward, sir," he said. "And repeat those words."

"Who'll make me?" demanded the voice.

"Why, I will," Haggard said, and stepped down from the platform. His heart pounded and he could feel the blood surging through his veins, but he was quite cool. He had not fought anyone for too long. Perhaps there was all of his trouble, the sole cause of his uncertainty. And this would be as vital a conflict as when he had opposed Malcolm Bolton. This crowd was not altogether against him, but they were not altogether for him, either. Now they parted willingly enough to let him through, while there was a brief scuffle at the rear and someone shouted, "Stand up to him, Jemmy, if you're so loud with your voice. He can't hang you for speaking."

Haggard reached the back of the throng. Jemmy Lacey. He might have known it. He wondered if Margaret was also here. "Well, Lacey," he said. "What do you have to say to me?"

The young man licked his lips, but he was realizing that he was surrounded by *his* friends, not the squire's, and that he was at least as big a man. "I said you was a lying lecher, Mr. Haggard. I'll not go back on that."

"Then back yourself with your fists," Haggard said, and hit him on the face, not hard, but just sufficient to sting.

Lacey gazed at him in astonishment for some seconds, then gave a grunt, lowered his head, and ran forward. Haggard clasped both hands together to use as a club on the nape of they young man's neck as he came up, but although Lacey gave another grunt, he was not stopped. His arms went round

Haggard's waist as his head crunched into Haggard's stomach with breathtaking force. The impact carried Haggard back, and he tripped and sat down, Lacey landing on top of him.

"Go it, Jemmy boy," someone shouted.

"Lay into him," shouted another.

Haggard struck down again, aware that he had only a few seconds of breath back, as Lacey continued to burrow into his stomach. Again and again he hit the young man, and at last there was a slight slackening of the grip. He rolled to his left, and Lacey went with him, this time underneath. Haggard managed to get a knee up, and the young man grunted and released him. They reached their knees together, Lacey once again grasping at him, but Haggard evaded the clutching hands and gained his feet. Certainly he could not afford again to find himself in that bear hug. He watched Lacey rising, and moved forward, balancing himself, leading a left hand which crunched on Lacey's chin and left a stain of blood, from his own torn fingers, Haggard realized. But now was no time to worry about that. While Lacey was off balance, he threw his right fist with all his weight behind it. The blow caught the other side of Lacey's chin with a jar which traveled right up Haggard's arm into his shoulder, left his right hand for a moment numb with pain. But Lacey was staggering. Haggard moved forward, hit the young man three times in the stomach, sinking the blows with all his force into the heavy coat. Then he switched back to the face, hurling three more blows, splitting Lacey's cheek and landing another in his eye. The young man gasped and fell to his knees.

Equally breathless, Haggard waited, each fist a mass of seething pain, heart throbbing, and head too, listening to the silence around him. "Up, Jemmy," he said. "Up."

Lacey remained on his knees, spitting blood. Haggard turned away, walked toward the trees; MacGuinness waited with his horse.

"Three cheers for the squire," someone called. "Who'll give three cheers for the squire? Hip hip . . ."

There was a surprisingly loud response.

"Fighting," Emma said. "Brawling, and with a man as far beneath you as the mud beneath your feet. Your clothes are ruined, and your hands . . ." She was extending them as she spoke, over a bowl of warm water held by Annie Kent, while Elizabeth Lancashire and Amelia hovered, armed with cotton and lint. "Are they very painful?"

"They ache," Haggard said, removing one from her grasp to take a drink of mulled wine. "What do you reckon, MacGuinness?"

"You did very well, Mr. Haggard. Well. There's not a man in the village won't respect you now."

"You have to fight people to gain their respect?" Emma demanded, opening the remains of Haggard's shirt. "My God."

There was a great red bruise on his belly where Lacey's head had ground into his ribs.

"These are Englishmen, Miss Dearborn," MacGuinness explained. "Fisticuffs is their natural way of expression, and they love to see a nob, if you'll pardon the expression, Mr. Haggard, who can handle himself. Oh, aye, I reckon you did yourself a power of good tonight, Mr. Haggard. And the schoolmaster a power of harm. Well, I'll be away home."

"Fisticuffs," Emma growled, and glanced at Roger, standing beside the maids, staring at his father with rapt attention. "A fine example for the boy."

"Did you really beat him to a pulp, Father?"

"I beat him, boy," Haggard said, "and there's an end to it. You'd have done as much."

"I should hope not," Emma said, carefully washing the last of the blood from the cuts on Haggard's hands.

"He will," Haggard said. "You'll remember you're Roger Haggard, boy, when you get to Eton. You'll never lie, and you'll never turn your back on any man."

"No, sir," Roger promised.

"And when you know you're right, boy, you'll fight, no matter however many are against you."

"Yes, sir."

"Men," Emma grumbled. But she nestled against him that night in bed. "Did you really fight because he insulted me?"

"He insulted *me*," Haggard pointed out. "But I fought him because the vicar insulted you. I couldn't very well fight Litteridge."

"Will he leave here?"

Haggard smiled. "Not before the election, I'll wager. After that, well, we'll have to see. I've more important things on my mind. MacGuinness tells me this Nash fellow arrives tomorrow."

"What I have in mind," Haggard explained, "is a tower. A

crenellated tower, high—I want to see over the trees—with a building attached."

The three men, MacGuinness and Haggard and the architect, stood on a knoll about a mile away from the manor, and on the far side from the village. The hills which separated them from the coal mine were close behind them, and the trees clustered thickly to either side. It was, to Haggard's mind, the prettiest spot in the valley, and the most secluded; before them stretched his own deer park. Now he watched the architect, pulling at his chin. John Nash was a short, spare man, only a few years older than Haggard himself, with thoughtful brown eyes and a disarming smile.

Which he now put to use. "You're expecting to stand a siege, Mr. Haggard?"

"I want it to look as if it might once *have* stood a siege," Haggard said. And smiled himself. "I'm a romantic, Mr. Nash."

"I can see that," Nash agreed, and led them forward over the sloping ground. "It would be cheaper over there."

"The cost does not concern me."

Nash nodded. "There is good news for an architect. You'll want your own accommodation in the tower?"

"That's right."

"Water closets?"

"What are they?"

"Privies, Mr. Haggard. But much more hygienic, as they can be plumbed in to give you a constant flow of water, as you require."

"Of course," Haggard said. "And a bathroom attached to every bedroom."

Nash frowned at him. "Now, there will be a real expense, Mr. Haggard. And why?"

"Just do it, Mr. Nash."

"Of course, sir."

"And a staircase," Haggard added.

Nash nodded. "I will let you have complete plans in due course, Mr. Haggard. I will delineate all the staircases."

"I mean a grand staircase," Haggard said.

Nash frowned. "How grand?"

"You've been to Almack's?"

"Indeed I have, sir. A facsimile of the main staircase."

"Not a facsimile, Mr. Nash. I wish an exact replica, in every way."

Nash sighed. "May I point out, sir, that it will take up a

great deal of room? I presume you are thinking of the entrance to the main withdrawing room."

"Which will be in the tower."

"Quite impossible. You'd not have a tower, Mr. Haggard. You'd have a citadel."

Haggard pulled his nose, then snapped his fingers. "I have it. The grand staircase will lead from the entry hall into the main withdrawing room, which will be partly situated in the lower building, to be sure. But that room will extend into the tower. In other words, the tower will grow out of the main building."

Nash scratched his head. "Which will make it entirely useless for defense."

Haggard smiled at him. "Whom am I going to defend it against, Mr. Nash? My own people here in Derleth? No, no. The exterior of the tower must appear as if it might once have been used for defense. But inside I wish it to be the most comfortable place you can imagine. And the master bedroom, which is to be on the top floor immediately beneath the roof, must be the most comfortable of the lot. Now, other things. I want a private pistol range in the basement. And I want a flower garden. Roses. Masses and masses of roses."

Nash regarded his notebook as if frightened of it. "With water closets in every room."

"Of course. And a bathroom."

Nash nodded. "I will prepare plans. But I am bound to say, Mr. Haggard, that this project will cost not a penny less than a hundred thousand." He peered at Haggard.

"Of course," Haggard said. "Now, come down to the hall for dinner."

"There are letters," Emma said, her voice curiously soft.

Haggard took the silver tray, sifted through the envelopes. Three from Cummings. One from Willy Ferguson. And one in a curiously upright hand, at once small and precise, and giving off the most delightful scent. A scent he recognized immediately.

"Is there anything of interest?" Emma asked carelessly.

"Business matters," he explained. "You'll excuse me." He carried them into the study, sat at his desk. Now, why was his heart pounding? He had seen through all of the schemes to ensnare him, and had rejected them. The business was at an end. Only a fool would ever reconsider that decision.

But he slit the scented envelope first.

Most esteemed Mr. Haggard,

Where modesty forbids me to utter a word, sheer remorse compels me to write to you. Am I then so wretched a creature? Did I offend you so deeply, or was I so immodest as to arouse nothing but horror in your breast? When we had laid dear Papa to bed—you will be pleased to know that he awoke next day with no ill save a slight pain in the forehead—it was *you* approached *me*. I had trusted you, Mr. Haggard, as a friend of my father's, and while I know it was remiss of me to allow myself into your presence wearing nothing more than a nightgown, I must beg you to believe that no thought of propriety crossed my mind in the instant of seeing my beloved father lying there unconscious, and for all I knew, dead.

You were kind to me, and you spoke words of endearment. Words I treasured, as I treasure them now. In the heat of the moment you made certain movements which I endeavored to resist to the best of my ability, without wishing to offend you, both because of my father's affection for you and because of my own understanding of the fine qualities which go to compose your character. Imagine my feelings on awakening, to be informed that you had fled our house, without leaving even so much as a letter behind. Such an act, Mr. Haggard, was scarce that of a gentleman, yet I do not reproach you, as I understand the differences between a Barbadian and an Englishman, and refuse to permit such differences to influence in any way my sure judgment of your worth.

Yet was I desolated, at once to have lost the pleasure of your company and to feel that I had in some way offended your sensibilities. It would be a great relief to me to hear from you to the affect that your abrupt and so far unexplained departure from my father's house was occasioned by circumstances beyond your control. Should this be the case, please be certain that should you ever care to visit us again, you will be most welcome, a sentiment with which my father and my sister wish to be associated.

Very sincerely yours,
A. Brand (Miss)

Haggard leaned back, the letter still in his hand, the perfume clouding up to clog his senses, his memory recalling the straight blond hair, the infinitely delicate features so strangely set off by the flaring nostrils, the touch of her lips and of her tongue, the gentle caress of her voice.

But the fact was, Emma was as much his wife as any he had ever had. Why, they had lived together now for nearly eleven years. He had even fought a man because she had been insulted. Alison could only be considered as a mistress. But what a delightful mistress she would make. Supposing it were possible.

Emma stood in the doorway. "If you have finished your letters, Mr. Haggard, dinner is being served. You have yet to tell me what Mr. Nash and yourself have arranged."

Definitely, Haggard thought as he got to his feet, she is as much a wife as any I have ever had.

"Are you nervous, Mr. Haggard?" Emma asked. It was a cold December evening, and the fire blazed in the upstairs withdrawing room. But because this was a special night, neither Alice nor Charlie had been sent to bed; Roger sat with them, keeping them from annoying their father.

Haggard stood before the fire, hands clasped behind his back. "What have I to be nervous about?" he asked. "It is a straightforward contest."

"I am nervous," Emma said. "It is . . . it's a vote of confidence, Mr. Haggard. In you. And a vote of acceptance, of me."

"Do they not accept you?"

"They smile at me, Mr. Haggard, and some even curtsy. They are pleased to see me in their shops, because I spend so much money. Your money, Mr. Haggard. I know not what they would do were I to be cast adrift amongst them."

"Do you suspect such a fate?"

She raised her head to gaze at him. "No, Mr. Haggard," she said. "I am merely making a point."

"Then remember this one," Haggard said. "Their vote, of confidence or of acceptance, is meaningless. Even were they to return Johnson, it would be nothing to me, and thus nothing to you. It is a contest, that is all. I shall be in the study."

He closed the door behind him, snapped his fingers to summon John Essex.

"Bring me a bottle of port," he said. He sat at his desk, leaned back with a sigh. He was spending more and more

time in here nowadays. Because it was the most comfortable
room in the house. Because he could be alone with his
thoughts and his desires. There was the fact of it. He had
been appalled by the effect England, and more especially, En-
glishwomen, had had on him. He realized that for a week or
so there he had been not quite himself. But it was idle to suppose that he no longer desired. It had been an act of will to
confine himself entirely to Emma for these past two months.
An act of will not to go to town. Time enough when he was
elected. If he was elected, as she feared.

But was this the sum of all those ambitions with which he
had left Barbados? Instead of a minister of the crown, a pair
of white thighs? Instead of the social lion of an entire county,
a pair of white breasts? Instead of a nationally known name,
a pair of red lips? Well, no doubt he had a nationally known
name, all right, but it was known as slave driver and lecher.
As for the others, they both were beyond his reach while
Emma lay like a deadening weight across his legs.

Emma. He got up, walked to the window. He had needed
nothing more in Barbados. But in Barbados he had worked
from dawn until dusk, had been eager to do no more than
find her arms when he returned to the house. Now he saw
her all day, unless he went out, but there was so little to go
out for. MacGuinness kept insisting he should inspect the
mine, but the thought of those naked, dust-stained white
bodies at once repelled him and beckoned him in the most
obscene of ways. The village was a no-man's-land at the
moment. He would not go among them until they either accepted him or rejected him. And he hated to look at the ugly
scars already marking the ground where the new hall would
arise. It would be the finest building in the land when it was
completed, but he did not wish to see it until then.

So Emma, a soothing, loving spirit, ever at his side. Perhaps there was an equal cause of his trouble. Sometimes he
wished to love savagely without feel for the object, only for
the satisfaction of his own desires. As he had loved Margaret
Lacey. As he had once loved Emma herself. But in Emma's
case, his conscience had reacted so violently against the harm
he had done her that he had been too gentle ever since. And
Emma liked gentleness. He could not suddenly begin to
savage her now, after eleven years.

How would Alison Brand wish to be loved?

"Mr. Haggard. Mr. Haggard." The door was open and

Emma stood there, MacGuinness and Roger at her shoulder. "The result."

Haggard stood up. "MacGuinness?"

"Eleven votes for you, Mr. Haggard. Four for the schoolmaster. My congratulations, sir."

Haggard shook hands.

"You're an M.P., Papa," Roger shouted. "An M.P."

"Aye." Haggard sat down again. "Four votes for the schoolmaster. You must discover who the other three were."

"I have already done so," MacGuinness said.

"You'll not punish them for voting against you, Mr. Haggard," Emma begged.

"I merely wish to identify those who would oppose me, sweetheart. He frowned at her. "You have not congratulated me."

"I am not certain there is cause for congratulation."

"In the name of God," he said. "An hour ago you were bewailing the possibility that I might not be elected."

"But now that you are," she pointed out, "you will be away in London nine months of the year."

Away in London. To Westminster itself, to take his place upon the national stage. Whenever he was permitted to do so.

"I must apologize for not submitting your name to the speaker," Pitt said when they met in the lobby after the first session of the new house. "But I am reserving you for whenever next Wilberforce launches one of his tirades against the slave trade, which I imagine will be at the conclusion of your lawsuit with Sharp. You have no real knowledge of India, have you?"

This having been the subject of the first debate.

"I have not, sir," Haggard said.

"And Philip Francis dreams of it day and night. He was there once, you know. Indeed, it was he who brought the indictment against poor Warren Hastings. Now, tell me, what do you think of our institution?"

I am overwhelmed, Haggard thought. To sit opposite men like Charles Fox and Dick Sheridan, of whom I have only ever read, to be standing here conversing with the prime minister, while other members pass us by and cast me envious glances . . . "Interesting," he said. "A trifle cramped."

"Ah." Pitt laid his finger alongside his nose. "It *is* cramped, of course. But designedly so, my dear Haggard. When we have a full attendance, when some issue of national importance is in debate, it electrifies the atmosphere to have insufficient room. Men are standing everywhere, pushing and heaving against the others, desperate to be heard and to hear. Were there comfortable seats for all, why, the Commons would be like a university debating society, with half its members permanently asleep." He gave one of his delightful smiles, which entirely relieved the somber cast of his features. "Even more than there are now. What did you think of his majesty?"

"It will give you some idea of my ignorance, Mr. Pitt, when I tell you he is somewhat smaller than I had supposed."

"Ah. Monarchs ever appear as larger than life in the imagination. But he has been ill, you know. Indeed. Most gravely. I will arrange an introduction for you, when you are settled in. There is something else we must arrange for you. You have no objection to joining one of our clubs?"

"I should be flattered."

"Good. I shall find you a proposer." He snapped his fingers. "Brand, of course. It will work very well. And a man must belong to a club, Haggard, if he is to prosper in London society. White's, I think. Then it will matter naught what the mob thinks of you." He gave a nod and walked away.

Now, what the devil did he mean by that? Haggard wondered. What have the mob got to do with me? As for being proposed by Brand . . . He saw the colonel starting toward him.

"John Haggard. I had not the chance to congratulate you on your election. We had heard there was some opposition."

"Inspired by Sharp." Haggard shook hands. "But it was easily disposed of."

"I am glad of that. There was a rumor the fellow saved his deposit."

"Well, what would you? I've an independent-minded community at Derleth. I'd not have it any other way."

"Of course not, my dear fellow. You'll sup with me?"

"Well . . . where?"

"At home, of course. The girls are waiting to renew their acquaintance. After your abrupt departure."

"Ah, well, I must apologize about that, Brand. There was urgent news from Derleth." How easily the lie slipped from his tongue. By God, he thought, this country is making me a degenerate.

"Of course, Haggard. I never doubted it for a moment. But

the least you can do is eat with us, and make your peace with Alison."

"And have you a comfortable place to stay, Mr. Haggard?" Alison Brand smiled at him, but he was not sure her pleasure quite reached her eyes. He was not sure of anything very much. His memory of her beauty had been quite inadequate, the more so as this night she had adopted the growing feminine leaning toward simplicity. No powder in her hair, which was arranged in a chignon on the back of her head, allowing only a few curls to descend onto her forehead. And no corset, either; her crimson gown, high-waisted but with a low and open bodice, which left only the bottom halves of her breasts concealed at all, lay against her thighs and outlined her legs as she moved. She wore a gold locket suspended on a chain round her neck, and no other jewelry. It was impossible to stop looking at her, just as it was impossible not to discover the most extravagant thoughts as he did so.

Emily, as ever, was a copy of her sister, in dark blue instead of red; but Haggard had eyes only for the original.

"My agent has secured me rooms at the Albany," He said.

"The Albany. Why, you could not do better." She raised one eyebrow, a disconcerting gesture at the best of times, but one indicative in addition of surprise that he should have done so well.

"Aye, well . . ." Brand drank the last of his port. "You'll excuse me for half an hour, Haggard. There are some letters to be seen to."

Haggard also rose. "Then perhaps I should leave. It has been a tiring day."

"Stuff and nonsense, my dear fellow. I'll not be longer than half an hour. Emily, you'll not forget that task you set yourself."

He was so heavy-handed it was nearly laughable. Yet Haggard found himself at Alison's elbow as they left the table and made their way into a deserted and somewhat darkened gallery which ran beyond the withdrawing room. "It is cool here," she said. "And quiet. Will you require anything else to drink, Mr. Haggard?"

" I have had sufficient, thank you, Miss Brand."

She nodded to the footman, who silently withdrew. "The last time we met, you did me the honor of addressing me by name."

"And with your permission I shall do so again." He held a chair for her, sat himself, opposite her.

"May I ask if you received my letter?"

"I did."

"And were offended, of course. You did not reply."

"I am no correspondent, Alison."

"What *are* you, Mr. Haggard?"

The question, asked in that soft, gentle voice, took him by surprise. He leaned back. "A man."

"An ambitious man," she said. "I am sure of that. As well as a wealthy one. Which means that most of your ambitions should be within reach. Will you share them with me?"

"To hold you in my arms," Haggard said. His heart seemed to leap from his chest into his throat and then sink all the way back to his belly. He had not meant to be as forthright as that.

Alison Brand gazed at him for some moments. She did not blush, nor was she smiling in embarrassment. "So you indicated at our last meeting, Mr. Haggard. Before fleeing into the night."

My God, he thought, she lectures me like my mother. But how pleasant, how delightful it was to be lectured by those lips.

"Aye, well, I doubted I would be doing you a service." Of course, he realized. This was the line to follow.

"Indeed?"

"As everyone points out to me continually, I am a wild colonial boy. That they accept me in even the smallest degree is due to my money. I do not dress as they. I refuse to wear a wig, or a corset . . ."

"In which direction you but anticipate the future, Mr. Haggard, as both wigs and corsets are going out of fashion, for men as well as women."

"Indeed? But those are only exterior points."

At last her face relaxed. "And are you also wild and uncouth in your personal habits?"

"Indeed I am," he said.

She regarded him for some moments, in a most speculative fashion. Her tongue came out and just touched her upper lip, before disappearing again. He had a sudden thought that the gesture reminded him of a snake, and as hastily rejected it. It was blasphemy to suggest there could be any reptilian quality about so much beauty.

"I do not suppose," she said, "that such a man would

be beyond the capability of a woman of sense and understanding."

"Alison . . ." he said, reaching for her hand, which was immediately withdrawn.

"Provided," she said, "that she could be sure of his love for her. That it was shared with no other."

He leaned back in his chair. "No doubt my domestic arrangements are the talk of London."

"You flatter yourself, Mr. Haggard," she said. "But they are common knowledge, to be sure."

"And you would change them?" He was beginning to be angry.

"I, sir? I have no interest in the matter."

"No interest?" He got up. "You have contrived this interview with me, Miss Brand, merely to tease me into using words I am already regretting. I shall bid you good night."

"Mr. Haggard," she said, "why do we always quarrel? I have heard it said that people who appear so violently to dislike each other are really attempting to conceal a much more sublime emotion."

He stood above her. How confident she was. But no doubt with reason, for how he longed to hold her in his arms. "I apologize."

"Then you'll stay and talk with me. At least until Papa returns."

Haggard hesitated, and sat down. "There are aspects of the situation which are not common knowledge."

"I do not seek to pry, Mr. Haggard."

"But you'd make certain conditions."

A trace of pink darkened her cheeks. "I am but a girl, Mr. Haggard, and know little of the world. But I do understand my own nature, which is as unruly and passionate as your own. And in addition, I am a woman. As a sex, we lack a man's aptitude for sharing, save with one other." She bit her lip to indicate she may have been too bold, but like everything else she did, it was clearly a studied gesture.

"Aye," he said, and got up again. "I *will* take my leave, Alison. Not in anger, I do promise you. I wish to think."

Her frown cleared. "And I would interrupt no man's thoughts, Mr. Haggard." She stood up as well. "I shall look forward to seeing you again." She held out her hand.

He took it, began to lift it to his lips, and then stopped. "When last we met, you allowed me the use of your lips."

Once again the tongue, just peeping through the barrier of

her teeth. "I apologize for my wantonness, sir. I was somewhat disturbed by my father's illness."

"Yes, having established such an understanding . . ."

She hesitated, then smiled, stood on tiptoe, and kissed him
on the mouth. His hands attempted to close on her shoulders,
but with an expert wriggle she slid from between them. Her
cheeks were pink. "May heaven aid your thoughts, dear Mr.
Haggard."

He doubted heaven was involved. And how to think coher-
ently when his mind was clouded with the scent of her perfume, the feel of her velvet flesh, the promise of all that lay
beneath that crimson gown. Thus night. But morning, with its
searching clarity, reminded him of what a plot it was. As if it
mattered. He was John Haggard. Alison Brand, or more
likely her father, might dream only of his fortune, but to at-
tain that she must grant him the use of her body. And that
was all he wished.

As he was a fool. He wanted more than that. But he did
not doubt for a moment that once he had possessed her body,
he would in the course of time possess her mind and her soul,
and her entire love, as well. Had he not achieved as much
with Emma, after a far less likely beginning?

But Emma. There was the point. He loved her, and she
loved him. If only he could still love her with the passion of
that first day when she had been tied to his bed. Oh, Emma.
Perhaps, if she could join him in London, he would feel less
disloyal to her. But that would be madness, and social and
political suicide. There it was; he was risking those fates all
the while. They had not mattered in Barbados, but in England, where acceptance was the entire key to a civilized existence, they suddenly clouded his horizon.

At the least it was not a problem to be faced seriously until
after he had regained Middlesex and settled with Sharp once
and for all; the case was scheduled for immediately after
Easter. Cummings had located a solicitor named Roeham,
who in turn had briefed a barrister by the name of
Broughton. "It is an open-and-shut case, Mr. Haggard,"
Broughton said. "I am amazed it has been referred to a Supreme Court at all. The man Middlesex is your property, and
there is an end to it. Property is inviolable."

"Which is what I told the magistrate," Haggard pointed
out.

"Oh, indeed, you did, sir. But, if I may be so bold, it is

nearly always a mistake to represent yourself at affairs of this kind. Magistrates, like judges, indeed, are accustomed to hear legal arguments put forward in proper legal jargon, and they become hostile very easily to laymen seeking to present their own cases. In this case, sir, you have nothing to apprehend, save that the man Middlesex may already have been secreted from the country."

"Sharp gave a bond," Roeham said.

"Indeed, Mr. Roeham, indeed. But then, Mr. Sharp is a wealthy man, and like all philanthropists, a trifle mad, in my opinion. It would matter not in the least to him to forfeit the bond, or even to be sent to jail for contempt, if he could make his mark with the public. This is your other problem, Mr. Haggard. The case has attracted some attention in the popular press, and it is possible that you may be subjected to the rigors of a hostile crowd. But then, after all, such an experience is nothing more than our noble prince suffers every time he rides abroad."

"I do not regard hostile crowds as being serious obstacles, sir," Haggard said.

"I did not think you would, sir. Well, then, see you in court, eh?"

But he was not really looking forward to such an ordeal, especially one which had attracted so much attention, and to decide such an open-and-shut case. But as Pitt himself had made clear, his political future depended upon it.

At least he was the first witness. He supposed indeed he would be the only witness, unless the defense called Middlesex himself. Nor was he in any way cross-examined by the defense counsel, who merely nodded as Broughton extracted each of the relevant facts in turn. But then how could he be cross-examined? Middlesex was his property, inherited by him from his father, and there was an end to the matter. He found the proceedings somewhat boring, for Broughton's arguments did not appear to be any advance upon his own at the earlier hearing, nor were the defense submissions in any way different. He preferred to study the face, and hopefully the attitude, of Chief Justice Mansfield, who made notes as each barrister presented his client's case, all with a quite expressionless countenance, only occasionally glancing at Middlesex, who sat with Granville Sharp immediately behind Barcroft, the solicitor. He never looked at Haggard at all.

Nor did he adjourn when the defense solicitor was finished, but merely considered his notes for a few minutes. Then he cleared his throat, and the courtroom, crowded to the very door—all three of the Brands were here, as well as several other gentlemen of Haggard's acquaintance—fell absolutely still.

"The case before me," the chief justice said in quiet tones, "is a simple one, in that we are not here today to consider any question of fact. My learned friend for the defense has not denied the essential claim made by my learned friend for the plaintiff, that the man Middlesex is, by West Indian law, the property of the plaintiff. This is indisputable. The question which I am asked to decide here today is whether such West Indian law applies here in England.

"Now, of course, when the West Indian colonies were founded, some hundred and more years ago, the gentlemen adventurers who so boldly created for themselves new homes in a new world carried with them the civilization they left behind, and the laws of that civilization. Thus the basic law of any British colony in the West Indies is English common law. But certain modifications were necessary to deal with local situations, and in addition, we must remember that these settlements *were* made more than a hundred years ago, and not all of the changes which have taken place in English law since that time, and in particular the Bill of Rights established by the Glorious Revolution of 1689, were translated into the laws of the different colonies.

"There was no slavery in the England of 1650. That situation, happily, has been left far behind in antiquity in this happy land of ours. Slavery, however, has been regarded as necessary in the West Indies since the establishment of the first colony, whether slavery of the indigenous population, the Indians, who did not survive such servitude, whether slavery of the indenture variety, to which convicted criminals from this country were attached, or whether it was imported slavery, that is, Negro slaves. The necessity was caused by the basic economy of the islands, which depended first of all on tobacco, and more latterly, and more successfully, on the growth of cane sugar, both industries which require a very high manpower. This situation has always been recognized by successive British governments, and although in recent years we have witnessed a growth of public opinion which is opposed to slavery on moral grounds, the question has not yet been decided by Parliament, and legal slavery remains in force in these colonies. It is not my place to go into the arguments for or against the system. That is the law as it stands today. In other words, no censure or obloquy can possibly be leveled against the plaintiff because he owns slaves. He is behaving in a perfectly legal fashion."

Haggard leaned back with a sigh. His apprehension had been groundless.

"On the other hand, there is no legal slavery in Great Britain. This state of affairs, as I have said, was ended many years ago, both because of public opinion, the ultimate arbiter of our laws, but also because the economic necessity for it has disappeared. For any man to attempt to enslave another human being—man, woman, or child, white or black or brown—inside this country is against the law. It is an illegal act. The question before me today is whether the laws of this land in respect of slavery are broken when a legal slave *outside* this country is imported into it. It has been put to me by my learned friend for the plaintiff, firstly, that the importation might be of a most temporary nature, and secondly, that a slave is a slave; slavery is a class of society, and a man cannot cease to belong to that class merely by crossing a boundary, any more than a prince ceases to be a prince merely by traveling to France.

"I will take the second argument first. It is specious. Slavery is not a class. It is an induced situation. The fact that, as in this case, the defendant's father and grandfather were slaves before him, is not, to my mind, sufficient to condemn his every descendant for the rest of his life of the world to perpetual bondage. This were a negation of every concept of ambition or advancement or common justice we hold dear, and the argument is further weakened by the fact that a slave owner may manumit any or all of his slaves, as he chooses, thus ending their state of servitude at one stroke."

Haggard began to frown as a rustle of whispers broke out behind him. Mansfield tapped his desk with his gavel, and the courtroom fell silent.

"Nor does the first argument appeal to me. Apart from the question as to the exact meaning of the word 'temporary,' it is again specious. Shall we suppose that a gentleman of this city, well known and respected, who puts to sea and commits piracy, is beyond the law because his was a temporary voyage, enabling him to return to his home and the safety of a respectable citizen? No, no, for the purposes of the law, the word 'temporary' does not exist. A crime, may it take only a fraction of a second to commit, and be it committed while in the grips of however *temporary* an aberration, remains a crime. Therefore the importation of any person or any goods into this country, for however short a period, remains an importation and is subject to the laws of this country.

"There remains, finally, the question of whether our laws here in Great Britain can be made to apply to citizens of another country, in civil matters such as this. Setting apart an obvious fact, that the plaintiff is actually a citizen of Great Britain, for Barbados is a colony and therefore a part of Great Britain, the answer to this must be in the affirmative. Should a Frenchman come here and commit libel, he is required to suffer for it under our laws. But there is an even more important aspect of the situation to be considered. The moral aspect. We in Great Britain worship freedom. It has been said we carry its worship too far, in that we permit unquestioned scoundrels to walk abroad merely for lack of evidence to convict them. Be that as it may, it is the cornerstone of our society, that a man is innocent until he is proven guilty, that a man is free to go wheresoever he should choose and work at whatsoever he should choose so long as he has not been proved guilty of any crime. My learned friend for the plaintiff has reminded us that the defendant borrowed a horse when he left Derleth Hall, but the animal has since been returned and a suitable sum paid for its use. This can be no issue here. My learned friend further contends that the defendant broke a law when he decided to run away in any event. But that is Barbadian law, not British law. To British law, as to British opinion, the concept that any man should own another is abhorrent, and I cannot but believe that to uphold so pernicious a doctrine, however legal it may be elsewhere, however necessary it may be to prosperity elsewhere, would be to undermine the very foundations upon which our society is so happily based."

Lord Mansfield paused to take a sip of water. The courtroom was absolutely quiet, but Haggard could feel the anger swelling in his belly. The chief justice put down his glass, glanced at his notes for a long time, and then raised his head again. "I therefore find for the defendant, James Middlesex, and pronounce him free of any taint of slavery or bondage."

Pandemonium broke out. People cascaded down from the spectators' gallery to shake both Sharp and Middlesex by the hand. Haggard remained seated. He was too angry to see or speak with anyone, apart from the humiliation, and the continued humiliation, because this case would make headlines in all the newssheets, be the subject of gossip for enough years, and more than that, as Broughton observed.

"A profound judgment, Mr. Haggard," he said. "In effect it sets a new law upon the statute books, all without the consent of that parliament Mansfield kept prating about. You'll appeal?"

Haggard looked up. "What for?"

"Well . . ." Broughton stroked his chin. "There are one or two of his interpretations of law I'd take issue with."

"You have already done so, and lost."

"Before Mansfield. A court of appeal, now, might take a different view."

Haggard got up, crammed his hat on his head. "I doubt that, sir. They would merely expose me to increased contumely. In defense of my own property," he said bitterly. "Truly, sir, I see England following the course set by the French, and coming to regard the ownership of property as a crime rather than a privilege. When that day arrives, sir, you may be sure I will renounce my citizenship." He walked away from them, paused as the Brands hurried from the gallery. "Have you come to gloat?"

"Mr. Haggard," Alison said. She was a perfect picture in a deep blue pelisse with a matching hood trimmed with fur.

"Damnably done by, Haggard," Brand said. "Damnably. Be sure, sir, that every right-thinking person will be on your side."

Haggard opened the door on to the steps of the court and faced the mob.

"Slave owner," they howled.

"Murderer."

"Beast."

"We must wait for them to disperse," Brand said.

"Perhaps there is another entrance," Emily suggested.

"I've not turned my back on a mob before," Haggard said. "You'll excuse me, ladies. Brand." He walked down the steps, while the yells and the whistles grew louder. There was a crunch on his shoulder, and he glanced at the egg which had just landed there; the evil-smelling yolk was dripping down his sleeve. He turned to face his assailant, and had his arm seized by Cummings.

"Your carriage is over here, sir."

"I'll have that fellow."

Another egg whistled through the air. Cummings ducked, and it hit the pavement with a splat.

"All of them, sir?"

Haggard hesitated. But to go into their midst would be to risk being beaten up with little hope of harming any of them. He allowed himself to be drawn away to the comparative safety of the carriage, although for several hundred yards their passage was obstructed by crowds who rocked the vehicle, frightened the horses, and peered at him through the windows to shake their fists and utter their curses and threats.

"The London mob," Cummings said, attempting a smile. "One has to get used to them, Mr. Haggard. Even the king has to do that. But once we get you back to your rooms and a hot bath and a change of clothing, and a full glass, why, sir . . ."

"Where can I drop you?" Haggard asked.

"Sir?"

"I am not going back to my rooms," Haggard said. "I am taking horse for Derleth today."

Cummings frowned. "Why, sir, do you suppose there may be repercussions there?"

"Aye," Haggard said. "There will be repercussions there, and I am going to cause them."

His anger was at a white heat. The entire venture of returning to England had proved a disaster. Instead of a welcome, there had been suspicion, save where people had wished to use him for their own ends. The climate was abominable. His election to Parliament, which he had been assured was a formality, had turned out as a slap in the face. He was master of a valley, and yet truly master of no one in it. And now he had been told that his own domestic slaves, people he had cared for and thought of since his boyhood, owed him no obligations at all.

No doubt his best course would be to abandon the whole venture and crawl back to Barbados with his tail between his legs. But he was John Haggard. No court of law was going to chase him away. If they wanted to make him into some kind of an outlaw, then, by God, they would see what kind of an outlaw he could be.

He rode north in a mood of black anger, leaving even his London valet, a cockney by the name of Simpson, behind, scarce stopped for more than a meal on the way, trotted through the high street of Derleth village and up toward the manor house, sat his horse and gazed at scar which was to be his house. Yardboys took his bridle, and he dismounted, stamped into the front door of the hall.

"Mr. John?" John Essex took his hat and coat. "But we ain't expecting you this time."

"Summon the servants," Haggard said. "The black ones. All of them." He went into the parlor, slapped his hands together in front of the fire; it was very cold out, and there was still snow on the ground.

"Mr. Haggard?" Emma stood in the doorway, her face a mixture of delight and concern. "Parliament has not been adjourned?"

"I doubt I have much place in that parliament. Well, come in," he shouted at the black people who were assembling at the door.

They filed in and lined up, John Essex, Henry Suffolk, Annie Kent, wearing her new apron, as she was straight from the kitchen, Elizabeth Lancashire, and Amelia. Emma frowned at them, looked questioningly at Haggard.

"You people are to leave this place," Haggard said. "There is the door. Get out."

The slaves exchanged glances.

"Where you want us for go, Mr. John?" Annie Kent asked.

"I do not care where you go," Haggard said, speaking very slowly and evenly. "You no longer belong to me. The court has made that clear. You are free people. Therefore I am free of you. I have no responsibilities toward you. You are to leave now."

"Oh, my God," Emma muttered.

"But, Mr. John, sir," Essex said. "We can't just go so. We ain't got no money."

"Man, Mr. John, but it cold out there," Elizabeth Lancashire said. "You ain't see that snow and thing?"

"But, Mr. John, how we going eat?" Annie Kent asked.

"That is your concern," Haggard said. "Not mine. Get out. Go to James Middlesex and ask him. He may obtain you shelter from his friend Granville Sharp." He pointed at the door. "Get out. I'll give you ten minutes to be gone, and one hour to be off my property, or I'll set Mr. MacGuinness on you."

They gazed at him for a moment, and Amelia started to weep. Annie Kent took her arm and escorted her from the room. Essex and Suffolk stood their ground, chewing their lips.

"Nine minutes," Haggard said.

"Man, Mr. John, sir," Essex said. "But this is wickedness

you doing. Be sure the Lord going see to you." He left the room, Suffolk at his heels.

"Mr. Haggard . . ." Emma grasped his arm. "John. Please. You cannot do this."

"Cannot?" He freed himself.

"I did not know the law decided for Middlesex. But he *wanted* to go. These people want to stay. They love you, John Haggard."

"I do not love them. Now, send one of the grooms for MacGuinness, and tell him we need new servants here. Tell him to organize it."

She stood before him. "You cannot do it, Mr. Haggard. I'll not let you."

Haggard raised his head. "*You'll* not let me?"

She bit her lip, flushed, and then the color faded again. "If . . . if they go, I'll go with them." Another bite of the lip. "You've forgotten, but my term of indenture ended last year. I'm as free as you are, Mr. Haggard."

"Your term of indenture ended March 17, 1790," Haggard said. "I am well aware of that. I assumed you stayed because you were comfortable here. Perhaps because you loved me."

"I do love you," she shouted. "But so do those people."

"Well, I do not love them, as I have said."

Emma inhaled slowly. "But you do love me."

"Whether or not I love you," Haggard said, "depends upon you. Now, fetch me MacGuinness."

Emma exhaled, equally slowly. "I meant what I said, Mr. Haggard. Those people are my friends. The only true friends I have. They are your friends as well. Apart from being cruel, it is stupid to let them go."

"Then go with them," Haggard said. "There is the door. Get out. You have ten minutes."

Chapter 6

The Bridegroom

"I've come to say good-bye, Mr. Haggard." Emma stood in the doorway. She wore her fur-trimmed crimson pelisse with the hood, and carried a single box. Henry Suffolk waited in the hall with two more. "I've taken only a few things. I hope you will not send me away naked."

Haggard smoked a cheroot and sipped a glass of port. He had adopted this role deliberately. Stupid girl. But was she now trying to appeal to his better nature? "Take what you will."

She hesitated, bit her lip. " 'Tis the children's clothes as well. I'll fetch them from the school. Will you wish them well?"

Haggard frowned at her. "You'll not see the children."

"They are my children, Mr. Haggard."

"They are mine, Emma. What would you? Take them off to starve?"

She stared at him as if unsure what she was hearing.

"Be sure I shall bring them up," Haggard said. "Educate them and see to their inheritance. Can you equal that?"

Still she stared at him. A single tear rolled down her left cheek. "What will you tell them of me?"

"I will think of something," He said. Give in, you silly girl. Throw yourself at my feet and beg my forgiveness. You shall have it. But give in. "What will you do?"

"I'll manage, Mr. Haggard." Her cheeks were pink.

"By whoring? Not in Derleth."

"I'll not stay in Derleth, Mr. Haggard."

But she had not denied what she might have to do to keep from starving. Haggard felt in his pocket, took out a handful of golden guineas, threw them on the desk. "You'll need money."

Emma's chin came up. "Not your money, Mr. Haggard."

"You've some of your own?"

But now she was as angry as he. "I will manage, Mr. Haggard. I'll bid you good-bye."

"Close the door," Haggard said. But she left it open, and he heard her heels on the stairs. He picked up the half-empty bottle of port, hurled it across the room, watched it shatter on the wall and scatter on the floor, leaving red liquid everywhere. The stupid little bitch. Why did he not run after her and seize her and carry her up to their bedroom, and love her into some sense?

Because he did not wish to. This crisis had loomed too long, and now it was of her making. She was gone, and he was free. Free, he thought. Free.

So, then, are you a bad man, John Haggard? How could you be otherwise, as your name is Haggard, as you are a slave owner? Oh, do not condemn John Haggard. Chief Justice Mansfield's own words. He was but born to a place in life and has lived that place to its hilt. By God, they'd not seen how he'd live that place. Not yet.

He got up, walked to the study window, watched them trailing down the drive. Emma walked at the back; John Essex carried her box; the children's had been left in the front hall. Would she really walk away without seeing them? And did it matter?

Their shoes left footprints in the snow. And he was free.

MacGuinness coughed in the doorway. "I've a list here, Mr. Haggard."

"I wish no list, MacGuinness. Just have the house stocked with staff."

"Yes, sir." MacGuinness twisted his hat between his hands. "About a valet, sir, it'll take time."

"Then take your time. I am returning to London tomorrow. Simpson is there."

"Yes, sir, Mr. Haggard. Then, there's a suitable cook . . . well, sir, Mistress MacGuinness was wondering if you'd care to sup wi' us this night."

"I'll not go out," Haggard said. "Surely you can find someone in the village, even if it's temporary."

"Oh, aye, Mr. Haggard." Once again the twist of the hat. "About the girl, Margaret Lacey. Do you wish her back?"

Haggard frowned. He'd be sleeping alone this night. Margaret Lacey. But did he want her, having had her? She was the sort of woman who would soon wish to dominate. And did he want her at all? Emma was gone. The weight was gone. He was more free than he had ever been in his life, he realized. Free to marry whom he liked. How his heart pounded at the thought of it.

And free, this night, to *do* what he liked. If he dared. But who would say him nay? He was John Haggard. A mean, vicious man. A slave owner. A very devil, as the London mob had called him.

"I'll think about it," he said.

"Yes, sir, Mr. Haggard." MacGuinness closed the door behind himself. Haggard waited for five minutes, until he heard the gentle clop of the hooves on the drive; then he got up and opened the door, remembered that Suffolk would not be there. He pulled the bell rope, and after a few minutes one of the downstairs maids came scurrying up.

"Yes, sir, Mr. Haggard," she panted, and was clearly terrified.

"Fetch my hat and coat," Haggard said. "And tell Ned to saddle my horse. Not the one I rode from London."

"Yes, sir, Mr. Haggard." She scurried off again. A young girl, but plump and perspiring. As if it mattered, when compared with what he had in mind. If he dared.

He went downstairs, and his outdoor clothes were waiting; the girl had reinforced herself with two others. No doubt they all knew how he had laid Margaret Lacey within twenty-four hours of arriving here. Or perhaps they were afraid he would throw them into the snow as well.

He mounted, nodded to Ned, the head groom, who waited patiently if resentfully in the cold—he had been growing fond of Miss Dearborn. He walked his horse out of the drive and up the slope slowly, nonchalantly, a squire going over to inspect his new hall.

The workmen touched their hats, gazed at him surreptitiously as he rode on. The rumor of what had happened was spreading. He found Nash seated at a trestle table poring over his plans, a clerk at his side; the architect had taken a room at the inn to be near his greatest project.

"Cold, Mr. Haggard," he said. "Damn near freezing."

"I'm here for a progress report," Haggard said. "Not a lecture."

"Aye, Mr. Haggard. You're not a man for lectures," Nash agreed. "Well, sir, the foundations are going in, as you see. But 'tis a long and difficult task. You'd have done better to wait until the summer."

"You'd do better to finish the job, Mr. Nash, and leave the worrying to me. When will you complete?"

"Ah, well, we're talking about next autumn at the earliest."

"A year?" Haggard demanded. "To build me a house?"

"I wouldnt' exactly call this a house, Mr. Haggard. And to get it right will take time."

Six more months, Haggard thought, as he turned his horse and rode away. But probably that was all to the good. Six months of courting Alison Brand. Time enough. She'd be eighteen. There was a better age to be married. And I'll be nearly forty, he realized. But still young. Still virile. Still crying out for womanhood, as he did now.

And perhaps, after six months, he'd have exorcised this demon in his belly. Perhaps he could do it now. If he dared.

He turned into the cut between the hills, rode on to the mine. It was nearly dark now, and the air was biting at his ears and nose.

"Mr. Haggard, sir." The foreman touched his forelock. "Bitter weather."

"Aye," Haggard said. "But I'm told there's a summer in this country." He was amazed at the evenness of his voice, while his throat was clogged and his heart was pounding. If he dared. "When do they knock off?"

"Aye, well, I was about to ring the bell, Mr. Haggard."

"Then do so." Haggard dismounted, stretched his legs, listened to the clanging. "How far down do they go?"

"A hundred foot and more, Mr. Haggard. But they hear the bell."

Haggard stood above the ladder, watched the first heads beginning to appear in the cold dusk. As usual, the men came first. They glanced at Haggard in surprise, one or two touched their foreheads, the rest put on their coats and made their grimy way back down the road to the village. And they had accused him of being a slave owner, Haggard thought bitterly. Was he not just as much a slave owner now? Only this was legal. He paid these people, just enough to live on, so they would have to continue working. And as he was here at all, they were as much his to do what he wished with as any black in Barbados.

Saving only his own conscience. Well, he had had a conscience in Barbados too, and that had prevented him from ever giving way to any of his more excessive moods. Until Emma. Then it had been Emma herself, keeping him in check. But now she too was gone, and he was a free man. So, the devil with his conscience. He was here for a purpose.

The children clambered out of the pithead, bobbed their

heads anxiously at the squire. Ten and eleven, he estimated their ages. In the main. But as he remembered from that first day, there were others. It was difficult to decide looks, the possibility of beauty, in the dusk and the dirt. He waited for them all to get out, the older ones bringing up the rear. "You," he said.

They all stopped and turned, insensibly huddling closer together. Haggard pointed. "I mean you."

The girl looked to left and right in bewilderment. She was one of the oldest of the children, going on her size. She was the one he especially remembered; he was sure of that. She had yellow hair, matted and coated with dust, and was somewhat taller than her companions. She had breasts, too, to which the dust clung entrancingly, and a pouting belly, and narrow thighs. It was impossible to decide whether or not there was pubic hair, because of the dust which coated her belly. But she had good legs, long for her body and sturdy. Coal dust dribbled down them as she shivered.

"What is your name?" Haggard asked, heart pounding fit to burst.

"Mary, your worship. Mary Prince."

"There's a pretty name," he said. "I am short a parlor maid at the hall, Mary Prince. Would you like the job?"

Once again the quick glance to right and left, while her tongue came out and went in again quickly.

"I'd have to ask me mum, your worship."

"Would you like the job, Mary Prince?"

"Oh, aye, your worship. But I'll have—"

"First let's see you know what you're at," Haggard said, and indicated his horse. "You can mount up behind me."

She gaped at him, mouth open; then she looked down at herself. "I'm that dirty, your worship."

"Clean dirt," he said. "Ha ha." God, how he wished he could snap his fingers and transport them both to the privacy of his bedchamber, away from the staring eyes, from the foreman's sly grin. But he'd not give up now. He was Haggard. Nothing he could ever do in the future would change that simple fact, for these people, for everyone in England. Not to behave like Haggard would do him no good, and leave him without any pleasure at all. Besides, this was something he *wanted*, as he had not wanted since seeing Emma for the first time. Everything he had done, almost everything he had thought, he realized, since arriving in this misbegotten land, had been conditioned by this single overwhelming want.

He swung himself into the saddle. "Come along, Mary Prince."

She glanced at her companions once again, then at the foreman, who shrugged. She put on her threadbare coat and approached the animal. Haggard put down his arm for her.

"I'll dirty your clothes, your worship."

"I have others," Haggard said.

Her fingers closed on his arm and he lifted her from the ground. He felt her hands on his back.

"Hold me round the waist," he said.

Her arms went round his waist, and he looked down on her hands, clasped together in front of him. They were dirty hands, but well shaped. He looked to either side, saw a long coal-dust-stained leg dangling there. She was sitting astride, wearing nothing but a coat.

He kicked the horse forward, and they trotted down the road. Behind them the other children walked, still staring.

"How old are you, Mary Prince?" Haggard asked.

"I'm thirteen, your worship."

Younger even than Emma had been, Haggard thought. But they were already through the gap, and there were candles burning in the hall windows. Haggard rode up the drive, dismounted by swinging his right leg over the horse's head, held up his hands for the girl. She swung her leg over in turn, dropped onto him; he caught her under the armpits and set her on the ground. For a moment she leaned against him, then hastily stepped back.

Ned was there, taking the horse's bridle. He did not speak, merely touched his hat. Haggard held the girl's arm, took her into the lower hall. The maids came scurrying out of the pantry, gathered in a group at the far end.

Haggard nodded to them. "I will need a hot bath," he said. "For this young lady. Start boiling up. Half an hour."

"Yes, sir, Mr. Haggard." They continued to stare. Haggard released Mary Prince's arm, indicated the stairs. She peered at the other girls for a moment—no doubt she knew them all, as they knew her—then scurried up the steps. Coal dust scattered onto the floor.

Haggard walked behind her. "And the next flight," he said as she paused on the landing. She looked down at him, then resumed her climb. He watched her feet disappearing above his head. He was back in Haggard's Penn, with Emma and Annie Kent above him. Emma and Annie Kent. He wondered where they were now, what they were doing. What they were thinking. But with this girl there would be no need for ropes. And no risk of daggers after.

"Father." Alice ran along the corridor, Charlie as usual tumbling at her heels. "Father." Her cheeks were stained with tears. "Mama was at school to say good-bye."

"She said she was going away," Charlie accused.

"She *has* gone away," Haggard said.

They stopped, faces slowly crumpling.

"Your mother has gone away," Haggard repeated. "It was her choice. But you're here with me. There is naught to concern yourselves with. There is cake for your tea."

He reached the third floor, looked down. They stared after him, tears running down their cheeks. He realized he did not even know the name of their new nurse. But he had no time for them this night. Mary Prince was waiting, hands clasped in front of her, looking at the dust which was gathering about her.

"I'm awful dirty, your worship."

"The floor can be cleaned." He stepped past her, opened the bedroom door. "In here."

She hesitated, then stepped past him. Haggard closed the door.

"Take off your cloak." His voice was thick as he lit the candle, set it on the table, turned to face her. She held the cloak in her hands, uncertain where to lay it. "The floor will do."

The cloak slipped to the floor. She faced him, inhaling slowly. Suddenly he did not know how to continue, what her reaction was going to be. Slowly he took off his own coat, pulled his cravat free. He watched her tongue come out, lick coal dust from her lips.

"I'm awful dirty," she said again.

"Yes," he said. "That's what I want from you. Dirt." He undressed quickly, while she stood there and gazed at him. "Have you not seen a man before?"

"I've seen me dad," she said.

He realized with a disturbing start that her dad was probably no older than himself. But nothing would stop him now. Haste, haste, haste. He stripped off his stockings, threw them behind his shoes, took her in his arms. Coal dust, and woman, clutched against him. Her breasts were big enough to feel, her groin squirmed against his, trapping his penis between, bringing it even harder. He threw her on the bed, lay on her. She tried to kiss him, but he did not want to kiss. He thrust his hands beneath her, held her buttocks, lifted her up while he found her slit and drove himself inward. He waited for a cry or a moan, and found only her eyes, huge and glooming at him, and her mouth, vaguely open, and coal dust, scattering across the snow-white sheets. He came in a tremendous explosion of pent-up passion and anger and self-disgust, throbbed on her belly for some seconds, then lay on it, listened to her gasping for breath.

He rolled away from her, lay on his back. Christ, he thought. What have I done? He had not thought that for a very long time.

Mary Prince sat up. "Must I go now, sir?"

Haggard turned his head, frowned at her. Sanity was back in control, and it was necessary to lay plans, correct mistakes. He got up, went to his trousers, felt in the pockets, discovered a guinea. He held it out, and she stared at it for a moment before taking it.

"You'll be a housemaid here," he said. "And every time you . . . you come in here with me, I'll give you one of those."

"Cor," Mary said, and lifted it up to give it a gentle bite. "Cor. Me mum will like that."

"You'll not tell your mum," Haggard said. "Or there'll be no more guineas. You'll tell her I offered you a job here."

Her head lifted; the coin was already secured inside her fist.

"Do you understand me, Mary?"

"Yes, sir, your worship." She stood up.

"There's a bath waiting for you downstairs. Have it. Then tell the girls to find you something to wear. Then you can go home and explain to your mum."

"Yes, sir, your worship."

Haggard looked down at himself. Coal dust stained his chest, his belly, his penis. Something he had wanted since he had first seen those children. Something he now had experienced.

Then what had she experienced? Why, nothing at all. She was stooping to pick up her coat; there was no blood, and she had shown no discomfort. Thirteen years old?

"Who've you known before?"

She straightened. Her tongue peeped for a moment, as usual. "Well, your worship, we all sleeps in the one bed . . ."

Haggard frowned at her. "You've brothers?"

"Oh, no, your worship. Just me sister, and me mum and dad."

"By Christ," Haggard said. "By Christ." He sat on the bed.

"But I'll not tell me dad," Mary Prince said. "I'll not give him the money."

"Aye," Haggard said. "You keep the money. We'll share a secret, Mary."

"Yes, sir, your worship." She looked pleased.

And I am dirty, Haggard thought. Dirty, dirty, dirty. "When you go down, Mary," he said, "tell the girls to send me up a hot bath as well."

As if it mattered. Had he not always known that incest was a fact of life in the logies at Haggard's Penn? That these people happened to have white skins was irrelevant, however much it had confused *him*. He was John Haggard. He was, in the eyes of English public opinion, the greatest blackguard on earth. He need fear the criticism of no man, after that.

Then what of woman? This he must find out. But he could not do so while looking over his shoulder. And how he wanted her, now. Because she was beautiful, and because she was of his own class, and because she would not submit to his every wish. And because she was clean. There was an indictment of his past relationships with women.

The grooms took his bridle, and he dismounted stiffly. He had ridden from Derleth at the same breakneck speed, after only a day at home. Each muscle in his body seemed to have a life of its own; he had not even been to his rooms to change. It occurred to him that since arriving in England he had been doing little but galloping from here to there, pursuing, or running, chasing the Haggard image, or attempting to escape it. Now was a time to call a halt, to settle his life down to the calm, confident, omnipotent existence he had known in Barbados. And the first essential toward accomplishing that goal was to have at his side a wife who would support him in everything he wished.

"Mr. Haggard, sir," said the butler. "Will you come up, please?"

Haggard gave his hat and coat and riding crop to a footman, followed the butler up the stairs. Alison waited at the top; she wore a pale blue gown with a ruched hem, and her hair was loose.

"Mr. Haggard. Is all well at Derleth?" Her tone suggested genuine interest.

Haggard took her hand and kissed it. How good she smelled. He had never known a woman with so beautiful a scent. "All is well, Alison. All is better than it has ever been."

She gave him a quick frown, then gently extracted her hand from his, led him into the withdrawing room. "You'll take a glass?"

"In fifteen minutes."

She nodded thoughtfully. "You'll bring in some wine, Partridge. In fifteen minutes."

"Of course, Miss Alison." Partridge closed the doors behind him.

Alison stood before the fire, facing Haggard. Her hands were clasped before her. "You look like a man who has ridden all night."

"I have ridden all night." He stepped closer. "Alison, I wish you to marry me."

"Mr. Haggard . . ." She sounded genuinely shocked, and Haggard, reaching for her, checked.

"I had supposed you regarded me with some favor."

"I do. But . . . you have *not* spoken with Papa."

"I am a Barbadian, remember." He held her hands, brought them toward him, pressed together. "I must have an assent from your lips, not forced by your father."

She smiled. "My father would force me into nothing, Mr. Haggard."

"Well, then . . ."

"I have explained to you my feelings, Mr. Haggard." She did not seek to free herself this time.

"And I have understood them, Alison. Listen. You will have heard I am building a new house?"

"All London has heard that, Mr. Haggard. At outrageous expense."

"A house fit only for the most beautiful girl in the country, Alison. A house being built especially for you. And you will be mistress of it, Alison. No one else."

Alison freed her hands very gently, sat down in the chair by the fire. "And the present manor house?"

"I shall probably pull it down. The new one will be complete by the autumn. We could be married then."

Alison appeared to consider. Then she raised her head, looked directly into his eyes. "What has happened to Miss Dearborn?"

"I have sent her away."

"A sudden decision."

"One to which I have been inclining for some time."

"But a decision," Alison Brand said.

"I am not a man to change my mind, Alison."

"You've children," she pointed out.

"My children. I'll not let them go. But you'll have children, Alison. I promise you that."

"Not to inherit."

"There'll be enough to go round." As her father had said, she had an old head on those beautiful shoulders, he thought. But did it matter? She was the woman he wanted, as much for her old and steady head as for her body and her lips. "I had supposed you wanted to," he said.

"We must talk with Papa."

"But you . . ." He knelt before her, held her hands again, brought them to his lips. "Will you not say yes to me now?"

She smiled. "After we have spoken with Papa," she said.

"Haggard." Brand squeezed his hands. But his eyes would not meet Haggard's gaze, kept dropping away.

"Alison will have told you?"

"Oh, aye. Splendid news. What I've always hoped for."

"Then I suggest you look the part."

"You'll take a glass of port?" Brand pulled the bell. "I've sent the girls out for the morning. Best, eh?"

"Of course," Haggard agreed, and sat down, stretching his legs in front of him. "I'll confess I am in no practice at playing the suitor."

"So I have gathered."

"But you've no objections?"

"To you? Man, I'd choose no other. Ah, Partridge." The port was poured, the decanter left between the two men. "First things first, though. I'm a straight-up man, Haggard. You'll have noticed that."

"Indeed I have," Haggard said, somewhat dryly.

"If you'd not come to me, I'd have come to you."

"About Alison?"

"Eh? God no. About you. You'd no trouble at Derleth?"

"None I couldn't handle."

"There's good news. The case has set London by its ears."

Haggard grinned at him, and drank some port. "And I am the most unpopular man in the kingdom."

Brand leaned forward, his face serious. "True."

"So you'd not see me as a son-in-law."

"I said, first things first. With a big program in view, Billy doesn't want distractions."

Haggard's turn to frown. "I'm not sure I understand you."

"It's politics, you understand. I doubt you have such things in Barbados."

"We have some."

"Not like here. 'Tis the ladies, you know. Every one dabbling away, influencing their husbands. To say a man is a Tory is not to say he'll always support us. No, no. There's a deal of feeling that runs through this community, which will find expression."

Haggard poured some more port. "Brand, you are babbling. Come to the point."

"The point. Yes. Well, Billy feels, we all feel, that perhaps it would be best were you to absent yourself from Parliament for a while."

"Eh?"

Brand produced a brightly colored kerchief, wiped his forehead. "Well, you see, Haggard, parliamentary procedure being what it is, the next time you appear in the house, in the immediate future that is, some damned Whig is going to put down a question about slavery, and slave owners being permitted to sit in the house . . . they're very devils. Next thing you'll be impeached, like that poor devil Hastings."

"I have done nothing for which I can be impeached," Haggard said. "I have broken no laws. Nor can I be impeached, while I am a member."

"True. True. But Billy feels there could be some terrible time-wasting, and maybe some to be too closely identified with the party."

Haggard got up. "No one mentioned this before. You were happy to have me. You knew I was a slave owner."

"Don't go getting the wrong idea. I've nothing against a slave owner. None of us have. But we assumed you'd win your case. As you should have done. But there it is. 'Tis public opinion we have to consider. England is ruled by public opinion. Important."

"So I'm to be ostracized because a madman like Granville Sharp has stolen one of my people."

"Too strong," Brand protested. "Too strong. You wish to be a Tory, Haggard. The party comes before anything else. Before country."

"That's a damned unpatriotic thing to say," Haggard said.

"Well, not before *country*," Brand said. "If it came to that.

But before anything else. And it's only for six months, Haggard. Billy is sure on that. It won't affect your seat. It's past Easter already. Soon Parliament will be rising for the summer. When they resume, in November, why, no one will even remember the name of James Middlesex. London is like that."

Haggard finished his port, poured himself a fresh glass. "And what of Alison?"

"My dear fellow, I am overjoyed. And it will work out rather well. You will have the time to prepare for the wedding." He leaned forward, slapped Haggard on the knee. "Tell your lawyer to prepare a settlement, and we'll consider it done."

Perhaps, Haggard thought, if I offered sufficient money to Wilberforce, I'd even be allowed to take my seat in Parliament.

They sat around the table. At Brand's request, Haggard had brought with him both Roeham the solicitor and Cummings; they were on either side of him. Colonel Brand sat opposite, Alison on his right, his own solicitor, by the name of Wooding, on his left. It was more like a business conference than a wedding proposal. But then, it had always been a business proposal, Haggard realized. Why else should a girl like Alison wish to marry a man more than twice her age? But at the end of it all, she would belong to him. All of her.

She wore a high-necked pink gown, and this morning her hair was up as well, and concealed beneath a mobcap. Her face and neck were exposed, and utterly magnificent. There were pink spots on her cheeks, but he suspected these had been assisted by rouge, as they neither deepened nor faded. He had no idea what might lie under the gown, save for the shadowy limbs he had seen beneath her nightdress. But he did not doubt for an instant. She would be his, at the end of it.

"Colonel Brand will settle upon his daughter an income of six hundred pounds a year," Wooding said. "It is a small sum, but the colonel is not a wealthy man. He hopes Mr. Haggard will understand this, and not permit Miss Brand to find herself in an embarrassing position."

"Mr. Haggard has been entirely generous," Roeham said in turn, consulting his own paper, "and means to settle upon Mrs. Haggard an income of one thousand pounds a month for the rest of her life."

"One thousand pounds," Brand said. "Bless my soul. There is generosity, Haggard. I thank you, man. I thank you."

Haggard looked at Alison, who for a moment returned his gaze. Her lips parted in what might have been mistaken for a smile.

"And the issue of the marriage?" Wooding inquired.

"Ah . . ." Roeham continued to study his paper. "Shall be recognized as heirs to the estate of Mr. Haggard in the event of the death of the existing heir, Mr. Roger Haggard, and in any event, from the ages of eighteen onward, shall be in receipt of an income of not less than two hundred pounds a month each."

"Generous," Colonel Brand said. "Oh, generous. Well, my sweet girl, are you content?"

Now Alison did smile. "I have always been content with Mr. Haggard's proposals, Papa," she murmured.

"Then shall we sign?"

The papers were exchanged, and Haggard appended his signature. Like buying a horse or a house, he thought. But what an animal.

"There we are, gentlemen." Brand pushed back his chair and stood up. "Now I suggest we all adjourn to the withdrawing room and enjoy a glass of wine. 'Tis a cause for celebration," he added, perhaps as an afterthought.

"We will join you in a moment," Haggard said. "But first I would like a few minutes alone with my fiancée."

Alison's mouth opened in surprise, and she glanced at her father.

"Well, of course, that is entirely correct," Brand said. "Only a few minutes, now, Haggard, eh? A few minutes."

They bustled from the room, and the door was closed. Alison remained seated at the table.

"Are you happy?" Haggard asked.

"I am overwhelmed, Mr. Haggard. As Papa has said, you have been far too generous."

Haggard got up, walked round the table, stood behind her, inhaled her perfume. "Would you have refused me, had I been mean?"

"John Haggard is not a mean man," she said. "Or I would never have been his friend."

Haggard rested his hands on her shoulders. For how long had he wanted to do that. "Now you are to be his wife."

Her head tilted backward, so that she could look up at

him. "I desire only your love, Mr. Haggard. As I shall give you mine."

He lowered his head, checked when he was an inch away from her. But she did not move. Relief spread outward from his heart and his belly. He dropped his lips onto hers. They were closed, and he stroked them with his tongue. For just a moment they parted, and he was able to touch hers. Her hands came up and closed on his arms, squeezing; then she released him, and her mouth was gone.

She stood up, and the pink spots in her cheeks had at last grown. "I am happy, Mr. Haggard," she said. "Very happy."

"Then you will call me John."

"John," she said, and held out her hand. "Shall we join Papa?"

"But where is she *now?*" Roger insisted. "Please, Father."

Haggard sighed. How big he was for sixteen years of age; why, they were roughly the same height. "I do not know where she is now, boy. You understand the situation between us?"

Roger nodded. "Emma explained it to me herself. But she said she loved you. And she said you loved her."

"Well, of course we loved each other. Then. But love sometimes grows cold. And we were not married. So when she wished to leave me, I had no means of keeping her here."

"But *why?*" Roger asked. "Why should she *wish* to leave you? Where could she possibly go that was better than here?"

Two terms at Eton had filled out his mind as well as his body. Made him into a true Haggard, Haggard suspected. He would have to be carefully handled.

He leaned back in his chair, gazed out of the open window at the brilliant sunlight streaming into the study. This was more like it. He could at last understand why England was occasionally described as the most beautiful country in the world. But June was only thirty days long. Would July be as kind?

Still, there was no better month for Alison to see Derleth for the first time.

"You do understand," he said, "that Emma was not your mother."

"Of course I do, Father. But she was my friend. And now . . . I don't understand why you wish to marry again."

"Aye, well, you will when you are a few years older," Haggard said. "I will explain it to you then. Now, come along.

Miss Brand will be here in a little while. We must go out to meet her."

He was determined that Alison, on her first visit to Derleth, should not be disappointed. Everything that had gone wrong with his own arrival had been corrected, so far as he was able. Now he mounted his favorite mare, and saw that the children were also suitably horsed. He led them through the street, MacGuinness bringing up the rear, inspected the bunting hung from the houses, at his direction and paid for with his money, made sure that the Reverend Porlock—Litteridge's replacement—had the church looking sufficiently welcoming.

He drew rein at the inn. "Is all ready, Mr. Hatchard?"

The publican was on the doorstep, in his best suit. "Aye, Mr. Haggard," he said. "All is ready. I'm just giving them a drink, to cure the heat, like."

Haggard nodded and rode on. He wondered what they really thought of him. They had had no reason to love the black people, and they had heartily disliked Emma. Even those who had opposed him in the slavery issue had been whipped into it by Parson Litteridge. Since that troublemaker's departure he had been greeted mostly by smiles, even if he often caught them whispering surreptitiously behind their hands. But they could whisper what they liked. He was Haggard. He had established that fact as firmly here as he ever had in Barbados. No doubt they were each relieved that the girl he had picked out of the mine had been Mary Prince rather than one of their own. But they'd not criticize. Not even Henry Prince did anything more than touch his hat; he had too great a liking for golden guineas.

And no doubt that went for the country as a whole. Six months, Pitt had said. Well, the six months would be over in September, and in September he would be married. It would be time to turn his back on discord and quarreling, and begin a new life with his new wife. With the most beautiful girl in the land.

And there she was. The carriage was in sight, rumbling up the London turnpike, and turning to the left to take the road into Derleth. Haggard stood in his stirrups and waved his hat, and handkerchiefs fluttered from the windows of the berlin.

"Wave," he commanded the children. "Wave, damn you."

They obediently waved their own hats, and the carriage scraped to a halt. Inside were both Alison and Emily and their maids. Alison leaned out of the open window and gave him her hand. He leaned from the saddle to kiss it and squeeze it. "Welcome to Derleth," he said. "Oh, welcome to Derleth."

"I feel as if I am coming home," she said. "And are these the children?"

"Roger, my elder son," Haggard said.

Roger raised his hat.

"Give me your hand, Roger," Alison said.

"And this is my daughter, Alice."

Alice, a perfect replica of Emma, even at ten years old, gave a nervous bob to her head.

"I am pleased to meet you, child," Alison said, but this time she did not shake hands. "And that will be Charles. He sits a horse well."

"Haggards," Haggard said. "Ride on," he told the driver.

The whip cracked, and the berlin raced down the hill, followed by its cavalcade. "She's lovely," Alice cried. "Don't you think she's lovely, Roger?"

Roger did not reply.

"I don't think she's as lovely as Mama," Charlie said, and bit his lip as Haggard turned his head.

"Hush," Alice said. "You'll annoy Papa."

They were entering the village, and the men were streaming out of the pub to cheer and clap as the carriage rumbled by. Everyone had a foaming tankard in his hand; Hatchard had done his work well.

"Hooray for Mistress Brand," someone shouted.

"Hooray for Mr. Haggard," shouted another.

Hats were thrown in the air, beer was spilled, and the whole mass moved along beside the carriage, shouting and cheering.

"They love you at first sight," Haggard said.

Alison merely smiled. But it was a more contented smile than he had ever seen before.

They left the village behind and approached the manor. Beyond, the new house was taking shape, the tower built and dominating the countryside, the adjoining building a gaunt skeleton of wooden uprights only slowly being covered with planking. But already it was making the old hall resemble a barn.

"Your future home," Haggard said, and dismounted to open the door for her.

Alison Brand stepped down, inspected the lined-up grooms and footmen, Pretty the butler, restored to his old position, the housemaids and parlor maids, marshaled by Mistress Wring, Peter's mother, who had come to the hall as housekeeper. The girls kept their eyes dutifully lowered, Mary Prince included, Haggard was pleased to note.

Alison swept by them and into the doorway, Emily and Haggard at her heels. In the doorway she stopped and turned. "I like Derleth," she said. "I like you all." She smiled at Haggard. "I will be happy here."

"I can see it's going to be magnificent," Alison said. They had dismounted, the better to inspect the works, stood together at the foot of the tower, which rose forty feet above their heads. "Can we get up there?"

"Can we?" Haggard looked over his shoulder. Nash had remained a discreet distance away.

"Only by ladder at the moment, I'm afraid, Mr. Haggard."

Alison's tongue came out, circled her lips. "I have never climbed a ladder. Could we, Mr. Haggard?"

"Of course." He led her inside the shell of the main building; at the far end, the inner wall of the tower was open, as if breached. On this, the ground floor, they looked at what would be cellars. A ladder led up to the extended drawing room on the second floor.

"It looks awfully steep," Emily complained.

"Well, then," Haggard said, "you stay down here with Roger. Alison and I will make the climb." It was quite impossible to get rid of the girl. Or, come to think of it, of his son.

Alison already had her foot on the bottom rung. "You'll stay close behind me," she said.

Haggard stepped onto the ladder; her skirt brushed his face. He inhaled her perfume, watched her neatly laced boots emerging and disappearing again as she climbed. Her riding habit was in midnight blue, with a matching tricorne. As ever, she looked good enough to eat. Certainly to rape. But what a strange thought about his future wife. He had only to be patient.

She paused for breath halfway up, and to look down at the people beneath her.

"Be careful," Emily called.

Alison laughed, and climbed again, scrambled off the ladder and onto the floor, waited for Haggard to join her. "It's going to be magnificent," she said.

"There's another," he pointed out. "Leading to the bedchamber."

She glanced at him, crossed the floor, and started climbing again. Now they were out of sight of the people below. Up they went, and through the opening onto the upper floor. Here the room was almost complete, although the windows needed to be glazed. Alison stood at the nearest, looked out at the rolling countryside, the trees clustering over the slopes of the hills; the window looked away from the village. "What an absolutely splendid view," she said. "I feel like a Norman chatelaine, waiting for the onslaught of the Saxons."

"A good time to be alive," Haggard said at her shoulder.

"Do you think so? I am happier now."

He put his arms around her waist, brought her back against him. "Do you know this is the first time we have been alone since our betrothal?"

"Well . . . you are such a passionate man, dear Mr. Haggard." Her hands were on his arms, seeking to free them. Gently he spread his hands, allowed the fingers to wander upward over the hardness of her corset and just to touch the underside of her breasts. She gave a little shiver, and this time exerted her strength to free herself and move away.

"And you are not a passionate woman, Alison?"

She turned, eight feet away, and faced him, hands clasped in front of her. "I do not know what I am, Mr. Haggard." She shrugged. "How could I?"

But there was a peculiar expression in her eyes, which he could not understand. He moved toward her. "You can permit yourself passion with me, my darling."

Her hands came up between them. "When we are married, Mr. Haggard. It is only three months now."

"Three months," he said. "An entire summer, just sitting here, with naught to do . . ."

"You could join a hunt," she said. "I know it is too early in the year, but you could train up a pack of hounds, break in some horses."

"Hunt," he said. "I suppose I could."

"I recommend it highly," she said. "Where is the nearest pack?"

"I have no idea."

She frowned at him. "But . . . your neighboring gentry?"

"I have never met them."

"They have not come to call, Mr. Haggard?"

"Why, No, they have not." He shrugged. "I suppose they approve neither of my being a slave owner nor of my earlier liaison."

"Well, they will have to change," Alison decided. "As they will be happy to, once we are married. Mr. Haggard, I have the most splendid news."

He took her hands. "Tell me."

"Papa has secured us invitations to the Duchess of Devonshire's ball, at Almack's. Can you believe it, Mr. Haggard?" Her eyes glistened. "The prince will be there."

"Damn and blast the thing," Haggard complained, surveying himself in the mirror. "I see no point to it. Especially in the summer."

"Hit must be worn, Mr. 'Aggard," Simpson explained, carefully adjusting the wig for the third time. "There is no 'elp for it. Now, sir, does that not look proper?"

Haggard sighed. The thing was at least straight. But it made him look absurd, and every time he moved his head, a spray of powder scattered across the shoulders of his black coat.

"Hevery other gentleman will be wearing one, sir," Simpson pointed out.

"I suppose you're right. My cane."

" 'Ere we are, sir. And the 'at."

All brand-new. There was a pun for you. Brand had himself seen to his future son-in-law's clothes. Now he waited while Simpson pulled the tails straight, gave a last brush to the shoulders—the only hope of keeping them clean was for Simpson to attend him to the ball itself—and stood back.

"There we are, sir."

Haggard descended the stairs, to where Brand was pacing up and down the hall.

"Ah, Haggard, there you are. My word, but you look splendid. Quite splendid. You'll be the sensation of the ball. I do declare. And 'tis important, mind. Important. Everyone has heard of you, not enough have seen you and talked with you."

"I am surprised I am allowed in at all," Haggard observed.

"Ah, bah, I told you that London society has a short memory for detail. You will take them by storm. Yes, indeed."

Haggard found himself once again before a mirror, peering at himself. The wig was still in place, and by keeping his head very still he could reduce the powder landslide. But why did he bother? Why was he vaguely excited and why were there butterflies in his belly? He was John Haggard. If he really wanted to, no doubt he could buy Almack's itself, and impose his own rules upon their silly functions. If he wanted to. But it was necessary to remember that, or these haughty duchesses and their lackeylike followers would reduce him to a jelly with their stares. How Bridgetown society would laugh could they but know the truth of it.

"If only the girls would be ready," Brand grumbled. "Ah, there you are, my dears. Come along, now. You know we mustn't be late. We'll be turned away if we're late."

For the first time that evening Haggard forgot about himself. Descending the stairs toward him was the most marvelous sight he had ever seen, Alison Brand wearing an ice-pink evening gown, slashed in a low décolletage, and with her hair quite disappeared beneath the towering white wig in which were embedded a variety of precious stones—rubies and emeralds and sapphires—his engagement present to her. But even the jewels seemed irrelevant. The absence of hair from her neck and shoulders left them as well as her face quite exposed, and far more lovely than he had ever realized them to be. Suddenly he was almost afraid of her. All that beauty, and soon to be his.

He hardly noticed Emily, wearing pale green, although he had supplied her jewelry as well.

"Am I suitable, for the future Mrs. Haggard?" Alison asked, and extended her left hand to allow the huge diamond to sparkle in the light.

Haggard kissed her knuckles. "You are suitable to be the queen of England," he said.

She smiled at him. "You'd best not suggest that to the prince," she said, "or you might lose me."

"Come along, come along, do," Brand said. "We shall be late. I know we shall be late. Turned away from Almack's. My God, what a disaster. We shall never hold up our heads in society again."

Haggard followed him through the door. "You forget I have already been turned away from Almack's, and am doing quite well at holding up my head."

Brand did not reply, climbed into the coach even in front of his daughters; he was clearly very agitated, and in a curious way his concern soothed Haggard's own nervousness. He could sit beside Alison and enjoy the evening—it was still daylight—and enjoy too the sensation of possessing so much beauty.

He could even enjoy once again encountering the formida-

ble Martin, as usual flanked by an army of footmen, all gold
and green and powdered wigs, bowing as he took Brand's
card.

"Colonel Brand, and the Misses Alison and Emily Brand,
and . . . Mr. John Haggard," he said. The information was
hastily passed up the stairs, immediately in front of them,
and was announced by the majordomo.

"Look at them," Alison said, without appearing to move
her lips, which were fixed in a smile.

Haggard surveyed the scene in astonishment. He had not
supposed the ballroom could be so large—and it could only
be a fraction of the whole area, for archways led away to
other rooms in which there were tables laden with cold foods,
other tables laden with champagne and chilled wines, and yet
other tables covered in green baize and surrounded by chairs;
clearly every possible taste was catered for here.

But for the moment it was the ballroom which was the
center of attention; this was packed, with women, every one
as magnificently dressed as Alison, although not one as good-
looking, with men, the majority in black suits and white shirts
and cravats, like himself, but with a smattering of red-coated
and high-collared army officers, and even one or two in the
dark blue and gold braid of the navy. He knew none of
them, although he had been told Addison would be here—but
every head was turned in his direction, and as he watched, a
woman came toward them, and the whole room seemed to
diminish in splendor.

She was about thirty-five years of age, he estimated. Her
natural good looks—and she must have been a rare beauty in
her youth,—were enhanced by her air of absolute confidence
and indeed arrogance, as much as by her gown, which was in
midnight blue with sequined hem and sleeves, or by her
décolletage, which was breathtaking, or by her jewelry,
which even Haggard's somewhat inexperienced eye—West Indian women seldom displayed much wealth—could be costed
at several thousand pounds. She moved across the floor in a
long glide, and allowed Brand to take her hand

"Colonel Brand." Her voice was a very gentle caress.
"How good of you to come. And your utterly charming
daughters. Why, they grow more beautiful with every passing
day." She stood before Haggard. "And this is Mr. Haggard,"
she said, her voice slightly lowered. "My evening is guaranteed success, Mr. Haggard. All London has been waiting to

see you. And no one is going to be disappointed, I am sure. Allow me to introduce you."

He realized that she was offering him her arm, and that she was escorting him down the line of ladies and gentlemen, rather as if he were visiting royalty, which he supposed he very nearly was. Their names flowed around him, their smiles seemed to bathe him, their jewels and their breasts winked at him, but he heard and saw none of them. His brain seemed suffocated by the scent and the aura of the woman on his arm. What misfortune, he thought, that I should have become engaged to Alison before meeting her; what an affair we could have had.

If she chose. But as they reached the end of the first row and she smiled at him, he could not doubt that she would choose.

"I must leave you now, Mr. Haggard," she said. "To greet my other guests. But be sure I shall find you again."

"On the contrary, your Grace," he said, bowing over her hand. "It is I shall find you, as soon as I may."

"Why, Mr. Haggard," she said, "I had no idea our colonials were so gallant. I shall look forward to it."

She withdrew her hand and returned toward the head of the staircase. Haggard found himself surrounded by people he had apparently just met, eager to talk about Barbados, which they seemed to confuse with Jamaica or Antigua; about sugar planting, of which they knew even less; and about the new hall he was building at Derleth, of which they seemed to know more than himself. He smiled at them and made what he hoped were suitable replies, and was rescued by Addison, who gently eased him from the throng and obtained them each a glass of wine from a passing footman.

"Well, Haggard, your triumph, what?"

"I confess I do not understand it at all."

"Society is like the mob, my dear Haggard. Fickle as a pretty woman. But while you please them, why, it is like living in perpetual sunlight. Miss Brand, how beautiful you look."

"Thank you, Mr. Addison. The prince is arriving."

They turned, with everyone else, and the ladies curtsied while the gentlemen bowed. Haggard found himself impressed. Prince George was just past thirty. Perhaps he was a trifle overweight, and his cheeks were too flushed, as his nose was too large, but he was a splendid figure of a man, with the height to carry any stoutness, and a magnificent *air*, which quite matched Georgiana's.

"Does he come down the line?" he muttered.

"No, no," Alison said. "We are presented to him as the evening goes on. Those of us the duchess chooses."

"But you will be amongst them, Haggard," Addison promised. "No doubt of that."

"The music," Alison said. "Will you dance with me, Mr. Haggard?"

"Wait for the prince," Addison warned.

But the Prince of Wales was already on the floor, the duchess in his arms. Haggard led Alison out; certainly they made a marvelous couple, and he observed the prince's head turning as they joined the parade. He had not danced for twelve years, since that disastrous night at the Boltons'. But had it been disastrous? That night had set in motion a remarkable series of events. But for those events, would he be here now?

Alison smiled at him as they parted, and was still smiling as they came together again. Her whole body seemed to be smiling. This was the life she truly appreciated, truly loved. Then he must be sure they enjoyed a great deal of it, at Derleth. The great room at the hall might have been intended for dancing; indeed, he had created it with that half in mind. Alison would be in her element. And after his triumph tonight, Derleth would be the center of all that was worthwhile in Midlands society.

The music had stopped, and he was escorting her back to where Emily sat with her father. "You dance divinely."

"As do you, Mr. Haggard. I am so happy."

"Haggard. The moment is here." Addison, smiling at him.

"You'll excuse you," he murmured, gave Alison's hand a hasty squeeze, followed his friend across the room, aware that he was being watched by everyone present.

The prince was surrounded by his gentlemen, none of whom Haggard had met; but also in the group was the duchess.

"Ah, Mr. Haggard," she said, and took his hand. "Sir, I would so like you to meet Mr. John Haggard, late of Barbados, but now of Derleth Hall, in Derbyshire."

Haggard gave a brief bow, straightened, found the prince staring at him. "You're the planting fellow."

"That is so, sir."

"The slave-chasing fellow, what? Dicky Sheridan has been telling me about you."

"Indeed, sir?"

"It won't do, Haggard. It won't do. No indeed. This is a free country."

Haggard opened his mouth and then shut it again. He had been quite unprepared for such an attack. He could feel his cheeks burning, but it was nothing compared to the sudden burning anger in his belly.

"And then, this other business," Prince George said. "Turning your people out into the snow. Gad, sir, that was barbaric. Barbaric. You'll know one of them died."

Haggard took a long breath. "I did not know that, sir. Nor do I accept it."

"You'd call me a liar?"

"Why, sir . . ." Fingers were closing on his arm.

"Sharp told me so himself, sir," the prince said, also very red in the face. "One of the women just fell down and died. Gad, sir, it made my blood boil. Called you a damned scoundrel, he did, and I'm not sure I don't agree with him."

The huge room was utterly silent. The men to either side of the prince seemed paralyzed. The fingers remained on Haggard's arm, but they no longer gripped. Haggard could only stare at the florid face in front of him; the Prince was showing slight signs of embarrassment, as if he had not quite intended to go so far.

But he was the prince. "I am sure, sir," Haggard said, "that you must therefore find my company obnoxious. You'll forgive me if I withdraw."

"Of all of the damnable things." Brand paced his own withdrawing room, waving his decanter of port.

"He was drunk, of course," Addison pointed out. He was also putting away as much port as he could swallow.

"Drunk?" Alison cried. "What does it matter what he was? We walked out of the Duchess of Devonshire's ball. We *walked* out. It is unbelievable."

"We shall never be invited anywhere again."

Haggard sighed. Although he had consumed quite as much port as either Brand or Addison, he was perfectly sober. "I had not intended you to follow me."

"What else was I to do?" Alison demanded, hands on hips. She looked less like a beautiful girl than a reincarnation of

Medusa, especially as she had taken off her wig and her undressed hair was scattered.

"Anyway, I'd not have had us do anything else." Addison said. "I think he used the opportunity for a deliberate attack upon Haggard, and through him on the Tory party. He more or less admitted he'd been put up to it by Sheridan. 'Tis nothing but a Whig plot. And you gave as good as you got, Haggard. Oh, aye, you met him fair and square, and did not even lose your temper."

"We'll never be presented at court," Emily moaned. "Never."

"I should like to know where I stand," Haggard said. "It seems that if you marry me, Alison, your social future is dead. Therefore I feel it is only right that you should decide."

"To . . ." Some of the color faded from Alison's cheeks, and she glanced at her father.

"My dear fellow," the colonel spluttered, "of course Alison means to marry you. What, refuse the . . . the best fellow in all the country because our scoundrel of a prince insulted him?"

Had he really been going to say "the wealthiest man in the country?"

"Treason." Addison grinned.

"And you, sir?" Haggard demanded.

"Oh, I am on your side, Haggard. Entirely."

"Well, then, the decision must rest with Alison."

She stared at him, her cheeks once again pinkening. Then her shoulders rose and fell. "Of course I wish to marry you, Mr. Haggard. Oh, how I wish it could be today. Thank God it is only a short while."

Only a short while. And indeed the summer had passed very quickly, Haggard thought. There had been the hall to be completed, and there had been the preparations for the wedding, the food and the wine and the lodgings to be prepared. Over the past week there had been the arrival of the guests, the rehearsal, with Emily taking the part of her sister, the meetings with the Reverend Porlock, who was in a state of high excitement, the practices with the children, who were each to have an important part to play, the knowledge that every day Alison was coming closer. Nothing mattered besides that single fact. Not Pitt's refusal to attend—affairs of state, by God—nor indeed the somewhat muted response of London society; the local gentry had been happy enough to have an excuse to end their ostracism of him, to inspect the new hall, to meet the squire himself. There were guests enough, even without Pitt. It had been quite a revelation to realize that so many people in this amazing country disliked the prince, were actually prepared to take *his* side in the quarrel.

So London society was apparently closed to him; he was not even prepared to be angry about that anymore. Politics were irrelevant to an impatient groom. How had he contained himself? Indeed he had not, entirely. But the housemaids were nothing more than a panacea. They relieved the pressure on his penis, the demands on his belly. But they did nothing for his mind, left him as anxious to dream of Alison immediately after a tumble as he had been afraid to do so before. And for the last week he had touched none of them.

And now it was over. All the waiting was behind him. He stood at the head of the aisle, listening to the music, conscious of Henry Addison, acting as best man, at his shoulder, head half-turned so that he would gain an early glimpse of her. Behind him the little church was packed to the door, and filled with a gigantic rustle, which slowly died as everyone stood and the music rose to a crescendo.

Haggard traced the advance of the white-clad figure from the corner of his eye. Only her face was uncovered, as the gown itself was high-necked and her arms and hands were lost in the long lace gloves. Behind her Emily was a splash of blue, and Brand, like himself, wore black. How slowly they moved. But he could wait forever, now. She was here, and she was about to be his. His entire body was swollen with desire for her. With love for her? Well, love had to be based, first and foremost, on desire. But how could he not love someone as beautiful, as soft-spoken, as purposeful as Alison Brand?

She smiled at him, and her hand was in his. Porlock was beginning his preamble, and the church had fallen silent. Haggard scarce heard a word that was spoken; Addison had to nudge him to make the correct responses. He thought all of his life might have been a preparation for just this moment: the boy who had stumbled into marriage with Susan Brett; the young husband who had near gone mad with grief at her death; the lonely savage planter who had nightly drowned his sorrows in a jug of sangaree; the careless marksman who had killed a man for very little reason; the eager lecher who had plucked Emma Dearborn from the noose; the determined individualist who had set all Barbados at defiance; the bewildered colonial who had sought a new life in England; the slave owner who had become the most unpopular man in the land—all of these different facets of his personality had led up to the complete Haggard. They were behind him now, and for the second half of his life he would be content to be Squire Haggard of Derleth Hall, John Haggard, M.P., and above all, Mistress Haggard's husband. So he had often been a bad man. But that was behind him as well, No more outrageous tempers, no more pandering to outrageous desires, no more coal dust on his penis. Only Alison, Alison, Alison, and all the joys that Alison would bring.

"You may kiss the bride," Porlock suggested.

Haggard awoke as from a dream, lowered his head, kissed her on the lips. For just a second she allowed her tongue to rest on his; then she was away, and the parson was waiting to escort them into the vestry to sign the register.

"My God, but I was nervous as a kitten." Brand took off his wig to wipe his head. "And to think I must experience that again with Emily."

Haggard beamed at them all, even at Roger, with his solemn, serious face. The two younger children, carrying Alison's train, were wildly overexcited. It would have to be an early night for them; but that could safely be left to Nurse Halling. It was going to be an early night for him as well.

"Shall we go?" Alison squeezed his arm. Pray to God that she was passionate. It was not a thought that had really troubled him before. But she was a lady. Had Susan been passionate? He could not really remember, but he did not think so, because he had known so little about passion himself. She had been willing, had accepted him, but had she ever responded? Alison was no older. It was he who had changed.

The organ broke out into the wedding march, the crowded church stood and smiled at them and greeted them and welcomed them. Alison's fingers were tight on his as they emerged into the midmorning sunlight, to blink and wave at the entire population of Derleth, today swelled by many from the neighboring villages and valleys. A society wedding was not something to be missed by anyone who could find any means of transport. Haggard beamed at them all, looking along the row of faces, Peter Wring, raising his hat, Jemmy Lacey, standing beside his sister—even she was smiling— Hatchard the publican, other faces he recognized without being able to put names to them, Emma Dearborn . . .

Haggard stopped at the foot of the church steps. He felt quite incapable of moving, his belly filled with lead, his heart suddenly pounding.

"Mr. Haggard?" Alison spoke in an urgent whisper; the two children had nearly bumped into her back.

Haggard had closed his eyes. He opened them slowly, looked at Emma again. There could be no mistake. She wore a bonnet which concealed the most part of her hair, and in place of the crimson pelisse she had worn when last he had seen her there was a light brown cloak, of considerably cheaper material. Her face was thinner than he remembered. But it was Emma. And now she had seen him looking at her. He watched her lips move, and not to smile. She was saying something. Pronouncing a curse, by God.

"Mr. Haggard." Alison's voice was sharp.

"MacGuinness," he said. "Where is MacGuinness?"

"Who?"

He recovered himself, looked away, hurried forward. The open coach was waiting for them, and MacGuinness was himself standing by the door to help them in.

"MacGuinness," he said. "Follow me to the hall. Quickly."

"Sir?" MacGuinness frowned at him.

"To the hall, MacGuinness." Haggard sat down beside Alison, and the coachman flicked his whip. They were turned away from where Emma had been standing, and he would not look back.

"Whatever is the matter, Mr. Haggard?" Alison asked. "I had supposed you had had a seizure."

He looked down at her, smiled at her. Emma could not harm him, not even with her curses. She had tried before. Hadn't she? He kissed his wife on the forehead, and the crowd cheered. "Nothing is the matter. No seizure."

She leaned back, still clutching his hand tightly. In front of them the new hall crowned the hill. Haggard's Folly, some unkind wag had called it. But it was a splendid building, dominated by the tower on the outside, and on the inside by the huge marble ceremonial staircase which curved from the entry hall to debouch into the ballroom. Here the servants were gathered, lining the steps, the maids to one side and the footmen to the other, waiting to throw rose petals at their master and their new mistress, before hurrying off to the mammoth task in front of them, of serving champagne and food to a hundred people.

Haggard and Alison climbed the stairs slowly, took their

places at the top. "MacGuinness," Haggard muttered. "Where the devil is MacGuinness?"

But the other guests were already arriving, headed by Emily and her father and Alice and Charlie. Had they looked into the crowd and seen their mother? They gave no sign of it. Nor did Roger. And MacGuinness was submerged in the mob streaming by, shaking hands and kissing, according to their sex, showering congratulations, faces he knew, faces which were strange to him, friends and relations of the Brands, every one with gaminlike features, shrouded in a head of waving auburn hair. Christ, the bitch. The utter bitch. Returning after more than six months to make a sport of his wedding. She'd not get away with it. Not so long as his name was John Haggard.

"MacGuinness." The crowd had at last departed from the head of the stairs, and Alison had also left, to circulate among her guests, to enjoy their amazement at the splendor of the hall, at the paintings and the draperies and the upholstered furniture and the acres of polished floor, to discuss the architectural splendors of the tower, to bathe in the aura of being Mistress Haggard of Derleth Hall. "Did you see her?"

MacGuinness, his black suit clearly too tight for him, his face crimson with wine and heat, mopped his brow with his handkerchief. "See whom, Mr. Haggard?"

"Emma Dearborn. She was in the crowd."

"Oh, aye, well, she would be."

"Eh?"

"Seems she's taken up with Harry Bold."

"Who the devil is Harry Bold?" '

"Well, sir, Mr. Haggard, he's a tinker who—"

"A tinker?" Haggard shouted. Heads turned, and he lowered his voice. "A tinker?"

"That he is, sir. Well, he works this neighborhood, up north a bit, then down a bit. I had heard he was around these parts."

"And you never told me?"

"Well, sir, I didn't suppose you'd want to know. Not right at this moment."

"I know now," Haggard said. "And I'll not stand for it. I don't want that woman and her . . . her lover on my land. Understood?"

"Yes, sir, Mr. Haggard. But they'll be moving along anyway, I should think."

"And then coming back again? MacGuinness, I want them discouraged."

The bailiff frowned at him. "I'm not sure I understand you, Mr. Haggard."

"You understand me very well, MacGuinness. Find out where they are living, take some men, Peter Wring and his friends, and get over there tonight. You'll never have a better opportunity, with this rout going on until near dawn. A tinker, you said. He'll travel by wagon."

"Aye, sir, that he does. But—"

"Destroy it," Haggard said. "Smash it up. And tell him if he ever sets foot on my land again you'll smash him up as well."

"Mr. Haggard, Harry Bold ain't the sort of man to frighten easy."

"You'll have my people at your back, MacGuinness. And if he attempts to resist you, beat him up."

MacGuinness wiped his brow. "And the lady?"

"Emma Dearborn is no lady, MacGuinness. She was transported for theft. You want to remember that. See that it is done, MacGuinness."

MacGuinness sighed, and nodded. "As you wish, Mr. Haggard. I'll discourage them. You'll excuse me."

He receded into the crowd, and Haggard took another glass of champagne. Emma, and a tinker. He had not been so angry since Mansfield had given judgment for Middlesex. A tinker, an itinerant who probably never washed and was riddled with the clap. My God, how low, and how quickly, could a woman sink. Had this Bold also been in the crowd? He would have been standing next to Emma, of course. But he had not noticed him.

"Father."

Roger looked unnaturally solemn. Now, how long had he been there? Haggard rumpled his son's hair. "You've been at the champagne, I'll wager. And why not, on this occasion?"

"Father." Roger licked his lips. "Is it true that Emma has come back?"

Haggard frowned at him. "You've been eavesdropping. That's no occupation for a gentleman."

"I'm sorry, Father. I just couldn't help overhearing. You won't harm her, Father?"

"Now, don't you trouble yourself with Emma, Roger. You have a mother now. A proper mother."

"She's only two years older than I," Roger protested.

"All the better. You'll be friends as well. As for Emma, you want to forget her. It's I have to apologize to you, boy, for inflicting her upon you all of these years. But there it is. A man does many stupid things."

"Inflicting her on me?" Roger cried. "Then what of Alice and Charlie?"

"They're my children," Haggard said. "And I love them dearly. Not so dearly as you, maybe, but just the same . . . You'll not mention their mother to them. It would only make them unhappy."

Roger gazed at him for a moment. "You're going to send her away again."

"Of course I am. We don't want Emma lurking behind every bush in Derleth, now, do we?"

"And suppose she won't go?"

Haggard smiled and slapped his son on the shoulder. "She'll go, Roger. She'll go. I'm having MacGuinness see to that. There's naught for you to concern yourself with. Now, come along and we'll have another glass." He slapped him on the shoulder once more. "She'll go."

At last. After four interminable hours of speechmaking and drinking and dancing, of coarse jokes and coarser allusions, the time was come. The bouquet had been thrown expertly into the arms of Emily, and the bride had been removed up the stairs to her bedchamber. Convention demanded the groom should be changed elsewhere, and Haggard had been escorted along the upper gallery of the house proper to one of the guest bedrooms, where his clothes had been ripped off and a nightshirt dropped over his shoulders, to the accompaniment of a good deal more ribaldry, and now he had to run the gauntlet of the entire assembly of guests, through the ballroom, while his back was slapped and his nightcap was whisked away and people trod on his toes and shouted obscene remarks at him. But he cared for none of them. After an eternity of waiting, and wanting, all of that beauty was to be his.

Hands assisted him up the stairs, many of them female, lubricated by the wine and the champagne and the sense of occasion, slapping and squeezing his thighs, seeking to do more, and one certainly succeeding with a blow which had him gasping for pain. Then he was in the doorway, being greeted by the shrill cries of the ladies who had acted as maids, and gazing at Alison, sitting up in bed, a bedjacket over her nightgown to assist her modesty, her golden hair loose and resting on her shoulders, her cheeks pink, her mouth slightly open, with just a trace of equally pink tongue. All his.

Words swirled around his head, but he heard none of them. He had himself had far too much to drink. But he could concentrate on what was about to come into his possession. He laughed with the crowd, and endured the hand-shakings and the back slappings, and suddenly found Alice thrust into his arms.

"You'll say good night to your father, Alice." Thus Mistress Wring.

Haggard hugged the girl, kissed her on both cheeks, did the same for Charlie.

"Where's Roger, then?" he demanded, his voice thick.

"Roger?" They looked from left to right. "Where's Roger Haggard?"

"Slumped in a corner, no doubt, full of champagne," Brand said. "We'll find him, John. But it's bed for you."

"Aye," Haggard said. "When you've all left."

"We're to see the consummation," someone said, very drunk.

"You'll not." Haggard bundled them toward the door.

" 'Tis the fashion," a lady cried.

"You'll not rob us of sport," a voice complained.

"Have your sport downstairs," Haggard suggested. "Consummate anything you like." He pushed the last protesting body through the door, slammed it shut, turned the key, and leaned against it. "Christ, what a rout."

"Was it not like this at your first wedding?" Alison asked.

"Oh, aye. But I was younger then." He frowned. "I'm sorry. I'd not meant to remind you of that."

"Of what?"

He crossed the room slowly. He supposed she could see the thrust of his penis almost coming through the linen nightshirt. "Of the difference in our ages."

Alison smiled at him. "I'd surely not wish to find myself in bed with any tyro."

She was his. He sat on the bed, took her in his arms. She came to him slowly, and he kissed her on the mouth; while he did so, he reached up and slipped the cap from her head, stroked the hair, held her close, felt the touch of her tongue entering his mouth, reluctantly released her as she slid away, frowned at her expression. For just a moment her face had been filled with distaste, even a suggestion of repulsion. But then she smiled, and was as lovely as ever.

"Be gentle with me, Mr. Haggard," she whispered.

Roger Haggard lay in his bed and listened to the sounds of revelry coming from the ballroom. He would not have slept in any event, not only on account of the noise, but because he was still not used to his new bedroom, so much grander than the one at the old hall. But tonight there was no chance of sleeping, anyway. Emma was here. She had not disappeared, as Father would have it. She was here, to watch her lover be married. Then she must love him still. Then everything Father had told him and Alice and Charlie must have been a lie.

Because of Alison Brand. What hold could she have over Father, to make him do such a terrible thing? But he had done it, and now he was going to send Emma away again, without allowing her to see them, breaking up her wagon— why Emma should be traveling in a wagon was beyond his comprehension—perhaps even injuring her.

He sat up, heart pounding. Father himself had always drummed into him: Do what you know is right, without looking right or left, without hesitating. Obeying that simple precept had involved him in more fights than any other boy at Eton. But it had also earned him total respect far more quickly than any other new boy, as well. And Father would himself agree, whenever he escaped from Alison's power. Because it had to be some sort of power. There was simply no other explanation.

He thrust his feet out of bed, dragged on his clothes, carried his shoes in his hand. He opened the door; there was no diminution in the music, the raised voices, and the laughter coming from below him; the celebrations were not likely to end before dawn. He tiptoed along the corridor, went into Alice's room, drew the draperies, and shook his sister by the shoulder. "Ally. Wake up."

She grunted, rolled toward him, and opened her eyes to peer into the darkness. "Who is it?"

"Me, stupid. Listen. Get up and get dressed."

Alice Haggard pushed hair from her eyes. "Whatever for?"

"I'll tell you later. Just do it. I'm going to wake Charlie. No noise, now. Wait for us here."

Charlie's room was immediately beyond. He got his brother out of bed, helped him dress, then they both returned to Alice; she was also dressed and waiting for them, sitting on the side of her bed and yawning. "I don't understand. I was fast asleep."

"Listen," Roger said. "Emma is in Derleth."

"Emma? Mama?" Alice's voice rose.

"Ssssh. Yes. She was in the crowd at the wedding."

"But Father said—"

"Never mind what Father said. She was there. But she's going to be sent away again tonight. Would you like to see her?"

"Mama," Charlie said, and began to cry. "Mama."

"Be quiet," Roger insisted. "Or I'll leave you behind. Come along, now. Follow me. But be *quiet*."

He opened the bedroom door, stepped into the empty corridor, listened; all sound was submerged by the cacophony from the ballroom. And most of the servants would be there too. He turned to his right, away from the main part of the house, went along to the back staircase, cautiously made his way down. Here there were candles burning in their holders along the walls, and the smells of habitation; they were close to the pantries. But there was not a soul in sight. Down the next flight he went, to reach the ground floor. The side door stood wide, allowing the night air to drift in and send the candle flames guttering, throwing huge shadows against the wall and across the floor.

"Ooooh." Alice grabbed his hand. "It's scary."

"Ssssh," Roger commanded, and looked out of the door. To his left the blaze of light from the ballroom threw itself across the front garden and the carriage park, absolutely filled with equipages in neat rows. To his right the crowded stables, containing several times their usual number of inhabitants, was a seethe of restless movements. But the grooms and yardboys had been given the night off, and were all at the inn in the village; from down the hill there was more distant carousing. The only danger lay in crossing the yard immediately by the house, lit by the glow from the ballroom; the rest of the drive was in darkness.

"Now, when I say the word," Roger said, "run across the light. Quickly, now."

They nodded, got their breathing under control, and heard Rufus growl. The mastiff came slowly round the corner of the house, no doubt seeking some relief from the noise. Now he stood facing the door, front legs spread, nostrils twitching as his teeth bared.

"It's me, silly," Roger said, and the hound came forward, wagging his entire rear quarters, to have his head stroked. "You'll come with us," Roger decided. For to tell the truth, he *had* been a little apprehensive of exploring Derleth Valley in the dark. But no one would dare molest them with Rufus along. "But you mustn't bark. Promise?"

Rufus licked his hand and panted.

"Come along, now," Roger said. "All together. Go."

The children dashed across the lighted area. Rufus gave a joyous yelp and ran behind them, barking excitedly; midnight games were something he had always wanted to enjoy. They tumbled into the darkness, hid behind the last of the berlins, crouched there panting. Rufus lay down beside them.

"Oh, *Rufus*." Roger said.

"They must have heard that din," Alice pointed out.

But amazingly no one came out to discover what was exciting the dog. Derleth Hall was not concerned with intruders this night.

"Come on," Roger said, and led them into the darkness, walking now so that Rufus would have no more excuses for barking. They made their way down the drive, reached the road leading to the village. "A wagon," Roger said. "She's in a wagon."

"I saw a wagon parked in the meadow behind the church," Alice said. "When we were there this afternoon."

"That must be it. We'll cross the cemetery."

Now Rufus led the way, apparently knowing where they were going. The children huddled behind, casting nervous glances at the headstones, at the willows which loomed above the church. There was no moon, and the night was very dark.

"It's scary," Charlie kept saying.

"We can't come to any harm with Rufus here," Roger promised him. "Rufus would never let anyone hurt us." But he was grateful to discover the end of the trees and the low wall which marked the limit of the church property. And there was a wagon, parked by the remains of a fire, its horse hobbled a little distance away, raising its head to give a nervous whinny as it scented the dog.

"Who's there?" a man called.

Roger inhaled, stepped away from the wall, Alice and Charlie at his back. "Roger Haggard."

"Haggard?" Now they could see the man, leaning over the tailgate of the wagon, just as they could make out the pots

and pans and other goods dangling from the roof above him.
"Keep that dog away from my horse."

Roger snapped his fingers. "Come here, Rufe. Come on, boy."

Rufus returned, tail wagging.

"It's Haggard," the man said over his shoulder, apparently in response to a query from inside the wagon.

"Haggard?" Emma's voice. A moment later she joined the man at the back of the wagon. "Mr. Haggard?"

"Roger," Roger explained. "With Charlie and Alice."

"Roger," Emma cried, and leaped down the steps. She wore a nightgown, and her hair was in plaits. "Alice." She seized the children, hugged them against her. "Charlie." She wept quietly, holding them close. "Oh, you *darlings*. But you shouldn't be out here in the middle of the night. Whatever will your father say?"

"We had to see you, Mama," Alice said. "Father said you weren't ever coming back. He said you'd run away. Did you run away, Mama?"

"Did you run away, Mama?" Charlie asked. "Did you? Did you?"

Emma chewed her lip, glanced at Roger.

"I know you didn't run away, Emma," he said. "It was that girl Alison, wasn't it?"

"Why . . . I suppose it was," Emma agreed. "Although I didn't know it at the time. But to have you here . . ." Still hugging them, with Rufus trying desperately to lick her hands, she turned back to the wagon. "My children, Harry. Would you believe it? They've come to see me. My children. This is Mr. Bold, Roger. Harry, this is Roger Haggard. And Charlie and Alice."

"Haggard," Bold said in disgust. He was a short, heavyset man with a thick black beard and mustache.

"He's not like his father," Emma said. "And he's brought my children to see me. Come down and shake his hand."

Reluctantly Harry Bold came down the steps, grasped Roger's hand.

"I came to warn you, too," Roger explained.

"Warn me?"

"Father saw you at the church this afternoon. At least, he saw you; Emma. He's given instructions for you to be thrown out of Derleth. For your wagon to be destroyed."

"He did, did he?" Bold said. "We'll see about that. Who's going to do this piece of dirty work?"

"Mr. MacGuinness and some men from the village."

"When?"

"It was to be done tonight. Why . . ." He turned his head. They could hear the sound of people approaching, stumbling and cursing over the uneven ground, voices high and interspersed with nervous giggles. The horse gave a neigh, and Rufus an angry growl.

"They're drunk," Emma said.

"Aye, they would be." Harry Bold chewed his lip. "But there's an awful lot of them. Emma, you'd best into the woods. You be off, children, your pa won't want you to be discovered here."

"What are you going to do?" Roger asked.

Bold sucked some of his beard into his mouth. "I don't rightly know."

"Fight them," Roger said.

"Eh? One man against a dozen." Because the approaching men could be seen now, the burly figure of MacGuinness at their head. "I've not even a weapon, save a stick."

"I'll help you," Roger said.

"A boy?"

"There's Rufus."

Bold frowned at the dog. "Will he obey you?"

"Rufus will do anything I say."

"You can't, Roger," Emma said. "It would be going against your father. And you'll likely be hurt."

"Those men are coming to hurt *you*, Emma," Roger pointed out. "They're going to break up your wagon. Father told them to. But I know he didn't really mean it."

"He did mean it," Emma said. "I can't explain now, Roger. But don't suppose your father doesn't know his own mind. Now, you take the children and hurry out of here, before—"

"There they are," MacGuinness shouted, his voice thick. "Awake, lads. Let's at them."

The men surged across the field.

"Get them, Rufe," Roger shouted. "Sick 'em, boy."

Rufus gave a long baying bark and hurtled away from the wagon like a cannonball. MacGuinness saw him coming and jumped backward, bumping into Peter Wring, immediately behind him.

"Sticks," Roger shouted. "You said you'd sticks, Mr. Bold."

"That I have." Harry Bold grasped a stout club and ran down the steps.

"And for me," Roger said.

"Me, too," Charlie bawled, jumping up and down.

"You come in here," Emma commanded, seizing her son by the arm and dragging him into the wagon. "And you, Alice."

Rufus had scattered the posse as if they had been toys. His snapping jaws could be heard even at a distance, and the one man who had attempted to stand his ground had gone down with the mastiff's teeth in his calf. The rest were tumbled left and right, slowly getting to their feet as Harry Bold and Roger Haggard reached them.

"Now, you listen to me," MacGuinness bellowed, getting up, to stare at Roger in total amazement. "Master Roger. What in the name of God . . ."

"Got you," Roger shouted, and hit him across the head with all the considerable strength he could muster. MacGuinness went down without a sound.

"And you," Bold cried, swinging his club from side to side to fell two other men as they attempted to get up.

"Help me," screamed the man being savaged by Rufus. "For God's sake, help me."

"Let him go, Rufe," Roger commanded. "Try another one."

Rufus reluctantly unclamped his jaws, and his victim staggered to his feet, gave a wailing cry, and fled back across the meadow, hopping on one foot. It was the signal for the end of the fight. The rest of the expulsion party ran behind him, such as could move. Roger Haggard and Harry Bold stood together, Rufus panting at their side, while Emma came up with a bucket of water, which she emptied over MacGuinness. The bailiff sat up, rubbed his head, and winced, slowly clambered to his feet.

"The squire will hear about this," he said. "By God he will."

"I'll tell him myself," Roger promised.

"He'll be very angry with you," Emma said.

"He won't. I know he won't. But maybe you'd better move on anyway, just in case."

"Aye. The lad is talking sense," Harry Bold said. "We won't go far, Emma. But we'll be off Haggard's property."

He grasped Roger's hand, gave it a squeeze. "Maybe one day we'll be welcome here, eh? It's been a pleasure, Mr. Haggard. A real pleasure. If you ever need a helping hand, be sure to call on Harry Bold."

Chapter 7

The Stepmother

Haggard opened his eyes, was for a moment unsure of where he was. Golden hair, tickling his face, brought back memory. Not altogether pleasant memory. He had spent the night with the most beautiful creature he had ever seen, who was also his wife, had had all of those soft curves at his disposal, and was yet left with a feeling of dissatisfaction.

Because she had so obviously not enjoyed herself, had been doing nothing more than her duty. But that must have been because it had been their first night together. She had at the least not been afraid of him. And now . . . He leaned on his elbow to look down at her. Sleeping, her face was even more lovely than when she was awake; the slightly predatory glitter he had observed at their first meeting was absent.

Gently he blew on the long lashes, watched them flutter and half open, then close again.

"Wake up, sweetheart," he said. "We're on our honeymoon."

"Let me sleep, Mr. Haggard. Please let me sleep." She rolled over, her back to him.

Haggard sighed and rang the bell. He continued to gaze at the serrated line of vertebrae marking the pale skin. Her back reminded him of . . . By Christ, he thought. Emma! By now MacGuinness would have carried out his orders. The wagon would have been broken up, and the tinker driven from the valley. Emma! But she had been cursing him. Why else should she have come back?

But did it matter? He did not believe in curses, so how could she harm him? He had behaved stupidly, because he had been nervous about his wedding. He hoped she hadn't been harmed in any way. But he had still done the right thing. It would be quite impossible for him to enjoy life were she allowed to return to the valley whenever she chose, to stare at him from behind hedgerows, to attempt to reach her children, to utter curses.

There was a tap on the door, and he hastily covered Alison up, pulled on his robe. Simpson entered, followed by Mary Prince bearing a tray.

"Good morning to you, Mr. 'Aggard, sir," Simpson said. "I 'ad no hidea you wished to rise early."

"I wish to see Mr. MacGuinness," Haggard said. "Send someone out for him, and tell him to meet me in the office in an hour. Thank you, Mary."

Mary Prince put the tray on the table, bobbed her knees in a curtsy, staring at Alison's indistinct form beneath the bedclothes, and withdrew. Simpson followed her.

"What can you have to do this early in the morning?" Alison demanded, suddenly sitting up.

" 'Tis a vast estate I have here." Haggard handed her a cup of chocolate.

"And a vast bailiff you have to manage it for you," she pointed out.

"Aye, well, there are certain things I must see to myself." He drank his own chocolate, kissed her on the forehead, endeavoring to caress her breasts, and watched her lie down again and roll herself into a cocoon, and went next door to his dressing room, where Simpson already had his clothes laid out. "What does the ballroom look like?"

"Ah, well, Mr. 'Aggard, there's been a ball, hall right. Oh, aye, there's been a ball."

Haggard went downstairs. The maids and the footmen had already been marshaled by Pretty, and were moving slowly to and fro over the floor with huge mops, gathering scattered pieces of wedding cake, the remains of shattered champagne glasses, and even various articles of clothing which had been discarded by the guests. The whole place stank of stale alcohol and stale perfume. Haggard was glad to escape it, down the great staircase into the lower part of the house, where the doors and windows stood wide and the air was clean.

"Haggard." Brand had been walking up and down the terrace.

"Good morning to you. Sleep well?"

"Eventually. And you?"

Haggard smiled at him. "Not a wink. Did you expect me to?"

"Ha ha," Brand said, and slapped him on the shoulder. "There's a man for you." But the smile did not reach his eyes. "I'd like to have a word."

"Come into the office." Haggard held the door for him,

closed it behind them. "You've something on your mind." He seated himself behind the huge desk.

Brand sat opposite him. "I'm a happy man, Haggard," he very obviously lied. "Alison married to the best chap I can think of, why, I've no reason to be unhappy."

"But you are," Haggard said.

"Aye, well, there's no justice in this world." He chewed his lip, blew his nose.

"If I can help you, Brand, you have but to say."

"God Almighty, man, 'tis not I need helping. No, no. Haggard . . . I'd not tell you before, in case it spoiled the wedding." He raised his head, gazed at his son-in-law. "You've been blackballed."

"Eh?"

"At White's Club. By God, man, I was that upset. I've resigned myself."

Haggard frowned at him. "There was no need to go that far."

"Ah, well, it's obligatory. Where one's candidate has failed, one is considered to have resigned."

Haggard brought his hands together, rested his chin on them. He could feel the anger swelling in his belly. Blackballed. "Is there a reason?" he inquired, speaking very softly.

"Well, of course, the committee is under no necessity to give a reason. But . . ."

"But you know what it is. The prince?"

"Aye, well . . ." Another honk on the nose. "It's that business at Easter, throwing your black people into the snow. In the name of God, why did you do it?"

"I had just been informed that they were no longer slaves of mine. As I had brought them from Barbados *as* slaves, I could seee no reason to maintain them any longer. I prefer white servants in any event."

"But Christ, man, the cold-bloodedness of it. And then, one of them dying. Of exposure, you know."

"I'm sorry to hear it," Haggard said.

"But you'd not regard it as any business of yours?"

"No," Haggard said. "Not once they ceased to belong to me. You'd do better to quarrel with your laws than with me."

"I seek no quarrel with you, Haggard. I'm entirely on your side. But there it is. 'Tis events in France, to my mind. The sight of all those stiff-necked *ancien régime* people voluntarily handing over their rights and privileges, well, it has given many a reasonable man over here cause for thought.

There's talk of a new bill being brought in to outlaw the slave trade. You'll have heard that?"

"I know of it," Haggard said. "And I'll be there to speak against it. On behalf of the Tory party. I was promised that by Harry Addison. And by Pitt."

"Oh, aye, we'll speak against it, and you'll lead. You may be sure of that. On economic grounds at the very least. But there it is. I'm sorry about the blackball."

"So am I." Haggard listened to the knock on the door. "If you'll excuse me, Brand."

"Of course, my dear fellow. Of course. I'll see you at dinner, no doubt."

"No doubt." Haggard stared at MacGuinness, whose head was enveloped in a bandage. "What the devil has happened?"

The bailiff waited while Brand, also giving him a curious look, left the room. Then he closed the door.

"Well?" Haggard demanded.

"Set upon, we were," MacGuinness said.

Haggard frowned at him. "By whom?"

"Well, sir . . ."

"You had men with you?"

"Oh, aye, sir. There were ten of us. But it was this dog . . . barely escaped with my life, I did, and again just now."

Haggard sat up. "Rufus attacked you?"

"Indeed he did, sir. Encouraged by Master Roger. Master Charles and Miss Alice were there too, sir."

"Let me understand this," Haggard said. "You and ten men went to evict that gypsy, and were set upon by my children?"

MacGuinness flushed. "Well, sir, Bold helped them."

"You were defeated by a ten-year-old boy?"

"Well, no, sir, Master Charlie and Miss Alice didn't take part in the fight. It was Bold and Master Roger, sir."

"A man and a boy," Haggard said.

"And the dog, sir. Why, there was no one going to fight that dog. Peter Henery has half his calf gone. Like to die, he is. And besides, sir, we didn't know what to do. How to set about it, sir. You'd not have had us break Master Roger's head, now, would you?"

"Roger," Haggard said. Oh, it would have been Roger. Always taking Emma's side. More fond of her than he had been of the memory of his own mother. "Where is the gypsy now?"

"Well, sir, he left anyway."

"With Miss Dearborn?"

"I reckon so, sir. She's not to be found. I did hear he was seen over in Plowding."

Which was the next village.

"Waiting to come back, no doubt," Haggard said. "The moment my back is turned." Oh, she had cursed him, all right. Blackballed. And that fool Brand had not told him immediately. But all the guests would have known. Addison certainly. He got up. "You'll shoot that dog, MacGuinness."

"Yes, sir," MacGuinness said gratefully.

Haggard opened the door, encountered Pretty. "Where are the children?"

"I haven't seen them, Mr. Haggard. Still in bed, I shouldn't wonder."

"After being out all night," Haggard growled. His own children, adding to the long list of those who defied him and sought to bring him down. Oh, undoubtedly he was bewitched. Emma had done it, the first day she had entered his life, for all of his scoffing. And not content with him, she bewitched his children and even his dog, turned them away from their duty as Haggards.

He climbed the stairs, passed some of the houseguests, who greeted him and stopped to stare after him as he ignored them.

And leading the rout was Roger. The very last Haggard, until Alison should give birth. If he could be sure of that, he'd a good mind to cut the boy off. As it was, they'd all had far too easy a life. He'd been an indulgent father, there it was. Indeed, he thought, as he started on the second flight, leaving a trail of staring housemaids behind him, he'd not been sufficient of a father. The fault was his. He had left their upbringing to Emma, had not understood that once she left he would have to play a more positive part. But leaving them to Emma had been the mistake. Witchcraft apart, they had absorbed her ideas, and she had never lifted her hand to any of them, would not have dreamed of it. She had very nearly ruined his children.

He stamped along the corridor, threw open Alice's door. The girl was just sitting up, being served her breakfast by Halling, the new nursemaid.

"Father?" Her eyes were wide.

"Out of bed," Haggard commanded. "Get into Roger's room." He went next door, to where Charlie was still asleep. "Up," Haggard shouted. "Go into Roger's room."

Charlie crawled out of bed, gazed at his father. Haggard grabbed his shoulder and half-threw him into the corridor. Then he opened the door of Roger's room.

"Father?" The boy sat up.

"Get out of bed," Haggard said. "You . . ." He pointed at Alice and Charlie. "Come in here."

They filed into the room; Charlie's eyes were already filling with tears.

"I understand you went to see the tinker last night," Haggard said.

"Mama was there," Alice said.

"I took them, sir," Roger said. His head jerked at the sound of an explosion. "Father?"

"That is MacGuinness shooting Rufus," Haggard said.

For a moment the children stared at him; then Roger ran at him, fist swinging. "You'll not kill Rufus," he shouted. "You'll not."

Haggard threw up his left arm to catch the blow, threw a right himself. His fist landed on Roger's chin, and the boy fell backward, hit the bed, and sat down heavily.

"You'll not kill Rufus," Charlie shrieked, also running forward. "You'll not."

Haggard caught his wrists without difficulty, pushed him away.

"You didn't kill Rufus, Father? Not really?" Alice's eyes were also full of tears.

"I'll not have any animal savaging my people," Haggard said. He unbuckled his belt, pulled it from round his waist. "I'll not have my children disobeying me. And I'll not have you seeing that whore again. Is that understood?"

They stared at him. Charlie was sobbing openly now. Alice's face was set; only a single tear rolled down her cheek. She looked so like her mother, Haggard wanted to flee. But he had to make them understand that he was their father, that he was Haggard, that they must grow up to be like him. And he had to subdue Roger. The boy was slowly climbing to his feet, his chin already an angry red stain. He started to put up his hand to rub it, then made himself stop.

"You first, Charlie," Haggard said. "Bend over that bed."

Charles Haggard glanced at his sister, seeking support. But there was none to be had. He walked to the bed.

"Nightshirt up," Haggard commanded. The boy obeyed, leaning over the mattress. Haggard sent the belt whistling through the air, and Charlie screamed and hopped up and down. Haggard hit him again, the strap leaving an angry weal across the white flesh.

"Ow," Charlie bawled. "Owowowow." He began to shake with fear and anger and pain. Haggard hit him twice more.

"Now, stand over there," he commanded. "You're next, Alice."

She gazed at him for a moment, licked her lips. He had never beaten Emma, but he was about to beat her now. Because here was the same stain of auburn hair, the same eager features. The same slender body, the same long legs, as she hitched uper her nightgown and leaned over the bed.

"Mr. Haggard? Whatever are you doing?"

Haggard's head turned in anger as the door opened, but it was Alison, wearing an undressing robe, frowning her disbelief.

"I am disciplining my children, madam," Haggard said. "I'd be obliged if you'd not interfere." He turned away from her, the belt already scything through the air. Alice had been starting to rise, supposing herself saved; the flailing leather caught her while she was off balance and threw her back onto the bed, a startled murmur escaping her lips. Haggard hit her again, watched the white flesh inflaming. Alice's fingers clawed at the bedclothes and her toes drummed on the floor as she pushed herself up.

"Keep still," Haggard commanded. He struck her again, watched her head turn and her mouth sag open. From the corner of his eye he saw Alison putting her arms around the still-weeping, still-wriggling Charlie. The fourth blow brought a wail from Alice's lips, and for the next two she shrieked her agony, while tears stained the bedclothes.

"Get up," Haggard said.

Slowly Alice pushed herself away from the bed, but she seemed unable to rise, remained on her hands and knees. Roger had to help her to her feet, and she leaned against him and wept loudly and uncontrollably, her shoulders shuddering.

"Whatever have they done?" Alison inquired.

"They have been consorting with tinkers and gypsies," Haggard said.

"We went to see Emma," Roger said, face pale.

"Aye," Haggard said. "Now it's your turn."

Roger looked at Alison. "I'll not scream, Father," he said. "But I would prefer us to be alone."

"Get on with it," Haggard growled. "Alison is your mother now."

Roger hesitated, then turned away, raised his nightshirt, leaned over the bed. Haggard's arm swung rhythmically, crashing the belt into the muscular buttocks, watching the flesh redden, watching the boy wince, watching him biting his lip, and watching too his penis harden with the first couple of blows before sagging again. He glanced at Alison from the corner of his eye. Her tongue was showing between her teeth and her nostrils were flaring.

He gave the boy twelve strokes of the belt, and was then exhausted. He threw the belt on the floor. "If it happens again, it'll be double," he said. "Now, you'll spend the rest of this day in your rooms, and there'll be no dinner." He turned away from the boy, who still knelt, not looking at him.

"I hate you," Charlie screamed. "I shall always hate you."

Haggard turned back.

"You have done a hateful thing, Father." Roger spoke evenly, as if he had not felt the blows. Haggard felt his anger, dissipated by the emotional exhaustion of the whipping, returning to seize his mind. If his discipline was not enough for them, then he'd discover a discipline which *would* suffice.

"Then you'll have cause," he snapped. "Eton, by God. That is for the sons of gentlemen." His hand stretched out, the forefinger pointing. "You'll leave school now, and take a commission in the army. I'll see to that. And you . . ." He pointed at Charlie. "You're for the navy. We'll see how you like that."

"You can't," Alice shrieked. "Charlie is only ten."

"Time enough," Haggard said. "And you, miss, watch your tongue or I'll find somewhere for you as well. Are you coming, madam?"

Alison Haggard seemed to awaken from a trance. She released Charlie, went through the door Haggard was holding for her. Outside there were half a dozen maids and even some of the guests. They stared at Haggard as if they were seeing a ghost.

"The coach is ready, Mr. Haggard." Ned stood in the study doorway, hat in his hands.

Haggard nodded, went outside. Charlie was weeping as usual. Roger's face was firmly set. In the month since his flogging, had his face ever been less than firmly set? Haggard did not know; his children had avoided him for that time. Behind the two boys Alice was also crying.

"You'll stop that," Haggard commanded. "You'll do well, Charlie. Just remember you're a Haggard. You'll tell the truth, and you'll turn your back on no man, and you'll do what's right. You understand me?"

Charlie's head started to come up, and then he gazed at the floor again. "Yes, sir."

"And stop that beastly weeping. You'll look after your brother as far as Portsmouth, Roger."

"Yes, sir," Roger said.

"Here's a guinea, no, here's two." He felt in his pockets for the coins. "One each. Spend it wisely. Now, have you said good-bye to your mother?"

Roger shook his head. "No, sir."

"Why not?"

"We don't know where she is, Father."

"Stuff and nonsense." But the fault was Alison's, he knew. She seldom left her bedchamber before two of the afternoon, although she knew the boys were leaving this morning. "You'll come along with me."

He led them up the stairs again, Alice dutifully trailing behind. They had not forgiven him. *They* had not forgiven *him*. But today he was in a good humor, not disposed to be annoyed by his children, even prepared to see their point of view. He would have resented a beating like that. He had never had one. His father had been too kindly a man. Perhaps had he used his belt, John Haggard thought, I might have been less of a monster.

But they would get over it, and he could make it up to them. There was time enough for that.

He gave a brief knock on the bedchamber door, opened it, was rewarded with a cry of alarm and annoyance from his wife. "Alison?"

The draperies were drawn around the bed. Now Alison's face peeped through. "You gave me a start, Mr. Haggard."

"I've brought the boys to say good-bye. You did remember they were leaving today?"

"I had no idea it was so early," Alison grumbled. "Well, come over here and give me a kiss."

Haggard stood beside the bed, jerked back the draperies, gazed in surprise at Emily Brand. Like her sister, she was still in a nightgown; her face was flushed and she gave him a nervous smile. Once again he was struck with the resemblance between them.

"Now you've frightened Emily," Alison said.

"I'm sure I haven't," Haggard said. "Don't you suppose you should get up?"

"I don't see why," Alison objected. "I like lying here gossiping."

"I like gossiping," Emily said.

The two boys were shifting from foot to foot with embarrassment.

"Come along, now." Alison held Charlie's hand, kissed him on the cheek. "And you." For Roger was if anything retreating. Now he presented his cheek, to be seized by his stepmother and hugged against her. "You are going to be a *big* boy," she said. "Like your father. I adore big men. Now, have a good journey. Off you go."

The children sidled out. Haggard remained standing just inside the door, gazing at the two girls. They made him think less of sisters gossiping than of lovers. What a remarkable thought. And an absurd one.

"Well?" Alison demanded. "Aren't you going to wave the boys good-bye, Mr. Haggard?"

"Harrumph." Colonel Brand strolled up and down the terrace, hands clasped behind his back. "I feel like the man who has overstayed his welcome."

Haggard was seated in one of the comfortable chairs overlooking the deer park. He smoked a cheroot, and frowned at the hills in the distance; already the November mists were gathering. "Nonsense," he said absently. I shall be glad to see you go, he thought. I wish to be alone with my wife. Or do I?

"Yes, well, duty calls, what? There's a new session to be prepared for."

"Am I allowed to attend?" Haggard asked.

"My dear fellow . . ."

"I am perfectly serious," Haggard said. "I'd not embarrass the Tory party."

"And you can hardly sit with the Whigs, eh, what? Ha ha."

Haggard flicked ash. "When are you leaving?"

"Well, tomorrow morning. If you'll permit me?"

"My dear Brand, my house is your own. Come and go as you please."

"You are a damnedly civil fellow, Haggard." Brand sat

beside him, took out his handkerchief, wiped his brow and neck. "The fact is, if I have tarried this long, it is because I was waiting for the last of the other guests to leave, so that you and I could have a chat."

"What about?"

"Harrumph. I don't know how to put it."

Haggard, who had been thinking about Alison and Emily—he had done little else this past week—frowned. "Are you in trouble?"

"Trouble, my dear fellow? Good God, no, not trouble. The fact is . . . my God, Haggard, I went overboard for this wedding. Trouble. My God."

Haggard nodded. It had been longer in coming than he had supposed would be the case. "How much?"

"My dear fellow, I could not possibly—"

"Brand," Haggard said, "I would take it most kindly were we always to be absolutely straight with each other. Nor would it please me greatly to have a father-in-law sold up for debt. How much?"

"Well . . ." Brand got up again. "This places me in a most terribly humiliating position."

"Not at all," Haggard said. "I would do as much for my own father. For God's sake tell me how much."

"Well . . . ten thousand. There was the trousseau, and some entertainments I was required to undertake in consequence of Alison's betrothal, and there was—"

"You shall have a check before you leave," Haggard said.

"My dear fellow." Brand seized both Haggard's hands, squeezed them. "You really are the very best fellow in the world. I knew it the very moment I laid eyes on you. And hardly done by. Oh, indeed, hardly done by. Believe me, I shall not take these matters lying down, sir. I shall seek to establish you at the very apex of London society. You may rely on that, sir. And I have a scheme to increase your wealth. Indeed I do."

"Have you?" Haggard inquired somewhat dryly.

"You've heard of Hargreaves?"

"Vaguely."

"He has invented a machine which spins cotton far faster and more effectively than any human being. Do you know cotton spinning?"

"No."

"Well, let me tell you that where it takes ten spinners to

produce enough yarn for one weaver, Hargreaves' machine does all of that work and more. Now, to be sure, power was a problem, but Watt has solved that, eh? Water, there's the answer. And you have the Derleth River just going to waste through those hills. Now, do you know what the wives of your tenants, and all the women in these parts, do with their spare time?"

"I shudder to think."

"They spin cotton cloth," Brand cried, slapping Haggard on the knee. "'Tis a lucrative business. Now, Haggard, suppose you were to build a factory, here in Derleth, fill it with Hargreaves' machines, and start a cotton-spinning business of your own?"

"Where'd I find the labor?"

"Your housewives, don't you see? They'd not be able to compete with you in price or quantity. You'd put them out of business, so they'd *have* to work for you. What do you think of that?"

"I have a factory already, Brand. In Barbados. And that is sufficient of a headache, believe me. Besides, this pin money the women earn keeps them happy. 'Tis best to let them get on with it."

Brand sighed. "Oh, well, it was but an idea. And a good one, I'll swear. At least I'd recommend you consider it. In the meanwhile, I must leave you in the care of my two lovely daughters, who I know will see to your every want. My dear, dear—"

Haggard freed his hands. "Is Emily not accompanying you back to London?"

"Why, no," Brand said. "She thought it best to stay on and keep Alison company for a while." He frowned at Haggard's expression. "Well, you know, you are so busy, and the girl is in a strange part of the country . . ."

Emily, spending every morning in Alison's bed gossiping. Two sisters who had always appeared like twins. Who dressed alike and spoke alike and smiled alike and ate alike . . . and loved alike? My God, he thought, what a conception. An utterly absurd idea. "I think Emily should return with you, Brand," he said. "After all, you need looking after as much as I. And Alison will have to get used to being alone here at some time. Besides, there is Alice to keep her company. Alice is going to be equally lonely with her brothers gone."

"Ah," Brand said. "They seemed so happy with the idea."

Haggard pointed. The two girls could be seen strolling out of the orchard, huge straw hats almost brushing each other, hands intertwined.

"What a charming picture they make," Brand said.

"Indeed," Haggard agreed. "But we shall explain the situation to them now." He stood up. "Alison. Emily."

Their heads turned, and they changed their direction to approach the terrace.

"Your father has just been telling me that regrettably he must return to London tomorrow," Haggard said. "I shall be sorry to see you go, Emily."

"Me? Oh, but . . ." She looked at her sister, mouth open.

"Emily isn't going, Mr. Haggard," Alison said. "She is staying on for awhile."

Haggard shook his head. "She is going with her father."

Alison's brows slowly drew together. "But I wish her to stay."

"And I wish her to go," Haggard said very quietly.

"Now, Alison," Brand said. "I am sure—"

"Oh, be quiet, Papa," Alison snapped. "Why do you wish her to go, Mr. Haggard? Emily and I have never been separated. Even for a moment."

"But you knew you were *going* to be separated, my darling," Haggard explained. "When you married me. Emily has her own life to live, and she has her father, your father, to care for. You'd not have your father pining away in loneliness in London, now, would you?"

Pink spots were gathering in Alison's cheeks. "And what of me? What of my loneliness, confined in this great dreary house in this empty valley?"

"Alison—" Brand began.

"You have me," Haggard pointed out. "And a great many duties to undertake, in which I am sure Mistress Wring would be happy to instruct you."

"Instruct me?" Alison cried, and suddenly she was crying, great tears rolling down her cheeks. "I want Emily to stay. I won't let her go. I won't, I won't."

"Alison . . ." Brand said. Emily was shifting from foot to foot and chewing her lip, but she too was on the verge of tears.

"I think it would be a good idea if Alison and I had a word together," Haggard decided.

"Of course, my dear fellow. Of course. Come along,

Emily. You'll want to pack your things." He seized his younger daughter by the arm and hurried her off."

"What are you going to do?" Alison demanded. "Flog me like your children?"

"If I did, it would be entirely because you are acting like a child. Did you suppose your sister was gong to move in with us permanently?"

Alison sat down. "Of course I didn't. But . . . it *is* lonely here. There is no one to talk to. You are so busy. You never come near me."

"When I do, you only wish to do one thing. You never want to talk."

"Well, she said sulkily, "we are still honeymooning. John . . ." She seized his arm. "We could go upstairs now. It is only an hour to supper."

"Now, don't be absurd, Alison. You cannot possibly want it this often."

"I am not being absurd," she shouted, getting up. "I'm a woman. I need to be loved. I love to be loved. It's . . . it's all I like doing."

Haggard frowned at her. All she liked doing? When every time he lay with her she seemed to be undergoing an experience like a visit to the dentist.

She discovered his expression, flushed, and sat down again. "I'm sorry. I didn't mean to shout. I . . ." She bit her lip. "I can't help how I feel. I should have thought you'd love me the more for it."

"The question is, do *you* love *me*, Alison?"

"Of course I do. I married you."

"Would you say you loved me as much as you loved Emily?"

"Why . . ." Her flush deepened. "What a remarkable question to ask. She's my sister."

Haggard caught her wrist. "And not your lover?"

Alison stared at him, gave a little gasp, tried to free her wrist. "Let me go."

"When you answer me."

"You . . . let me go." She gave an ineffectual tug. "I shall scream."

"Go ahead."

Her lips pulled back from her teeth, her tiny nostrils flared. "Are you jealous of her?" she hissed.

"I'd like to discover just what I married."

"Ha," she said. "I've given you everything a woman can. To a man."

His grip tightened, and she winced. Tears sprang to her eyes. "You're hurting me."

"Be fortunate I don't break it," Haggard said. "Is Emily your lover?"

"You . . ." Another tug. "Let me go."

"Tell me."

"We . . . we've been alone. Always. Ever since Mother died. That was ten years ago. There's only been Emily and me."

"Tell me."

Her head came up. "What do you want to know, Haggard?" she snarled, her lip curling. "Where she puts her finger?"

Haggard threw her hand away from him. She rubbed it for some seconds, while her color slowly faded.

"What are you going to do?" she asked.

"Get up," Haggard said.

She hesitated, then slowly rose.

"Now, go upstairs," he said.

"Brrr." Alison Haggard gave an exaggerated shiver. "This place is cold. Cold, cold, cold. Pretty, can't there be more wood on the fire?"

"Coal, madam. We use coal," Pretty said, and signaled a footman to empty one of the hobs into the grate.

"Our own coal." Haggard sat at the opposite end of the dining table, with Alice in the center and to the left, facing the fire, and looking from one to the other of her parents.

He wondered why he wasted the effort to speak. For the past month, indeed, he wondered why he did anything at all.

But he loved her. There was the amazing consideration. Or perhaps not so amazing. She remained the most beautiful thing he had ever seen. He did not love *her*; he loved her body, her face, her hair, her lips. Even her disdainful eyes and her flaring nostrils were things to be loved. He hated *her*, but he loved her body.

A fact of which she was well aware.

"Coal," she sneered, drinking wine. "What an occupation for a gentleman. Have those invitations gone out?"

Haggard nodded. For she was determined to entertain. He wondered how many replies they would get.

"Boring people." Alison commented. "I shall be bored out

of my mind here. We must pay a visit to town, Mr. Haggard.
Of course we must. You must take your seat in the house."

"In good time," Haggard said. He had made up his mind
not to return to Parliament until Pitt begged him to. Nor did
he have any desire to experience either the pity or the pretended concern of Brand and his friends. They considered to
be blackballed from White's the greatest catastrophe that
could happen to a man. Well, he didn't give a damn for their
silly clubs. He had never belonged to a club in his life. But
now he had an additional reason for remaining in Derleth.
He had no intention of taking Alison back to within reach of
her sister. But to tell her that would be to provoke a scene.
Better to leave it, he thought, and wait for events.

"Oh, bah." Alison turned to Alice. "Have you heard, Charlie has gone to sea?"

There was no end to her cruelty. Tears immediately sprang
to the girl's eyes.

"Oh, stuff and nonsense." Alison declared. "It will make a
man of him. Indeed it will. Little crybaby. They'll tan his
backside for him. They'll have him climbing to the masthead
in January, with icicles hanging from his fingers. You won't
know him when he comes back."

"Stop it," Alice screamed. "Stop it. You're horrid. I hate
you. I—"

"Mr. Haggard," Alison said. "Are you going to permit this
child to speak to me like that? She should be whipped."

"You'd best go to bed, Alice," Haggard said. "Charlie will
be all right. I promise you that."

Alice sniffed up the last of her sobs, pushed back her chair,
left the room without a word.

"Your indulgence does you no credit and the girl no good
at all," Alison pointed out. "If you do not wish to flog her,
you should let me. Her rudeness is beyond belief. I have
never heard of a child allowed to leave the room without saying good night."

"I would not let you touch Alice with a ten-foot pole,"
Haggard said.

Alison glared at him for some seconds, her eyes pinpoints
of angry amber. Then she pushed back her own chair and got
up. "No doubt I also should be sent to bed. I will say good
night, Mr. Haggard."

She swept across the floor, and one of the footmen hastily
opened the door for her. But before she got there, she

checked, and frowned. One hand went up to her forehead, and she swayed.

Haggard leaped to his feet, but the footmen were there before him. They caught Alison as she fell, gently deposited her in the nearest chair.

"In the name of God." Haggard stared at his wife, the suddenly pale cheeks, the gasps of breath. "Fetch Mistress Wring, quickly."

He fanned her with his napkin, held a glass of wine to her lips.

"The floor moved," she muttered. "I swear it."

"You all but fainted," he said.

She pushed the wine away. "Ugh. The smell nauseates me. Ugh."

"Mr. Haggard?" Mistress Wring stood in the doorway.

"The mistress is ill," Haggard said.

"No," Alison said. "I'm not ill." She attempted to push herself up, sat down again, and suddenly vomited over the front of her gown. "Ugh. Oh, God. Ugh."

"Wring!" Haggard shouted in alarm.

Patience Wring smiled. "Not ill, Mr. Haggard." She came across the room. "If madam will permit me, I will help you to your room." She raised her head. "'Tis but the morning sickness, Mr. Haggard. You are to be a father."

There was a moment's silence in the room.

"A father," Haggard said. "Well, great God above. There's a happy event."

Alison raised her head; vomit still trailed from the corner of her mouth. "Happy?" she asked. "Happy?" she screamed. "I don't want to be pregnant. I don't want to have a child. Oh, Christ in heaven, I don't want to have a child."

Haggard smiled at her. "'Tis the business of a wife, my darling. Patience, you'll assist Mistress Haggard to her bed."

Because there of course was the answer to all of his problems. All of Alison's problems too, even if she refused to recognize them. Pregnancy was a wife's natural state, and he was eager for children, children who would love him and respect him, not those who would hate him and fear him.

As her slender body became distorted, and as her face fattened as well, it was possible for him to regard her with more detachment. She remained an utterly beautiful girl, but he saw less of the beauty and more of the girl. There was the main cause of their trouble. She was still only approaching

nineteen. Had he been of the same age, he would have been
more willing to wean her away from her obsessions, from her
unnatural love for her sister. But he was approaching forty,
and not inclined toward patience and understanding. Yet am
I understanding now, he thought with some pleasure. Once
she is a mother, and again a mother, and again, and once she
is past twenty and growing into a woman, why, then she will
be all I desire. He remembered how Emma had matured
from a suspicious little girl into a loving and lovable woman.

If only there was someone in whom he could confide, discuss his fears and his hopes. He had never known loneliness
before. It occurred to him that he *had* been lonely, as a
young man, after Susan's death. That indeed loneliness had
accounted for a great deal of his misanthropy. How percep-
tive Adelaide Bolton had been, after all. But he had not
recognized it then, with the shallowness of youth. And once
Emma had appeared on the scene, he had had no time to be
lonely.

Emma! He wondered what she was doing now, if she lived
or died. Certainly the tinker had not attempted to return to
Derleth. But that was no indication that Emma still lived
with him. Undoubtedly she would have further descended the
scale of human existence, was now probably an utter whore.
Dear Emma. She had come into his life at a most opportune
moment, and he had loved her. But she had been setting herself up as a wife, without any of the rights of one. They had
parted at the best time. It was a pity it had been so bitter.

But, oh, what a pleasure it would be to have her to confide
in, just for a few hours. He was even tempted by Mary
Prince, as, with Alison indisposed, he found himself able to
humor the girl once again, to her gratification. But Mary
Prince could not possibly be a confidante. She was a servant.
She had to be nothing more than an extension of his personality, there when he wished her to be, out of mind as much
as sight when he wished her to be.

He wondered if Alison was also nothing more than an extension of his personality. But she was his only hope for the
future. In time, when she grew older, she would be able to
talk with him and understand him, and dissipate his misery.

There could be no one else. Roger and Charlie had vanished as if they had left the face of the earth, so far as he
was concerned. He kept track of them, from Roger's colonel
and Charlie's captain. Roger was in barracks with his battery
in Kent, as the international situation deteriorated, and was

making a fine soldier, so it was said. Charlie had already made one voyage to the West Indies and back, would no doubt be an admiral in due course. But while his ship had been paid off in Portsmouth, and he had been entitled to a month's shore leave, he had remained on board. "Perhaps," Captain Trowbridge had written, "you would care to visit us here in harbor, Mr. Haggard." What, crawl to his own son? Charlie would discover, eventually, where his bread was buttered.

But they would never be friends, any more than he could be friends with Alice, who existed in a tightly knit dream, never smiling, never speaking except when spoken to, often weeping. Marriage was the only solution for her. The very moment she was sixteen, which, he reflected, was not too far distant.

Nor was it possible to be friends with any of his parliamentary acquaintances. Where had that dream dissipated? In the scene with the prince which had resulted in the blackballing at White's? In his obvious contempt for them, or in their obvious dislike of him? It would be different, Brand said, when Alison was again out and able to play her part. "You should take a town house for next season," he said. "Entertain. Show them that you are not such a bad fellow after all." And had flushed as Haggard had stared at him. "They don't understand foreigners," he had mumbled, adding insult to injury.

They had listened to his speech against the abolition of the slave trade. He did not suppose he had ever spoken better or more forcefully, and Pitt had congratulated him afterward. But he doubted he had convinced many of them. The bill had been lost, to the discomfort of Wilberforce and his supporters such as Clarkson and Sharp, but it had been lost mainly because the growing excesses of the French democrats were offending all right-thinking opinion in Britain, not because John Haggard had persuaded them that slavery was less morally wrong than economically essential to the well-being of the sugar crop. Once again they did not understand, were too wrapped up in their own affairs to see any importance in the world beyond the white cliffs of Dover.

And having said his piece, he had not been required to speak again, had been returned to that outer darkness reserved for back-benchers who were also named Haggard and were slave owners. Well, bugger them, he had thought, and abandoned Parliament altogether. If Haggard was to be ostracized, then there was sufficient for him to do in and about Derleth. As indeed there was, to a man brought up to the intimate details of managing a sugar plantation.

He at last persuaded himself to descend the mine. If he no longer had any temptation to have coal dust on his penis—or if he *was* tempted, he could exorcise it in the arms of Mary Prince—the economics of mining, the understanding that this wealth did not have to be planted, but was just there, had been there for thousands of years, and would be there for thousands more years, no matter how much of it he took, was remarkably comforting. Of course, coal did not produce a tenth of the income of sugar. And he had to pay people to mine it for him. But inexhaustible wealth, even if in a low key, was fascinating.

As were the other occupations of his tenants. He became an active farmer, to his mind a far more rewarding pastime than senselessly chasing foxes round the countryside. Indeed he barred Derleth to both the neighboring hunts, and made himself as unpopular with the local gentry as with their London betters. Instead, he developed a herd of milch cows on his own estate, at the same time as he followed with interest the activities and prosperity of the seven other farms in the valley. Not a week passed but he made a tour of inspection, and was happy to assist with money whenever it was needed. Soon all of Derleth was sporting the new red roofs and the clean white walls which had been his pride at Haggard's Penn. Here at the least he was needed and wanted. His villagers might have regarded him with suspicion at first. They might not have forgotten how he had taken Mary Prince from the mine—but then, the widow Prince was one of the most prosperous in the entire village as her store of golden guineas grew. They might not have forgotten how he had thrown his domestics out-of-doors on a winter's day, never to be heard of again—but they had been black people and not really important. They might not have forgotten how they had been encouraged to oppose him by Parson Litteridge—but neither had they forgotten how he had walked into the midst of them to seek out and defeat Jem Lacey, straight up and man to man. And they knew that in his capacity as magistrate his judgments were given without fear or favor, and strictly according to the rule of law. He had achieved the respect he wanted, at least in Derleth. As he had been respected by his slaves in Barbados. Which did not mean they would ever lift a finger to save him from drowning. But at least it gave him a feeling of belonging in his own valley, which he knew nowhere else in England.

But if they were friends in their fashion, they were not friends to whom he could speak, in whom he could confide, who could in any way alleviate his lonely bitterness. Which but grew as Alison grew, and became more bitter herself, and more plaintive.

"If only Emily were here," she moaned. "You are the hardest man in all the world, Mr. Haggard. What harm could it do, with my belly at this hideous size?"

"You knew I was the hardest man in all the world when you married me," he pointed out with savage humor. "And Emily will not enter this house again."

"You will drive me insane," she shouted, throwing her pillows on the floor. "Insane, do you hear, insane."

" 'Tis of course a grievous hardship," Dr. Harrowby explained on one of his weekly visits from Derby. "For any woman, but for a young girl who is in all the prime of her beauty, why, I know not how they put up with it. On the other hand, the rewards, the feeling of the babe in their arms, are usually sufficient to compensate for the long months of misery. Usually. We must hope and pray that it will be so in this case."

"Hope and pray?" Haggard demanded.

"Well, Mr. Haggard, there is no question that your wife is taking it harder than most. She tells me she did not wish the child, does not wish it now."

"Neither of us had expected a pregnancy so soon," Haggard said.

"Of course, sir. But it is the future that must concern us now. Your wife must want to have the child, or the risk, to both mother and babe, will be greatly increased. Mrs. Haggard is in a most unhappy state of mind. She says you do not go near her."

"To be screamed at?" Haggard demanded.

"Can you not look on her as unwell, Mr. Haggard? Once the ordeal is over, she will be herself again."

"Then I will be happy to be with her," Haggard said.

Harrowby sighed. "Well, then, sir, would it not be possible to accede to her request and have her sister to stay, at least until the confinement?"

"It would not be possible," Haggard said.

"As you say, sir. But I feel I must warn you that it is impossible for me to guarantee a successful delivery unless I am actively assisted by the mother."

"You cannot guarantee it even then, Dr. Harrowby," Haggard pointed out. "So do you do your best, and leave the rest to God."

Did he want her to die? he wondered. Of course he did not. He wanted to hold her in his arms again, even while she seethed with sexual discontent. But he had been speaking the truth; he did not really think it made any difference at all whether or not the mother wanted the child. No one could have wanted Roger more than Susan, and it had done her no good at all. And as for having Emily back in the house—that would be to lose Alison altogether.

Anyway, he reminded himself, it is only for a short while. Then it will be over and forgotten. As indeed it was. Harrowby was in attendance with a midwife, and the birth was amazingly easy. "A son, Mr. Haggard," the doctor said. "You'll not lack for heirs."

Haggard held the tiny little boy in his arms. "This one," he said, "this is my true heir." He handed him over to the midwife, sat beside Alison. Her eyes were open, but she scarce looked alive, her hair matted with sweat and sticking to her head and shoulders. "Happy, my sweet?"

"Leave me alone," she said. "Just leave me alone, Haggard."

Haggard looked at the doctor, who shrugged. "I imagine Mrs. Haggard wishes to rest, sir," he explained. "But I suggest you allow the boy to suck, ma'am, if you will. Your milk will not be in yet, of course. but 'tis best he gets into practice, so to speak."

"To suck?" She raised her head. "You expect me to give my breast to *that*?"

"Well, ma'am, it is nature's way."

"You'll find a wet nurse," she said.

"But ma'am . . ."

"Just get out of here," Alison Haggard commanded. "All of you. Leave me alone."

Leave me alone. Haggard knocked softly and then turned the door handle. But the door was locked. As it was locked most of the time nowadays. He had not slept in his own bed for near a year. She was playing the spoiled brat again. But how did she exist, a woman so febrilely sexual, alone in her bedchamber?

His bedchamber, and he had been patient long enough. He knocked again.

"Go away," she said.

"Sweetheart," Haggard said, "if you do not unlock this door, I am going to break it down." He could feel the anger simmering in his belly. So what would he do to her? He could not throw her out as he had done Emma. Besides, when he saw her again . . .

The key turned, and the door swung inward. He stepped into the room, watched her climbing into bed. It was early December, and she wore both a nightgown and a robe, but not even the heavy garments could hide the sliver of figure, the pink soles which he could remember from the night they had put Brand to bed.

She settled herself beneath the blankets, looked up at him. "Well?"

Haggard closed the door behind him, once again turned the key.

"What do you want?" she asked in some alarm.

"To sleep with you," he explained, undressing.

"You can't," she said. "I am not yet recovered."

"It is three months," he pointed out. "Harrowby says you will be as well as ever in your life."

Her tongue showed for a second, then disappeared again. "I am still full of milk. Look." She opened her bodice.

"What do you do with it?" Haggard asked. His belly was swelling, with a terrifying mixture of desire and anger.

"I squeeze it out. Like this." She took the nipple between thumb and forefinger, pressed very gently. The milk trickled onto her stomach.

"It seems a waste," he said, keeping his voice even with an effort. "When the boy could use it."

"The boy does not starve," she said. "That girl has more than I could ever produce. And would you have me with sagging tits?"

He removed the last of his clothing, stood by the bed. "It would scarce matter, as I am not allowed to touch them."

"Mr. Haggard . . ." She hesitated.

He sat beside her, took her in his arms. He slid one hand between them to touch her breasts, to feel the sticky wetness crossing his palm as the nipples rose against it. He kissed her eyes and her nose, fastened on her mouth, felt her fingers biting into his back.

"Mr. Haggard," she said, "I'll not be pregnant again."

"'Tis unlikely so soon," he agreed, reaching down to spread her legs and finding them tightly clamped together.

"I'll not," she gasped. "It will be rape."

"A man cannot rape his wife." Haggard sat up. "You'll not pretend you don't want it."

"Want it?" She raised herself on her elbow. "Give me your hands, Mr. Haggard. Oh, give me your hands." She herself pulled the skirt of her nightgown to her waist. "Please, Mr. Haggard."

He moved closer, obliged, had his fingers imprisoned in that warm wonderland, watched her eyes turn up and her tongue loll. He kissed her mouth, very gently extracted his hand.

"My turn," he whispered.

"No," she gasped. "No." Her knees came up and she rolled away from him as he would have come on top.

"For Christ's sake . . ."

"Let me use my hands, Mr. Haggard. Please. The sensation will be no different. It will be better."

"I am not to enter you again?"

"No," she said violently. "No." She bit her lip. "Please. Not for a while. I could not endure it, Mr. Haggard. I would go mad. I could not stand it."

"My cock?"

"The pregnancy, Mr. Haggard." Her legs slowly straightened, and she turned to face him again. "Not you. The pregnancy. Let me, Mr. Haggard." She reached for him, but he rose to his knees above her and just out of reach.

"You are behaving like a silly little girl," he pointed out, the anger returning. "For God's sake, you had the easiest of deliveries. You are perfectly healthy in every way. Can't you understand? 'Tis just in your mind."

"I won't." She shut her eyes. "I won't, I won't, I won't."

"Silly child," Haggard said, and moved toward her. Her eyes opened, as did her mouth.

"No," she shouted, and threw up her hands. He caught her wrists and flattened them on the bed, lay across her, driving her knees flat. He got his toes between her ankles, slowly prized her knees apart, forced his own knee between—but she wriggled her hands free and scratched at his cheek. The pain made him gasp and half-rise, and another wriggle sent her onto her face, trying to crawl away from the bed.

He threw himself on her, pressing down on her shoulders. She gasped and squirmed, attempted to kick. Her legs were spread. Haggard pushed himself between, caring not where he made his entry, his anger and his desire and his frustration mingling together into a tremendous climax which hurled the girl flat to the bed and kept her there, driving the breath from her body, making her bite the sheet, bringing a thin trickle of sound from her mouth.

"No," she moaned. "No, no, no."

Haggard gasped, and lay still, his weight pressing her flatter yet.

"No," she whispered. "No, no, no."

The self-distaste spread over him. It might have been Mary Prince lying here, with coal dust staining the bedclothes. But it was his wife.

He pushed himself up, got out of bed, went to the washstand. "I apologize," he said. "You have kept me waiting for too long."

Alison made no reply.

Haggard dried himself, went back to the bed. She had not moved. Her feet dangled over the edge, her bare bottom seemed to shiver, but perhaps with cold. He gathered her feet and turned her straight, lifted the sheet and placed it over her, got into bed himself.

"You'll not sleep here," Alison whispered, her back to him.

"It is my bed, my darling," he said. "As much as your." He attempted a smile. "At least you'll know you are not pregnant."

"You have abused me in a most unnatural fashion," she said.

"Oh, come, now. It was an accident, brought on by your own stupidity."

Alison rolled over and sat up. She gathered her bed jacket over her breasts, got out of bed.

"Where are you going?"

"As you have pointed out, Mr. Haggard, this is your bed. Therefore, I must find another."

He felt his anger returning. She really was in the most absurd mood. But it was a mood she had been in for too long. "You want to remember that the entire house, and every bed in it, is mine."

She turned to face him, her arms folded to hold the bed jacket close.

Haggard pointed. "As you are my wife."

Her chin came up. "I wish to visit London. I wish to visit Papa."

Haggard frowned. "You wish to leave Derleth?"

"Yes."

"You wish to leave me?"

Her tongue came out, went back in again. "For a season."

"Do not suppose your father will be pleased to see you. Who will settle his debts, should he quarrel with me? Or will you tell him you have been abused? Even that will hardly equal his desire for money."

"My father is no more contemptible than any other man," she said.

"Or do you propose to shout from the rooftops that you have been buggered by your husband? Do you suppose even that could possibly make me less popular than I am? You cannot ruin me socially, Alison. I am ruined socially, merely by being Haggard. So do not be a fool. Come back to bed."

Her eyes gloomed at him. "I wish to visit London, Mr. Haggard. I have been confined here for upwards of a year. It will be Christmas in a month. I wish to visit London."

"You wish to bed your sister, you mean."

Once again the tongue showing for an instant. "We do not harm each other, Mr. Haggard. Nor do we quarrel. Nor are we cruel to each other. I wish to be away from this . . . this coal dust. Just for a season." This time she licked her lips. "If you will let me go, Mr. Haggard, I will be good to you when I come back. I give you my word."

"You will be good to me," Haggard said, his anger once again mingling with the returning desire, as he watched her standing there. The most beautiful girl in England. And she was his. There was nothing she could do about that. Nothing anyone on earth could do about that. So why was he afraid of her moods, of her angers and her scorns? Why was he even afraid of her perversions? They were all equally his, equally to be enjoyed. Why, indeed, did he not take her back to Barbados? There was the answer to all their problems. Surely Emily could hardly follow them there. But his instincts warned him that Alison's reaction to such a proposal would be hysterical. Time enough for that when she had had more children.

And in the meantime, he suddenly realized, she could be enjoyed the more by humoring her perversities.

"You will be good to me first," Haggard said. "You will come back to this bed now, and make love to me, and then you will sleep here with me. You will sleep with me every night for the next three months. At the end of that time, I will allow you to visit London. I will give you to your sister. For six weeks. Is that not an equitable arrangement? For every twelve weeks you spend with me, behaving as a wife should, I will allow you six in London."

She stared at him for some seconds. "I hate you," she said at last in an almost matter-of-fact tone. "I hate everything about you."

Haggard patted the bed beside him. "And take off those stupid clothes."

Slowly Alison released the bed jacket, shrugged it onto the floor behind her. Then she lifted the nightgown over her head, threw that also on the floor, inhaled to fill her lungs. "You're an old man," she said contemptuously, slowly approaching the bed. "You'll not be stiff enough to enter."

He held her wrists, pulled her onto his chest, kissed her mouth. "I am not going to enter you, my darling. As it displeases you. You may use your hands, after all. Pretend I'm Emily. Be loving, Alison, my sweet. Be loving."

"I hate him." Alison Haggard nestled deeper into the double bed, her chin on her hands. "Everything about him. His age. It's horrible. Do you know he's over forty? Even Papa is only a year or two older. If I loved a man at all, it would have to be someone young. Someone even younger than myself. Someone who could keep it up for hours and hours. I suppose *some* men can do that."

Emily lay beside her, gently stroking the long golden hair. "Did he really, well . . ."

"He did." Alison rolled on her back, arms and legs flung wide. "The strange thing is, I rather enjoyed it. I'd never felt anything like that before." She rose on her elbow, clutched her sister's hand. "Em, do you suppose . . ."

"No," Emily said. "I never heard of anything so ghastly. Anyway, we'd hurt each other. Didn't he hurt you?"

"I don't know," Alison said seriously. "I suppose he did. But it was different." She leaped out of bed as the drum and fifes started again; it was the sound of martial music which had first awakened her. She stood at the window, pulling the drapes just wide enough to look through at the red jackets and the gleaming bayonets, the horses and the officers with their gold braid . . . young men, she thought.

"War." Emily stood beside her, put her arm round her sister's waist, was rewarded with an equally warm embrace. "Isn't it terrible?"

"Oh, you think everything is terrible," Alison complained. "I think it's splendid. All of those young men, all going to be blown to bits, just pieces of mangled red flesh everywhere . . ."

"Ugh," Emily said, and crawled back into bed.

"Or think of the King of France, kneeling there, waiting to have his head chopped off. Wouldn't it be marvelous to watch King George have his head chopped off? I suppose it would be boring. He's so *old*. But Prince George. Or that Freddie. Wouldn't that be splendid?"

"Come back to bed, do," Emily begged.

Alison crossed the room slowly. "What do you suppose it must feel like to kneel there and know you are about to die, that all around you are people who hate you, jeering and laughing at you? What do you think it feels like as the knife hits your neck?"

"You are in a horrible mood," Emily protested. "I don't suppose you feel anything at all."

"You must feel *something*," Alison insisted. "You can't die and not feel anything. Imagine it. Em, you and me executed, the man holding up our heads, with our hair trailing and the blood dripping from our necks."

"Stop it, stop it, stop it," Emily screamed, pulling the pillow over her ears.

Alison knelt beside her, kissed the nape of her neck. "I was only supposing."

"Well, don't. I've never known you in such a mood."

"Ha," Alison said. "You haven't had to spend nearly two years locked up with John Haggard. He never talks, he hardly ever smiles, he doesn't play any games, he won't entertain, God, I may as well have married my own father. But I don't have to see him for six weeks. Six whole weeks. God, I want to . . . to . . . I don't know what I want to do. I want to flirt and I want to make love and I want to dance. Get up, get up, get up," she shouted, pummeling her sister's back. "Papa is taking us to Almack's tonight. Didn't you know?"

"I don't see how we can," Emily said. "I don't see how we *dare*."

"Oh, nonsense. It is Haggard they hate, not us. Besides, the prince won't be there. But the officers are going to be there before they sail for Holland. Get up, get up, get up."

The music rippled across the giant ballroom, set the crystal chandeliers to tinkling, had the myriad candles guttering and flaring. The colors were dazzling, the ladies in whites and pinks and pale blues and greens, the officers in their red jackets, with here and there a sprinkling of black-coated riflemen or gold-and-blue-clad artillerymen to add contrast; there were even one or two naval officers present, and of course a smattering of drably dressed politicians and young men-about-town. It was too early in the year, and yet everyone who was within reach of London was at Almack's this night. Tomorrow the army embarked. Once again it was war, with France. Why, the intervening ten years might never have been. War with France was a natural state of affairs.

But this war would be different, was already different. This was a punitive war, a determination to punish the upstart lawyers and doctors and merchants who had dared to overturn the established order of things, who had dared to execute their own king, who had dared to challenge the rest of Europe to follow thier example. Who had dared to overrun the Netherlands. Which was where, however dark the secret, everyone knew this army was destined. Alison, seated against the wall behind her fan, watching Emily dance with a guards officer, wondered what John Haggard thought of it all.

"War," Papa had said. "You had best return to Derleth."

"Whatever for?" she had asked.

"Well, 'tis a serious matter."

"How can it possibly affect Mr. Haggard?" she had demanded. "So there will be French privateers and some of his sugar may be lost. He survived the last war, he is always telling me, even more prosperous than he began it."

"Your two sons are in the service," Papa had pointed out.

"*His* sons," she had answered contemptuously. "Mine is safe at Derleth."

But she might as well have gone home, she thought angrily. She was the most beautiful woman in the room. In her pink satin gown, the ostrich plumes which dominated her headdress, in the pearl necklace she wore or the diamonds on her fingers—all paid for by the Haggard wealth—she was the best-dressed woman in the room. And she knew she was the best dancer in the room. But she had not once been asked. Because she was Mistress Haggard. Because everyone knew of her husband. Because he had quarreled with the Prince of Wales.

While Emily, wearing last year's gown, had not missed a dance. I may as well be home, she thought, her anger

growing. By marrying Haggard, by securing Papa's debts and
my own future, as he would have it, I have taken on a mill-
stone to hang around my neck and leave me bereft of friends
or entertainments for the rest of my life.

She was so angry she wanted to stamp her foot, and could
not resist the tears which suddenly sprang to her eyes. It was
so *unfair.*

"Ma'am . . ." said the young man.

Alison raised her head, blinked at her stepson in consternation. "Roger?" She frowned. "It cannot be."

He sat beside her, while her eyes glowed at him. Haggard
must have looked like this once, she thought. Except that
Haggard had never been so handsome, nor so superbly displayed by his uniform. Haggard had never been a soldier. But
Roger wore the dark blue coat with the red facings and the
masses of gold braid of an officer in the Royal Artillery; with
the white stock and the high black boots, with a sword at his
side, he was quite the best-looking man in the entire room.

"Roger," she said. "What a pleasant surprise."

"And for me, ma'am," he said. "I had not supposed you in
London."

"I had to visit my father," she said. "He is not well."

"Oh, but I have just seen the colonel . . ."

"Indeed you have," she agreed. "He is at the tables, is he
not?" She peered through the archway to her left. "But there
is the trouble. He will continue to live his normal life, however poor his health. But I am sure you did not attend Almack's to discuss my father's health?"

"Oh, no, ma'am . . ." He bit his lip. "Would you care to
dance?"

"I should be honored."

The room whirled about them, as she left her hand resting
on his shoulder, feeling the epaulet beneath her fingers, inhaling the faint aroma of leather, gazing into his handsome
face. Roger Haggard. She gave him a smile, but he allowed
her only a brief grimace in reply. Nor did he speak. He was
concentrating on dancing.

"You are a very naughty boy," she said as he escorted her
back to her seat. "You have not written. Why, I will wager
you do not even know you have a new brother."

"I did know, ma'am," he said. "And I wish to offer you my
congratulations. May I say . . ." He ran out of words and
flushed.

"That I have not changed? I have endeavored not to, to be sure. Now, do sit down and tell me about life in the army."

"I . . . You must excuse me, ma'am. My fellow officers are waiting for me. Excuse me."

She watched him walk across the room. He had performed his duty. Really, he was after all very like his father. Except that he was only . . . She frowned as she calculated. Seventeen years old. As she was nineteen. He could be her brother. Or her lover. A seventeen-year-old boy, with a dick as hard as any in the land, she'd be bound. Her stepson. My God. No relation at all, really, merely the son of the man to whom she was married, the man she hated with utter loathing.

Therefore she should hate the son as well. He would undoubtedly grow up into a copy of his father. Save that they had quarreled. Now, where did that leave Roger Haggard? she wondered.

"There is a brown study." Emily sat beside her. "And after such a handsome partner, too. However did you let him get away?"

"Didn't you recognize him? That was Roger."

"Roger who?"

"My son, you silly goose."

"Good Lord. Well, I only saw him twice, and that was two summers ago. He looked quite different. I suppose it is the uniform."

"Not entirely. It is the army, as well. He has twice the confidence I remember. Em . . ." She seized her sister's hand. "I want him."

Emily frowned at her. "Whatever do you mean?"

"I want to bed him."

"You must be insane."

"For God's sake," Alison said, keeping her voice low with an effort. "Why does everyone accuse me of being insane all the time? I want to bed him. There is nothing insane about that."

"He's your stepson. It would be a crime."

"Against his father. Oh, yes. That's why I want him. You have no idea what that great lout has inflicted upon me these past three months. He would be bad enough, but the thought of again becoming pregnant . . . I've had a syringe up me more times than I've had Haggard."

"And you don't suppose this boy could make you pregnant?"

"I'll use the syringe again, you silly goose."

"Anyway, he'd never agree."

"Of course he won't agree, goose. That's why I'm telling you."

"Me?" Emily shook her head. "Oh, no, oh, no, no, no."

"You said he was handsome."

"He is. But . . ."

"And you'll have him too, all to yourself, when I'm finished. If you'll just do as I tell you. We'll both have him, and he'll never know the difference. Please, Em. Don't let me down."

Emily Brand stared at her sister as if she'd never seen her before in her life. "You must hate Mr. Haggard very much," she said at last.

"I do," Alison said.

Roger Haggard drank champagne punch and watched his stepmother through the archway. How utterly beautiful she was. He wanted to loathe her as the woman who had displaced Emma, who had replaced his own mother. But it was impossible to hate such radiance. And now she was a mother herself. Father's possession. As everything in Derleth, everything on Haggard's Penn, was Father's possession.

She had rebuked him for not writing. For not returning to Derleth in a year. For not inquiring after his new brother. Could it really be possible that Father missed him? Wanted him back? He finished his punch, took another glass, felt the room gently swaying beneath his feet; he had never been drunk before. But if Father wanted him back, he had only to send for him. Thert could be no question as to which of them was in the right. Even Father must recognize that now. It had been drummed into him since birth, be a Haggard, do what you think is right, turn your back on no man. Except your own father. But how could he do otherwise than turn his back on Father?

The point was that he still loved and admired the old tyrant. He admired everything the name Haggard stood for, everything Father represented. He knew little enough about the rights and wrongs of slavery. His memory of Barbados was a happy one, of smiling faces and eternal sunshine. Whatever reason Father had had for sending the black people away from Derleth, it had not been their fault. He had sent Emma at the same time. Therefore the cause had been Alison Brand. There could be none other. That had been wrong, and it would continue to be wrong as long as Alison was mistress of Derleth Hall. It would be wrong until he could find Emma again, and in some way make it up to her, all the misery and humiliation she had suffered. But he had no idea how to go about it; she had vanished as completely as if she were dead. Perhaps she was dead. Then would Father never be forgiven. Certainly by Alice and Charlie.

But what of him? How magnificent it would be to be able to return to Derleth, to know the comfort of his own home, to be loved by Father. How magnificent to share the house with so lovely a stepmother.

He started guiltily, raised his head, and stared at her. And then realized that it was not her, but her sister.

"Roger Haggard," Emily said. "How absolutely splendid to see you. You'll dance with me?"

"Why, ma'am . . ."

"Emily," she said firmly. "You'll be pretending I'm your aunt, next. Dance with me, Roger." She held his hand.

He put down the cup, held her hand in turn. They fitted into the parade, lost each other and found each other again, turned away from each other and came back at the arch, ducked together and brushed their shoulders against each other, reached the end of the floor laughing with each other. Roger gave a hasty glance at where Alison had been sitting, and discovered she was gone.

"To bed," Emily said. "My sister takes her duty as a wife and a mother seriously, and never remains after midnight. But you do not have to hurry off, Roger. Do you?"

"I must report to my depot at six tomorrow morning."

"Well, then, you have yet seven hours. You do not wish to waste any one of them in sleeping. Who knows how long it will be until you are again at Almack's dancing? Why, there goes the music again."

Once again she was in his arms, and this time, reinforced as he was by several glasses of punch, he could appreciate her more. She was a remarkably pretty girl. Not as beautiful as her sister, to be sure, but with the same finely chiseled features, a slightly darker yellow in her hair, somewhat more placid nostrils and eyes. But better than any of those things, she was unmarried, and only a year older than he.

"You'll call me Emily," she insisted, as they obtained some more punch.

"You are my aunt."

"What absurdity. I am your aunt by marriage, which is no

aunt at all. How can I be your aunt, when we are almost the same age?"

So she had been considering the matter too. "You *are* my aunt," he said owlishly, once again feeling the room tremble. "But I would have no other. You are a very beautiful aunt."

"And you are a rogue, Roger Haggard. I can tell it. I think you should take me home."

"Home?" He blinked at her, desperately trying to focus.

"Home," she said firmly. "By now, you see, Papa will be hopelessly drunk. I must therefore either wait here until the small hours or make my own way. I would not like to have to do either. But there is no reason at all why you should not see me home, as we are so closely related."

He found himself in the open air, and felt vastly better. It really had been very close in there. But really, he supposed he should play the man, and not permit Emily Brand to do all the organizing. She had already secured a carriage, and was waiting for him to hand her up. He sat beside her, took off his shako; he could not remember having regained it from the porter, but he must have done so.

"Miss Brand . . ." he said.

"Emily."

"Emily. I fear I am cutting a very poor figure. The fact of the matter is, I am unused to strong drink."

"You have not had any strong drink," she pointed out. "Only champagne cup, which is perfectly harmless. And I do not think you are cutting a poor figure at all. I think you are a perfectly splendid figure. I could not wish for a better nephew."

"You are too kind."

"And I do wish you would stop being formal. We are friends, are we not?"

"Oh, indeed, we are, ma'am."

"Emily," she reminded him.

"Emily."

"And therefore I wish you to treat me as a friend. Here we are, two friends, alone in a carriage, traveling at midnight through the streets of London, and you sit there prating about cutting a poor figure."

"I am sorry, Emily."

"So you should be," she said severely, and then smiled, allowing her teeth to flash in the gloom. "Do you know what any other friend would be doing now?"

"I have no idea. Telling you a story."

"God give me patience," she muttered. "He would be kissing me."

"Kissing you?"

"I suppose you have never kissed a girl."

"Well . . ." he began.

"It's done like this." She held his arms, kissed him on the mouth. She took him by surprise, for in fact he *had* never kissed a girl before; when, with the other junior officers in the regiment, he had been laid on top of a whore, only a few weeks ago, she had neither offered her mouth nor had he wished to kiss her. But here was a tongue licking across his own, gently sweetened with champagne, as was the breath which rushed against his. He discovered his eyes were shut, and opened them again to stare at her face, so close, to feel her hands sliding across his uniform jacket, to feel his own arms going round her. But what to do with his hands? He touched bare flesh and gave a little gasp until he realized that it must be her shoulder. But how wonderful it felt.

The cab was slowing and turning into the gateway. Roger felt a sense of panic that this heavenly moment was about to end. He clung to her the more tightly, sent his own tongue questing after hers, felt, to his amazement, her hands slipping lower on his body, wondered with desperate anxiety whether he dared do the same. She turned away from him as the cab finally pulled to a halt, and his hands slid across the bodice of her gown. He sat back and gazed at her as the door was opened and the interior filled with light from the link torch held by one of the Brand footmen.

"You'll not leave me now," she whispered, and stepped down, drawing her cape about her shoulders. Roger found himself at the foot of the front steps, paying the cabby, the entire night revolving about him. Emily had already gone inside, but the footman was still holding the door for him. He ran up the stairs, into the front hall, found her already halfway up the next flight of stairs.

"Your coat and hat, sir," the footman said.

He tore them off, handed over his sword as well. He could not believe it was really happening. But was it not what he had always wanted to happen? His aunt. But only by marriage. A lovely girl only a year older than he. Why, he thought, how wonderful it would be if she would marry me. What a sensation that would cause.

Whatever would Father say? But it was impossible, and Father must never know.

Emily was waiting for him at the foot of the next flight of stairs. "I should not be here," he mumbled inanely. "My regiment . . ."

"You said you were free until six of the morning," she said. "That is still more than five hours. But I do not think we should waste a second of them." She held out her hand, and he took it. She led him up the stairs.

"But . . . that fellow. The servants."

"Are my servants. I act as housekeeper for my father. They will not say a word. I promise you."

"Well, then, your father . . ."

"Will be brought home drunk, and will scarce awake before noon. By then you will be on your ship."

"Alison . . ."

She gave a little tinkle of laughter. "Alison is asleep. Do not worry about Alison."

"But . . ." He checked in horror as they reached the next gallery, and were met by a maid.

"Good evening, mum. Shall I attend you?"

"Not tonight, Rose, thank you." Emily opened the bedroom door. "*You* shall attend me."

He stood in the doorway, shifting from foot to foot as she disappeared into the gloom.

"I . . ."

She turned to face him. "Don't you like me, Roger?"

"I do. I . . . I adore you. But . . ."

"You adore me." She came closer, put her arms round his neck, kissed him on the mouth. Her body seemed to fasten itself on his, sliding up and down his uniform. "And I adore you. We shall adore each other." She stepped away from him. "And if you say one more word about our being related, I shall scratch your eyes out."

"I really . . ." He sighed. "I suppose I just can't believe it is happening. That you should want to . . . well . . ."

"I do want to. I have wanted to since I saw you at my sister's wedding. Perhaps I also never believed we would meet again like this. But we have. And I don't want to waste a moment of it." She held his hand, pressed it on her breast, and he realized that while she had been talking she had unfastened her gown and allowed the bodice to fall round her waist. He touched satinlike flesh, had his palm scraped by a hardened nipple, felt he was going to burst with desire . . . but she was away again, half-lost in the darkness.

"There is a pot," she said. "Do you undress, and get into bed, my darling Roger. I will be back in a moment."

"But . . ." He reached after her in the gloom, but she was too far away, opening an inner door which apparently led to a dressing room.

"Go to bed," she said over her shoulder.

The door closed, and he was alone. As if he could ever be alone while her scent was whirling about his head, filling every recess of his lungs. He tore at his clothes, sent them flying about the floor, sat down to pull at his boots. His fellow officers had boasted of evenings like this, unbelievable conquests, of girls who actually wanted to surrender . . . but they had usually been married women. No unmarried girl was going to risk her reputation or her virginity by taking a man to her bed. Then was Emily Brand a whore? She could not be. She was Alison's sister.

He parted the curtains, got into the bed. Here her scent was even more pronounced, and the sheets were warm, as if someone had recently been lying on them. More likely the warming pan had only just been removed by the maid they had met on the stairs. He lay on his back, gazed at the dimly visible white tester above his head. Emily Brand. Emily Brand, Emily Brand, Emily Brand. My God, he thought, I am in love, and was suddenly nervous. His erection was not yet full. He had not considered that before. But suppose he did not come hard. Would she not scoff at him? Emily Brand. An unmarried girl, but if she was so free with him, had she not been equally free with others?

He leaned on his elbow, staring at the drapes, watched them move. He could only just see her in the darkness, but he could smell her. It was not a scent he would ever forget.

"Emily," he whispered, and reached for that white blur. She came closer, kissed him on the mouth; her hair flopped across his face. His hands slid over her shoulder blades, attempted to hold her breasts, and were unable because she was pressed against him, slipped down her back to her buttocks, felt her spreading her legs to allow him between, while she gave a little moan and wriggled, and her fingers sought and found his penis. No doubts about hardness now. He rolled her onto her back, and her legs came back together, trapping one of his between.

"So soon?" she whispered.

"I . . ." He slid off her, and her breath rushed against him as she smiled at his ignorance. She held his hand, guided it down to her pubic bush, moved it up and down for him, left him to his own devices while she caught his head and brought it close, to kiss him again. He had never believed such a freedom would be granted by any woman. Certainly not by a lady. But she actually wanted him to touch her as he chose, gave another of those little wriggles, and broke out in a fine sweat against his chest.

"Oh, Emily," he whispered. "I love you, Emily. Emily, Emily . . ." She closed his mouth with another kiss, and her hands were back at him, stroking and rubbing until suddenly he realized that he would not be able to stop himself. "Emily," he gasped. "Not now. Emily . . ." But it was too late. He lay against her, quite paralyzed with alarm, waiting for her disgust, for her to flee him, and instead heard a low gurgle of happy amusement.

"You are a potent fellow," she whispered. "If you will put your hand through the drapes, you will find a towel."

He obeyed, still feeling her against him, mind utterly confused. "I . . . I don't know what to say."

She took the towel from his fingers, dried herself and himself. "Then why say anything? There is naught to be ashamed of. It is what I wanted."

"Wanted? But . . ."

"You would like to enter me. You cannot do that. But you may use your hands again, and soon you will be hard again, and I will be happy again."

He rested his head on the pillow, on strands of her hair. His confusion was complete. No one had ever warned him there might be a woman like this. A woman who wanted to touch and to feel and to hold, just like a man, but not necessarily to consummate. Should he be repelled? Should he be disgusted? Should he be angry? What would Father be? Oh, angry, certainly. Father would take her by force, in such a situation.

But was he not having the best of all possible worlds? He loved the feel of her fingers, as they now returned, gently stroking him while she nuzzled his cheek. And he was doing her virginity no harm. Nor was there any risk of a pregnancy. That could wait until after they were married. Because they must marry now. He could not envisage ever loving any woman save for this magnificent creature, who knew so surely the way to his happiness, and had no doubts of her own.

"Emily," he whispered. "Oh, Emily, Emily, Emily. Marry me, Emily. Say that you will?"

Once again the gurgle of amusement. "I can't marry you, silly," she said. She released him, raised herself on her elbow. "But if you wish it, we can tumble like this whenever you are at Derleth."

"Derleth?" He was sliding his hands to and fro between her legs, her thighs clamped on his fingers. "Do you spend much time in Derleth?"

"I spend all my time in Derleth," she said. "And it is a dismal spot, I do promise you, with only your father for amusement. But when you return from the wars, my darling Roger, why, then we shall have sport. And it will serve the old monster right."

He moved his head to stare at her, as realization burst across his mind like an explosion of gunpowder.

"Well?" Haggard demanded. "Out with it, man. What have you?"

George Cummings stood first on one foot and then the other. His face was pale, and not entirely with fatigue. He licked his lips and looked longingly at the decanter of port on the table by the desk. "There is some news, sir. But . . ."

"I am not a boy, Cummings. You do not have to stammer at me. He's dead."

"No, sir. Well, sir, I cannot say for sure. The news of Master Roger is not so definite. But, sir . . . there is a letter."

"Letter?" Haggard frowned at him.

Cummings took the envelope from his pocket, held it out. Haggard's frown deepened as he saw the black edge. "Dead," he said.

"Well, sir . . ."

Haggard slit the envelope with his thumb, took out the single sheet of paper, gazed at the embossment: the Admiralty. Charlie. Slowly he raised his head to gaze at his agent. And realized that his eyes were filled with tears. It could not be. It was simply not possible. "What does it say?" He did not recognize his own voice.

Cummings sighed. "The frigate *Antiope* was lost at sea, Mr. Haggard. A most gallant action it was, sir, but against a superior French force. And finally a shot in the magazine . . . it is supposed, sir. She blew up. There were no survivors."

Slowly Haggard leaned back in his chair. The letter fell

from his hand and sifted down to the floor. He supposed he was dreaming. He had supposed he was dreaming from the moment the news had been brought to him that Roger had deserted the colors on the day before his regiment had been due to sail. He had attended a ball at Almack's, and then just disappeared. Roger. A coward. Because there could be no other explanation. Unless he had been set upon by footpads. Either way, Roger, lost. Susan's child. Yet had his grief been assuaged by the memory of their sudden enmity, the fact that Roger had taken Emma's side, had steadfastly opposed him. He had anticipated endless quarrels, endless opposition, as the boy had grown to manhood. He had not anticipated cowardice. And there had always been the others. If Alice seemed determined to be on Roger's side, Charlie, younger and more pliable, would surely be a prop in the years to come.

Charlie. Floating about at the bottom of the Mediterranean Sea. My doing, he thought. I sent him there. Just as I sent Roger into the army. Just as I elected to come to England at all.

He raised his head. Cummings still stood there. "You spoke of news."

Cummings licked his lips. His distress had given way to terror. "We . . . we have traced certain of Master Roger's movements, sir, on the night he disappeared."

Haggard nodded. "Go on."

"Well, sir, in company with several other young men from his regiment, he had attended Almack's—"

"I know that, for God's sake," Haggard snapped.

"Well, sir . . ." Cummings' despair appeared to increase. "We have ascertained, sir, that he left the ball in the company of Miss Emily Brand."

Haggard stared at him for some seconds. "Emily? But . . . he saw her home, of course."

"Indeed, sir. That is the information I have been given by Miss Brand. That Mr. Haggard accompanied her home, and then left again."

"Well, at least we may be able to obtain some clue as to his mood." It was essential to keep living, keep acting, keep searching, for Roger. Charlie was dead, dead, dead. But Roger might be alive. Might not have run away. Might still be his son.

"Yes, sir. Miss Brand did not apparently notice anything unusual about Mr. Haggard."

But he had not finished. Haggard raised his head again. "There is something more?"

Cummings licked his lips. "Well, sir, Mr. Haggard, you told me to spare no expense and no feelings, provided I found Mr. Roger."

"I'll not deny my own instructions."

"Well, sir . . . notwithstanding what Miss Brand had to tell me, I spoke with the servants, sir, clandestinely. It was necessary to disburse some currency, you understand . . ."

"Of course," Haggard said. "Go on, man."

"Well, sir, one of the maids confided to me that Mr. Roger did not leave immediately after accompanying Miss Brand home. That he stayed for some time, sir, upstairs, alone with Miss Brand, and that eventually he left in haste, sir, barely half-dressed, trailing his clothes behind him." Cummings paused for breath and to mop his brow.

Haggard continued to stare at him for some moments. His brain seemed to have atrophied. Charlie was dead, dead, dead. And Roger . . . had raped his own aunt by marriage?

But he had been invited there in the first place. Conspiracy, conspiracy, conspiracy. It was the only sure fact about the Brands. All was conspiracy.

He pushed back his chair and got up. Cummings hastily backed to one side of of the room. "The girl did not know where he went after that, sir. But my people are still looking."

"Tell them to cease," Haggard said, and opened the door. Conspiracy. Not on Roger's part alone. Emily Brand. A girl who wanted only the embraces of her own sister. Unless it be the embraces of her nephew by marriage. Emily Brand, a crawling thing, a snake . . . no, it was Alison he had once compared to a snake. A hateful thought, as hastily rejected. But Alison had been in town then, even if she had come hurrying back to Derleth the moment she had learned of Roger's disappearance. Learned of it? She had been there.

He stamped up the stairs. What was he going to do? What *could* he do about Emily Brand? He could not call her out. He could not have Cummings' people waylay her and slit her nose. By God, he *could* do that. Perhaps he would do that. Emily Brand. To have her here . . . He opened the nursery door, gazed at his wife and son playing on the floor. My only son, he thought. Of them all, my only son.

"John?" She frowned at him, then scrambled to her feet. She wore only an undressing robe, and her hair was tucked out of sight beneath her mobcap. It was far too early for Alison Haggard to dress. "News of Roger?"

"Aye," Haggard said. "And of Charlie."

"Charlie?" Her frown deepened.

"Is dead."

She stared at him for some seconds, while her jaw slowly slipped open. "Oh, my God," she said.

"Drowned," Haggard said. "The entire ship's company."

"Oh, Mr. Haggard." She got to her feet, while John Haggard junior lay on his back and stared at his parents with deep, thoughtful eyes. "I am so sorry."

"Are you, madam? Does it matter to you in the slightest?"

"John," she protested, "how can you say that?"

"How can I?" he snapped. "My entire family has been destroyed. With a single snap of the fingers, your fingers, madam, I have lost both of my sons."

Suddenly she was watchful, taking a step backward, to find herself against the cot. "I have no idea of what you are speaking."

"Have you not? Had I never seen you, I had never quarreled with my sons. Had I never seen your sister, I would still have Roger, at the least."

"Emily?"

"Can you deny it was she left Almack's with Roger? Can you deny it was she seduced him, there in your own house, left him so ashamed he deserted his regiment and his honor? Can you deny it was she destroyed him?" He pointed at her. "I will tell you this, madam. Should that sister of yours ever set foot in my presence again, I will take my whip to her. There you have a promise. And one I shall keep."

"You are being absurd," Alison said. "How on earth could Emily destroy Roger? Even supposing she did seduce him?"

"Supposing?" Haggard shouted. "Can there be any doubt about it?"

"You persist in seeing him as a child," Alison shouted in turn. "Well, he is not. He is a man grown, will all the appurtenances of a man. I cannot help it if he is so confused and uncertain that he does not know his own mind. He fled before . . ." She checked, and bit her lip.

Haggard frowned at her. "You were there?"

"I . . ." Again she bit her lip.

"By God," Haggard said. "You were there. You are no better than your sister. Well, I have always known that. You are an unnatural whore at heart. By Christ, a snake. I knew it when first I saw you. A snake."

"A snake," she snarled. "And what are you, John Haggard? A stupid old man. A cuckold in his own home, by his own son."

Haggard's head jerked. "By God," he said.

"Oh, yes," Alison shouted. "It was I seduced your precious son. Oh, I destroyed him, all right. I didn't mean to. I meant to use him to destroy you. But what difference does it make? He jumped from my bed and fled the house when he realized it was me. He abandoned his home and his regiment and his honor. Oh, he is destroyed, Haggard." She paused for breath, and to pant, amazed at her own temerity. "What are you going to do?"

Haggard stepped round the amazed babe.

"You'll not whip me," Alison said. "By God, you'll not. I'll walk Piccadilly naked to show the world your stripes, Haggard."

Haggard reached out, seized her wrist.

"You'll not," she spat at him.

"I'll not whip you," Haggard said. "There would be a waste." Slowly he drew her toward him, then thrust down his other arm to encompass her knees and lift her from the floor. "I am going to bed you."

"To . . ." She stared at him.

"As you have robbed me of two of my sons, Mistress Haggard," he said, "I am going to make sure you replace them, as soon as possible."

BOOK TWO

The Son

Chapter 1

The Industrialist

George Cummings twisted his hat in his hands. He was getting too old for breakneck journeys up and down the London turnpike, especially when they were invariably the result of bad news. Nor was he ever sure of his reception. John Haggard's moods were notoriously unpredictable.

But this morning the squire merely leaned back and frowned. He frowned so often nowadays, there were permanent grooves on his forehead, just as he drove his hands into the graying dark hair so often that it was receding, to extend the forehead itself higher and higher. He was no youngster himself, Cummings remembered. Why, he had to be fifty-six years old. He could hardly believe that it was nineteen years since this man had abandoned his plantation and come here to live. He wondered what Haggard really thought of that decision, in retrospect.

"All gone," Haggard mused. "What were the navy doing?"

"Well, sir, Mr. Haggard, the convoy was first of all scattered by a storm. And then it was just bad luck, I reckon, for them to have fallen in with a line of battleships. Why, I didn't know the frogs had one left."

"Neither did I," Haggard said.

But why shouldn't they have a fleet again? he wondered. It was sixteen years since this dreary war had begun, four even from Trafalgar, and there was no prospect of an end in sight. Indeed, with Bonaparte controlling all of Europe west of Russia, and Russia itself his firm ally, with both the men who might have found an acceptable formula for peace, Pitt and Fox, dead, it was difficult to see how it could ever end. Bonaparte could not be beaten, but on the other hand, he could not defeat England, at least in the field.

Haggard pulled his chin. But the French might hope to do so by commerce raiding, by the destruction of English trade. It was the fifth crop he had lost since the struggle began. These were absorbable. What was far more serious was the

243

closing of the European markets for West Indian sugar. By Napoleonic decree the helpless French and Germans and Belgians and Hollanders and even Austrians now sweetened their coffee with sugar obtained from beets. Sugar which he and his father had supplied, twenty years ago, and which represented their true profit.

"What are you going to do, Mr. Haggard?" Cummings asked.

"Do?" Haggard pushed back his chair and stood up. He suffered from rheumatism in the winters, but with the coming of spring his bones and muscles regained a great deal of their former elasticity. In the spring he was as happy as it was possible for him to be. If it was possible for him to be happy. "I shall have to consider."

"The plantation is now showing a loss, sir. I cannot remember that ever happening before, not even during the American War. And all this Whiggish agitation . . ."

"I know of it." Haggard stood at the window, looked out at the apple trees. Agitation to oppose which he would make one of his rare treks to Westminister. Since Pitt had resigned over the king's refusal to admit his Irish proposals—how long ago was that night when they had discussed his ambitions over Brand's port—he had attended Parliament but once. He loathed and hated the city, as perhaps he feared it. And since his defeat over the trade, he had loathed it even more. So Wilberforce had finally had his way, and Sharp must have rolled in his grave with glee. Haggard wondered what Middlesex, supposing he still lived, thought of it all. But Wilberforce was like a terrier. Having pushed the abolition of the trade through Parliament, despite a speech which Haggard had been assured was the most brilliant he had ever made, the mad fool was now seeking to strike at the very institution of slavery itself. For the sake of a principle he would ruin the West Indian plantations, one of the main sources of British wealth, the wealth upon which men like Wilberforce depended to fight the French. He'd not succeed there. Not all the Whigs were that hog-headed. But once again it would be a matter of journeying to London, of making speeches, of defending the interest of all those stiff-necked idiots in Barbados because they were his interests as well, and of continuing to be the best-hated man in England, merely because he sought to defend his own property, his own rights.

And for what? If the Whigs had an iota of sense, they'd have realized by now that Bonaparte was winning their battle for them. With the European markets closed, and with his cruisers snipping away at each homeward-bound sugar fleet, another five years would see even Haggard's Penn on the verge of bankruptcy.

Cummings shifted his feet. He had ridden all night, and could barely stand.

"You'll spend the night," Haggard said. "And dine with me. But get some rest."

"Thank you, Mr. Haggard. If there is anything . . ."

"I'll tell you," Haggard said. He went down the stairs and out the side door. It was time to think.

Ned was waiting for him, a horse saddled as ever. " 'Morning to you, Mr. Haggard."

"I'll walk today, Ned," Haggard said, and strolled down the hill, cutting at the daisies with his stick. Time to think. He stood on the shallow brow of the hill, looked down on what had once been the hall. He had had the old building pulled down sixteen years ago. Then it had been a scar on the green face of his valley, but now there was almost no evidence that it had ever been there. He had planted it with poplars, and in the center he had erected the family vault. Parson Porlock had objected to that, but he had been over-ruled, had consecrated the ground after all. No one living in Derleth dared object to anything the squire proposed. His money, his willingness to repair their houses and finance their projects and pension their fathers and mothers, in exchange for their unswerving loyalty and obedience, had proved too formidable a weapon. Haggard the slave owner, he thought with a grim smile. He owned these people, by virtue of his purse, as much as he owned the blacks on Haggard's Penn.

But such ownership depended entirely upon his wealth. He thought he would like to see Bonaparte and Wilberforce, together, squirming in hell.

He walked toward the grave, his terriers snapping at his heels. Why? Why torment himself? He could hear her as he approached, as he sometimes heard her at night, wailing around the eaves. "I hate you Haggard," she screamed at him. "God damn you, Haggard. I hate you. May you die in a gutter, Haggard." She had screamed that every time he had entered her, and she had screamed like that the day she had discovered her second pregnancy, and she had screamed like that seconds before she had given birth, and died. The most beautiful woman in England, lying at his feet, destroyed. Once he had wanted to destroy beauty, and had found he could not. Although, no doubt, he had destroyed Emma Dearborn as much as he had ever destroyed Alison Brand. He had destroyed all the Brands, the colonel through drink, and Emily, so it was said—and he could believe—from sheer grief at the death of her sister. Haggard the destroyer.

Because he had destroyed more than that. He stood before the white marble, gazed at the door and the inscription. There was only one coffin within that vault; they had buried the babe with its mother. But there should have been at least three. Charlie, moldering bones at the bottom of the sea; Roger, moldering bones no doubt in some gutter. Haggard the destroyer.

And equally, Haggard the indestructible, he reminded himself fiercely, blinking back the tears. How Alison, from her perch on a cloud or from her burning furnace, must seethe with rage at the sight of the man she had hated proceeding on his way. His hair was gray, and his waist had thickened. There was no further evidence of age. Not even the maids could discover any lessening of the essential power that had always been his; they weren't to know that he wanted them less and less—they would put that down to increasing preoccupation with other things.

"So hate away, my darling," he said to the stone. "You cannot touch me. And I have Johnnie."

Because there was the greatest irony of all. Alison, by merely living, had robbed him of Charlie as much as by her very hate she had robbed him of Roger. Had she planned it she could not have more securely established her own son as the Haggard heir. What a triumph that had been for her, and she had recognized none of it. She was dead, and Johnnie lived, and as he remembered nothing of his mother, nothing of the hate, he could love his father. Why, Johnnie Haggard was Roger all over again, but with a vital difference: he had not been neglected. No father could ever have lavished more love on a child. No father could ever have educated a son more carefully. And no father could ever have been better rewarded. Johnnie Haggard might be only seventeen, but he had already completed his schooling at Harrow, and was in his first year at Cambridge. So he possessed certain traits unique for a Haggard and not altogether welcome: poetry was a form of expression Haggard had never ever been able to understand, much less appreciate. But for Johnnie to scribble verses was better than for him to be riddled with the clap all the time.

"So hate away," he said again. "You'll not harm me, my darling."

He left the tomb, slowly continued on his way down the hill. He did this often, took a constitutional to the church and the village. The people liked to see their squire, and he liked to see them. However hard times might have become, as prices rose and the government tried to keep wages steady, there was a certain security in Derleth. Haggard regarded them all as his family. Even the Laceys, even Margaret, unmarried and her beauty fading into wrinkles. He had seen them die, and he had seen them born, and he had seen them wed, every birth and every wedding attended by a handsome present from the squire. He had bought their affection. And not even the combination of Wilberforce and Bonaparte could change that. The Haggard millions might be dwindling, but they were good for his lifetime. He had merely been feeling pessimistic earlier.

He stopped, frowning down the main street. *His* lifetime. He had never considered very deeply what might happen after that. He had been born Haggard, and he would die Haggard. That single goal had stretched before him, when all the other, ephemeral goals—the ministry he had dreamed of, the social lion he had once thought of becoming, even the presentation at court which had never happened—had fallen by the wayside, regretted only for a passing moment. And that goal would be achieved. There was no force on earth could prevent it being achieved, unless he renounced his birthright, and he could perceive no signs of dementia in himself.

But what of after? What of Johnnie? Poetry or no, the boy was a Haggard through and through. He had been brought up to that, would undoubtedly fulfill every ideal necessary to the name, certainly once he had rid himself of the Whiggish notions common to every young man. But his future must be equally safeguarded. It was not enough to reflect that *his* fortune would see him out; it had to stretch into the distance, for the support of Johnnie and of Johnnie's children, until the end of time. If for no other reason than that to allow the family to decline would mean that Alison, from her gutter in hell, would have gained a victory. Or worse, that Emma's curses—for if she was still alive, she was undoubtedly still cursing him—would have been successful.

He walked down the street, the dogs continuing to frisk at his heels. Men touched their hats and the women curtsied. If they feared him, they also loved him, in their own way.

Many stopped, for occasionally the squire himself stopped for a chat. But today he did not wish to speak with any of them. Today he wished to think.

What was the answer to his problem? Why, to pick up Haggard's Penn, bodily, and transport it to somewhere beyond the reach of Napoleon's cruisers, and to replace his sugar with something less perishable, something which could be stored and sold whenever the continental markets opened again, or whenever new markets were discovered. There were no new markets for sugar. However much the world was opening for western trade, the Indians of the Americas or the Negroes of Africa or even the Chinese of Asia did not put sugar in their coffee, because they did not drink coffee at all.

So there it was, a simple solution, really, were he a god. But he was Haggard.

He opened the door to the inn. It was still early in the morning, and the taproom was empty, save for old Hatchard, polishing glasses behind his bar.

"Mr. Haggard? Good morning, sir, good morning. You'll take a glass of ale? Martha? Martha? Bring some bones for the dogs, there's a good lass."

Haggard sat down, took the foaming tankard, sipped. He had developed quite a taste for ale, however unsophisticated a drink it might be when compared with sangaree. The dogs deserted his boots for the mutton bones of Martha Hatchard.

"A fine day, Mr. Haggard, sir," Hatchard commented. "It'll be a good summer, I reckon."

Haggard drank some more beer. Haggard's Penn could not be transported, but a new factory could be built. There was answer number one. But who would do the field work? No slaves were permitted in England. He would have to pay wages to a vast labor force. And where would he get the acreage, save by plowing up all his farmland, and all his tenants' farmland as well. And what could he grow? Sugar needed heat.

"There's no ill news, Mr. Haggard?" Hatchard inquired.

Haggard ignored him. So the crop, whatever it was, would have to be low labor intensity, and amenable to this climate. Just as it had to be nonperishable. Whoever heard of nonperishable food?

Wheels rumbled, dogs barked, brakes squealed. Haggard raised his head.

"The northbound stage, Mr. Haggard," Hatchard said apologetically. "There'll be passengers."

Haggard nodded, took his ale into the corner, sat down again. The doors were flung open, three men came bustling in, red-faced and cloaked against the spring winds and rain, calling for ale and for food. Behind them came an elderly married couple, obviously sore and cramped from sitting in the coach. And behind them again came the coachman himself, humping a small chest.

"For Jem and his friends," he said. "You've the payment?"

"Oh, aye, right here." Hatchard produced a bag of coin.

"Good business," the driver said. "Good business." He turned as Haggard approached. "And a good day to you, Mr. Haggard, sir. Why, 'tis a pleasure stopping at Derleth, indeed it is."

"I'll apologize for the disturbance, Mr. Haggard," Hatchard said. "But these people are here for dinner."

Haggard nodded. "I'll not clutter up your taproom, Hatchard. What's in the box?"

"The box, sir?"

"That one."

"Why, cotton fiber, sir."

Haggard frowned at him. "Cotton fiber?"

"Oh, aye, sir. Jemmy has quite a cooperative going. Didn't you know, sir? There are twelve families in on it. The women spin the cotton, you see, sir, and the men weave it into good cloth, and then the buyer comes, oh, regular, and pays coin for it. 'Tis a thriving community we have here, Mr. Haggard."

Haggard continued to frown. "But where does the fiber come from?"

"Why, from the Americas, sir. The colonies what were. The United States. 'Tis a thriving trade."

"Cotton fiber," Haggard said. "By God." He finished his ale. "You'll give everyone here a drink, on the squire, Hatchard. I'm pleased to see them, that I am.

Haggard strode up the hill, regardless of the spring drizzle which had suddenly started. He was still Haggard. He had but to put his mind to a problem, and it was solved. The door was opened for him by one of the underfootmen, and he marched through, the dogs still excited at his heels.

"Mr. Haggard," Mary Prince was thirty years old now, and housekeeper of Derleth Hall ever since the death of Patience Wring. She had put on far too much weight, and had never been very beautiful. But if she understood she would never again be for his bed, she was happy enough to supply him with those of her inferiors as he fancied—her son had emigrated to the Canadian colonies with his pockets full of Haggard guineas. He would not return. Haggard had no intention of ever recognizing a bastard again. But Mary was content enough, and fussed over her master as if she were still his mistress. "You're soaked through, that you are. You should take care, Mr. Haggard." She pulled off his coat. "And your shirt."

"The devil with my shirt," Haggard snapped. "Tell Morton to prepare me some mulled wine. Where is Mr. Cummings?"

"Why, sir, he's asleep."

"Send someone to wake him up and tell him to come down to the office. And send one of the lads for MacGuinness. I want them both in my office in ten minutes. Haste, now." He slapped her bottom and climbed the stairs, stopped halfway up, gazed at the woman standing above him. Oh, indeed, he would never again recognize a bastard. Alice remained a massive weight lying across his mind and his pleasure. And the strange thing was that he was content it should be so. He had wanted to marry her off, once. He had produced a string of suitors, and she had turned them all away. She was a pretty young woman, prettier at twenty-eight than ever she had been as a girl. She possessed her mother's hair, and wore it loose, as Emma had done, no doubt the more to remind him of that particular crime, as she would have it. And he had to admit she managed his house with supreme efficiency. The girls were terrified of her, as indeed were the footmen and even Nugent, the butler. If she chose to live and be a spinster, why should he quarrel with that? It was the most convenient for him.

But she never smiled, never shared a single thought. Apart from seeing to the household duties, from sitting at his table, she preferred her own company, either in her room or riding alone through the trees and over the hills.

"You're wet, Father," she said.

"Aye, well, I've just had a lecture from Mary Prince. Some hot wine will take away the chill."

"You must change."

He glanced at her. Don't you want to see me die? he wondered. She at least did not seem to hate Johnnie. "I have business to attend to."

"After you've changed," she said.

Haggard sighed, but he knew she would have to be humored. He climbed the next flight of stairs, where Simpson was waiting.

"Mr. 'Aggard, sir, you are hall wet."

"If you say that again, I shall break your neck," Haggard remarked, and allowed himself to be stripped of his shirt and breeches and wrapped in his undressing robe. Then it was the warmth of his study, where a fire blazed, and where Nugent had placed the jug of steaming wine. And where, to his surprise, Alice was waiting for him.

"You'll sit down."

"I'd prefer to stand, Father."

Haggard sighed, drank some wine. There was no point in offering her any, because she did not drink alcohol. "You are not my servant, you know. You should understand that."

"Yes, Father."

"Well?"

"I have had a letter from John."

"Have you, now. The young devil. I haven't. When is he coming home?"

"He isn't."

"Eh?"

"He's away to some place in Nottinghamshire . . . Newstead, it's called, with some of his varsity friends."

"Newstead," Haggard said. "Byron. There's a minority."

"Not anymore," Alice said. "This Lord Byron has just become of age, and is leaving Cambridge to take his tour. But before he does, he wishes to entertain some of his friends at the abbey—"

"The abbey?"

"Newstead was an abbey once, before the Reformation. It's still known by that name. Well, that is where John is going for Easter."

"Aye, well, I doubt we'd be able to provide equal entertainment here," Haggard said. "Lord Byron, is it? I'll wager young Johnnie knows more of the aristocracy than I do, already."

"Father, I think you should write to John and tell him to come here for the vacation instead."

"Why?"

Alice flushed. "I have heard of this Byron person. And his other friends." She consulted the letter. "Skinner Matthews, and someone called Hobhouse. They are utter rakes."

"How do you know?"

"I have heard," Alice said primly.

"Stuff and nonsense. They are young men with oats to sow. Nothing worse than that. It will do Johnnie good."

"They are also Whigs," Alice said.

"Every man under the age of twenty-five is a Whig. Well, almost," he added, thinking of young Canning, who had apparently been born a Tory; he had recently earned himself some unwanted notoriety by fighting a duel with Foreign Secretary Castlereagh, over the prosecution of the war. "They grow out of it. It will do him good. Ah, Cummings. Where is MacGuinness?"

"Here, sir," said the bailiff, appearing behind the agent.

"You'll excuse us, Alice," Haggard said. "Sit down, gentlemen. Sit down. Have some wine. I'm sorry to have awakened you, George, but I've solved our problem."

"Problem, Mr. Haggard?" Cummings sat down, filled glasses for himself and MacGuinness. Alice withdrew to the doorway.

"How to replace this loss we are suffering in sugar," Haggard explained. "It came to me like a flash of lightning. Gentlemen, I am bound to say that I think cane has seen its day."

"Mr. Haggard?" MacGuinness was frowning.

"A great day it has been. And I may be wrong. It may pick up again. But now the slave trade has been abolished, and with Wilberforce promoting his abolition plank for all he is worth, I doubt the fight can be maintained a great deal longer."

"You'll abandon Haggard's Penn?" Cummings scratched his head.

"I will not abandon Haggard's Penn. As I have just said, I hope I may be wrong, and things there will improve. Abandon Haggard's Penn? That is my family birthright, Mr. Cummings. I'd as soon abandon the name. But we must expand in another direction." He paused, looked at their faces, even smiled at Alice, who had remained standing in the doorway—well, she would, as it was her future as much as Johnnie's he was discussing—took a sip of wine. "Cotton."

"Sir?" MacGuinness was looking even more confused.

"Hargreaves' machines," Haggard said. "Fool that I was, I did not take it up when it was suggested to me, damn near twenty years ago. But by God, I'll take it up now. We'll build a factory."

They goggled at him.

"I shall build a factory," Haggard said slowly and patiently. "Into which I shall put the spinning machines . . . what are they called?"

"Jennies," Alice said from the doorway.

"That is it. I shall fill the factory with spinning jennies. There is sufficient spare labor going begging in this valley and the valleys around us. We shall turn raw cotton into cloth."

"Begging your pardon, Mr. Haggard," MacGuinness said. "That is already being done in Derleth and the neighboring valleys. 'Tis the main support of the people. The women work at it, while the men farm or go down the mine."

"I know that," Haggard said. "But they will produce much more cotton working in a factory, on machines, than in their own parlor on hand looms." He gazed at their bewildered faces. "Don't you see? It will mean that the profit comes to us instead of being dissipated amongst a hundred separate homes."

"It's been done," Cummings said, half to himself. "Oh, aye, it's been done."

"Nottingham," MacGuinness said. "There were riots, mind."

"Riots?" Haggard demanded.

"Aye, well, sir, the people didn't like the idea," MacGuinness explained.

"The people, well, they don't like newfangled things," Cummings explained.

"They don't like having their livelihood taken away from them," Alice Haggard said, coming back into the room.

"Now, don't you start talking nonsense," Haggard said. "I shan't be taking anyone's livelihood away from them. I shall be giving them increased security. Guaranteed work, in my factory. Guaranteed wages in my factory."

"At a fraction of what they are now earning."

"Rubbish."

"But that doesn't matter," Alice cried, placing her hands on his desk. "Don't you understand? You would be taking away their independence. You'd be turning them into slaves, wage slaves. You'd change the entire character of the valley. You can't do that."

"Can't?" Haggard demanded, feeling the anger suddenly starting to bristle. The girl was nothing more than a reincarnation of Emma, sent to plague him.

"You'll make them hate you," Alice said. "For heaven's sake, Papa, for everything wrong you've done, you've done your best by this valley. I've watched you, earning the respect of these people. There cannot be a better landlord in all England. It's the one good thing you've done all your life. You can't destroy that now. You can't."

Haggard gazed from MacGuinness to Cummings. The two men were scarlet with embarrassment.

"The one good thing I've done," Haggard said, speaking very slowly. "By Christ. You'll leave this room, miss. Get to your own room and stay there. Be thankful you don't feel the weight of my belt."

Alice slowly straightened. "You are evil, after all," she said. "Evil. And you can whip me if you wish. You are *evil*." She turned and walked from the room.

Cummings shifted his feet noisily. "Young women, Mr. Haggard, well, you can never tell how they're going to behave."

"I can tell how my daughter is going to behave, by God," Haggard said. "She is going to oppose everything I think is best for the family, for the valley. By God, I am cursed at that. She's my curse. But I've survived her this long. I'll not let her upset me now. We'll need a site."

"We'll need an architect," MacGuinness said.

"For a factory?" Haggard cried. "For God's sake, man, four walls and a roof."

"You'll be employing women as well as men, Mr. Haggard," MacGuinness said. "Now, there's a difficulty."

"What difficulty? I employ women as well as men down the mine. I have employed men and women in Barbados. Four walls and a roof. Only the site matters. It should be near running water; that will be our power source. And I don't want to have to look at it all day. Over the hill is best. Close to the mine. Aye, we'll keep all the industry in the valley in one place." He pointed. "I'll leave that with you, MacGuinness. But I want it started right away. I want to be in production by the autumn. You'll also settle the rates of pay and secure the labor."

MacGuinness gazed at the floor. "You'll not get it here, Mr. Haggard. The lass may well be right. They're independent-minded people in Derleth, who like to earn their own money."

"Nonsense. Labor goes where the money is. The wholesale buyers aren't going to deal with a lot of cottage industries when they can obtain their goods in bulk from us." Haggard leaned back in his chair, pointed at MacGuinness. "I want work to start on the factory now."

●   ●   ●

"There you are." The sixth Lord Byron leaned from the window of the coach, pointed at the buildings before them. "Newstead Abbey."

The other young men stared from both sides of the coach. " 'Tis awful decrepit," remarked Wedderburn Webster.

"The abbey," Byron agreed. "The house is not too bad. You'll see it in a moment. It's built away from the ruin."

"But where are the trees?" Skinner Matthews inquired. For the road down which they were traveling was lined on either side with only stumps, and indeed there was hardly a tree to be seen in the entire park.

"Ah, well, my great-uncle, may the devil bless the poor old sod, cut them down to settle his debts," Byron commented with a brief laugh.

"And left you with naught with which to meet yours," Cam Hobhouse shouted.

Byron nodded, a frown flitting over his face. " 'Tis a problem, to be sure. Wake up there, Johnnie lad. What do *you* think of it all?"

John Haggard scratched his head. He had not been asleep, but he supposed he was dreaming. To have been befriended by these men at all—because they *were* men, every one at least twenty, while he was a freshman of seventeen—had left his head in a whirl. The invitation to spend a week's holiday with them had been like a summons to ascend Olympus. Apart from having completed their university careers, while he was but beginning his, they were so sophisticated and so talented. Webster was a bit of a bore, but no one could doubt that he was a man of the world, if only a tenth of his stories were true; Francis Hodgson, the sixth member of the party, was quiet and withdrawn, but obviously very learned; Skinner Matthews was all fire and wit and bubbling energy; Cam Hobhouse was much more serious, but had considerable ability as a writer, it was said; and then, their host himself. John Haggard was still unsure what to make of him. Remarkably handsome, to be sure, in a raffish fashion, as far as face went, with a somewhat heavy body rendered the more clumsy by his permanent limp—but his right leg was not something to be discussed without driving his lordship into one of his frequent moods of violent bad temper. Remarkably talented, too, it was claimed, but at writing poetry rather than prose, and John was no judge of that. And remarkably wicked? John had no idea. This was the first time he had been admitted to intimacy with any of the group; all the rest was hearsay. But Byron had a peculiar way of looking at people, and particularly himself, John realized, which seemed to shroud them in the aura of his personality. "You must come to Newstead," he had said. "It will only be for a week, because at the end of that time Hobhouse and I are off on our travels. Turkey and the East, there is our destination. Why, my dear Haggard, we may never return. You must come to Newstead."

"I am sure I will be boring," John Haggard had protested.

"You, my dear Haggard, could never be boring. Because you are rich, or will be, and we are poor. Because you are gay, and we are sad. And because you are the most handsome little devil I have ever laid eyes on, and we are ugly." And he had squeezed Haggard's hand in a peculiarly intimate way which had sent a thrill right through his system.

He had never thought of it before, but he supposed Byron was absolutely right. He *was* going to be immensely rich when he inherited. Everyone had heard of John Haggard senior's millions. And almost everyone else at Cambridge *was* most terribly in debt. As to gaiety, he really did not think he was any happier than Matthews, for example—save that he was *genuinely* happy, completely contented with his lot and his future, while Matthews' gaiety had an air of desperation, as if he knew he was laughing on borrowed time. And he supposed he was handsome. He had often been told, and not only by his father, that his mother had been the most beautiful woman in England. He had inherited a great deal of those small, exquisitely carved features, just as he had inherited his father's height and cool blue eyes and lank black hair.

But had he really been invited to join five men at Newstead because of his looks?

"I was but thinking what a splendid place this could be," he confessed. "It is larger than Derleth."

"Aye, but not so prosperous, I'll wager," Byron said. "Still, perhaps it will *look* as prosperous one day. Now, then, lads, let's discover the secrets of my ancestral home."

The carriage was stopping, and footmen were waiting to assist the young gentlemen. Also waiting was a bevy of housemaids, all young and remarkably pretty—"Chose them myself," Byron boasted—and a large shaggy dog which assaulted its master with every evidence of affection.

"Mind how you go," Byron advised.

John was last down, pausing to admire the abbey itself, the

roofless main hall of which stretched away from the side of the house before dwindling into tumbled cells and cloisters. Now he followed Matthews through the great doorway, to hear his friend give a startled exclamation. "For God's sake. Rescue. Rescue."

John ran forward, checked at the sight of the large brown bear, controlled to a certain extent by the chain around his waist, but into whose clutches Matthews had inadvertently strayed, and who now appeared to be attempting to kiss the young man.

"Byron," John shouted, "help us!"

Byron limped into the hall, caught the bear a resounding thwack across the nose, at which the animal reluctantly released its victim and turned its attention to its master. But Byron was too quick for it, retreating out of reach with another pat, this time less violent.

" 'Tis only Bruin," he explained. "Why, down to last year I had him at Cambridge with me."

"At Cambridge?" Webster shouted. "What did the fellows say?"

Byron winked. "What *could* they say? I wished to take one of my dogs, and was forbidden. The rule was there, and I was helpless. But the rule specified *dogs*. So when I went out and bought myself Bruin, *they* were helpless. Why, I even put him up for a degree, as he spent several terms in residence. But they've no humor. Now, come along, lads, the girls will show you to your rooms, but no dalliance." He laid his finger on his nose. "That comes later. Tomorrow we will start to dig."

"To dig?" Hobhouse inquired.

"Why else are we here? Think of it, man. This place was an abbey back in the sixteenth century. Before it was ever given to my ancestors. Now, do you not suppose, when the monks heard the tramp of armored feet approaching, Great Harry's minions, no less, come to strip them of their wealth, that they went out and buried it? I swear this place is standing on top of a gold mine, can we but find it. And you'll not deny I need to discover a gold mine more than most? Tomorrow we dig."

His enthusiasm, his tireless energy, flowed over them like cool water. And the house was comfortable enough. John tried the bed, bounced on it while the maid stood just inside the doorway and watched him. "Will that be all, sir?" she inquired hopefully.

He must act the part for which he had obviously been invited. "For the moment," he said. She gave a little simper and withdrew. What would she say, he wondered, what *will* she say, when she discovers I am quite virginal? And was suddenly nervous. He had ever been too concerned with games, with cricket and football and swimming, to bother himself too much about women, and during his first weeks at Cambridge he had resisted the temptations which had been thrown in his way by his elders. But he was about to become a man here at Newstead.

He sat up as the door opened. "Well, Johnnie lad." Byron limped into the room, closed the door behind him. "Comfortable?"

"Indeed I am."

Byron sat on the bed beside him. " 'Tis the second-best room in the house."

"Oh, but . . . what of Cam?"

"Is farther away. I have had you put next to me. After all, you are my protégé, are you not?" Once again the long, serious stare.

"Well, I . . ." John felt his cheeks burning. "I wish I knew why."

"Have I not told you?"

"Nothing I could believe."

"You are too modest. But there is more. I remember you from Harrow."

"Do you? You were in the sixth."

"And even then had a reputation for misanthropy, I'll be bound. But I do remember you. I remember your first night, when we made you get up to those antics."

"I hated you all," John confessed.

"And I thought, there is the prettiest lad I have ever seen. I was all of a mind to pull your cocker for you." He paused, staring at his friend. "Would you have hated me the more for that?"

"I would have blacked your eye for you." John flushed. "Or at least tried."

"Spoken like a man," Byron said, and got up to wander the room in his slow and embarrassing fashion. "And then, after I had left, I could not but hear how you were prospering. captain of cricket . . ."

"*You* played for the school."

"Ha ha. But once, in that game we had with Eton."

"And top scored, as I remember."

"Second highest, to be sure. But we were thoroughly thrashed. No, no, I am no athlete, Haggard. How could I be?" His face twisted as he slapped himself on the thigh.

"I . . ." He could think of nothing to say.

"Byron had come back to the bed. "It is a pleasure to have you at Newstead," he said. "A great pleasure." He stretched out his hand, stroked the side of John's face. "I will enjoy your company."

Now what the devil had he meant by that? John Haggard wondered. But it was not something to be considered this night. Or even believed. Byron's face was relaxed under the influence of the wine he had been drinking, the conversation which had flowed through the meal and was only now beginning to dry as their brains became fuddled.

"Ah, she was a beauty," Webster said, leaning back in his chair. "Better than the other one. But I should tell you . . ."

"No more," Matthews said. "I beg of you, my dear Wedderburn. No more."

"I was going to recount how I had them both together. *There* was an occasion."

"Sir, you disgust me," Hodgson said, pushing back his chair and rising somewhat unsteadily. Like his host, he was lame.

"Now, Francis, where are you off to?" Byron demanded.

"To my room to study," Hodgson said.

"For God's sake, it is barely midnight."

"Aye, and the conversation degenerates. I have no doubt the conduct will soon follow. I will bid you all good night." He stumped to the door, nodded to the footman.

"Now, there, you wretched man," Matthews said. "You have offended dear Frank."

"Wretched man?" Webster bellowed. "By God, sir, you'll not repeat those words."

"Wretched man, wretched man, wretched man," Matthews said.

"By God, sir, my second will call upon you."

"By God, sir, you'd not find anyone to undertake the task."

"Now, lads," Byron interrupted.

"I shall fight him," Webster cried, getting up and thumping the table. "I am determined on it. I shall fight him, or my name is not Wedderburn Webster."

"Is it really Wedderburn Webster?" Hobhouse inquired around a yawn.

"I shall fight him," Webster shouted, apparently trying to convince himself.

"And so you shall," Matthews agreed, also getting up. "But not until I have thrown you out of that window."

"Eh?" Webster leaped backward so fast he overturned his chair. "Byron . . ."

"Got you." Matthews seized Webster's shirtfront. "Now, for the window."

"Byron," Webster screamed, wriggling to very little purpose, as Matthews was at once bigger and stronger. "You'll not permit it, Byron."

"My dear Wedderburn," Byron said, leaning back in his chair to laugh and to wink at Haggard, "if Matthews says he is going to throw you out of the window, he will certainly throw you out of the window. But I should not take it to heart. There can never have been a window so intended for defenestration as that one. Four feet to the ground, and a flowerbed at the bottom of it. Mud, my dear Wedderburn. Soft, glutinous mud."

"Put me down," Webster begged. "Put me down. I don't really mean to fight you, Skinner. For God's sake, we are all friends together."

Matthews hesitated halfway to the window, both arms around Webster's waist to lift him from the ground.

"Oh, let the fellow go," Hobhouse suggested. "I am sure we can think of better things to do than listening to Wedderburn's screams."

"Aha." Byron leaned forward, his face suddenly intent. "We are in an abbey, thus it behooves us to be monks."

"Monks?" Matthews inquired, with so much interest that he released his victim, who hastily ran to the far side of the table, sheltering behind Haggard.

"Indeed. The habits are waiting for us in the next room. Let us don them." He wagged his finger. "And only them, mind." He led them from the table, already removing his coat and loosening his cravat.

"And then what?" Webster demanded.

"Why, then, my dear Wedderburn, we act the part. Were there ever monks who were not up to mischief?"

They tore at their clothes, laughing and joking among themselves while the alcohol in their brains dispelled their inhibitions. *Whatever am I doing?* John Haggard wondered, but he was certainly not going to stop now. He was almost the first of them naked, his body already flaming into an erection at the thought of the untold pleasures before him.

"There's an anxious man," Byron said with a shout of laughter, and he hastily dropped the habit over his shoulders, adjusted the cowl.

"And now, action," Byron commanded, and led them in a rush along the corridor. "We seek a virgin. Well, to be sure, there is little prospect of discovering such a creature in Newstead, but as long as she *looks* like a virgin, we shall be satisfied. There."

One of the upstairs maids could be discerned at the next corner. The young men gave a whoop and chased at her. She gaped at them for a moment, her smile changing to alarm as she understood their drunken passion. She turned and ran for the stairs, scattered down them, her cap falling off, and with it one shoe, which left her on her hands and knees on the next level. Before she could regain her feet, they were upon her, seizing her arms and her legs to lift her from the floor.

"Oooh," she squealed. "Oh, sirs. Oh, *sir*, whatever are you at?" as a hand slid up her leg under her skirt.

"To the dining room," Byron shouted. "To the dining room. We shall make a meal of this one."

He cannot mean it, Haggard thought, but how his heart pounded. He had been at the back of the rush, and could only now catch hold of a handful of toes, which wriggled and squirmed in his fingers, while her gown had been thrown back above the knees to reveal her legs; it came as a shock to Haggard to realize that he had never seen a woman's legs before—he could remember at one stage in his life, not so very long ago, doubting whether his half-sister, Alice, even possessed any. But here were legs, short and plump, to be sure, and lightly covered in brown hair, but nonetheless female legs, leading to . . . He discovered they were in the dining room, and the gasping, giggling girl had been laid in the very center of the as-yet-uncleared table, in and out of half-demolished plates of tarts and blancmanges. Byron was upending a bottle of wine over her face, so that she gasped and licked as she attempted to swallow some of the liquid.

"Now, then," Byron shouted. "The wench must be stripped and prepared. Lay on, my lads. Lay on."

They surged up her arms and legs to reach her body itself, grasping handfuls of material to pull and tear it. Haggard found himself staggering backward from the table, holding half a yard of skirt. He threw himself into the fray, found some petticoat beneath, ripped this off instead, and gazed at the naked body of the girl, almost still now as she had entirely run out of breath. The plumpness spread upward from her thighs into her hips, and her belly was quivering like a jelly, as were her breasts. But Haggard was fascinated by the seething mass of hair on her groin, the suggestion of what lay beneath.

"Now for the moment," Byron shouted. "Who . . . ?" He looked around them, pretending to make up his mind, as if his mind had not been made up from the beginning. "Young Johnnie here. I'll wager he's a virgin."

"Well . . ." Haggard began, but he was not going to confess that. Not that it would have made any difference. Hands seized him in turn, pulled the habit from his shoulders and threw it on the floor, and he was lifted and deposited on the girl's body. Whatever must she think of it? he wondered, but her eyes, wide and staring, hardly seemed to notice him at all.

"The scoundrel isn't hard," Matthews said.

" 'Tis the excitement," Hobhouse panted.

"We must assist," Byron said. Someone's hand touched his penis, he did not know whose, and gave it several gentle caresses. His hands gave way and he was lying on the girl's breasts. He wondered if he should kiss her, and felt her legs closing on him while her lips parted and her tongue came out to lick his cheek. He seized her mouth even as he felt himself sinking into her, in and in and in into a warmth he had never known before. Only a second later he was shaking with a convulsive passion, while someone was patting his buttocks and someone else was shouting in his ear.

"Oh, good lad," Byron shouted. "Good lad. You went into her like a veteran. Now, who's to be next?"

John Haggard found himself in a chair, still naked, while Byron held a glass of wine to his lips. "You did well, lad," he said. "Well. I can see we are going to be the best of friends. When I come back from my tour."

"And did you discover any buried treasure?" Haggard asked.

"No, sir," John said. "We found a variety of skeletons. Including a skull of great size. Lord Byron said he was going to have it made into a drinking cup."

"Ha ha," Haggard shouted. "Sport, eh? What sport. By

God, we had none of that in my day." He fell serious, brooding into his glass. "*I* had none of that," he said thoughtfully. "There was none of that in Barbados."

John gazed across the table at his sister. As usual she had been silent throughout the meal. Now she looked even more sad than usual. He endeavored to signal her with eyes and eyebrows, but although she returned his gaze, her expression did not change.

"Aye, well," Haggard said. "It sounds like a splendid couple of days. I had supposed you'd be staying longer."

"I think that was the intention. But they soon got to quarreling. Matthews, mainly, he quarreled with everyone. So the party broke up. And it's good to be back in Derleth."

"It's good to have you back." Haggard leaned across to squeeze his son's hand. Then he pushed back his chair and left the room.

John Haggard finished his wine. "Why do you and he never speak?"

"We speak when we have to," Alice said.

"But you hate him. I wish you'd tell me why. He couldn't have known Charlie would die. Or Roger either. If either of them were alive, I'd be happy to go into the army or the navy. I think it's a man's duty, with a war on."

"I do not hate him because of Charlie," Alice said. She also got up. "I hate him . . . because of what he is, what he does. What he has always done."

"Such as?"

"Oh, you would hardly know. Anyway, it was before you were born. But he is being hateful again now. Do you know what he plans? To build a factory."

"Here in Derleth? I say, what fun."

"Do you really think so?" She stood above him. "He means to spin cotton, on those machines. He means to put all the villagers who supplement their incomes by hand weaving right out of business. They'll have to work for him or starve. And do you know why? Just so his millions won't become a million less."

"Well . . . I suppose that makes economic sense. Machines will spin much more cotton than any person could do."

"They'll be slaves," Alice said. "Johnnie . . ." She rested her hand on his shoulder. He could not ever remember her doing that before. "I'd be so very grateful if you'd have a word with him."

"Me?" He gazed at her. What a lovely young woman she

was. Compared with her, that girl on the table in Newstead Abbey had been a carthorse. That girl on the table, at Newstead. He could remember everything about it, and yet nothing about it. He had been so ashamed, and the next day when he had encountered the same girl in one of the corridors, while she had broken into a fit of giggling, he had turned and walked the other way. Run the other way.

But she was the least of the problems which had arisen from that evening. What would Father say, just for instance, if he knew the truth of it, how Byron had held his cock, how he had, indeed, suggested they do more than that. Byron had been equally unsure. There was the point. It was a great crime he had proposed, and the moment he had discovered no immediate response, he had changed the subject. But he had come back to it, with hints and innuendoes, time and again. Had the others ever felt that way? Webster and Hobhouse and Hodgson? What absurdity. Matthews perhaps, because Matthews would try anything once.

Anything once. Did I wish to try it? he wondered. Does wishing to try it make me less of a man? And try what? He had no idea.

Anyway, he reflected, so long as I can discover beauty, even in my own sister, there is nothing the matter with my manhood.

"He adores you," Alice said. "If you'd oppose this scheme, he might just not do it."

"Father? Put off a scheme for increasing his wealth because I didn't like it? There's a likely possibility. Anyway, as I said, I think he's probably right."

She gazed at him for some moments, her face somber. "Will you ride with me this afternoon?"

It was the first time she had ever asked him to do that, and he, like everyone else in Derleth, was aware of her solitary expeditions. "Would you really like me to?"

"I have asked you to," she said. "We'll leave as soon as you are ready."

The weather was warm for Easter; the sky was blue, as the clouds of a week ago had cleared away. Alice Haggard's habit was in pale green, showing off the color of her hair, the pink and white of her cheeks. John felt quite proud to be riding at her side as they turned away from the hall and the village and took the cut through the hills for the mine.

"What does it feel like?" she asked. "To know that one day all of this will be yours?"

"It gives one a very pleasant feeling of security," he said, and watched her frown. "Believe me, Alice, I know how lucky I am. Nearly all of my chums are head over heels in debt."

"Even Lord Byron?" she asked.

"Even Lord Byron. He more than most, in fact."

"Yet he is going on his tour."

"On borrowed money."

She touched her horse with her heels, cantered away from him, waited for him to catch her up. They stood on a knoll looking down on the mine, listening to the clanking of the air pumps, watching the donkeys coming out of the shaft entrance, each with its two panniers of coal, the grimy men emptying the buckets onto the ever-growing pile in the bottom of the first barge.

"Don't you find that hideous?" she asked.

"It's our wealth."

"Wealth," she cried. "Is that all you think about?"

"Did you bring me out here to quarrel?"

Once again the appraising stare. "No," she said at last. "No, I did not do that. I wished to speak with you. I had supposed Cambridge was a place of liberal views. Father accuses it of being so. He says you have been imbibing dangerous ideas."

John Haggard smiled. "I suppose by his notions they are dangerous enough. We oppose the continued Tory dominance of government, the way they trample on the people. We abhor the continuance of the war with France. Britain and France are the two most civilized nations in Europe. We should be allies in opposing Russian barbarism, not fighting each other. Certainly we should not be trying to pull down the greatest man of our age."

Alice's mouth had fallen slightly open. "Do you really discuss things like that?"

"What would you have us discuss?"

She made a helpless gesture with her whip. "Things that matter. For God's sake, if we were not fighting Napoleon, we would be fighting somebody else. Has there ever been a year when the English were not fighting somebody? You prate about freedom. What about those poor souls down the mine? Will you give them their freedom when you inherit? What about the people Father is about to enslave in his factory? You won't raise a finger to stop him."

"Now, that doesn't make sense," he protested. "If I no

longer mine the coal, not only will our wealth—yours as much as mine, Alice—diminish, but those people will merely be put out to starve. You'd not have that happen? And as I said, I cannot believe the idea of the factory is a bad thing. It will guarantee employment for these poor creatures."

"Poor creatures?" she cried. "You speak of them as if they were different species. They are men and women, like us. It is not their fault they were born poor."

"But there you have it," he argued seriously. "They *were* born poor. I do not know who decided that. But it was so decided. And you and I were born rich. It is our business to maintain and if possible increase our wealth, that in the spending of it all may benefit. It would do no one any good at all for us to attempt to lower ourselves to the level of the poorest person in the kingdom. There would just be wholesale starvation."

"And what of raising them to our level?"

"A Utopian dream." He smiled. "It is not possible. Were they capable of being so raised, they would have accomplished as much by themselves over the years, surely."

Alice Haggard turned her horse without replying, flicked her whip to send the animal galloping into the hills. John Haggard hastily kicked his own mount into following, cramming his tall hat onto his head. "Wait," he shouted. "You are leaving the valley."

She looked over her shoulder. "Afraid?"

Away she charged, through the hills and out the other side, crossing the turnpike, which hereabouts made a loop before entering the next village, galloping across a succession of fields, taking the stiles in superb style, red hair flowing behind, slowing only to enter the wood beyond, twisting in the saddle to avoid the branches, occasionally looking over her shoulder to make sure he was following. But she knew where she was going, while John was utterly lost; he had never ventured from Derleth on horseback before.

The trees thinned, and there was another field, and on the far side a lane, and hard by the lane a trim little cottage, smoke issuing from the chimney, and with roses creeping up the wall. The very epitome of rural England, John thought, as he caught her up, for she was pulling her horse to a halt.

"This is very beautiful," he said.

She glanced at him, urged her horse once again forward, trotted across the field and onto the road, turned down the little path leading to the cottage. Instantly the front door was

thrown open, and John Haggard stared in amazement at the
woman who stood there, the gaminlike features, hardly
touched by lines, although he reckoned she could not be less
than forty years old, the still-slender body, the auburn hair,
exactly the same color as Alice's, only slightly streaked with
gray.

Alice was already dismounting, running up the path to embrace the woman. She looked over her shoulder. "Get down,
John," she said. "Get down, sir. I'd have you meet my
mother."

John Haggard dismounted more slowly, felt the gravel
crunching under his boots. He continued to stare at the
woman, his brain tumbling as he took off his hat. He could
feel the heat in his cheeks, and did not know what to do with
his hands.

Emma had given her daughter a quick interrogatory look,
and received a brief nod. Now she came forward. "You'll be
John," she said. "Alice has told me a deal about you."

John's turn to glance at Alice. "I . . . I had supposed you
dead, ma'am."

"Is that what your father says of me?"

"Why, no. My father has never spoken of you. But neither
has Alice."

She nodded. "My decision. She will have to tell us both
why she has spoken of me now." She stretched out her arms.
"Will you not at least take my hand?"

John slowly extended his own arms, held her fingers; they
were cool and dry. "I am totally confused."

"Then come inside." She released him, led him toward the
open door. From within he could hear the gentle murmur of
plucking strings and rustling cloth. He ducked his head, entered the front room of the cottage, gazed at the three people
who sat there, now abandoning their looms to get up.

"I'd have you meet my husband, Harry Bold," Emma said.

The man was short and thickset, twice the size of his wife,
although he only came to her shoulder. His hair and beard
were black speckled with gray. His eyes were watchful, but
not hostile. John shook hands.

"My son, Tim."

A copy of his father, perhaps a year older than himself,
John estimated.

"And my daughter Meg."

John turned, hand outstretched, and found his mouth
opening. Margaret Bold was equally a copy of her mother,

without any of the off-putting cragginess of the Haggards, such as afflicted Alice. Here was pure beauty, not like the portrait he possessed of *his* mother, where the very perfection of the features had suggested coldness, but in a warmth of her rounded chin, her short nose, her wide mouth, her sparkling blue eyes. And like both her mother and his sister, she had wavy auburn hair, loose and stretching almost to her waist.

But Alice is *her* sister as well, he realized with a start of dismay. And looked around him in amazement. The people were simply if cleanly dressed—the women wore gowns with aprons and slippers, their bodices modestly high-necked—as was the cottage simply furnished.

"He's in a tizzy," Alice said, not unkindly. "My mother is not dead, as you can see, John. Your father, our father, threw her out when she had served her purpose."

"That is not altogether true," Emma said.

"Why must you defend him? He is an utter brute."

"I will not have you tell lies about him. Have you heard of me, John?"

"A little." John Haggard could not keep his gaze from returning to the girl, as no doubt her parents observed.

"You'll take a glass of cider," Harry Bold said.

John's head turned in surprise; never had any man with such an accent addressed him without saying "sir." But why *should* Harry Bold call him "sir"?

"I would like that very much," he said.

"And you'll sit down, and tell us why Alice has brought you here," Emma said. "Your father will not be pleased. He'll not be pleased to know we are within even ten miles of Derleth."

"Then I shall not tell him." John watched the girl sit down and take up her cloth. "You are industrious."

Emma sat beside him. Harry Bold gave him a mug of glowing cider. " 'Tis a sight better than traipsing the country. And it is a good living."

"Which Father would destroy," Alice said.

"What's that?" Harry Bold demanded.

"It is his latest scheme. Apparently he has lost an entire sugar crop to privateers and weather . . ."

"That would *not* please him," Emma said.

"He is determined to replace the loss, to shift the emphasis of his wealth, as he says, from the West Indies to England.

As I told you, he has never got over being defeated on the slave-trade question."

"And how can that affect us?" Emma asked.

"He is building a factory," Alice explained. "Into which he is going to put the machine looms. He intends to take over the cotton weaving for this entire area. He will put you out of work."

Emma frowned at her daughter.

"But it is our livelihood," Tim Bold protested.

"Do you think that matters to my father?" Alice cried.

"And how do you stand in this, boy?" Harry Bold asked.

"Why, I . . . I knew nothing of it, until an hour ago."

"But he assumes Father must be right," Alice said bitterly.

"I . . . I had not properly considered the matter," John protested. "Be sure that I will consider it now. I do promise you."

"Why, then, I am sure we have naught to bother about," Emma said. She rested her hand on top of his. "And you'll come to see us again, John Haggard. You will always be welcome here, I promise you."

John gazed at her, found his eyes sliding away from her face to look at Meg, just visible over her shoulder. In twenty years' time, Meg would look like this. Why, she would be just as lovely then as she was now.

"I'll come to see you again, Mistress Bold," he said. "You have my word."

Chapter 2

The Soldier

Low clouds gathered above the Sierra do Mondedal, shrouded the mountain peaks, dipped down into the valley as scything April rain. The huge drops cannoned onto the burnished helmets of the dragoons, splattered from the barrels of the great cannon creaking along the road, embedded themselves in the bearskins of the guards, dripped from the brims of the shabby shakos which denoted the bobbing heads of the infantry of the line.

"Bleeding weather," grumbled Private Corcoran. "Don't the sun ever shine?"

He was a replacement. His jacket was a crisp crimson, his trousers a fresh gray rather than a nondescript brown. His cross belts were still white and his musket gleamed; his shako still possessed a strap. He had joined the army as part of a draft from England, after the passage of the Douro had sent Marshal Soult tumbling back from Oporto in disarray. He knew nothing, as his immediate comrades knew nothing. As yet.

But they would learn. Already from in front of them there came the rumble of gunfire and the hoarse sound of men shouting.

"On the double, the Twenty-ninth." Captain Llewellyn came trotting down the disordered column. "Close up, there, close up. Sergeant Major, take that man's name."

For Corcoran was trailing his musket by the strap.

"Corcoran," the sergeant major snapped. "Pick it up, boy. Pick it up."

Private Corcoran hastily shouldered his musket, broke into a trot with the rest of his fellows, eyeing the sergeant major who ran alongside him. Sergeant Major Smith. There was more to him than first met the eye. He was a young man, still in his early thirties, and his accent was unplaceable, a trace of brogue littered with the remnants of what might even once have been a toff. But he was a veteran. He had crawled over

270

the sand dunes of Walcheren as a private, and he had seen Abercrombie die outside Alexandria as a corporal. As a sergeant, only a year ago, he had marched with Moore over the mountains of this selfsame land into the haven of Corunna, and instead of sailing home with the battered remnants of that army, he had volunteered to change his regiment and remain with the nucleus around which had been formed this new army, Wellesley's army. His skin was burned the color of mahogany, and his mustache drooped like that of a froggie. But he was a man. Far more so than any of the perfumed officers on their high trotting horses.

"What's the shooting, Sergeant Major?" inquired Private Withers, on Corcoran's left.

"Rear guard," Smith grunted. "They've not better than that left in Portugal."

Now they could see the houses, what remained of them; wisps of smoke still rose into the damp air. And now too they could see the dragoons galloping out the far side of the village, waving their swords.

"Column." Captain Llewellyn came down the line.

The men fell into columns of four, tramping along the rutted road, splashing in and out of puddles.

"Keep time there," Sergeant Major Smith bawled as the drummer took up the beat. "Left, left, left right left. God damn you, don't you know your left foot?"

Captain Llewellyn and Lieutenants Portman and Mayhew had taken their place at the head of the column, the sergeants flanked the recruits. For now too they could smell the stench, and not only of burning timber. They could see the gallows, where the three bodies hung, swaying gently, perhaps still warm; the French had only just evacuated their billets. And nearer at hand there was a dead woman, her skirts thrown above her head, her legs strangely white and twisted. Even in April, the bees were gathering above the great rent in her belly.

Someone vomited. "Keep time, there," Sergeant Major Smith commanded. "Keep time."

"When will they stand and fight, Sergeant Major?" someone asked.

"They'll fight when they're ready," the sergeant major said. "And you'll know about it. Keep time."

The Worcestershire regiment tramped through the shattered village, and Captain Llewellyn held up his hand.

"We bivouac over there," he said.

"Begging your pardon, sir," Sergeant Major Smith said. "May the lads use wood from the village?"

Llewellyn considered for a moment, then nodded. "Very good, Sergeant Major." He wheeled his horse and rode across to the next company, where battalion headquarters was to be found.

"Fall out," Smith commanded. "You heard the captain. Let's have some fires, now. Fall out."

The men broke into excited chatter as they stacked their muskets, discarded their belts and knapsacks, prepared their foraging tools.

"Pickets," Smith said. "You, Corcoran."

"Me, Sergeant Major? Why me?"

"Because I'm saving you from a flogging, that's why, boy. You and you. Go with Corcoran. That hummock over there. Face the east. There's our enemy. You, there. Muskets are stacked, not left to lie in the mud. You, sir, get that hat on."

He wondered what they'd fight like, when the time came. But he didn't suppose it was really a reason for concern. He had taken enough recruits and molded them into fighting soldiers during the past few years, and this lot certainly didn't lack enthusiasm.

Hooves. "Fall in there," he bawled. "Fall in." A hasty glance across the sodden field assured him that this was not merely Captain Llewellyn returning, and not even Colonel Hallam accompanying him, but that they were both escorting the general of division himself, Sir Rowland Hill. The sergeant major felt his heart pounding. It was his bad luck that the Worcesters had been brigaded under Hill, a man with whom he had once played cards. But there was really no cause for alarm; the combination of seventeen years, of his mustache, and of all commissioned officers' tendency to regard NCO's as NCO's rather than as men protected him.

"At ease." The general's cheeks were pink, as ever, and his mouth was smiling. Now he pointed at the hills to the east. "Over there, lads, is Spain. Tomorrow we'll be there. But you want to remember, lads, that they are our allies. Just as much as the Portuguese. I'll hang the first man who takes without paying, and the first man who lifts a skirt without invitation. We're here to fight the frogs, lads. And I can tell you this, they aren't far away. But if they won't fight us, why, we intend to march on Madrid and send Joseph Bonaparte home, on his ass. That's our plan, lads, so keep your powder dry."

"Three cheers for the general," shouted Captain Llewellyn. "Hip hip . . ."

The Worcesters responded with a will, the little cavalcade rode on, leaving the captain behind.

"Dismiss the men, Sergeant Major," Llewellyn said, and dismounted himself. "And bring me that fellow who was trailing his musket."

Smith remained at attention. "I have given him picket duty, sir. Tonight and every night for the next week."

Llewellyn frowned, and then added. "Saves the waste of time of a flogging, eh, Sergeant Major? Punishment confirmed. Fall out the men. And tell them the general means what he says. It's Madrid for us, and then the end of the war will be in sight. You tell them that, Sergeant Major."

The end of the war. It was not something Sergeant Major Smith had ever seriously considered. This war had lasted too long for it ever to end. But it occurred to him that he must have considered it once. He could hardly remember. He had fled Alison Brand's bed—strange how he could only think of her as Alison Brand, rather than Alison Haggard—blindly, fearfully, aware only that he had committed as ghastly a crime as it was possible to consider. That he had been innocently involved, that the real crime was hers, had not seemed relevant. She had been Father's wife, Father's young and beautiful wife, and there could be no doubt of his love for her, of whose side he would take.

Even if she could be proved to be hardly better than a whore? But how to prove that?

So, then, what it came down to was fear of Father rather than remorse at what he had done. He had merely anticipated what Father would have done to him, by running away without a shilling in his pocket, by deserting his commission, which at any time would have left him an object worthy only of contempt, and also by deserting his regiment in time of war, which left him worthy only of a hanging. Then he had sought death, but without the courage to take his own life. Then he had presumed that as a front-line soldier he would soon stop a bullet, and be forgotten.

Seventeen years ago. He had been surprised, at once by the realization that however much of a moral coward he might be he was certainly not a physical one, and even more by the realization that he liked the army life. Even the aimless marching and countermarching amid the canals and in the rains of Holland, with malaria fever making his teeth chatter at every step, or the searing heat of the Egyptian desert, had been enjoyable. As he expected to die, wished to die, he had lived every day for itself, had fought every battle as his last. And as was the whim of fate, had prospered. Nor had he ever doubted that the peace of 1802 was more than a truce. The war would not end until Napoleon had beaten the English or was himself beaten by the English. That was obvious.

By which token the mere expulsion of Joseph Bonaparte from Spain would mean very little. Yet after seventeen years even he must realize that the war had to end someday, and that he might very well survive that day. But why should it make any difference? He was a professional soldier. As a company sergeant major he was nearly at the top of his particular branch of his profession, and Great Britain would still need an army, even after peace with the French. He would remain with the colors. No man could ask for better anonymity.

"Ah, 'tis a wonderful place," Corcoran commented, tramping as usual at his shoulder. The contrast with Portugal was nothing short of miraculous. Instead of burned and looted villages, here were clean and prosperous towns; instead of starvation rations of whatever they could carry in their knapsacks, here were marketplaces filled with produce; instead of mayors and town clerks hanging from improvised gallows at every crossroad, here were haughty officials who regarded the British soldiers with a mixture of suspicion and contempt. And instead of the tormented and mutilated bodies of young women in the gutters, here were dark-eyed beauties hiding behind shawls and mantillas, peering down at the marching soldiers from wrought-iron balustrades, sometimes tossing flowers for the men to catch. No French army had as yet retreated through this pleasant land.

And what of the pleasant land you have forsworn? Roger wondered. He had no idea. He had no idea what might have become of it in seventeen years. The exploits of John Haggard made little impact upon the national scene, as he had turned his back upon that scene, nor would Roger ever inquire. He knew his father lived, because he had read of his impassioned speech against the abolition of the slave trade only two years ago. How his defeat on that occasion must have angered the old man. But for the rest, he knew nothing. He knew nothing of Charlie, whether he was by now a captain or even an admiral. He knew naught of Alice's marriage.

He knew nothing of Alison's amours, and of her children. He knew nothing of what had happened in Derleth Valley, save that he did not doubt it would be as prosperous as ever. He sometimes wondered if his room remained as he had left it, what he would feel like were he to reenter it. Childish thoughts, because only a child had ever dwelled there.

"Fall out." The order came down the line. The men moved more smartly now, at once because of their increased experience and because of the crowd watching them.

"Sergeant Major, do you suppose . . . ?" Corcoran was exchanging smiles with two Spanish girls across the street.

"You'll make your own decision about that, Private. But remember what the general said. He's a man of his word."

Corcoran winked. "And what about you, Sergeant Major? Don't you ever feel the urge?"

"A clapped soldier is no damn use to anyone," Roger remarked, and walked away. He messed by himself, although his tent was next to the company sergeants'. They knew better than to attempt to penetrate his reserve; Sergeant Major Smith was a law unto himself.

But didn't he ever feel the urge? Especially now, on a warm summer's day? Gone were the rains of the spring and the icy blasts which had accompanied them from the mountains. Now the sun shone out of a blue sky, and the land through which they had marched was already turning to brown dust, which eddied above the column and obscured the brilliance of their uniforms while denoting the passage of troops for miles around. But he had turned his back on woman, years ago. Not intentionally. As a private soldier he had taken his turn in line for the few whores who had been available, and suffered the humiliation of impotence as Alison's face had risen before him, as her scent had clouded around him. No women for Sergeant Major Smith. He was a man of iron. There was a subtle joke, appreciated only by himself.

But how he wished this marching would end, and they could again see their enemy. It made sense, of course. If Marshal Victor would not assault them until he was sure which way they were moving, there was no need for Sir Arthur Wellesley to assault Marshal Victor until his army had been brought up to strength, until his ammunition wagons had been replenished, until his veterans had been rested and his recruits assimilated. But that was done. Roger could look down at the glowing red of his jacket, the gleaming white of his belts; he had even been presented with a new staff, and his shako was a crisp brown instead of a disintegrating gray. And no one could doubt that Corcoran and the others were as trained as they would ever be, barring only the experience of actual combat. Too much more of this lying about in cantonments, and discipline would suffer.

"Pensive, Sergeant Major?"

He came to atteniton. " 'Tis good campaigning weather, sir."

"Indeed it is," Captain Llewellyn agreed. He was young for a captain. His army career had only begun in 1803. Had I remained an officer, Roger thought, I might well be colonel of this regiment now, and he be calling me "sir." Except that had I remained an officer, I would also have remained with the artillery. But thoughts of that nature were a waste of time. "And we shall be campaigning," Llewellyn said. "The general returned last night, from Cuesta's camp. 'Tis a combined operation we're after, Sergeant Major. Victor must be crushed."

"And will the dons fight, sir?"

Llewellyn frowned. "Do you doubt that? 'Tis their land."

"I meant, sir, in our fashion. Will they obey General Wellesley?"

"We shall have to wait and see. But I doubt it matters. 'Tis the numbers that are important. Why, we shall outnumber the frogs by at least two to one. They'll not escape us this time."

"As you say, sir," Roger agreed. He had had sufficient experience of fighting alongside inexperienced or self-centered allies; they were less nuisances if they had not been there at all. Still, he had no reason to doubt Sir Arthur Wellesley's dispositions. That long-nosed old bugger had led him to three victories, so far, in two years. He seemed to know what he was about.

"Mind you," Llewellyn said, chewing his lip, "it will be a risky business. There is talk that Soult is hovering over there . . ." He pointed to the mountains fringing the north. "Just waiting to descend on our flank. And then, the Light Brigade has not yet come up . . ." He was definitely agitated, for all his attempt to suggest that he was looking forward to the prospect of a fight.

"I am sure Sir Arthur keeps Marshal Soult in mind, sir," Roger said. "I'd but wish, if you'll excuse the liberty, he kept our grub more in mind as well. This last week we might have been back in Portugal."

"Aye, well, there is a war on, Sergeant Major."

"The dons don't look as if they're starving to me."

Llewellyn nodded. "Difficult. They do not understand us, to be sure. They do not understand anything. Even when we offer them money, they prefer to hoard their food. But Sir Arthur is working on them, you may be sure of that. Now, you get the men ready to march."

Forward, once again, into the heart of Spain. The day was July 16, 1809, and no weather could ever have been so hot, even in Egypt. Every footstep dislodged a puff of dust, and the cavalry, out to either flank, as well as the artillery bringing up the rear, created clouds which hung above the column and showed no tendency to dissipate in the windless air. Men coughed and choked as their red jackets became orange, while officers riding up and down the column were shadowy, half-visible figures, nuisances because they created yet more dust.

"Column will halt and fall out." The order was received with a clatter as men sat or lay by the roadside. And here was relief. Immediately men materialized from the yellow murk, great muscular fellows with sun-browned skins sheltering beneath enormous sombreros, every one with a full barrel on his back and a cup in his hand.

"*Limonada*," they called. "*Limonada fresca.*"

Immediately the weary men were back on their feet or their knees, holding out their own tin mugs to be filled with the enormously refreshing liquid. Roger waited his turn. He knew there would be sufficient for all.

"Christ, but that tastes good." Corcoran squatted by the roadside, sipping his cupful with great care. "How much longer, Sergeant Major? Four days. By Christ, another week and I'll have lemonade in my veins instead of blood."

"We'll be in Orepeso by sundown," Roger said. "So you'd best spruce up. There's to be a parade."

For General Cuesta was coming to see his allies for himself. The Worcesters took their place in the line beside the Forty-eighth, the Northamptons, with the other line regiments farther along. They had dusted their jackets and waxed their belts, and their muskets gleamed. They looked good, and they knew it. But what were they to make of the Spaniard, captain general of Estremadura, held on his horse by two pages, wearing old-fashioned trunk hose and laden with gold lace

and glittering medals? Before he even reached the Twenty-
ninth, indeed, he was overcome by his ailments—he had been
ridden over by his own cavalry a few months before—and
was forced to take refuge in his coach, from the cushions of
which he peered out at the amazed Englishmen.

"Christ, what a crew," Corcoran muttered, staring less at
the general than at his escort, whose prancing shaggy ponies
hardly suggested the horse guards any more than their officers, dressed in a variety of uniforms, armed with Toledo
blades so long they all but dragged on the ground, and
chewing tobacco or openly smoking cigarillos, suggested an
Englishman's idea of an officer.

"Hold your tongue, God damn you," Roger growled. But
his heart was sinking. Were these men capable of standing
before Napoleon's veterans?

Cuesta's departure was followed by a visit from the commanding general himself, Sir Rowland Hill at his heels.

"Do you see those mountains?" demanded Sir Arthur Wellesley. "That is the Sierra de Gredos. That's where the French
are, my lads. That's where you'll have your fight." He rode
on, and Roger squinted at the forest slopes, seeming to shim-
mer in the heat. At the foot of the nearest hill there was a
sizable town.

"Talavera, it is called," Captain Llewellyn said when the
parade was dismissed. "That's our destination."

But of course the Spaniards had to be given the honor of
clearing it of the French. The British stood to their arms and
watched the dragoons, the first regiment wearing blue jackets
and the second green, go clattering past, and immediately
there was a great hullabaloo from in front of them, shrieks
and musketry interspersed with cheers of *"Viva España!"*
while soon enough the inevitable crowd of men and women
and children came flooding down the road to greet the advancing army and to convey, with bloodcurdling gestures, just
what they had done to the French.

"I tell you what, Sergeant Major," Corcoran muttered.
"I'm glad these chaps are on our side, that I am."

Suddenly the morning was overcast with the growl of artillery, and a moment later the Spanish dragoons came strag-
gling back from the far side of the town, wailing their fear.

"The Twenty-ninth will deploy." Captain Llewellyn rode
up and down the column, while Sergeant Major Smith and
his assistants formed the men into line and dressed them.

"The Twenty-ninth will advance. Fix bayonets."

With a gigantic rustle and clatter the regiment prepared for battle, the various companies coming up into the line, while beyond the houses they could see first of all the river and then the hills beyond, but for the moment no sign of the French.

"Where are they, then, where are they?" someone muttered.

"On the far side of the river," someone else said.

"That's a river?" Corcoran demanded. In the July heat the stream had dwindled to a few yards across and clearly only a few inches deep.

"That's the Alberche," said someone else, more informed than the rest. "'Tis a tributary of the Tagus."

"Nah," Corcoran objected. "The Tagus is in Portugal."

"It begins here," Roger told him. "But you're right. It'll be no obstacle." He looked for his officer. The regiment was excited and ready to go. They had heard the sound of enemy guns, but they had lost not a man. At the command they would wade that river, and he was sure, drive away anyone opposed to them.

But the bugles were sounding and the command was being passed down the line. "Fall out. Prepare to bivouac."

Roger saw his men setting up their tents, sent out pickets, waited for Llewellyn to come up. "What a way to fight a war," the captain said as he dismounted. "You won't believe it, Sergeant Major, but the Spaniards weren't ready to fight today. So we don't."

The dons were not ready to fight on the morrow, either. The British lay to their arms, while endless staff officers, and even Sir Arthur himself, visited Cuesta's headquarters, without apparent avail. Nor did the French seek to cause trouble, and indeed they were nowhere to be seen.

"Ten to one they're already halfway to Madrid," Llewellyn grumbled.

"They'll be concentrating, sir," Roger pointed out. "We surprised them, but not any longer. We're going to have a fight on our hands."

Which earned him a startled glance from the captain. And on the next day the Worcesters were awakened by a great noise: the entire Spanish army was at last on the march, an amazing sight, as the advance guard was composed of what appeared to be brigands dressed in a variety of garments not one of which could be called a uniform, and armed with a

variety of weapons; behind them came the regular soldiers, a
gleam of blue and scarlet marching in perfect order with
arms sloped as if on parade, and behind them a nondescript
horde of priests and women, cattle and pigs, sheep and chickens. It made Roger think of tales he had read of Hunnish
hordes on the march.

"And where are they going, Sergeant Major?" Corcoran
wanted to know.

"To find the French," Roger said.

"While we stay here?"

The men were restless and disappointed, as Roger reported.

"Aye, well," Captain Llewellyn remarked, somewhat relieved to find himslf still behind the river, "Sir Arthur wants
to fight as much as anyone. But not by marching blindly at
those hills. So far as he knows, there are better than fifty
thousand frogs over there, and now they know we're here.
Nor do we have a tenth of the carts promised us by the dons.
You mark my words, Sergeant Major. Those fellows will be
back, and with their tails between their legs."

For once he was absolutely right. Only two days later the
Spaniards came hurrying down the road in a chaotic,
shouting mass, screaming that the French were at their heels.
The redcoats clustered outside their bivouacs and stared at
the mob in amazement, which only grew, as, having fled pre-
cipitately from a single contact with the French, Cuesta suddenly halted the retreat on the *other* side of the Alberche and
stubbornly refused to bring himself and his men to safety for
another twenty-four hours, while Wellesley begged him and
pointed out his danger.

Which was real enough. Now the dust clouds were moving
toward Talavera, and the distant firing showed that the
French were dispersing all rear guards that might be left to
oppose them. So rapid was their march, as they discounted
the Spaniards and knew they outnumbered the British by two
to one, that the rumor ran up and down the ranks that the
general himself had been taken while at a reconnaisance. But
Wellesley reassured his troops by cantering down the line,
while the British slowly spread themselves across the plain.

"Because, you may rely upon it," Roger told his company,
"that river wouldn't stop us, so it won't stop the French either." And indeed, the more he regarded the situation, the
less he liked it. The allied right was in Talavera itself, and
was secured by the Tagus. Here the Spaniards had been
posted; even they could surely hold the town walls. But the

British were extended across an open plain, with only a stream, the Portina Brook, another tributary of the river, in front of them, and their left anchored, if such a disposition could be so called, on a little hillock which rose from the plain, the Cerro de Medillín.

"I want them two deep," Captain Llewellyn said.

"Very good, sir," Roger agreed, but never had he seen such a thin line.

"We're overextended, that's what we are," Corcoran commented, suddenly very knowledgeable. "We'll not stop anything at all."

"Well, the enemy ball will pass through that much easier," Roger reminded him, but he gazed at the distant dust with increasing apprehension. Never had he felt quite so exposed, not even when retreating across the mountains with Moore last winter, and certainly not under Wellesley, who invariably chose the very best defensive positions for his troops.

But there could be no question of retreat. Behind them was open country, and the French had far too great a preponderance of cavalry. Besides, there could be no doubt that were the Spaniards forced to abandon the walls and houses of Talavera, they would dissolve into the rabble they suggested.

"We're here for a day or two, lads," he said, strolling along the line of bivouacs. "So sleep easy tonight, and be sure the frogs will still be there tomorrow."

He reached his own tent, where he found Captain Llewellyn.

"Good evening to you, Sergeant Major. I have just come from General Hill. He wishes us to occupy the hillock first thing in the morning. There's a compliment, eh? But that position must be held, and the Twenty-ninth and the Forty-eighth are the best infantry in the army. His words. Gad, I feel twice my size."

"Yes, sir," Roger agreed. "But should we not occupy it this evening?"

"No, no. That isn't in the least necessary. There's a company of the King's German Legion up there now, and you may be sure the frogs won't attack without a proper reconnaissance, at dawn. We've time, and the men are exhausted. Let them sleep."

"Yes, sir," Roger said, and saluted as Llewellyn walked into the darkness. He had no doubt the officers knew a great deal more about battlefield strategy and tactics than he. And the French did not usually attack at night, to be sure, at least without a proper understanding of what they were about. But he did no more than take off his boots and his jacket, lay down with both staff and musket close at hand, slept deeply, and awoke with a start at the crash of musketry and the peal of a bugle.

He was on his feet and into his jacket in a moment, seized his rifle and his boots, dragged on his belts and his water bottle, crammed his hat on his head.

"To arms," he bawled. "Fall in, the Twenty-ninth."

It was utterly dark, save for the flurry of sharp lights where the musketry was coming from, both in the center of the English line, some half-mile to his right, and from the Cerro de Medillín itself. But where the devil were their officers? Men poured out of their tents, some with and some without their equipment, hastily forming rank, heads turning from left to right as they listened to the fire.

"Who's there?" Roger shouted, presenting his musket as hooves thundered through the night.

"Rowland Hill, damn your eyes," came the reply. "What regiment is this?"

Roger came to attention. "The Twenty-ninth, sir."

"Thank God for that. You'll follow me, on the double. Extended order."

"Extended order," Roger shouted, heart pounding. It was the first time in all his long years in the army that he was actually going into battle under the immediate command of a general officer, and what an officer, for Hill was bareheaded and his tunic was open at the neck. But his sword was drawn, and now he dismounted and put himself at the head of the advancing line.

"Do you wish bayonets, sir?" Roger asked.

"No. Musketry must do this work in the beginning. There are the devils."

Men could be seen on the slope in front of them, engaged in driving the last of the German Legion from the hillock.

"The Twenty-ninth will present," the general called in a clear voice. "Aim, now, lads, those are frogs. Fire."

The explosions came almost as one, a hail of lead which swept up the slope and sent the French marauders scattering back in dismay.

"The Twenty-ninth will load and advance," the general said.

Roger hurried along the ranks, slapping men into action. "Get that ball home. Haste, now. Load up."

Some scattered shots were fired in return, and a man fell with a ghastly whistling sound. Those around him hastily knelt to his aid.

"Up." Roger cracked his stick across their backs. "Load. You heard the general."

"The Twenty-ninth will take aim." Hill continued to march at their front, turning now to face them. "Steady, lads." Still bullets pinged around them, scattering dust, and striking home again by the cry which came from farther down the line. "Fire."

Once again the hail of lead swept forward, and the French on the hilltop, hastily endeavoring to form line to meet the advancing British, could be seen to waver.

"Now the Twenty-ninth," General Hill shouted. "Now. Fix your bayonets. Follow me."

Steel rasped, and Roger hurried up and down the line, forcing it straight, barking encouragement. The men ran forward, and it was time to fight himself. He threw down his staff, drew his sword, ran with them. Shadowy figures formed up and raised their own weapons. They also had fixed bayonets, but too many of their number were already retreating down the hill. The shock of the Twenty-ninth's charge completed their discomfort. Those still on their feet turned and ran for the brook and the safety on the French line.

"Halt there," bellowed Hill. "Sergeant Major, fetch those fellows back."

Roger stumbled down the hill behind his men. "Halt there," he shouted in turn. "To me, the Twenty-ninth. Fall in. Fall in, the Twenty-ninth."

Reluctantly the men came to a halt, panting and gasping.

"I got one," Corcoran shouted excitedly. "I got one, Sergeant Major. Right through the belly. Look at that." Even in the darkness the blood could be seen staining the bright steel of the bayonet.

"So you did," Roger agreed. "Now, back up the hill, or you won't live to see your grandchildren."

"Is that the end of the battle, Sergeant Major?" Withers inquired as the company tramped back to where General Hill was standing.

"That?" Roger gave him a grim smile. "That wasn't even the beginning, lad."

"Well done, the Twenty-ninth," Hill said as they came up.

"Oh, indeed," agreed Captain Llewellyn. "Well done, the Twenty-ninth."

"Where the devil have you been, sir?" the general demanded.

Llewellyn glanced at his two subalterns, who stood one to either side. "Well, sir, as the company was bivouacked, I took myself into Talavera for a glass of wine. I saw you on the road, sir."

"Aye," Hill agreed. "But when the shooting started, I seem to have got back here the faster, eh? You're to congratulate your sergeant major, Captain Llewellyn. He had his men well in hand."

"Oh, indeed, sir, there is no better sergeant major in the army than Smith." Llewellyn cleared his throat. "What orders have you for us now, sir?"

"Why, sir, to stand fast. This hill is where you are, and this hill is where you'll be, God willing, this time tomorrow night. I'll bid you good night, sir."

He walked down the slope. Llewellyn produced a handkerchief and mopped his brow. "Gad," he grumbled. "How was a fellow to know? Sergeant Major Smith. Will they come again, d'you suppose?"

"Not this night, sir."

"Then you'd best fall out the men."

"Very good, sir. If I may suggest, sir . . ."

"Yes, yes, go on."

"It wants only three hours to dawn, sir. No one is going to sleep now. So we may as well make ourselves comfortable. I'd like to send a party for the rest of our gear, sir. And I'd also like to detail a squad to roll these corpses down the hill; if the frogs don't come on at first light, there's going to be an awful stink."

"My word, but you're right. See to it, Sergeant Major. See to it."

Roger supposed, after all, that he had dozed off. In two hours the hilltop had been cleared of most of the corpses, which now formed a mound at the bottom, half in and half out of the brook; from above they looked like a heap of blue-bottles—he could hear the buzzing of the real things as well. And his men were fully dressed and armed. And blooded now, as well. He was pleased with them. They'd play their part. Then what had awakened him? It was dark, with the chill blackness of the hour before dawn, and there was no movement from in front of him.

But behind him. He leaped to his feet, listened to the

creaking and thumping, the snorts of the horses, the muttered curses of the men, and the whispered commands of the officers.

"Fall in, the guard," he said, and stepped forward, as Llewellyn also sat up and hastily reached for his sword. "Who comes?"

"Friend," said an English voice. "The general wishes this hill held at all costs."

He blinked into the darkness, saw the caissons trailing behind the horses, made out the gold-and-blue jackets. A battery of horse artillery. His own regiment, before his world had come to an end. He wondered if in some way this was an omen for his impending death; however many battlefields he had shared with these men, this was the first time he had been commanded to fight next to them.

The noise had awakened most of the battalion, the men were sitting up and making themselves a hasty breakfast, as dawn was so obviously close at hand. But now there was a rustle through the entire force, and people scrambled to their feet, as Sir Arthur Wellesley himself, accompanied by four staff officers, came to the top of the hill and sat his horse there, peering into the darkness. "Mark me well, Hill," he said, his voice clear in the stillness. "This will be the critical point. If we lose here, we lose everywhere."

"We'll hold," Rowland Hill replied.

"I'm relying on that." The general looked around him. "I'm relying on you all," he said. "Good fortune." He turned his horse and walked it back down the slope, his officers jingling at his heels.

"Sergeant Major," Corcoran whispered. "When will the battle start?"

"As soon as you've had your breakfast, lad," Roger told him. "So you'd best eat up." He pointed at the sudden lightening of the sky behind the eastern mountains. For now the light came on apace, and he could hear the sharp intakes of breath from the men to either side of him as the French army was revealed, already arrayed in order of battle, more than forty thousand of the finest soldiers in the world.

Close at hand, just on the far side of the Portina Brook, there was a swarm of *tirailleurs* waiting the command to advance. At the rear was squadron after squadron of cavalry, their casques gleaming in the first light, which also illustrated the many-colored pennants and picked out their lanceheads. In between were the solid masses of blue-coated infantry, bayonets already fixed, drummer boys waiting expectantly. And it was perfectly easy for the British watchers to see that while the country opposite Talavera and the Spaniards was thinly held, the main body of the French was concentrated against the twenty thousand British and Portuguese holding the allied center and left, just as the main part of that concentration was below the Cerro de Medillín.

Corcoran spat into the dust, looked from right to left. The hill was also held in strength, no fewer than six battalions of the Twenty-ninth and the Forty-eighth, the Northamptons, with support from the King's German Legion as well as the artillery batteries placed during the night—but they were terribly few compared with the mass in front of them. "Will we beat them, Sergeant Major?"

"We'll bloody well try," Roger grunted. Now that the moment was at hand, irrelevant thoughts, of past or future, had drifted away. Only the present need concern him. He was here to do a job of work, as they all were, and nothing else could interest him until afterward.

"Look there," someone called. From the middle of the French army a single puff of smoke curled into the sky.

"Wait for it," Roger snapped as the men commenced to rustle. But he had no sooner finished speaking than every gun in the French army seemed to fire at once, a tremendous rolling explosion shrouded in huge clouds of black smoke. Almost before he could turn his head there was an enormous whistling sound and a chorus of curiously abbreviated cries; he looked to his left and saw two huge scythes cut right through the lines of redcoats, sudden gaps composed of mangled arms and legs and heads and trunks, all suddenly without meaning.

"Back, fall back," came the order, and Roger turned his head in surprise, to see Sir Arthur himself, with his staff, coming up the hill.

"Damn, Arthur," shouted Rowland Hill. "You told me to hold it."

"And I am still telling you to hold it," Wellesley replied. "But there is no need to expose the men. Have them lie down behind the brow. Smartly, now."

The redcoats withdrew, while the French cheered and their skirmishers started to cross the brook.

"Down you get," Roger commanded. "On your bellies."

"Those fellows make a target, Sergeant Major."

"You'll have your targets. Down, lads."

"Funny way to fight a battle," Corcoran commented, nestling on his stomach.

Roger rolled on his side to look at the regimental standard behind him, at Hill and Wellesley and the staff officers, at the cannonballs which continued to come bounding over the hill-top, but now doing very little damage. He watched Wellesley give a brief nod and then ride away, followed by his staff. The moment was at hand, and now, indeed, he could hear the rat-a-tat of the drums and the shouts of *"Vive l'Empereur!"* coming closer. His blood began to tingle, and he found that his hands were wet. He wondered what the French thought as they approached an apparently empty hill-top. How they must be hoping that the British had indeed withdrawn. And how unpleasantly surprised they were going to be.

And there was Wellesley again, returning up the slope, having satisfied himself that the rest of the line was holding. Now he took in the situation at a glance and raised his hat. "Now, Hill."

"Up, lads," Rowland Hill bellowed, his voice rising even above the mutter of the drums.

"The Twenty-ninth will rise," shouted Captain Llewellyn, and similar orders rippled down the line. The men stood shoulder to shoulder, gazed at the massed French column, officers in front, proceeding as if on parade and scarce a hundred yards distant.

"The Twenty-ninth will take aim," called the captain.

"Straighten up, there," Roger snapped, marching down the line behind the men, tapping the laggards on the shoulder. "Close up."

"The Twenty-ninth will fire," Captain Llewellyn shouted, and the muskets crashed in unison. The French column halted, the leading men on their knees or already on the ground, muskets thrown away and shakos rolling in the bloodstained dust.

"The Twenty-ninth will load," Captain Llewellyn said. "Haste, now, lads."

"Haste, there, haste," Roger snapped. The French were beginning to recover, their officers were waving their swords, and the drums were again starting to beat.

"The Twenty-ninth will take aim," Llewellyn said.

Roger reached the end of the line, pointed his staff. "Careful, now, lads," he said. "At this range, you cannot miss."

The French were very close, their bayonets bristling in front of them, their faces contorted with anger and hate.

"The Twenty-ninth will give fire," said Captain Llewellyn. Once again the same orders had been issued at the same moment in every company of every one of the six battalions. Now the enemy were only fifty yards away, and not even Napoleon's mustachios could withstand that hail of lead. Once again the heads of the column crumbled, and this time the dense masses behind lost their cohesion. Gaps appeared, and some of the men started to look over their shoulders.

"Now, Hill," Wellesley called.

"Advance, the Twenty-ninth," shouted Hill. "Advance, the Forty-eighth. Clear me this hill."

Roger threw down his staff and drew his sword.

"Charge those fellows," shouted Captain Llewellyn, also drawing his sword. He and the two lieutenants put themselves at the head of the line, Roger kept his place at the end, to maintain dressing, and the whole mass surged forward, yelling at the tops of their voices.

"*Sauve qui peut.*" The cry was begun by a single faint-hearted throat, and then taken up by others. The redcoats crashed into the blue, the bayonets seethed against each other. A thrust went under Roger's arm, tearing his coat and his flesh as well, for he felt the sting of pain. But he knew he was no more than scratched, and his own blade had sunk deep into the belly of his assailant. Down he went, and Roger tugged at the sword, saw another blue-coated man lunging at him, reckoned he was about to be at least seriously wounded, saw Corcoran thrust in turn with his own bayonet, parrying the blow and turning it up, swinging his musket as he did so, to catch the Frenchman a blow across the chin with the butt, throwing the man backward with a sickening crunch.

"On, the Twenty-ninth" bawled Captain Llewellyn, sword bloodied and face flushed. For now they were descending the far side of the hill, driving the French in front of them. They scattered down the slope, splashed into the shallow brook, turning the water brown and red with their blood and the dust on their feet.

"Halt there," bellowed General Hill, having dismounted to accompany his men. "Fall back."

But the battle was ended for the moment. The French had returned to their original positions, and the English were gasping and panting, suddenly aware of the heat, for although it

was just eight of the morning, the sun was already high and
hot, and the hillside was covered with corpses.

"Water," Corcoran grunted. "I must have water."

Several of his comrades were already kneeling. On the
other side of the brook, not twenty feet away, a few of the
French were also drinking, scooping the bloody liquid in
their hands and conveying it to their mouths.

Roger looked back up the slope. Not all of his men had
broken ranks to drink; most were pulling over the dead and
dying, some calling for stretcher bearers, others out to discover what they could.

"Come on, lads," he said, tapping Corcoran on the shoulders. "Up you get. We can't stay here all day."

"Look what I've found," bubbled Lieutenant Portman,
more excited than anyone else at the outcome of his first engagement. He held out his hand, showed two crosses of the
Legion of Honor. "Took them off a dead officer up there.
Must have been a rare hero, eh?"

Llewellyn glanced at Roger, slowly took the two medals.

"I beg your pardon, sir," Portman objected. "The spoils of
war, what. They belong to me."

"They belong to the French, sir," Llewellyn said, and
waded into the stream, hands outstretched. After a moment's
hesitation a French officer came to meet him. "*Pour vous,*"
Llewellyn said uncertainly.

The officer gazed at the crosses for a moment, then took
them. "You 'ave the thanks of France, monsieur," he said,
and saluted.

How hot it was. The sun was past noon high, and scorched
the field. There had not been time to bury the dead, and they
were already starting to bloat as they were assaulted by a
fresh horde of flies. The Twenty-ninth and the Forty-eighth
had regained their hilltop and stood to their arms, as did the
rest of the army on the plain between them and the town.
And as did the French on the far side of the brook. The only
noise, apart from the humming of the insects, was the occasional crack of a musket from away to the south, where the
French skirmishers were potshotting at the Spaniards.

"What are they waiting for?" Corcoran wanted to know.

"Why don't they go away?" someone else demanded.

"Ah, they ain't going," said a third. "They still have us by
two to one."

Or more, Roger thought as he walked by the group. Perhaps they were waiting on Soult to debouch from the mountains in the British rear. Just as Sir Arthur Wellesley was certainly waiting for the arrival of Black Bob Craufurd with the three regiments of the Light Brigade, hurrying over the roads behind them. The battle was a long way from being over.

And there it was again. Another puff of smoke, immediately enveloped in a rolling black thunderclap. "Take cover," shouted Captain Llewellyn, hurrying back from an officers' conference. "Behind the hill. Smartly, now."

Roger used his staff to hasten men into moving, get them away from their canteens and their salted meat, out of sight of the artillery. But apparently the French were no longer interested in the Cerro de Medillín. Few cannonballs came up here, as the main weight of the coming assault seemed to be directed at the men on the plain. Roger stood with Llewellyn and Portman to watch the French surging forward, to watch the Fourth Division, commanded by Major General Campbell, charging in a counterattack and actually overrunning three French batteries before being recalled. This was worth a cheer, but nearer at hand, almost at the foot of the hill, things did not go so well. Here the First Guards Division and the Hanoverians took their bombardment with admirable courage, held their fire as the Twenty-ninth had done, and then rushed forward with the bayonet to disperse the attacking French in fine style. But they had not been kept on as tight a rein as the Worcesters, and continued their charge even across the brook.

"Great God almighty," remarked Rowland Hill, coming to stand with the other officers to watch the disaster looming below them. "Those fellows will suffer for it."

Roger watched, and felt his belly roll. The disorganized mass of redcoats was commencing to break up and straggle, just as a compact column of blue-coated French was launched against it in a counterattack. Now he realized what their own assault must have looked like, seen from a distance. Only, this time the roles were reversed. The First Guards attempted to form line to meet the assault, and were scattered by a devastating volley. The Hanoverians simply dissolved; Roger watched their commanding general riding his horse into the midst of a melee and tumble from the saddle to disappear. The rest fled every which way. The Guards were retreating in better order, but a good third of their men lay scattered in and out of the brook, and behind them there was a great gap in the British line.

"Can't we get down there, sir?" Portman begged. "The army will be cut in two."

"The battle will be equally lost if we abandon this hill, Mr. Portman," Hill said. "Pray do Sir Arthur the credit of having allowed for such a misfortune."

"There, sir," Roger said, pointing, and they watched General Mackenzie's reserve division hurrying toward the break in the line. How few they were, hardly two thousand men, while at least ten thousand French were marching on the gap. But the three regiments of the reserve, the Twenty-fourth, the Thirty-first, and the Forty-fifth Foot—the Warwickshires, the Huntingdonshires, and the Nottinghamshires—took up their places and began delivering volleys with deadly haste and equal accuracy, while staff officers scurried around to shepherd the retreating Guards and the remnants of the Hanoverians back to their positions.

"Noble lads," Rowland Hill said. "Noble lads."

"Will they hold, d'you suppose, sir?" Llewellyn inquired.

Roger stared down the hill at the thin red line. Many of them were not even properly dressed, were still wearing the uniforms of the militia regiments from which they had so recently been drafted. But they were showing no signs of fear. And now there came the clatter of hooves and the Fourteenth Light Dragoons hurled themselves against the French flank, swords flailing, helmets gleaming in the afternoon sun.

"Stapleton Cotton, by Gad," Hill cried. "There's a cavalryman."

"Now, Hill," Sir Arthur said from behind him. "Send the Forty-eighth."

Roger and Llewellyn turned in disappointment, but the orders had already been given, and the Northamptons moved down the hill in line, sending volley after volley into the French flank; the Worcesters had to watch the French column wither and start to ebb back across the brook.

"Oh, gallant Northamptons," shouted Rowland Hill.

"It should have been us," Llewellyn muttered, and judging by the scowls on the faces of his men, the rest of the Twenty-ninth felt the same.

"We should give them a cheer, sir," Roger suggested. "They'd do as much for us."

"Of course you're right, Sergeant Major," Llewellyn

agreed. "Three cheers for the Northamptons, lads. Hip hip . . ."

The Worcesters tossed their hats in the air. Surely the battle was finished. Surely the French, having been repulsed wherever they had attempted an attack, would call it enough. But even as the cheers broke out from the hilltop, fresh firing commenced on their left, at the extreme end of the British line.

"Stand to your arms," General Hill commanded. "They'll be here next."

"Form line. Stand to." Roger hurried through his company, slapping exhausted men to attention, paused at the far end to gaze down the valley, where two French divisions had crawled up the ravines in their attempt to turn the British left. He watched staff officers galloping away from Wellesley's side, and a moment later saw the Twenty-third Light Dragoons together with the First Hussars of the King's German Legion moving forward to charge the as-yet-disorganized French.

"There goes the cavalry, lads," he shouted. "Give them a cheer."

Once again the Worcesters responded, only to have their cries die in their throats as they watched in horror the entire leading squadrons of the charging cavalry disappear into an unsuspected ravine, men and horses plummeting to their deaths in a mass of waving arms and legs and swords, of cries and neighs, of commands by the remaining officers as they brought their men under control, wheeled to the left, and continued their charge.

"Brave men," Llewellyn said. "Brave men."

The French had formed square, and the horse, instead of vainly assaulting the bristling bayonets, rode round them to disperse a regiment of chasseurs coming to their rescue. Thus isolated, the French began to retreat.

"There it is." General Hill had remounted, and stood behind them. Now he pointed, and in the distance they could see the rearmost French troops beginning a movement back along the road to Madrid. "We've won, boys. We've held them off. Three cheers for Old England."

Once again the men responded with a will, but Roger, standing away from the main body, suddenly felt his nostrils twitch. He turned to look down the hill, where the dead and wounded lay scattered in and out of the brook, left there not only by the encounter of the early morning but also by the more recent action of the Guards. There a spark had ignited the parched grass, and now tongues of flame were licking upward, and the cries of agony were redoubled as the wounded discovered themselves about to be burned to death.

"Captain Llewellyn, sir," he said. "Permission to attend the wounded with a detail."

Llewellyn followed the direction of his pointing finger. "My God," he said. "What a fate. General Hill . . ."

But Hill had seen it too. "Aye," he said. "If you can find some volunteers, Sergeant Major. But take care, man, take care."

"Who'll come with me to help those poor fellows?" Roger shouted.

"Oh, I will, Mr. Smith," Corcoran cried.

"And I," called another, and then nearly the whole company hurried forward.

"The French may come again," General Hill pointed out. "You may take no more than a dozen men, Sergeant Major."

"Very good, sir." Roger pointed. "You, Corcoran, and you and you. Come along, now, lads. Let's make haste."

They slung their muskets and followed him down the hill. Now the flames were high and very bright, and the heat seemed redoubled, while the cries of the wounded grew ever more piteous.

"Help, for God's sake, help me," someone cried.

"Over there." Roger directed the men, continued on his way. He knelt beside a gasping guardsman. "Easy, now, old fellow. Help is coming."

"Help me, *monsieur*," another voice shouted.

He turned, gazed at the flames. He sucked air into his lungs, discovered it was impossible to take a proper breath, pushed through the yellow wall, which licked at his legs and scorched his jacket. A French officer lay at his feet, blood and intestines trailing away from the terrible wound in his belly. No help was possible for him. But he could die more easily.

"I'll get you out, *monsieur*," he said, and stooped, raising the man's arm and placing it over his shoulder, reaching down through the blood and mess for his legs, checking as he heard a movement behind him. He turned his head, gazed at the other Frenchman, whom he had supposed dead, but who was now raising himself on his elbow and thrusting forward his musket.

"Easy, old fellow," Roger said. "I'll be back for you in a moment. Easy."

The musket exploded into flame.

Chapter 3

The Crime

"There you are, Mr. Haggard. " MacGuinness pointed at the heap of rags, dried twigs, and paper, fire-blackened to be sure, but never really allowed to develop into a bonfire. "Real amateurs, they were."

Haggard tilted his head back to look up at the walls of the factory. The roof had just been completed, and it was all but ready. And someone had tried to burn it down.

"Who are *they*?"

"Well, sir . . ." MacGuinness stroked his chin.

"Wring?"

Peter Wring scratched his head. "I wouldn't like to say, Mr. Haggard."

"Who was watchman last night?"

"Harry Crow. You come over here, Harry."

Crow was a large, slow-moving man. He blinked at the squire uneasily.

"You disturbed them, Crow," Haggard said. "You must have seen who they were."

"Well, sir, Mr. Haggard, it were mighty dark."

"But at least you can tell me how many there were?"

"Well, sir, two or three. I couldn't be sure, they ran off that quick."

Haggard gazed at the man for a moment, then nodded. "Very well. You may go home now." He kicked the rubbish with his boot. "Get rid of this mess, Wring."

"Right away, Mr. Haggard. Right away."

"It was a hopeless business from the start, Mr. Haggard," MacGuinness said reassuringly. " 'Tis too damp to burn, down here."

Haggard went inside the huge empty shed. It was a late-September morning, and it had been a dry summer, yet MacGuinness was right, inside the factory smelled damp, and felt damp. He had deliberately built the mill in the next shallow valley to the coal mine, where the Derleth River came rushing down from the hills. This had always been wasted land. Now it was to be put to good use. Alice had said it would be impossible for anyone to work here in the winter, because of the damp and the cold. But Alice objected to everything he did, on principle. What really annoyed him was that she seemed to have enlisted the help of Johnnie these past few months. But Johnnie's opposition was never prejudiced. He was always willing to listen, preferred to argue than merely to oppose.

Anyway, the factory could hardly be any damper than the mine, and the men and children worked down there all winter. Rheumatism was a fact of life. And not only for the working class, he thought, as a twinge crept up his leg.

"Aye," he said. "Damp. Derleth people, d'you suppose, MacGuinness?"

"Well, sir, I wouldn't like to say, for sure."

"Come straight with me, man, goddammit," Haggard snapped, for the first time revealing the anger which was burning at his belly. "You'd know if there were strangers in the valley. Three men? You'd know, MacGuinness."

"Yes, sir. There are no strangers in the valley. Leastways, none I've noticed."

"Derleth people," Haggard said. "Arson. There's a hanging offense, MacGuinness."

"Attempted arson, Mr. Haggard."

"Transportation, at the least. You'll find them, MacGuinness. Mark me well. You find them."

"Yes, sir, Mr. Haggard."

Haggard nodded, went outside, mounted his horse. Wring released the bridle, and the horse walked down the path toward the mine. One of them? Haggard reined in, sat for some moments gazing at the steady activity, the pit ponies with their loads of coal, the surface workers humping the bags toward the barges, the bargemen making sure the cargo was properly stowed, all shrouded in the miasmic dust which always hung over this hell on earth.

Bargemen. They came and went from the valley as they chose. MacGuinness would not notice *them*. Was he so reluctant to admit that three of his own people had turned against him? Cummings said there had been riots in Nottingham when the factory had been built there, and Nottingham was not so very far away. He almost smiled. He had spent the first half of his life preparing himself to meet a slave revolt which had never happened. Would it happen here in Derleth, in his twilight? Well, they'd find that Haggard was equally prepared to deal with that.

He nodded to the foreman, walked his horse through the cut toward the hall. But it might be a good idea *to* prepare. The machines were due to arrive in a few weeks' time. In Nottingham they had turned out the yeomanry. But that would mean sending to Derby, admitting to the entire county that Haggard could not handle his own affairs. There were enough men here, Wring and his friends, who would support him no matter what happened. Even against their own kin, if it came to that? He pinched his lip, dismounted, threw the reins to Ned.

"There are letters, sir." Nugent waited for him at the top of the stairs with the silver salver. Haggard nodded, took the envelopes.

"Is Mr. John in?"

"Why, no, sir. Mr. John went for a ride."

"By himself?"

"Yes, sir."

As usual. Where the devil did he go every day? He was becoming far too like his sister for comfort.

Haggard went into the office, sat down. Nugent hastily appeared with the decanter, poured his master a glass of port.

Haggard riffled through the envelopes. Most of them were the usual reports, from Cummings and from Ferguson. But there was one he did not recognize at all; it had been franked by the British Army Headquarters at Lisbon. He frowned, slit it open, took out the sheets of paper.

My Dear Mr. Haggard:

I hardly know where to begin a letter such as this, save to invite you to prepare yourself for a very great shock, but one which, I know, will bring much happiness in its wake.

You will by now have heard of the check given by Sir Arthur Wellesley's army, of which I am proud to be a member, to the French under Marshal Victor on the field of Talavera last July. The victory, for such it was, as we remained in possession of the field, was not attended by the continuing success we had anticipated, as owing to the dilatoriness of our Spanish allies, and our own severe want of food and munitions, we were unable to march on Madrid, as we had intended, and indeed, as you will see from the address on this letter, have re-

turned once again into Portugal to prepare ourselves for
a winter's defensive campaign. No doubt this is also
familiar to you.

But what you will not know is that the division which
I had the honor to command in the late battle was composed of the King's German Legion, the Forty-eighth
Foot, the Northamptons, and the Twenty-ninth Foot, the
Worcestershire regiment. All of these soldiers covered
themselves with glory in defending the key point in our
line, the Cerro de Medillín, but none more so than a
company sergeant major in the Worcesters, who boasted
the name of Robert Smith, and who it appears has been
a regular soldier since 1793. The significance of the
above date will not be lost upon you.

It was at the conclusion of the battle, when most gallantly trying to rescue some wounded men, French as
well as British, from a fire which had sprung up on the
plain below us, that Sergeant Major Smith was most
treacherously set upon by a Frenchman, and himself
badly hurt. I hasten to assure you, sir, that his wound is
on the mend, and that he will soon be able to take his
place once again with his comrades. But it was while
wounded, and temporarily bereft of his senses, that he
uttered words which astounded all those present, myself
included, and which informed me that here was a man I
had once been proud to call friend when we had both
been subalterns together. Indeed, sir, I must now be
straight with you, and tell you that this man is none
other than your son Roger.

Now, you may understand some of the amazement
and shock we all felt at this discovery. For, like you, we
had supposed him dead, or at best an outlaw who had
deserted his commission at the outset of this war. Now,
sir, I cannot pretend to know what caused Roger to undertake so strange a course, but I do know that far from
deserting the colors, he merely abandoned his commission and immediately reenlisted as a private soldier. In
fact, sir, he has campaigned more often and more successfully than anyone else I know, as will be understood
from his rise to the highest noncommissioned rank.

The facts of the case were immediately conveyed to
the commanding general, as I was in any event duty-
bound to do. On the one hand, we had a deserter,
worthy only of a firing squad, and on the other a hero,

worthy only of a medal and promotion. You will be as overjoyed as I was to learn that Sir Arthur has inclined toward the second view of the matter, and in order to regularize the situation, has issued a brevet commission as ensign to Mr. Roger Haggard.

Now, sir, I come to the difficult part of this letter. The above transactions took place while your son was still grievously ill, and no one could be sure whether or not he would die. He has since recovered, as I say, and although he will not be fit for duty for some weeks, yet he anticipates being able to resume his career on this higher level. I would be misleading you did I not reveal that his immediate reaction to his exposure was one of alarm and dismay, but this has now been overcome. What has not been overcome, however, is his total refusal to communicate with you, or indeed to return to Derleth, as was suggested to him by Sir Arthur, during his period of convalescence. He has preferred, as you will have gathered, to remain in Lisbon.

Now, sir, I repeat, I have no knowledge of the cause of Roger's original desertion, but the above forces me to suppose it was the result of a family difference. I have therefore taken it upon myself, quite without your son's knowledge, to write you this letter. I do not know in what regard you hold your son at this moment, nor do I see how it would be possible for you to meet him at this time, even supposing you wish to do so. On the other hand, this war must end eventually, and then we shall all be happy to come home. So, sir, I have placed you in possession of these facts, that you may decide for yourself your future course of action.

Should you consider that circumstances would permit you to extend the love of a father toward your son, may I suggest that you write to him care of myself. In this way, not only will you be sure your letter will reach its proper destination, but I will be able to act as your advocate should Roger continue to feel uncertain as to his next move. On the other hand, should you wish to leave matters as they are, I shall of course entirely understand.

I trust you will pardon this intrusion into your private affairs and believe that it was motivated entirely out of admiration for your son.

Yours faithfully,
R. Hill, major general

Haggard continued to stare at the paper for some moments, aware that his eyes were slowly filling with tears, that they were rolling down his cheeks and soaking his vest, that his heart was pounding and he was having difficulty in breathing. Slowly he got himself under control, drank some port, got up, went to the door. He wanted to shout at his very loudest. He wanted to shriek the news to the world. Instead he climbed the stairs, still moving very slowly.

"Alice."

His voice echoed in the upper hall, and Mary Prince came out of the withdrawing room.

"Mistress Alice is in the kitchens, Mr. Haggard."

Haggard nodded and turned away, but not before she had commenced to frown. But did it matter? Did anything matter? He went down the stairs.

"Alice."

She looked up at him from the foot of the servants' staircase. Her head was enveloped in a gigantic mobcap, tied beneath her chin, and there was grease on her gown. She habitually betrayed her true origins by wishing to take part in the cooking herself.

"Father? Whatever is the matter?"

Haggard went closer, held out the letter.

"Father?" Alice said again, staring at the tearstained cheeks.

"Read it."

She took the letter, frowned at it. Haggard watched her face changing expressions, from curiosity to interest to concern to delight. She raised her head.

"Roger is alive," Haggard said. "And a hero."

"Oh, Father." It was the very first time he had discovered warmth in her tone since she had been a small child. "Oh, Father."

She was in his arms, and he was hugging her close.

"Roger is alive," he said again. "And a hero."

"You'll write him, Father. Say that you'll write to him."

"Write to him? Of course I shall write to him. This very day." He gave her a last squeeze, released her as he heard the clip-clop of hooves on the drive. He ran up the stairs like a boy, burst out of the door to greet Johnnie. "Johnnie," he shouted, "Roger is alive. And a hero. Roger is alive. D'you hear, boy? Roger is alive."

Johnnie, cheeks flushed, no doubt from the wind, slowly dismounted, looked from his father to his stepsister.

"It's true, Johnnie," Alice said. "Father has had a letter from Sir Rowland Hill. Roger is alive. He has been wounded, but he will be well. Think of it. He has been fighting the French all these years. All of your life."

"All of my life," John Haggard said slowly.

Haggard threw his arm round his shoulder. "A surprise," he said. "A shock. You'll not worry, lad. Roger is my heir. But you'll never want."

Johnnie flushed. "I had not thought of that, sir. I am too happy that he will be coming home. He *will* be coming home?"

"In time."

"Believe me, sir, I am too happy. Will he like me, do you suppose?"

"Like you? He will love you, Johnnie." Haggard released him, gazed up at his house. "Roger is alive and well," he shouted, unable to control himself any longer. "Roger is alive and well." He looked at his daughter, still framed in the doorway, watched her face break into a smile and then a laugh. He could not ever remember having seen Alice laugh before.

"He *will* love you," Alice said. "Roger . . . why, he was the kindest, bravest, nicest boy I ever knew. You will never have met anyone like Roger. Why, he is like Father, with none of Father's sternness. You will love him, Johnnie."

"I have no doubt of it."

She studied his face. "But you do not like the idea of giving up the major part of your inheritance."

He caught her hands. "That has naught to do with it at all. My inheritance means nothing to me, Alice. Really and truly. I am just delighted to be able to give up the responsibility, of being the Haggard heir. Can you understand that?"

She frowned at him. "I suppose I can."

"It means I am so much more *free*, to do anything I wish, without the fear of disgracing the name."

Her frown deepened. "What an odd thing to say. How could you disgrace the name?"

"Well . . . you know I really have not been very keen on opposing Father. I felt it was disloyal for his only son, his heir . . ."

"You mean you'll do something about the factory?" Her grip tightened. "Oh, say that you will."

"Well . . ." He flushed. "It's just about complete."

"The machines aren't here yet. Father could still change his mind."

"I doubt it. And hadn't we better wait for Roger? He is the one Father is more likely to listen to."

"Oh, you . . ." She threw his hands away from her. "You're afraid of him."

"Well . . . aren't you?"

"No. I've told him what I think. But he just ignores me."

"And don't you suppose he'd ignore me? Believe me, Ally, Roger is your best bet."

"When he comes home," she said, and wandered to the window. But Roger. *He* had never been afraid to oppose Father. And now there could be no question that Father would listen to him. Roger.

John Haggard stood up. "You'll see that I'm right. And I promise you this: whatever Roger decides to do, he will have my complete support. Now I must be off."

She turned back to him. "Where?" The frown was back. "You aren't doing anything stupid, are you, Johnnie?"

He gave a guilty laugh. "Of course I'm not. I'm just enjoying riding over the countryside. In another week I'll be at Cambridge again. What a bore. I really am enjoying being free." He blew her a kiss, ran down the stairs, called for his horse, swung into the saddle and sent it racing away, through the cut in the hills, past the mine and around the looming shell of the factory, over the following hills and into the woods beyond. Free, he thought. Free of the burden of being the next Haggard. Free to do as I wish, think what I wish, feel what I wish. Free to love whomever I wish.

He pulled rein, slowed his horse to a walk. There was the nub of the matter. *Whomever* I wish. *Whatever* I wish. Supposing I know what I wish. Supposing I dared to think about it.

Supposing I could forget the gentle caress of Byron's fingers sliding over my cock. My God, he thought. I dare not. Sodomy carries the death penalty. But girls . . . he knew only the housemaid amidst the dirty plates. Then what of Meg Bold? A peasant girl, and therefore not one to see through his weaknesses, to do anything more than accept him. In what guise? She had given every indication of liking him, revealed nothing but pleasure whenever he called, which was as often as he could escape the hall. And Emma and Harry Bold had equally become used to his visits, and appeared to welcome them. But no doubt, encouraged by Alice, they counted him a firm and valuable ally in the looming crisis that they could see ahead. What would their reaction be? And again, to what? Because he *was* considering the girl in the guise of a wife. He *had* to marry beneath himself, someone who would submit and submit and submit. And besides, she was such a lovely girl. She actually made him *want* her, and he had never felt that about any girl before. The future, should he let her go, was unthinkable.

Then what of Father? That was something he had never considered, because marriage to Meg Bold had never seemed a possibility before. But Father was at last happy. Why, he had never seen him so happy, or seen him happy at all. And a happy father might well be a father who would welcome a reconciliation. So Meg was the daughter of a workingman. Her mother had been good enough for Father's bed.

But he had never married her. John Haggard plucked at his lip as his horse made its way into the open country beyond the trees. That had been his greatest crime. At least, according to Alice. And his greatest mistake. Had he married Emma, he would have lived a happy life. And I would never have been born, John thought. Or at least, I would be Emma's son, and Meg would be my sister. Oh, happy thought, that Father had been a *bad* man. And it would all turn out for the best. He had no doubts about that.

The cottage was in front of him; the roses still bloomed against the walls. He would always remember this cottage with roses blooming against the walls. And Meg was standing in the doorway to wave at him.

"Is your mother at home?"

"Why, of course, Mr. Haggard. Have you come to see her, then?" Meg flushed as she spoke, aware of her forwardness. John Haggard gave her a smile and chucked her under the chin.

"I have come to see you. But I've some news I know your mother would like."

Meg regarded him for some moments, a half-smile on her face; then she looked over her shoulder. "Mama. Mr. Haggard is here."

Emma Bold came outside, drying her hands on her apron. "And welcome you are, Mr. Haggard."

"I have great news, Mistress Bold. My brother Roger has been found."

She stared at him, a frown slowly gathering between her eyes. "Roger? You mean he is alive?"

"Indeed. He is in the army, in Spain. He has been in the army for the past seventeen years. He is all of a hero."

"Well, glory be," Emma said. "He was a fine boy. Your father must be very happy."

"I have never seen him so happy," John Haggard confessed.

"This is a great day," Emma said. "You'll come inside, Mr. Haggard, and take a bowl of broth with us."

"I . . ." John Haggard made a great fuss of securing his horse's rein to the ring in the wall. "It is such a lovely day, Mistress Bold, I thought I would take a walk."

Emma frowned at him. "You rode twelve miles to take a walk, Mr. Haggard?"

"Well . . . I thought Miss Meg might like to walk with me."

Emma's mouth opened and then closed again. She looked at her daughter.

"Could I, Mama? I'd like that. Really I would."

Emma looked from one to the next. She was flushed and seemed uncertain what to do. John Haggard could almost read her thoughts. The innate suspicion of the intentions of a gentleman added to the understanding that here was a possible crisis added to the consideration that the girl was almost his sister—completely set off by the fact that he was John Haggard.

"Please, Mama," Meg said.

"Mind you're not long," Emma said, and went inside.

"She likes you. I know she likes you, because she told me so," Meg said.

"She fears I may be too like my father." He held the gate for her. Her arm brushed his as she went through, and he inhaled her scent. No perfume for a tinker's daughter. But a magnificent freshness.

"And are you too like your father, Mr. Haggard?"

John Haggard walked at her side. "I'd like it very much if you'd call me John."

"You're Mr. Haggard," she pointed out very seriously. "One day you'll be squire."

"No. Don't you see? I can't be squire, now. I thought I had to be before. Everything I did had to be subject to that consideration. But now that Roger will be coming home, why, I'm nothing. I'm just a younger son. I'll probably be sent into the army or the navy. Or the church."

When she frowned, she looked just like her mother. "I wouldn't like to think of you in the army, Mr. Haggard."

"John."

She licked her lips, looked over her shoulder to make sure the cottage had disappeared. "John."

"I don't think I'm really cut out for the church." Their knuckles brushed against each other, and he allowed his fingers to extend. A moment later hers caught in his. Her hand was dry and strong. "I know. I could ask Father to find me a position in the city. Or better yet, of course, he can make me manager of the plantation in Barbados. There it is."

"Barbados?" she cried.

"Wouldn't you like to visit Barbados?"

"Me, Mr. Haggard?"

"John. Yes. You see . . ." His turn to look over his shoulder and make sure they were alone. They had walked down the road from the cottage gate, and there was a stand of trees between them and the house. He stopped, and when she turned to face him, he took her other hand as well. "Meg . . ." How solemn was her face, her eyes. And he knew he was flushing. "Do you know, I've thought of no one but you since I met you, back at Easter? All last term, I could do no work for thinking of you. And since seeing you again this summer, oh, Meg, oh, dear, dear, Meg, I have dreamed of you every night."

"Oh, Mr. Haggard," she said, flushing in turn and trying to free herself.

"Meg," he said, tightening his grip and bringing her closer. "I love you, Meg."

"Oh, Mr. Haggard." But she had stopped pulling.

"I want you to marry me."

"*Marry* you?" Her consternation was complete.

"Because we can marry, don't you see? I'd never lie to you, Meg. When I was Father's heir, well, I had to think of him, of the estate, I had to be prepared to marry as he chose, or certainly as he thought best. But now that Roger is coming home, why, I'm no longer important. I can do what I like with my life. And I can marry whomever I like. Whomever I love."

"Marry you," she muttered. "Marry Mr. Haggard."

"John."

"Oh, Mr. Haggard," she said, and came against him. Her head was tilted back and her mouth was open. He kissed it, felt her body against his, moving, her hands sliding round his shoulders, and realized that here, for the very first time in his life, was a girl asking him to take her. She was his, all his, to do with as he wished.

He held her arms, gently pushed her away from him. Her mouth was still open, her eyes closed, but they now opened in turn, in alarm. It could not be explained to her. He could not tell her about the girl on Byron's dining table, the whore at Cambridge. She would hardly appreciate that, and she might not understand, in the first flush of love, that he did not *want* to have her until they were married, that he wanted nothing sordid or amoral to enter their lives at all.

"You have made me so happy, Meg," he said. "The happiest man in all the world."

She closed her eyes again. "I love you, Mr. Haggard," she said, as if practicing.

"John," he reminded her.

"John."

"But you must listen, Meg. I have to go away to Cambridge the day after tomorrow. I won't be back until Christmas."

Her eyes opened again.

"But I will be back then. Only, you mustn't tell a soul about us, not now. Do you understand?"

Her chin moved up and down, but clearly she didn't.

"Because *they* might not understand, might not wish us to. Even your mother. You must leave the telling to me. When the time is right. Will you do that?"

"Oh, yes, Mr. Haggard. Oh, yes."

"John," he said, and kissed her again.

"Well?" Haggard barked. "Well?"

MacGuinness stood on the far side of the desk, shifted from one foot to the other. "They have been delayed, Mr. Haggard. Nothing more than that. Apparently they are delicate machines, and can easily go adrift. But they are on their way, I promise you. They will be here by the end of the month."

"By Christmas, you mean," Haggard grumbled. "And why are there no letters?"

"Now, that I couldn't say, Mr. Haggard."

"Well, then, is there news from Spain at all?"

"Only that the Duke of Wellington continues to retreat, sir. They are saying he intends to pull back all the way to Lisbon."

"Bah. The fellow does not seem to know what he is about. Unless he means to evacuate the army to England. Do you suppose he means that, MacGuinness?"

His eagerness was pathetic, MacGuinness thought. "I doubt that, Mr. Haggard. The country would not stand for it."

"I suppose you're right." Haggard leaned back. "What of that other matter?"

"Well, sir . . ." MacGuinness twisted his hat in his hands.

"I've lived fifty-six years, MacGuinness. Don't come over coy with me. It's a girl."

"Well, yes, sir, I imagine it is. Mr. John has been riding over in the direction of Plowding."

"Go on."

"Well, sir, one of my people followed him, as you instructed, on his last visit there, and we discovered that he went visiting at a cottage outside the village."

"Ha. The young devil. And here was I beginning to wonder if he'd any spunk at all." Then Haggard frowned. "A cottage, you say, outside the village proper? Does not sound like a whorehouse to me."

"It is not a whorehouse, sir."

"A yeoman? And he'd let his daughter mess with a member of the gentry?"

MacGuinness preferred not to comment, but he was back to twisting his hat again.

"You'll find out his name, MacGuinness. And continue to keep an eye on it, when Mr. John comes back."

MacGuinness licked his lips. "I have found out his name, Mr. Haggard. 'Tis Bold."

Haggard's frown deepened. "Bold? Bold. I have heard that before, I'll swear."

"Indeed you have, Mr. Haggard. It was in support of Harry Bold that Mr. Roger broke my head on your wedding night."

"By Christ." Haggard sat up straight. "Harry Bold. Great God in heaven. Sitting on my very doorstep, seducing my son. By God. How long?"

"Several years now, sir. He has given up tinkering, and spins cotton instead."

"He does, does he? We'll soon see about that." Haggard glanced at his steward, looked down at the desk again. "Is he . . . I mean . . ."

"He is married now, Mr. Haggard. But his wife is Miss Dearborn."

Haggard leaned back again. "Hum," he said. "Hum. Very good, MacGuinness. You've done well. Oh, aye. Now, fetch me those looms."

Emma. Emma Dearborn. Emma Bold. Emma of the glowing red hair and the twinkling eyes. Emma of the suspicious look and the sudden warmth. Emma, Emma, Emma. Why, she would be . . . forty-five years old. Emma, at forty-five. And several times a mother. She would be fat and flouncing, and undoubtedly reverted to her common ancestry. He doubted she'd remember which fork to use.

Then why was he here? Why was he behaving like a lovesick boy? Johnnie had apparently at least ridden up to the cottage without hesitation, while his father lurked in the trees and gazed at the little house with a pounding heart. But Emma. After all his years of loneliness, Emma. He had never been lonely with her at his side. He need never be lonely again. Undoubtedly he had made a mistake when he quarreled with her. Mistake? It had been a catastrophe. Save for Johnnie. But might not Emma have produced a Johnnie? He could not believe there was a great deal of Alison in the boy. He was too open, too good-humored. Alison would suggest a frightful flaw waiting to be exposed, and he had seen none of that. There were no flaws in Emma.

But she was married. Or said she was. To an itinerant named Bold. There was no problem, surely. It really was very doubtful whether it had been a legal marriage. Then *why* was he lurking here in the trees? Well, for one thing, Bold would undoubtedly not have forgotten who had sent the men to expel him from Derleth eighteen years before. And he had no means of telling whose side Emma would take. But that was stuff and nonsense. Would she seriously side with Harry Bold, when all of her future demanded she return to Derleth?

He watched the door of the cottage open, saw two men come out. A man and a boy, he realized, and the boy had reddish-brown hair. Emma's son, just as the bearded man had to be Harry Bold. It was something of a surprise for him to realize that he had never actually seen the fellow before. But they were going out, carrying a fowling piece and a net. Poaching, by God. Not on his land, at the least.

The pair disappeared into the trees behind the house. They'd not be back for some time. It seemed to Haggard that fate was conspiring to make his task easy. But fate would always have known that he was meant for Emma, as fate had sent him the girl in the first place. His heart began to pound, and he wiped a trace of sweat from his neck and forehead. John Haggard, squire of Derleth, nervous at the thought of visiting a tinker's wife. But suppose she was, after all, fat and blowsy? It was most likely.

He kicked his horse, walked it out from the trees, slowly approached the cottage. The sound of the hooves was deadened in the soft earth—there had been recent rain—but his approach had either been heard or seen; he watched a window open and then close again. He turned in through the gate, listened to the clucking of chickens from behind the house. There was no dog. He dismounted at the front door, and it opened. His heartbeat quickened still further as he gazed at the girl. Emma, reborn. Johnnie's doxy. Frowning at him as she took in the richness of his coat and boots, of his horse furniture.

"Sir?"

Haggard raised his beaver. To a tinker's daughter, ye Gods; he might as well be in France. "Is your mother at home?"

"Oh, yes, sir." Meg backed away from the door, leaving it open. "Ma," she cried. "Ma, there's a gentleman at the door."

"A gentleman?" Emma hurried into sight, drying her hands on her apron. Emma. Had she changed at all? She wore a cap, and he could not see her hair. She had thickened somewhat at the thigh—but then, so had he. But her face had not changed in the slightest; there had been crow's-feet at the corners of her eyes before they had left Barbados. "Sir?" she inquired, and frowned as she came closer. He remembered that she had always been a trifle nearsighted. She reached the door and stopped, and gave a little gasp. The color drained from her face, and then returned again in a rush.

"I happened to be passing," Haggard lied.

She licked her lips. "You knew where I lived?"

"Of course." Another lie. But was not the entire purpose of this visit a lie? How lovely she looked. How utterly everything he wanted in a woman.

She looked from right to left, patently uncertain what to do next.

"May I come in?" Haggard asked.

She stood aside. Her hands were back at her apron, twining themselves together. Meg continued to stand at the inner door, looking equally embarrassed. Haggard ducked his head and entered the cottage, closing the door behind him and looking around, at the hand looms, at the four straight chairs and the kitchen table which composed the furniture, at the curtains, worn but clean enough, as indeed were the walls and ceiling, at the glowing fire in the grate, the pot of rabbit stew hanging from the spit, the mushrooms and the turnips placed among the coal.

" 'Tis not what you are used to, Mr. Haggard." Emma seemed to be recovering.

"It looks comfortable enough. I'd like a word in private."

Emma glanced at the door.

"I've work in the yard," Meg said, and closed it behind her.

"She's a good girl," Haggard said. "And a pretty one. She takes after her mother."

Emma slowly lowered herself into one of the chairs. "Won't you sit down?"

Haggard sat down. "You'll have heard about Roger?"

She nodded. "I am very happy for you, Mr. Haggard."

His turn to lick his lips. "I did not know Charlie would die. He was a difficult child. Like his sister." He attempted a smile. "I do not suppose she is difficult, with you."

"No," Emma said.

Haggard got up, walked to the window, walked back again to his chair. "I wronged you, Emma. I wronged you more than any man can ever have wronged a woman. I wronged you from the moment I saw you." He paused; Emma continued to gaze at him. Her color had settled down, as had her breathing. He went toward her, picked up her left hand; she wore a thin gold band. "In a church?"

"In a church, Mr. Haggard."

He released her hand, sat down again.

"I knew my mistake almost the moment it happened." He shrugged. "But what would you? Pride, I suppose." His head came up. "You don't believe me."

"I had never supposed to hear John Haggard apologizing to anyone."

"Hum. Pride seems less important as one grows older. Emma . . ."

"I am married, Mr. Haggard. To a man I respect. A man who loves me."

"And do you love him?"

"I am married to him, Mr. Haggard. He is the father of my children."

"Am I not the father of Alice? And you could bring your children, Emma. I'd treat them as my own."

"Bring them where?"

"Emma . . ."

"No." She shook her head to emphasize her words. "No, no. no."

"Emma." He left his chair, knelt beside hers, took her hands. "You'll not refuse me."

"No one ever refuses John Haggard," she said with an attempt at humor.

"True." He began to draw her forward slowly. "I have never knelt to any woman before, either." Not true. He had knelt to Alison Brand. "I love you, Emma. I have always loved you. Christ, I have realized how much I loved you, day after day after day. Emma . . ." Her face was close enough to reach with his lips. She allowed him that; her own were parted. Then she jerked herself away from him.

"No."

"Emma." He'd not release her hands. "I'd marry you, Emma."

She pulled her head back, stared at him.

"I swear it. Emma Haggard. Isn't that what you've always wanted? Lady of Derleth. Can you do better than that?"

She tugged on her hands. "You buy, Mr. Haggard. Everything. Just as you bought me once."

"I've a mind to make that up to you. I thought you understood that."

"In your own fashion, Mr. Haggard."

"And that's not good enough for you."

Pink spots gathered in her cheeks. She had had enough experience of the suddenness of his anger, could discern the signs easily enough. "Harry Bold took me in, Mr. Haggard. When I was right to die, just as Annie Kent died in the cold and the snow, he took me in. He treated me as a woman, where you never treated me as anything save a handful of flesh. I loved you, John Haggard. I loved you because I had never loved anyone else. I loved you because I didn't know how to love. I loved you because you showed me a world I'd only dreamed of, in bed and out of it. I was prepared to love you to the end of my days."

"And you love as your mind directs," Haggard said.

" 'Tis better than not to love at all."

He pushed himself to his feet. "You'd starve, here in this cottage."

"We survive, Mr. Haggard."

"For how long, I wonder."

She smiled. "You're thinking of your factory? Harry can always go back to tinkering. I enjoyed the life, Mr. Haggard. I like new faces and new places."

He stared at her, brow a mass of furrows. Then he pointed at her. "You'll not forget I'm a magistrate in these parts, Emma. That husband of yours, and that son, are away poaching now. Don't lie to me."

"I'd not lie to you, Mr. Haggard. I don't know what they're doing at this moment. But my Harry owns this land. He paid for it, and he built this cottage with his own hands." She stood up in turn. "You'll leave it, if you please."

He stared at her in consternation. He had never been so addressed in his life.

"Meg," Emma called. "You'll show Mr. Haggard to his horse."

"You think to defy me?" Haggard demanded.

"No, Mr. Haggard. No one can do that. I am asking you to leave my house, as we have nothing more to say to each other, and I have a deal to do. I must spin all the cotton I can, before you take that right away from us."

Haggard gazed at her in impotent anger, then at the girl, who had crossed the room and now held the front door for him. He turned and brushed past her, swung into the saddle, kicked his horse toward the meadow. Too late he remembered that he had not discussed Johnnie's visits.

As if it could have made any difference. Emma had changed. She was in a mood to defy him. The prospect of her daughter enjoying his son would to her be an enormous victory. It would merely have humiliated him further.

His anger grew every time he thought about it, and he thought about it every day. He had been a fool to attempt to turn back the clock, and Emma, mean and vengeful Emma, intended to make sure he suffered for every wrong he had done her, real and imagined. He had apologized to her. He could do no more, and she had herself recognized how much that must have cost him. Just as she had recognized what a triumph she had achieved.

She would be crushed, he thought, as he watched the machines being unloaded from their wagons, watched them being set up inside the factory. She would come to him and pray for a crust of bread before he was finished with her. But

not so long as she was able to bewitch Johnnie. Because very
obviously she had, just as she had bewitched him all those
years ago. That problem had to be solved, or Johnnie would
always stand between the two families, rejecting the one and
protecting the other. He was a damnably quixotic youth.

And a damnably independent one, as well. To forbid him
ever to see Margaret Bold again would be a waste of time,
and would cause another of those family rows which distressed him so deeply. There was no doubt whose side Alice
would take, nor did he really suppose there was much doubt
whose side Roger would undoubtedly take, unless he had
changed beyond recognition.

Roger! The problem had to be solved before Roger came
home.

He had no legal jurisdiction over the Bolds, there was the
trouble, as long as they remained in Plowding. But there
would be no point in exercising such jurisdiction even if he
possessed it; that would only alienate Johnnie the more. It
needed to be something personal, something which would disgust Johnnie and turn him away from the Bold family.

Haggard paced the floor of his office, pulling at his chin.
Nor would it be any use harming Emma herself. That would
hardly do more than increase Johnnie's sympathy for her.
The girl Margaret had to be proved a whore. Would that
make any difference to Johnnie? It occurred to Haggard
that he did not know his son well enough.

But he was a young man of birth and position, who fool-
ishly imagined himself to be in love with a working girl.
There was no official betrothal to be thought of, no family
honor involved in marriage, come what may. It was an infat-
uation, which, suitably exposed to the realities of life, had to
die. So, then, could Johnnie really love a girl who had been
raped? There was the answer.

He sat behind his desk, stared at the door. Are you a bad
man, John Haggard? It was not a question he had asked himself for a very long time. But if I am a bad man, he thought
angrily, it is circumstances have made me so. And I will defend my family to the end. In any event, Margaret Bold was
a tinker's daughter. Really, there was very little difference between her and a Negro slave. She deserved to be punished for
seducing a boy who was her better; she was fortunate he was
not in a position to have her flogged. But *could* Johnnie love
a girl who had been raped? If only he could be sure. Then
consider the matter logically. The boy would hear about it,

from Emma and from a tearful Margaret. Would that not only kindle his sympathy, further increase his love? Further titillate him, as it was titillating himself at the thought of it. It was too simple a matter, to be titillated by rape, there was the problem. The disgust of it, the bestiality, did not enter the imagination.

Unless one had been a witness to it. Haggard sat up, slammed his fist on the desk. Because there was an added bonus: Margaret Bold would scarce fight. She might even acquiesce in the deed. Certainly she would beg for mercy, make herself a humiliated and repellent figure. While Johnnie would fight for her honor with all his strength, and defeated, watch her subjection with horror and disgust.

Fight with all of his strength. It would have to be carefully handled. But that was a detail.

And afterward? The disgust would remain. No doubt about that. It would of course be tempered by sympathy and by a sense of honor. He would be humiliated himself. Well, that was no bad thing; he was an arrogant puppy. It would also cause resentment. Haggard knew that of himself. He hated those who caused him to be humiliated, even if it was not their fault, even if they had suffered equally. Johnnie would hardly feel different. However great his sense of honor, it would be tempered by resentment. It was a question of which would gain the day.

But could it not be assisted? If at the very moment that Margaret Bold became an object of pitiful disgust to him, another, at least as lovely and with the added charm of being of his own class, were to suddenly appear . . . Haggard found himself smiling. Life was really a very simple matter when one had the means and the determination to make it so. The determination to tuck morality out of sight, when it was necessary to do so. The determination to be Haggard. It was as simple as that.

All that was needed was the girl. Alice? No, Alice had no friends, and even if she did, they would be too old. He needed to apply to one of Johnnie's friends. He remembered how enthusiastically the boy had talked about his week at Newstead. Well, Lord Byron and Mr. Hobhouse were away touring the Mediterranean. Skinner Matthews did not sound the sort of fellow to know anyone worthy of the name of Haggard. Francis Hodgson apparently knew no women at all. But Wedderburn Webster? Now, there was a likely prospect.

A man of the world. Johnnie had said so. And with it a gentleman.

Haggard rang the bell, sent for MacGuinness. "There is something we must do, MacGuinness," he said. "I wish you to order my carriage prepared. I am going to London."

MacGuinness concealed his surprise. "Very good, Mr. Haggard."

"And sit down," Haggard said.

This time MacGuinness's mouth opened in amazement. "Sir?"

"Close the door and sit down, MacGuinness," Haggard said. "I wish to discuss a very confidential matter."

It would be a cold winter. Even with a week to go to Christmas, the air was crisp and breath clouded before the nose, of horse as well as rider, while there had been a frost the previous night. As if cold mattered. John Haggard wanted to sing as he let his horse pick its way through the already leafless trees toward the meadow; no need to guide Constable; he had taken this way sufficiently often in the past.

Johnnie did not know how he had survived the Cambridge term. His every thought, every instinct, had been guiding him back to Derleth. He could not help but recall how George Byron had boasted that in three years he had spent only three terms actually in residence. "I had better things to do," he would say in that dry tone of his. But it was best not to think of George Byron, now somewhere in the Mediterranean. That was finished and done with. Only Meg mattered now. For the whole autumn he had done nothing but think of her, with determination at first, with delighted anticipation at the end. She would be his, he would be hers, and stupid, irrelevant, obscene desires would be forgotten. The temptation to flee his tutors and return early had been overwhelming. But it would be senseless to anger Father at this juncture. It was Father's mood he had waited upon, and not in vain. Never had the old man been in a better humor than at the commencement of this holiday. The letter from Roger, the very news that he was alive and would eventually be coming home had made him a changed man. Too much so, in fact, as he had insisted upon having a house party for Christmas. Such a thing had never happened in Derleth before, and the news had left Alice staring at her father in openmouthed disbelief.

And what a party. Wedderburn Webster, of all people. Johnnie supposed he should be grateful, as Father had obviously searched for one of his Cambridge friends. But Wedderburn, the greatest bore on earth? Why not Skinner? And Wedderburn was bringing a female friend, and her sister. "We shall have a young people's Christmas," Father had shouted, slapping him on the shoulder as was his habit.

And John had done his best to smile and look pleased. He did not want anyone cluttering up the place at Christmas, especially two young women who would have to be entertained. On the other hand, he would never find Father in a better mood. He had almost been inclined to broach the matter there and then, but had decided to put it off. It was an immense step, and he would need all his resolution to carry it through. Besides, it was necessary first to see Meg again, to hold her in his arms again, to know it was no dream, that she loved him as much as he loved her. It would only be a few seconds now.

He walked Constable up the path, dismounted, gazed at her, framed in the doorway, regarding him with a mixture of delight and disbelief.

"Mr. Haggard?" Her voice was hardly more than a whisper.

"Meg." He reached for her hands, but she drew away, backed into the house. "Mr. Haggard . . ." she said again, this time speaking more loudly.

Instantly her mother was at her shoulder, peering at him.

"I am no ghost," John Haggard said, now equally bewildered.

Emma Bold glanced at her daughter, then opened the door wider. "You'd best come in out of the cold."

Haggard ducked his head, entered the little room. "I doubted I was welcome," he said with a smile. "Or had you heard I was dead?"

Emma licked her lips. "I'm sure Mr. Haggard would appreciate a cup of cider, Margaret," she said.

John Haggard's turn to glance from one to the other. "There has been some catastrophe," he said. "Where is Mr. Bold? Where is Tim?"

"They are out," Emma said. "And there has been no catastrophe, Mr. Haggard. It is just that we did not expect you here."

He frowned at Meg. "You knew I was returning for my holiday?"

"Yes, but . . ." She glanced at her mother.

"Your father was here," Emma explained.

"Father?" Johnnie sat down, took the cup of yellow liquid, sipped. "Here? How did he know where you were?"

Emma shrugged. "He has his people everywhere. We do not hide."

"But . . . what did he want?"

Emma flushed, sat down in turn. "He wished me to return to the hall."

"He asked Mama to marry him," Margaret said.

"To . . . My God. But you are already married."

"That were hardly a problem to John Haggard," Emma said.

"But . . . you refused him?"

"Indeed I did."

"And he was very angry," Margaret said.

"And you thought he would stop me coming to see you? Well, he could not do that in any event. But he does not know of my visits."

"Are you sure?"

"Quite sure." He frowned thoughtfully. This afternoon, for instance, he had thought he heard hooves, and thought indeed he had seen some horsemen in the trees behind him. He had been grateful for the loaded pistol in his pocket; the countryside around Derleth was lonely enough, even if footpads and highwaymen were not generally found there. But no footpads would dare assault John Haggard. Father would tear the entire county apart to find them. "Quite sure," he said again.

"Still," Emma said, "he will find out eventually, Mr. Haggard. You'd not wish to quarrel with your father. There has been too much of that."

Haggard turned his gaze on Margaret. "You wish me to stop coming?"

"There has been bitterness enough," Emma insisted.

"There'll be no more bitterness, I promise you," Johnnie said. "So he was angry. Well, no man likes being turned down, Mistress Bold. And it goes to show that he must still be very fond of you, must regret most heartily what happened all those years ago. Oh, don't suppose I am criticizing your refusal, I am glad you did. He thinks he can snap his fingers and everyone does exactly as he wishes. It does him good to learn, from time to time, that not *everyone* is so compliant. And he has got over it, I do promise you. He is in the best of humors. So much so, that, well . . ." He hesitated, felt his cheeks burning, glanced at Meg. Who flushed in turn and bit her lip.

Emma commenced to frown. "You have something to tell me?"

"Something splendid. Mistress Bold. Something which makes me so happy you did not accept Father's proposal. Mistress Bold, I would like to marry Meg."

"To . . ." Emma turned to stare at her daughter.

"I . . . It was to be a secret," Margaret protested.

"For as long as was necessary. It is no longer necessary. Father really is a new man since he learned Roger will be coming home. I mean to approach him this Christmas, secure his consent—"

"Do you really suppose he will agree to your marrying my daughter?" Emma seemed dazed.

"He will. And if he will not, then I will marry without his consent, the moment I am twenty-one. I will never be penniless, you know. By the terms of the marriage settlement with my mother, Father promised me an income of two hundred pounds a year from my eighteenth birthday. It is a legal matter."

Emma gazed at Margaret. "And what have you got to say about this?"

"Why, Mama . . . I would be honored to be Johnnie's wife."

"Do you love him?"

"Oh, yes, Mama. I do love him."

Emma sighed. "Does that mean . . ."

"Oh, no, Mama."

"I love Margaret, Mistress Bold," Johnnie protested. "I would never harm her."

Emma's gaze turned to him for some seconds. She seemed able to see past his eyes and into his brain, and he remained looking at her with an effort. "You will have to ask Mr. Bold," she said at last.

"I intend to. I but wished to secure your permission first."

Emma drew the back of her hand across her brow. "I will give it, but not at the cost of an estrangement between you and your father. That were to create too many evils."

"You may leave Father to me," Johnnie promised. "I but wished to be sure that our proposal met with your approbation. Now you have made me the happiest man in the world. Why, Mistress Bold, I see Father and yourself again being friends, even now."

"I will say amen to that, Mr. Haggard. And now . . ." She glanced at her daughter.

"Perhaps you would permit Meg to take a walk with me."

"Is it not very cold?"

"The sun is shining, and it is all but warm. I do promise you. And besides . . ." He winked at her. "You may be sure we will not stay out too long."

"I'll fetch my shawl." Meg hurried for the inner room.

Emma sighed, got up. "You do understand what you are about, Mr. Haggard? Meg has had no such advantages as yourself. She knows naught of luxury. Why, the four of us sleep in a single room. As for fine clothes and rich foods . . ."

"Did you know of them when you met my father?"

Emma nodded. "I had observed them, Mr. Haggard, as a ladies' maid."

"And you will at the least have told Meg that these things exist."

"I suppose I have."

"Therefore your positions are analogous. I do not observe that a sudden elevation to prosperity affected your character in any way."

"I was thinking of *your* character, Mr. Haggard. Of your friends. Of your position. Your father was ostracized, both in Barbados and here in England, because of me. That is why I can never find it in my heart to hate him, for all the wrong he has since done me. I cannot help but believe that it was those years of isolation embittered his character."

"My friends are not Father's, Mistress Bold. Believe me." He smiled at Meg as she came out of the inner room wearing her shawl. How beautiful she was going to look, he thought, in satins and furs, with rings on her fingers, with her hair properly dressed, and smelling of perfume. How beautiful.

He held her hand as they walked down the path. "I think your mother is happy about it," he said. "About us."

"There is Papa to be considered," she pointed out.

"He will be happy too. I promise you."

"And are you happy, Mr. Haggard?"

"Is that any way to address your future husband?"

"I could not believe it was going to happen. I cannot believe it is ever going to happen."

"Try saying it. Margaret Haggard."

She licked her lips. "Margaret . . . Haggard."

"That was not very difficult. Margaret Haggard, Margaret Haggard. Margaret Haggard. Meg Haggard. It is a good name."

"Meg Haggard," she said, and she felt her fingers tighten on his.

"So, are you happy, Meg, soon to be Haggard?"

"I think I am dreaming. But it is a happy dream. A very happy dream."

He stopped, and she stopped also. They had turned the corner and were out of sight of the cottage. To their left was only the wood, and to their right the empty pasture across which he had ridden. Gently he brought her to him, watched her face turn up and her eyes close. She still could not believe it was to happen, could not look him in the face. He brushed her lips with his own, allowed his tongue to push between, touched her own, shyly emerging. Once again he knew a tremendous sense of sexual desire, compounded by the knowledge that she might well consent . . . and once again he rejected it. Sex with Meg could only be enjoyed in their own bed, after they were married. She was no giggling, squealing servant girl to be laid on a table, or on the ground either. She was the future Mrs. John Haggard.

He released her, and her eyes opened.

"I love you, Meg."

"I love you, John Haggard," she said. "Tell me about Derleth. Tell me about the hall. Tell me about Cambridge and London. Oh, tell me about it."

They walked hand in hand, while John told her about every aspect of his life he could think of. He told of Byron and Hobhouse, of playing cricket at Harrow, he gave her a minute description of Derleth Hall, he told her what he could remember of Roger, as told *him* by Alice. "You will adore Roger," he told her. "I am going to . . ."

"I adore *you*," she pointed out, and squeezed his fingers. "I think it is time for us to be going home."

He hadn't realized they had walked so far. Now he found the afternoon was drawing in. It was going to be a cold ride back to Derleth. They turned, still holding hands, and were alerted by the cracking of a twig in the trees. Meg stopped, glanced from left to right.

"Poachers," John said.

He released Meg and thrust his hand into his pocket to find his pistol, gazed at five men, roughly dressed but clearly dismounted horsemen, from their boots, and every one with a handkerchief tied round the lower part of his face, leaving only the narrowest of strips visible beneath the pulled-down brims of their flat hats.

"Oh, God," Meg whispered. "Oh, Mr. Haggard."

John Haggard licked his lips. His throat had suddenly gone quite dry, and he was aware of a great void in his belly. Think, he told himself desperately. I am John Haggard. They'll not touch John Haggard. Besides, I have a pistol, and they have only cudgels. But if I draw the pistol, and miss, they will beat me up. Five men. He realized with a start of utter horror that he was afraid of them.

But they'd not dare harm John Haggard.

He stepped away from the girl. "You'll leave," he said. But his voice trembled. "I am John Haggard. My father is squire of Derleth. He'll hang the lot of you." But the last sentence barely escaped his lips. He glanced to his left, watched Meg Bold slowly backing away from him, her face a picture of disbelieving consternation.

The men came closer, made no reply. Their silence was the most terrifying thing about them.

"Run, Meg," John Haggard shouted, and drew his pistol. But before he could level it, a cudgel tapped him on the wrist, and he gave a shout of pain and watched the pistol hit the dust. "Run, Meg," he shouted again. Desperately he swung his left hand, but that was caught in turn and twisted behind his back to join its fellow; he found himself on his knees, weeping tears of anger and shame. His hat had come off and his hair was flopping across his face. His wrists were being tied together with a length of rope.

He gazed at Meg. She had covered no more than fifty yards, hampered by her gown and her shawl, before the first man had caught up with her. Now she too was on her knees, her red hair tumbling past her shoulders, gasping for breath.

He was forced forward, his feet stumbling over the uneven ground.

"She's a lady," he gasped. "She's my fiancée. You'll touch her at your peril."

Meg had regained her breath. "Help me, Mr. Haggard. Help me." Her voice rose to a screech.

Haggard attempted to step forward, had his shoulders grasped by the man behind him, iron fingers biting most painfully into his flesh.

"Help me," Meg Bold screamed, her voice echoing into the empty trees. For now she was on her back. John Haggard blinked away the tears, saw the men holding her wrists and ankles, the other man kneeling between, turning up her skirt and her shift. He saw the girl's head twisting left and right, grinding her hair into the leaves, saw a leaf getting into her mouth and being expelled again by the rush of air, listened to another terrified scream hurl itself at the sky, watched the long, slender white legs being uncovered, the pale thatched groin, the heaving belly, listened to the laughter of the men, the obscene remarks, caught a glimpse of white backside as the first man released his breeches, lost sight of Meg save for kicking boots, heard her next scream fade in a gurgle of breathless horror, watched the man humping up and down, hands beneath her now, fingers lodged behind her buttocks, felt his own erection mingling with the horror and the fear cascading down from his chest, gasped himself as the man lay still, closed his eyes and opened them again as the man pushed himself up and he could see her again, the white flesh now discolored red with the weight which had lain on it. He could see no blood, as she had sunk even farther into the leaves, but there would be blood.

And now another man had taken the place of the first, and the slender legs were again kicking. But only for a few seconds; then they lay still. She was exhausted, and each man was fresh. He had to stand there and watch while four of them took their turns, while Meg's body became more and more stained with leaves and damp earth, while her very last struggle ebbed and she stared at the trees above her, even her tears dried.

The men were laughing as they came toward him. Once again John Haggard's belly rolled with fear, and he gave a great jerk, and to his utter surprise his hands came free, swinging round to the front as fists. The approaching men seemed to hesitate.

He looked from right to left, at the men, at the girl still lying motionless on the ground. His stomach rebelled and he wanted to be sick, and to be away, anywhere but here, anything but to be beaten by these louts. He gasped for breath, turned, expecting to be caught by the man behind him, but the man had also stepped away from him, pursuing some game of his own, no doubt. There was nothing before him but the tree fringe and then the meadow. He leaped for it, tripped and fell to his knees, regained his feet, and rushed madly for the safety of the open spaces. Behind him he heard laughter, but he cared nothing for it, bounded up the slope to the top of the first shallow rise, fell there, panting, made himself get back to his knees and look over his shoulder, saw to his relief that they had stopped following him. They had, indeed, gone back to Meg, were kneeling around her body, and it seemed to him that the fifth man was taking his turn.

He chewed his lip, felt his heartbeat begin to slow. What to do? Somewhere over there in the wood lay his pistol. But they would see him if he attempted to return there. Well, then, what about help? He could call for help. Here? He needed a horse, and his horse was at Harry Bold's cottage. Harry Bold himself might have returned by now. Alice had told him how Harry and Roger had put to flight a dozen men once upon a time.

So, then, he should run to the Bolds' house and say: Help me, I have left your daughter in the wood, being raped by five men.

He sobbed, and began to cry again. Life had been so perfect. Now it was too horrible to be considered. If only he could snap his fingers and wake up yesterday morning . . . No, this morning would do, with today never to happen. What to do? What to do?

He stared at the wood, realized that the men were no longer gathered round Meg. He rose to his knees, then his feet, heart again clanging with alarm. But they were not coming after him, either. They had melted into the wood. They had gone.

But they might not have gone very far. He took a step or two toward the wood, stopped, tried to peer through the trees, thought he could hear distant hoofbeats. Coming toward him? His blood congealed in horror, and he turned to run, before he realized that the sound was in fact fading. Once again he faced the wood. Meg still lay there. Perhaps she was dead. Perhaps they had killed her. Oh, God. But then he was overtaken by the strangest of thoughts, that perhaps that would be for the best, that she should be dead, that she should not have this terrible memory to look back upon . . . that she never be there to accuse him.

His steps quickened. He almost ran into the wood, stopped as he reached the trees, and the girl sat up. Slowly she raised her hand, gazed at him. There were no tears.

"Meg . . ." He stumbled forward, and she got to her feet.

"Don't touch me," she said.

He hesitated, chewing his lip. "Those men . . . they would have beaten me up. They would have killed me."

"Well, they didn't," Meg said, her voice remarkably quiet after the screams of an hour earlier. "You didn't let them."

Slowly she smoothed her skirt, her fingers making tight patterns on the cloth.

"Meg . . ." He came closer.

"Don't touch me," she said again. "Don't ever touch me, John Haggard."

Haggard stood at the foot of the great staircase to welcome his guests. Alice was at his side. And Johnnie had not yet returned. But Haggard did not wish to consider Johnnie's return. Time enough for that when it happened. He could only pray the boy was not hurt. But MacGuinness was a good man.

"Mr. Haggard, I can't tell you what a pleasure this is." Wedderburn Webster bustled, shook hands with Haggard, bowed over Alice's hand, turned to introduce the two young women who had traveled with him. "Miss Frances Annesley, Miss Catherine Annesley. Miss Frances is my fiancée."

The young woman gave a becoming simper. She was undoubtedly very pretty, dark-haired and petite, far more so than her sister, Haggard was disappointed to note. But Miss Catherine was also a good-looking girl.

"The pleasure is mine," he said, kissing their fingers in turn. "Ours. I have no idea where Johnnie is. He usually returns before dusk. Alice?"

"I hear him now," Alice said. They gazed down the drive, watched the horseman, swaying in the saddle, tumbling up to them. His hat was gone, there was mud on his cloak, and he fell from the saddle rather than dismounted. "Johnnie?" Alice cried, running forward.

"Johnnie?" Haggard also started forward, while Webster and the two young ladies stared in dismay.

Johnnie Haggard gazed at his father in horror, glanced at Alice, and made for the doorway.

"John," Haggard said sharply, "your guests have arrived."

Johnnie seemed to recollect himself, stopped, looked at Webster as if he had never seen him before in his life.

"John?" Webster asked. "May I present my fiancée, Miss Frances Annesley, and her sister, Miss Catherine?"

Johnnie Haggard looked from one to the other of the girls. His face seemed to crumple, and he turned for the inner stairs.

"John," Haggard snapped. "Whatever is the matter?"

Johnnie Haggard hesitated, licked his lips, brushed hair

from his forehead. "A fall," he muttered. "I was thrown. You'll excuse me, Father. I . . . I must change my clothes."

He ran up the stairs.

"A fall from his horse," Haggard explained. "Alice, you'd best go after your brother and see that he is not hurt. I expect him down for supper. Mr. Webster, the Misses Annesley, come along with me, come along with me, and I will show you to your rooms." He ushered them into the downstairs hall, allowed them to gush their pleasure over the great staircase, beckoned Nugent to his side. "Tell MacGuinness I wish to see him right away," he said.

"Well, sir . . ." MacGuinness twisted his hat in his hands.

"He's not hurt?" Haggard demanded.

"No, sir. The fact is . . ."

"Come along, man, spit it out."

MacGuinness sighed. "Yes, sir. Well, sir, the fact is, Mr. John didn't fight at all."

"Eh?"

"He ran away, Mr. Haggard."

Haggard stared at him in utter disbelief. Johnnie, a coward? But the distress on MacGuinness' face was ample proof. John Haggard, running away and abandoning a girl with whom he supposed he was in love? He *could* not believe it. He dared not think about it. It was necessary to pretend it had not happened, at least for the moment. "What of the girl?" His voice was thick.

"Well, sir, as you supposed would happen, she lay on her back like a good whore and took what was given to her."

Haggard poured two glasses of port. "Take one," he said, and leaned back in his chair. "There's no risk any of them will be recognized?"

"No, sir. Peter tells me—"

Haggard held up his hand. "I don't want to know who they were, MacGuinness. No, no. That will not do at all. Because eventually Johnnie will tell me what happened, and I shall have to agree to punish these fellows. No, no. I must not know their names. Just be sure Johnnie never discovers them either."

"No chance of that, sir. I can trust these men. And so can you."

Haggard nodded. "They got paid enough. He sighed. "And they'll never . . ."

"They can't say anything about Master John, sir, because that would be to betray themselves."

"Aye," Haggard said. But they'll know, he thought, that my son is a coward. Alison's child. But not my only son, by God. Roger is alive. And Roger is coming home. Suddenly he felt almost human again. Roger was coming home. There were other things to be considered than Johnnie's cowardice: the future of Derleth, for a start. He smiled at MacGuinness. "What of that other matter?"

MacGuinness permitted himself a smile also. "There is no cause for worry there either, Mr. Haggard. There has been a lot of talk, and some of it fairly radical, too. Jemmy Lacey, as you may suppose, sir, once he had a few pints in his belly, swore he'd never work for the squire, and Maggie Lacey said the same. But that was tavern talk, Mr. Haggard. When I told them the wages we was paying, and when I told them you'd negotiated with the buyers and that the only cotton that was leaving Derleth in the future was what was spun on our looms, why, sir, they didn't grumble for long."

"What of Lacey?"

"Headed the lot, Mr. Haggard. He'll be at the factory, come Monday morning."

" 'Tis as I had expected," Haggard said. "You've done well, MacGuinness. Well. I'll not forget it." He waited for the door to close, slowly lowered his head into his hands.

"Oh, Johnnie, Johnnie." Alice Haggard sat on her brother's bed and massaged his shoulders with her fingertips. "It could have happened to anyone."

"But I ran away." Johnnie raised himself on his elbows, stared at her. "Anyone else would have fought them." There was no point in trying to keep what had happened a secret from Alice; she would discover the truth of the matter soon enough from the Bolds.

"It was your first . . . well, fight, I suppose," Alice said. "It wouldn't happen again."

"It will happen every time again." He threw himself on his back. "I am a coward. There is no need to pretend. My God, what Father would say . . ."

"No one is going to tell Father," Alice said.

"But what am I to *do*?" Johnnie begged.

Alice sucked her upper lip beneath her teeth. She was still haunted, often enough, by the memory of slaves screaming as they had been flogged. But the only physical violence she had experienced had been a whipping from her father. She found her brain could not cope with the idea of being held on the ground and raped by five men. What Meg must be feeling like did not bear consideration.

But then, she realized, her brain could not cope with the idea of *any* man touching her body. It was an aspect of life she had always rejected utterly. Meg was different. Meg was more down to earth. Meg might even recover from being raped, where Alice knew *she* would have curled up and died.

But that Harry Bold and Emma would ever forgive Johnnie for what had happened was impossible. No amount of wishful thinking could change that certainty.

"It's so *unfair*," she said. "For God's sake, I have ridden over those meadows and through those woods for five years, visiting Mama, and I've never been molested. I've never heard of anyone being molested. . . ."

"There were five of them," Johnnie moaned. "Alice, I must go away and never come back. Otherwise I am disgraced forever."

"Oh, stuff and nonsense," Alice said, and held him close again. Five men, appearing from nowhere, to rape a girl. Five men who had disregarded the implicit threat in their victim being a Haggard. They could not have known he would prove a coward. They could not have known he would not have ridden back to Derleth and called out his father's people, scoured the entire countryside as far as Nottingham, if need be, to catch them and hang them. They could not have known.

She found herself staring past her brother's head at the mirror on the wall, was surprised by the expression on her face. Five men who had appeared from nowhere to commit a dastardly crime, a crime which might specifically have been designed to end the possibility that Johnnie Haggard could ever marry Margaret Bold.

"The first thing you must do," she said, still holding him close, "is get up and get dressed and come down for supper."

"I could not," Johnnie moaned. "I could not face anyone. Certainly not Father."

Alice shook him. "You *will* face Father. And you'll be charming to Miss Annesley. No one, but no one, must even guess what might have happened. Do you understand?"

He raised his head to look at her. "But . . ."

"You must *pretend*, Johnnie. I will help you. And I will

help you regain your self-respect, too. Can't you see, there is only one thing you can do. You must track these men down."

He frowned at her, through his tears. "Track them down?"

"And avenge Meg. And yourself."

"Avenge Meg?" he asked stupidly. "Find the men? But how can I find the men? They'll be miles away by now. Perhaps Father—"

"You are not to tell Father," she said fiercely. "Nothing. Let him suppose it *was* a fall from a horse. He'd never forgive you for being a coward. This is something you must do by yourself. Those men beat you. You must get your own back. I will help you."

"You?" He sighed. "Anyway, how can I? I have to go back to Cambridge."

"I told you. I will help you. I have my friends in the village, and I have my friends in Plowding. Besides, the Bolds will help me. I will discover who those men were, and then I will deliver them to your justice." She squeezed his arm. "And next time you will not fail."

He stared at her. "Could I? Do you really suppose we could?"

"We shall," she promised him. "If you will but play your part. Now, go and dress yourself." She kissed him on the forehead, left the room, closed the door behind her, and leaned against it. And I shall find out who *paid* those men, she thought, and deliver him also to your vengeance, dear Johnnie.

Chapter 4

The Prodigal

The two horsemen drew rein at the top of the rise, where the London turnpike branched into Derleth Valley. It was just noon on a June day, and the sun was high and scorching down on the village, and the duck-filled pond, and the green beyond, sparkling from the windows of the church, making the grotesque house on the far side of the valley glow.

"Home," Roger Haggard said.

"And right pretty it is, too, Captain," Corcoran agreed. He pointed. "But what might that be, your Honor?"

Roger smiled; he did this as easily as ever, for all the tightness induced in his face by the constant pain from the arm he carried in a sling. " 'Tis my home, you rascal, as you well know. Come on." He touched his horse with his heels, and the pair rode down the lane toward the inn. And Roger found himself frowning. A Friday in June. Already the cricket pitch should be being mown with scythes, and the jugs of ale and cider should be being prepared for the afternoon's match—but the green was empty, as indeed was the street.

"We'll stop at the inn," he decided.

"I'm all in favor of that, your Honor," Corcoran agreed. He was in favor of any suggestion which might come from his master. He knew that he had to be the most fortunate private in the entire British army to have found someone like Captain Haggard and to have been taken away from the marching and fighting, the killing and the dying, that was Spain, even if only for a season. He hastily dismounted and hurried round the horses to be there if needed. But dismounting was less of a problem to Roger than mounting; he did not use his right arm for that.

He went up the steps, pushed open the door, knowing that Corcoran would see to the horses. He stepped into the gloom, blinked, realized that it was the first time he had ever entered this place. He had shaved off his mustache, but he did not suppose there was the least chance of being recognized.

"Sir?" Hatchard peered at him from behind the counter, frowning at the crimson jacket and the gray trousers, the empty sword belt and the well-worn shako, the bandaged right arm.

"A mug of ale," Roger said. "And one for my man."

"Right away, sir." Hatchard had them on the counter before Corcoran could gain the room.

"Now, there's a happy sight, Mr. . . . ." He raised his eyebrows as Roger shook his head.

"What's the name of this village, landlord?"

"Why, sir, Derleth."

"Ah. And is it, then, derelict?"

"Bless you, sir, no. You'll not find a more populous community in the county."

"But everyone is away visiting."

"Working, sir. Working."

"On a Friday afternoon?"

"Aye, well, the squire is not a man to have idle hands about the place, sir. He reckons Saturday is enough to have free, what with Sunday as well, and who's to say he's not right."

Roger drank beer. "The squire being Mr. Haggard?"

"That's correct, sir. You'll have heard of the gentleman?"

"I have. But tell me this, landlord. What do the people work at? I'd heard there were coal mines about here, but you'll not pretend they occupy an entire village?"

" 'Tis the mill, sir."

"Mill?"

"Oh, aye, we spin cotton in Derleth, Captain."

Roger found himself frowning. "They always have spun cotton in Derleth."

Hatchard did not appear to notice the slip. "Indeed they have, sir. But on hand looms. Regular cottage industry it was, sir. Then the squire got to thinking about it, and decided it would be best for all, or at least best for himself and best for the wholesaler, if the business was put in order, you might say. So he built the mill. You'll not see it from here, it's over the hills by the coal mine. But it employs everyone in the village, just about. Leastways, all those not coaling or farming. Even brings in people from Plowding."

"But why should people spin cotton for my . . . for Mr. Haggard, when they can do so for themselves?" Roger demanded. "He can't be paying them that much."

"Well, sir, there's them that say he don't pay anyone

enough. But that's just gossip, sir. No, no, the fact is, Mr. Haggard signed a contract with the wholesaler that he'd buy only from the factory, so it was spin at the mill or not at all. The mill can produce so much more cloth, you see, sir, than any number of hand looms. Well, sir, what with rents going up, and the cost of grain, well, sir, there weren't much choice."

Roger scratched his head. "And the people didn't object?"

"Lord above, sir, 'tis the squire they're working for. Oh, there was some talk. There's been a bit of unrest farther north. They was burning frames in Nottingham and thereabouts, only last winter. And like I said, there's been talk. Wild talk. But not more than that. There's no man in Derleth, or for twenty miles about, would openly oppose Mr. Haggard. No, sir."

"A hard man, is he?"

"Well, sir, he has a way with him, that he has."

Roger finished his beer, signaled for a refill, and for Corcoran. "He's family?"

"Well, sir, yes and no. And there's the main part of the trouble, if you ask me."

"I am asking you. What trouble?"

"Mr. Haggard can be fierce, when he's a mood to it. But it's all to do with his misfortunes, I'd say. Sixteen years now he's been a widower . . ." Hatchard sighed. "And then, the boy being lost at sea, and the heir also going astray, although, mind you, sir, there is talk that he's been found, and will be coming back again. That's done wonders for the squire, that it has. Smiles nowadays, he does."

"There are other children?"

"Oh, aye, sir, well, there's young Master John. He's at university, he is. Strange boy. Very serious. And then there's Miss Alice . . ."

"Yes?" Roger had to suppress the eagerness in his voice.

"A lovely girl, sir. Lovely. But serious. Oh, aye, they're a serious family. You'll take another pint, sir?"

Roger shook his head. "We'll be on our way."

"You'll not find another inn for twenty miles, sir, and 'tis hard on dinnertime."

"We'll manage," Roger said. "Come on, private."

"Right away, Mr. Haggard, sir," Corcoran said, finishing his pint and bustling for the door, while Hatchard stared after the pair of them.

"Seems like your father has his people well in hand, Captain, sir," Corcoran observed as they rode up the empty street. "Like a good officer should."

"Save that my father was never in the army," Roger observed.

"Oh, aye, sir, but a man what would be a good soldier will always be a good soldier, regardless of whether he actually bears a musket. Wouldn't you agree, sir?"

"It's a point of view." They were out the other side of the houses now, passing the school, also closed, and the church. Here at the least there were signs of life; Roger saluted the verger sweeping down the path between the gravestones, and received a long stare in reply. Then he was approaching the stand of poplars, through which the sunlight glinted on the white stone of the tomb. He knew whose it was, from Father's letters. He wondered if he should dismount and pay his respects. To her? He rode on.

The new hall had weathered, the stone turned green and brown by the trees and the wind. He drew rein to gaze at it, and attempted to remember, and found it difficult. Rufus should be sunning himself outside the front door, but there was only an undergardener turning over a bed. Yet the house was active; most of the windows stood open, and he could hear voices. He turned his horse in at the gate, rode down the short drive, watched the grooms coming from the stable, headed by a man he did not recognize.

"You're expected, Captain?"

Roger dismounted. "In a manner of speaking. You are . . . ?"

The head groom frowned at him. "Ned's my name, sir."

Roger nodded. "Private Corcoran will help you unstrap our gear." He walked toward the door.

"You'll pardon me, Captain." Ned hurried at his heels. "But the squire likes his guests to be announced."

"I'll announce myself," Roger said. Ned hesitated, chewing his lip and looking relieved as Nugent came down the inner staircase.

"Sir?"

"Is the squire at home?"

"Indeed, sir. But I do not think he is expecting a visitor."

"Indeed he is," Roger said, and climbed the stairs.

"He cannot be interrupted, sir," Nugent protested. "Sir, I must ask you . . ."

Roger had reached the first landing and was opening the door to the office.

"Sir, I must protest," Nugent said in a strangled voice. But Roger was gazing past MacGuinness at his father, slowly rising from his chair.

"What? What . . . ? My God."

"Father?" He had not supposed any man could look so old or so tired. Certainly not John Haggard. And he was not yet sixty.

"My God," John Haggard repeated, and slowly sat down again. MacGuinness hastily got to his feet.

"You'll remember me, MacGuinness." Roger held out his left hand, and after a moment MacGuinness took it.

"My head still hurts, Master Roger."

"I'll apologize for that blow, to be sure." Roger went round the desk. "Father?"

John Haggard stood up again, held out his arms. "By God, boy, but it is good to see you. Good . . ." He held his son close, blinked at MacGuinness, who backed to the door. "But . . ." He stepped back, stared at the arm.

"A sword thrust."

"Crippled. My God."

"Hardly crippled, Father. But temporarily unable to defend myself. Else I would not be here."

"At Badajoz?"

Roger nodded.

"You must tell me of it. Was it as savage as the papers say?"

"It was savage, Father. Even British soldiers can be savage. But after, the duke gave me leave of absence. Until my arm is healed."

Haggard frowned. "Then you must go back?"

" 'Tis my profession."

"But I need you here. My God . . ." He seized Roger's hand. "I have waited for this moment, boy. You'll not desert me again."

Roger squeezed the fingers clutching his. "In a month or two you may tire of me."

"Tire of you, boy? . . . John Haggard slapped his son on the shoulder. "Tire of you. Christ, there is so much to say, so much to do . . . your room." He went to the door, "Mary Prince," he bawled. "Mary Prince. You'll see to Master Roger's room. Quickly, now, girl."

"I've a manservant with me," Roger said. "He has fought at my side these three years."

"And will always be welcome at Derleth. You heard Master Roger, Mary Prince."

"Indeed, sir." Mary gave a little curtsy. "Are you really Master Roger?"

"Why, so I am." Roger smiled. "I do not remember you."

Mary flushed. "I came to the hall just before your worship left it, sir. But it is so good to have you back."

"It is good to be back, Mary, I promise you."

"Ah, begone with you," Haggard growled. "She'll stand there the day when she has work to do. See to it, Mary Prince. See to it. You've seen Alice?"

"Why, no, sir. I came straight to you." How his heart was again pounding at the thought of her.

"She'll know you're here by now," Haggard said. "News travels through this house like fire through a canefield. Alice!" He went to the stairs, looked up.

Roger stood at his side, gazed up at the woman. Alice was thirty-one years old, he recalled, only five years younger than himself. But life had passed her by. In the wavy red hair, the slender body, the quiet house gown, she might have been ten years the younger; she reminded him of his last memory of Emma.

"Alice," he said, and climbed the stairs.

She made no reply at all, but as he reached her he saw the tears rolling down her cheeks. Then she was in his arms, hugged close, and crying unashamedly.

"You'll want to be careful of her," Haggard remarked. "She'll be enlisting your help."

Roger released her, held her away from him to smile at her. "And I shall give it, freely," he said. "You have but to name the cause."

Haggard gave a shout of laughter. "Against me."

"Father?" Roger frowned, looked from one to the other.

"It is Father's joke," Alice Haggard said quietly. "He is a great one for humor."

"No joke," Haggard said. "God, I wish it were. She opposes me in everything. But mainly it is the factory." He drew rein and pointed.

They sat their horses in the cut through the hills, with the mine close to their right, and to their left the great rectangular bulk of the mill. It reminded Roger of an immense tomb, something created by the pharaohs. Save that this was alive.

The clanking of the huge wheel, the rushing of the water, filled the morning.

"I'm not sure I understand the situation," he said. "You say it provides work for two hundred people."

"That it does," Haggard agreed. "We bring in labor from several of the surrounding villages."

"And Alice objects to this?"

"Ah, well, you see, in the old days, these people spun cotton by themselves. In their houses, you understand. A precarious living it was, and the profits were low. But it made them independent. As if that were a good thing. There's those born to be independent, and those born to be dependent. You agree with that?"

"I had never considered it," Roger said. But he *had* considered it, he supposed. There could be no clearer example of that philosophy than the army. There were those born to be officers, and there were those born to be private soldiers. He supposed his own career proved the point. He had been born to be an officer, had thrown away his birthright, and still had risen to the very top of the noncommissioned tree, without a favor from a soul. While Corcoran was a private and would remain one for all his life.

"But you're thinking of it now," Haggard said, and urged his horse forward.

"Indeed I was. I imagine you're right. Haven't you explained things to Alice?"

"Explain things? You cannot explain things to Alice. To any woman, by my way of thinking. Women feel, they do not reason. But Alice is more unreasonable than most. 'Tis a personal matter. You'd not know that Emma Dearborn is still alive."

"Emma?" Now, why did his heart start pounding all over again?

"She was a witch, all right. Still is a witch. She has a witch's power of survival. But she's alive, and lives just beyond the borders of Derleth." He gestured at the hills. "Just over there. Alice visits her regularly."

"And you permit this?"

"How would I stop her, without using force? I permit more than that, by God. How do you suppose Emma has lived, these past years? There's no money in witchcraft. Only satisfaction. She spun cotton with the rest of them. A regular spider's web of a community we had here. And she'd not come to the factory looking for work. But she'd not move on, either. She's still there, waiting for me to die, I'd wager. Alice supports her."

"Alice?"

"She has an allowance of two hundred a year, and nothing to spend it on. She must have accumulated a tidy sum. And she gave it all to Emma. Truly, boy, I am glad to have you back."

"Well . . . Emma *is* her mother," Roger said cautiously.

"So she is." Haggard dismounted before the huge door. "You'll come inside."

Roger felt strangely embarrassed. He also dismounted, gazed up at the wall and the roof, was again reminded of something prehistoric, or, more likely, he supposed, something out of the future, some monolithic society where only a few people were ever allowed to see the light of day.

But the doors were being opened, and Haggard was being welcomed. A bell was ringing, and the gigantic hum was slowly dying, to be followed by an equally gigantic scraping. Roger realized that the looms had come to a halt and everyone was getting to their feet. Because the squire had decided to visit them.

He stood just inside the doorway, stared at the machines, arranged in orderly rows, at the men and women who stood there gazing toward their employer, at the better-dressed men, obviously foremen, who were gathered round his father, explaining and pointing . . . It reminded him of the West Indies, save that the laborers there had been black, and that they had been slaves—and that it had been in the open air with a cooling breeze playing over them.

"My son," Haggard was saying. "Captain Roger Haggard. Lately back from Spain."

Their names swirled about Roger's head as he shook hands. "You'll explain all this to me, I have no doubt," he said.

"Aye, well, 'tis simple enough, Captain Haggard. 'Tis the water supplies the power, you'll understand. That keeps the jennies and the mules moving at speed, and the cloth is turned out far quicker than ever before. Oh, 'tis a simple operation."

"I shall study it," Roger said, and glanced at his father, who was wiping sweat from his forehead. Now he nodded, and they stepped back outside. The noise became almost pleasant.

"By God, 'tis hot in there," Haggard said.

"I wonder those poor people survive."

"People can survive anything they get used to."

"But would it not be possible to install fans? They could be worked by block and pulley, or even by the water power."

"Fans? You'll be sounding like Alice, next. Those people are there to work, not to enjoy themselves. I pay them enough, by God." He mounted, walked his horse away from the noise, drew rein again, gazed at the barges being loaded with coal. "You'll inherit this, Roger."

"I doubt I have the right, sir. What of Johnnie?"

"Johnnie?" An expression Roger could never remember having seen before crossed his father's face. "You're the eldest. You were always my heir. He gets his allowance, and that should be sufficient. But this wealth, the factory here and in Barbados, these mines, these will be yours to handle, soon enough."

"I doubt not you'll live to be a hundred, Father." Roger smiled. "You look fit enough."

"And I feel fit enough, to be sure. But no man lives forever. And sometimes I feel mighty tired." His turn to smile. " 'Tis a great strain, being hated. You will have to get used to that."

"Being hated? You?"

"Me, boy. And you, in time."

"Surely people have forgotten about Middlesex by now."

"Probably they have, but they hate me still. And in these parts they hate me for the factory."

"You're not the only mill owner in the Midlands?"

"Of course I'm not. We're none of us too popular. At least here in Derleth we've kept the peace. You've heard of the happenings in Nottingham?"

"Some."

Haggard urged his horse away from the mine and toward the hills which marked the limit of Derleth. "Luddites, they call them. Way back, before I even thought of building my factory, some poor half-wit named Ned Ludd burned his master's mill. Well, that was the act of a madman. But recently, as times have got hard, there have been enough radical spirits ready to resort to crime and violence, especially in these parts."

"Times *have* got hard, Father," Roger pointed out.

"The nation has been at war for twenty years. Times have got hard for everyone. They will get better when Bonaparte surrenders. But we'll not beat him by fighting amongst ourselves."

"Perhaps the people don't much care whether we beat him

or not," Roger suggested. "They'd rather have full bellies and warm houses."

"The *people*," Haggard said disgustedly. "You're sounding like your sister. That's why I want you to understand what you're about. The people? The people have no brains, no intentions. They are like the sea, which has no menace of its own. Left to itself, it just lies there, peacefully enough, and is a pleasure to bathe in or sail upon. But let the wind get at it, and all that changes. That's your people for you. You have to be sure you know what's best for them, for *your* people, and do it, no matter how much they grumble. That's what I've always done, and I have prospered. You'll do no less, boy. Even here in Derleth, while we've had our quarrels, we've had no riots. Some crazy fools tried to burn the factory before it was even built, but they didn't succeed. And since then, there's been no trouble. My people know I'd not stand for it. But the whole country is coming to my point of view. There's a bill before Parliament now, decreeing the death penalty for frame destroying, and giving the power to the local justices. That's me, boy, and you, in time. That'll soon put a stop to all this nonsense."

And Parliament truly represents the people, Roger thought, remembering the men with whom he had lived and fought for twenty years. There was a farce. But he didn't say it.

"What does Johnnie think of it all?"

"Johnnie?" Haggard snorted. "I'll not talk about Johnnie. He'll be back soon enough. You'll meet him then." He drew rein, reached across to take his son's hand. "Oh, 'tis good to have you back, boy. So good. I'd not admit this to anyone but you, but I was a lonely old man until I heard you were alive. Had I the power, I'd exhume that bitch and hang her from the highest gallows I could build." He paused, and flushed, perhaps surprised as much by his own vehemence as was his son. "But 'tis all in the past now. There's no value in looking over your shoulder in this life. You're back, and I'll love you the more for being away. This valley is yours. Roger, whenever you want it. I'll retire and watch you prosper."

"Ah, 'tis a splendid place, Captain, sir. A splendid place." Corcoran lovingly brushed the shoulders of his master's uniform jacket, adjusted an epaulete. "Why, sir, I'll never understand how you turned away from all this for so long." He paused hopefully.

"I doubt you would understand it, Corcoran." But it *is* a

splendid place, he thought, gazing out of the window, and frowning as he watched the people trooping down the road into the dusk. They came from both the mine and the mill, seemed happy enough. But then, it was Friday evening, and they had a weekend of holidaying to look forward to. As it was Friday evening, they would also have just been paid.

But twenty years ago, on a Friday evening, they would have been trooping back from the cricket field rather than the factory, and they would not have had to depend on the squire for their wages. They would have been less prosperous perhaps, but had they been happier? He supposed there was no way he could ever find out; they'd hardly talk frankly to a squire's son who was also a stranger.

Corcoran seemed at last satisfied. "There you are, sir. Enjoy your supper."

"And you?"

"Oh, aye, Captain, I'll enjoy mine. They eats well in this house, sir. I've never had such food, even below stairs."

Haggard went down the stairs. They eats well in this house. Times are hard, Father has said. Times had been hard in Barbados, from time to time. But they had never eaten less than well. He thought of the times he had lain to his arms, in the freezing rain, with hardly a hunk of black bread to keep from starving. Now, if rumor was to be believed, the entire country sometimes approached that terrible state. The people. But not John Haggard.

And therefore not Roger Haggard. Nor anyone else privileged enough to be taken under the protective wing of Derleth Hall. Not Roger Haggard's wife. He paused at the next landing in surprise. It was not a thought he had seriously entertained before. But he was home. He was again, marvelously and mysteriously, heir to the Haggard fortune. Therefore it was his duty to marry and have other Haggards. Who would it be? Who would wish to marry Roger Haggard? Why, every unmarried lady in England, no doubt, whether they gave a damn for him or not.

He heard the rustle of her gown, inhaled the very faint scent of her perfume, turned in sheer pleasure, all other women banished from the very recesses of his mind. "Alice." He held out his hand. "We've not had a moment to be alone together."

She squeezed his fingers. "I'm sure you have been very busy, learning all about Father's plans and projects."

Still holding her hand, he escorted her along the corridor

to the great withdrawing room. "Plans of which I gather you do not approve."

"I am sure you have no desire to discuss my approval or disapproval." She freed herself as the footman opened the door for them, seated herself by the open windows, allowed the gentle breeze to ruffle her hair.

"I do, actually." He sat beside her.

"It is very simple." She smiled at him. "Father believes it is his heaven-sent duty to be rich, and then richer, and then richer yet. He believes that everyone not exactly in his own class was put here to assist in that inevitable progress. That they may have some aspirations of their own concerns him not in the least. I doubt he even believes it."

"You enjoy his wealth."

She gave him a quick glance, and flushed. "I am a coward. Had I a spark of talent in any direction, I might be prepared to strike out on my own. As I have not . . ."

"You have your allowance. Sufficient to live on, I'd suppose. Father would certainly not cut you off were you to leave. I'd not let him."

Again the quick glance, and a deepened flush.

"That is, did you not squander it on charity," Roger said gently.

This time she turned her whole body. "Of course. Father has been quick enough to place you at his side."

"I belong at his side," Roger pointed out. "But I do respect what you have been doing. I think you have done it long enough, that's all. Father is making me a princely allowance. I can certainly spare some of it. I would like you to allow me to support Emma, and leave yourself free to do what you wish with your life."

Her color slowly returned to normal. "I doubt Mama would wish to accept charity from you."

"We were friends once."

"Perhaps you were less of a Haggard then."

"Perhaps. At least allow her to make up her own mind. Will you take me to see her?"

"No."

He frowned. "May I ask why not?"

"It would make her unhappy. God knows, this family has brought her sufficient of that."

"This family, as you put it, is also partly hers."

"Oh, bah. Anyway, it's immaterial. You're Roger Haggard. You'll inherit all of this. You cannot be anything other than

Father's son. We can all only hope you'll be more understanding. I don't blame Father, believe me, for what he is.
What he was born to. How could he be otherwise, with a
background like his?"

"You don't blame him," Roger Haggard said. "But you hate
him."

Her head came up. "There's a terrible thing to say."

"Yet you'll not deny it. It's in your every look."

Alice got up, walked to the window, looked out at the
park. "I hate him."

"Have you a reason, beyond his treatment of your mother?
Beyond the death of Charlie?"

She would not look at him. "Aren't those sufficient reasons?"

"I imagine they are. I'm trying to discover if there are any
others. Something even more personal."

At last she turned. "And if I told you?"

"Tell me."

She stared at him for several seconds. "I hate him," she
said at last. "I have sufficient reason."

"And I have offered you the opportunity to leave this
place, to live on your own, or indeed to live with your
mother if you chose. I'll have your allowance doubled,
tripled, quadrupled."

"Are you so anxious to be rid of me?"

"I shall never be rid of you. I merely seek your happiness.
It is not good for you to live here, hating. Good for neither
you nor for Father."

Alice Haggard's face twisted with anger. "I do not care
what is good for me or what is good for Father. I will stay
here, and one day I shall see him suffer. So help me God, I
will."

Empty words. She knew that now. Two years, and she was
no nearer discovering any proof of what she *knew*. Father's
people were too afraid of him, too thoroughly in his pocket,
ever to betray him. Two years in which she had watched Meg
turn inward, watched her seem to shrivel, in her mind if not
in her body, watched too Emma dwindle, as she had in turn
watched her daughter shrink from life; there was too too
much of the lady born into Emma, and thus too much of it
born into Meg, there was the trouble. Had she truly been a
tinker's daughter she would have shrugged off her rape as a
misfortune, like stubbing her toe or a toothache, to be forgot-

ten. But her grandfather had been squire of Derleth Hall no less than was John Haggard, and through her there ran a streak of gentility which ill fitted her for the brutalities of this world.

But it had been a disturbing, a frightening two years in more than that. It had been two years in which Harry Bold and his son, robbed of their self-respect by their inability to find a weaver for their cotton no less than by their inability to track down the men who had savaged their daughter and sister, had turned more and more openly into outlaws, men who went abroad only by night, who poached as a way of life, even if her money kept them from poaching as a necessity. But even they were left less than men by their fear of John Haggard. They never crossed the hills to poach Derleth land. John Haggard's gamekeepers were well armed, and were trained to shoot to kill, well woe betide any midnight rambler who was taken alive; he found himself on the next ship for the New South Wales settlement. No one could argue that John Haggard's justice was ever unfair; no one could deny that it was savage.

So what would he sentence himself when it was proved that he had arranged a rape? Supposing it could ever be proved.

And two years, finally, in which she had watched John stagnate. Or perhaps stagnation was too flattering a word. He had retreated from whatever he had been, and she was realizing that that had been little enough. But the idle youth who had scribbled verses and amused himself with the dissolute aristocracy now hardly even scribbled verses, while his holidays at Derleth, kept as brief as possible, seemed nothing more than dismal adventures in boredom. He seldom rode abroad, kept to the house and the tower, sat on the terrace and stared at the park, and when questioned as to his thoughts, gave a sly and secret smile. "There is much to be considered," he would say. "Much."

"Of what you will do when you leave Cambridge?" she would insist.

"Indeed. Of what I shall do when I leave Cambridge," he would agree.

"And do you not suppose it would be a good idea for you to visit Margaret? A kindness?"

"Oh, hush, for God's sake," he would cry, his alarm almost feminine. "She knows, don't you see? She knows I am a coward. Christ, how that thought haunts me. She knows."

That you are a coward, Johnnie boy. Therefore, why do I waste my energy in thinking of you? Why do I count upon you as my ultimate weapon against Father?

She had left the mine and the factory far behind, emerged beyond the hills, and now looked down on the trees. She was at the limit of Derleth, and would soon be entering Plowding. She had refused to bring Roger. But why did she not turn to Roger for support, as he had offered, or for the implementation of her vengeance? Because she knew he was too like his father? Because the years of discipline and comradeship in the army had changed him, and he was no longer the determined rebel of his boyhood?

A rabbit started out of the underbrush beneath her horse's hooves. Sparkle gave a terrified neigh, rose on her hind legs; desperately Alice shortened her rein, at the same time giving an instinctive flick of her riding crop against the horse's haunches. Sparkle gave another shriek of terror and leaped forward; Alice had to throw herself flat on the mare's neck to avoid being swept away by the first low branch, which removed her hat. "Sparkle," she shouted. "Whoa, girl. Whoa, Sparkle."

But the mare had seized the bit and was not going to be checked. Through the trees she stampeded, throwing her body this way and that to avoid injury, throwing Alice this way and that as well. She abandoned all idea of riding, and grasped the horn of her saddle. Her left foot came out of the stirrup and for some seconds she clung on by a sheer act of will. Dimly she heard shouts and the drumming of other hooves; then she could no longer keep her seat; the saddle slid sideways and she felt herself hurtling through the air for a moment before she struck the ground, landing, amazingly, on her feet, which immediately gave way beneath the impact. She hit the ground with her knees, rolled over twice, seemed to see a tree trunk hurtling toward her, and knew nothing.

For some seconds. Surely it had been nothing more than that. Her eyes opened and she was aware only of pain, in her legs, certainly, but that was nothing compared with the pain in her head. It seemed that a giant was standing immediately behind her, hitting her with a hammer. She screamed with the agony, closed her eyes, opened them again. Through the pain haze she gazed at men. One man. Peter Wring. Thank God for Peter Wring. But there were others. Two men. Three men. Four men. Five men.

She lay on the ground surrounded by five men. Memory of

the stammered tale Meg had told, of the horror which had imprinted itself on her brain, came rushing back to her, mingling with the pain. She would be raped, by five men, just as Meg had been.

By Father's gamekeepers? Her eyes opened again, and she stared at them in horror.

"Miss Alice?" Peter Wring's voice seemed to come from a far way away.

"Don't touch me," she said. At least, she meant to speak. But apparently she shouted. His head jerked, and fresh waves of pain crashed through her brain.

"You're hurt, Miss Alice," another man said. Another rapist. Another of Father's henchmen. "We must get you back to the hall."

"Don't touch me," she screamed. "Don't touch me." What to do? If only the pain would stop. If only she could think. They would rape her. There was an end to the matter. She was too tired, too much in pain to fight them. No doubt Meg had felt the same. Therefore she too would have to be avenged. She felt their hands on her arms and others on her thighs. Oh, God, she thought, it was beginning. "Don't touch me," she screamed, and lost them in a wave of blackness.

Seconds, only seconds. Her eyes were open, and the giant was back, hitting her and hitting her and hitting her. Oh, God, if only he would stop. And there were people all around her. Men, about to rape her. Peter Wring. "Don't touch me," she screamed. "Oh, don't touch me."

"Alice?" Father's voice, coming from a very long way away. She opened her eyes, and he was there. Father, helping his gamekeepers rape his own daughter. She had known all along it would come to that.

"Oh, God," she whispered. "Oh, God," she screamed. "Help me." Desperately she turned her head left and right, stared at Roger. Roger too. But that was obvious. Roger was Father's son. Roger was as much Father's creature as Peter Wring. Roger would soon enough be laying his body on top of hers, with Father. "Don't touch me," she screamed. "Oh, leave me alone."

"A sprained ankle and a twisted knee," said Dr. Harrowby. "Nothing more than that, Mr. Haggard. At least, nothing that I can see."

"You'd best speak plain," Haggard suggested.

"What of the blow on her head?" Roger demanded.

"Well, sir . . ."

"Oh, sit you down, man, and take a glass. There's port in that decanter. And you can pour me one as well, Roger."

He waited while the glasses were filled, sipped, sighed. The best part of the day. Ruined.

"Well?"

"Well, sir, Miss Alice undoubtedly took a blow on the head. A severe blow."

"How severe?"

"It is impossible to say, sir. I examined her skull, as you saw, sir, but apart from the fact that it seemed agony for her to be touched, it is very difficult to say. . . . The skull is a very hard thing, Mr. Haggard. The misfortune is that the brain inside is a very *soft* thing, and not securely anchored, one might say. It is as if, well, sir . . ." He shook his glass suddenly and violently. Port shot out of the top and landed on his sleeve. "You'll observe, sir, that my glass is unchanged. But the liquid inside . . ."

"But . . . my God," Roger said. "You mean *that* is what the brain does when the head receives a blow?"

"To a greater or lesser extent, Captain Haggard, according to the force of the blow. Now, none of us knows quite how hard Miss Alice struck her head. She is certainly concussed. If that were all, there would be no problem. But . . ."

"If that were all?" Haggard shouted.

"Well, sir, you'll have observed that she appears to be existing in some sort of a nightmare. She does not wish to be touched, and she gazes at everyone with absolute horror on her face. If only we could decide what is going on in her mind . . ."

"She keeps asking for Johnnie," Roger said.

"Indeed, sir, it might well be useful to send for Mr. Haggard."

"Hum," Haggard said. "Hum. What can you do for her, Harrowby?"

"Well, sir . . ." Harrowby flushed, drained his glass, gazed into it hopefully. Roger hastily poured.

"Yes?"

"Rest, of course. There is the physical matter of her legs. And constant attendance, that is essential. For the rest, we must be patient, and hope, and pray. There are, of course, hospitals intended for the treatment of cases such as this . . ."

"Bedlam?" Roger shouted.

"I'll not have it," Haggard snapped. "My daughter in a lunatic asylum? I'll not have it."

Harrowby sighed. "The place I had in mind is certainly not a bedlam, Mr. Haggard. It is a private sanatorium where she would be treated royally. I do promise you that. But I agree these are early days. That would be a last resort, if her nightmare does not end. We must hope that it will, and shortly." He stood up.

"But you do not suppose it will," Roger said. "Or you'd not have proposed your . . . sanatorium."

"No, sir. I believe the young lady will recover. It is just that, well . . ."

"Out with it, man," Haggard said.

"Well, sir, Mr. Haggard, her nightmare is not a nightmare to her, if you follow me. It is very real. Now, sir, it may have been induced by a blow, which has crushed something or dislodged something or just hurt something, but as the state is there, it is the state we must consider. And . . . well, sir . . . you'll have observed as well as I that the state appears to consist of a morbid mistrust, one might almost say hatred, of everything around her. Everyone around her." He raised his hand. "Of course this is a delusion, sir. But it is real to *her*. *I* only wondered if perhaps, removed to surroundings where all the faces will be unfamiliar, she might not recover the more quickly." His color faded as he came under the full force of Haggard's stare. "It was only a suggestion, Mr. Haggard. We must discuss it at some other time. Who knows, sir, by this time tomorrow morning the crisis may be over. Miss Alice may awaken her own true self. It will happen that way, when it happens. I'll bid you gentlemen good day."

Roger went with him into the hall. "But you'll come again?"

"The day after tomorrow, Mr. Haggard, I shall be back. Good day to you."

The study door closed, and Roger leaned against it. "I had hoped my homecoming would bring you nothing but joy. Instead I seem to have brought you nothing but catastrophe."

"Stuff and nonsense, boy. You did not cause the fall. Pour me another glass."

Roger obeyed, took one himself. "What are you going to do?"

"What can I do? Rest, that quack said. Rest."

"You'll send for Johnnie?"

"I doubt it'll do much good."

"On the contrary, Father. Not only will it relieve her mind, but it may provide an answer to what is in it."

Haggard frowned. "You'll explain."

"Well, sir, I've seen quite a few men hit on the head during my service. In some cases it has appeared to mean nothing, in others it has had a terrible effect, rather like what has happened to Alice. Those fellows have become demented, or reacted in various strange ways, But they have never *invented* their nightmares. They have invariably reached into their own pasts for some horrible memory, and allowed it to dominate them."

"Charlatanry," Haggard grumbled.

"Not really. It is more like logic."

"And you think Alice may be obsessed by something in her past? Ha. I can tell you what has come out of her mind. Her hatred for me. She has always hated me. Well . . . I threw Emma out. I was wrong. I admit it freely. I even tried to make amends a couple of years ago. You know Emma lives in Plowding?"

Roger nodded.

"Aye. Well, I went over there to see her. Invited her back. Humbled myself, by God. And she asked me to leave. Oh, Alice hates me, all right. I'm only sorry she seems to have extended her hate to you as well."

"We talked about it," Roger admitted. "About you. Perhaps I didn't make sufficient effort to understand. But why does she keep calling for Johnnie?"

"Oh, he's her friend, she supposes. I'm beginning to wonder if Harrowby may not be right, after all."

"You'd not send Alice to a bedlam. Even a private one."

"Of course I shall not. But it's a gloomy prospect for her. As Harrowby says, we must be patient, and wait."

Roger nodded. "What of that?"

"It is a bag of coins. Found lying by her. Good to know one's gamekeepers are honest men, eh?"

"She would have been on her way to Plowding."

"Oh, aye. I told you, she supports them."

"I would like to take it."

Haggard leaned back. "Eh?"

"It is Alice's money, Father. She has a right to do with it what she pleases. And besides, she is also Emma's daughter. I should like to go over there and tell Emma what has happened." He smiled. "Who knows, I may bring her back with me."

"You'll not do that," Haggard said.

"But if Alice is truly ill . . ."

"I won't have Emma Bold in this house," Haggard said. "That's her name, Roger. Emma Bold. She's turned her back on us. You'll not forget that."

Roger picked up the bag. "But you've no objection to my visiting them?"

Haggard sighed. "Do what you will, boy."

Roger opened the door, hesitated. "I'll get over there now. And, Father, you *will* send for Johnnie?"

Send for Johnnie. Haggard finished his port, slowly pushed himself up. Send for Johnnie. Because some nightmare out of her past had arisen to dominate Alice's brain. A nightmare with which Johnnie was connected.

He climbed the stairs slowly, opened the bedroom door. One of the maids had been sitting there; now she hastily got to her feet.

"Has she spoken?"

"No, sir, Mr. Haggard."

He stood by the bed, looked down on the girl. Harrowby had given her laudanum, had prescribed it whenever she started to shout. There was a blessing.

But what of the future? A nightmare from the past, concerning Johnnie. Of course she would have been told what happened to Margaret Bold, by Emma. Perhaps by Johnnie as well. Two years ago. He had supposed that one dead and buried. He should have known better, when his scheme to marry the boy to Catherine Annesley had failed so dismally; Johnnie had just not been interested.

But of course it *was* no more than a nightmare. Alice had made no accusations. She had allowed her imagination to run wild, and it had finally overtaken her brain. She had no proof. Unless Wring had said something. That could easily be ascertained.

Thus, what harm could there be in sending for Johnnie? Everyone knew that the girl was out of her mind, at least for the moment. Why, there was always a chance that when she recovered she might remember nothing of it. How ironical that she should have stumbled on the truth by sheer chance, through a blow on the head.

But Emma would also tell Roger what had happened. Why had he not considered that?

Would she? Did mothers, even Emmas, rush around telling

everyone: My daughter was raped, did you know that, my daughter was raped. Except that to Roger she could say: My daughter was raped while walking out with your brother. Nothing more than that, unless she suspected.

And even if she suspected, what could she prove? What could Alice prove? What could anyone prove? And did it matter *what* could be proved? He was allowing his conscience to play him tricks, and it was a very long time since he had suffered from his conscience. He was Haggard. He had always done what he had decided was right, for the Haggards. Harming Margaret Bold had been no more than commanding a Negro slave to be flogged for insolence. There it was. That must never be forgotten. Perspective. That was the essential to a successful life. The girl had committed a crime in seducing Johnnie, and she had been punished in the most appropriate manner. Because, despite her hatred of him, he loved Alice, he was becoming a weak old man. It had to be combated. It would be combated.

But it would do no harm to make sure. He nodded to the girl, went down the stairs. Nugent waited for him. "You'll send for Mr. MacGuinness, Nugent," he said. "And I want a word with Peter Wring, as well."

Roger Haggard walked his horse through the trees, looked across the turnpike at the meadow, and then the other trees beyond. So far he was recognizing all the landmarks he had been given. Would he also recognize the family?

He kicked his horse, cantered across the road and once more into the trees. Corcoran had wanted to accompany him. "You cannot ride abroad by yourself, Captain," he had pleaded. "Not with that arm. Why, sir, suppose you was to be set upon by footpads?"

"Footpads? In Derbyshire?"

"Oh, aye, Captain. You want to think about that. There's a lot of discontent in these parts. In the whole country, they're saying, but most especially in the north. There's no food, Captain, and no work, neither. 'Tis an unhappy country, England."

An unhappy country. Roger found that difficult to believe, as he cantered toward the trees, ducked his head to avoid the low branches, inhaled the smell of the sun-scorched leaves. And if it was, surely the people should be the more grateful to men like Haggard, who had provided them with employment and a certain security. Certainly he could not be held responsible for rising food prices.

In any event, it was no problem of his, at the moment. Father might wish to look to the future, but *his* business was to regain his health and return to his regiment; he could do nothing better for this country, and for its people, than bring Bonaparte to his knees as rapidly as possible. His problem was to deal with the Bolds. And how he wanted to do that, how he wanted to see Emma again, how he wanted . . . The click of the hammer brought his head up, his hand tightening on the rein. He had been so deeply in thought he had not observed the little house. But now he looked from right to left, gazed at the two men, each armed with a fowling piece, each pointing it at him.

"You've business here?" demanded the elder man with the beard.

"And you've forgotten me, Harry Bold?"

"I remember you well enough, Captain Haggard."

"But you've forgotten we once stood shoulder to shoulder."

"A long time ago, Captain Haggard. Now you're not welcome here. This is my land."

"Bought with my sister's money," Haggard said, beginning to grow angry.

"My land," Bold said again. "It's legal, Captain Haggard. You'll leave it when I say so."

"Alice sent me."

Harry Bold glanced at his son.

" 'Tis a fact she did not come yesterday, Pa."

"What's happened to her?" Bold demanded.

"A fall from her horse. Nothing more serious than a sprain. But she knows you're waiting for this." He slapped the bag at his belt; the jingle was loud enough in the stillness of the morning.

"Then give it to me," Harry Bold said, coming closer.

Roger shook his head. "I'm not likely to hand over money at gunpoint, Harry Bold. Besides, the money's for Emma. No doubt you'll follow me to the house."

He touched his horse with his heels, walked it past the two men. He could feel the sweat on his shoulders, but he did not suppose they'd do anything violent. He had not harmed them, yet. But the Haggards had. Were memories really that long?

He turned in at the gate, walked his horse toward the front

door, watched it open. Slowly he dismounted, tethered the reins to the ring. "Have you no words for me?"

"Roger? Can it really be you?" Emma had lines on her forehead and running away from the corners of her eyes and her mouth. Somehow he was disappointed; he had not expected Emma ever to age.

"The bad penny." He went toward her, watched her eyes drift away to the meadow behind him. "They let me through."

"They'd not stop Roger Haggard." Her tone was suddenly breathless, and now her gaze was shrouding him. "Your arm?"

"Is useless, at the moment. But useful, in another fashion. But for it I'd not be home."

"But you are home." She clutched his left arm. "Oh, Roger, my darling, darling Roger."

He held her close, kissed her cheek. "And finding a great deal to puzzle over."

"Nothing for *you* to puzzle over, Roger. But . . . does your father know you are here?"

"Of course."

She frowned. "Did he not try to stop you?"

"I'm not a man to be stopped."

She moved her head back the better to look at him. She is thinking he is as arrogant as his father, he realized. But only someone as arrogant as John Haggard could possibly deal with John Haggard as an equal. That was where all the others, Emma herself, had made their mistakes. "Will you not ask me in?" He allowed the bag to jingle. "I have something for you, from Alice."

Emma released him. "She'll have told you that we exist on her charity."

"She has told me very little." He drew a long breath. "She has had an accident."

"She's hurt?" Emma's voice rose.

Roger had already determined on his approach. If Emma could not visit Alice at the hall, then she must not be unduly alarmed. "A fall from her horse. She has sprained an ankle and twisted a knee. She will be in bed for a few days."

"Nothing more serious than that?"

"Of course not."

Emma peered at him; he realized that she was nearsighted. "You'd not lie to me, Roger."

"I'd not lie to anyone, Emma." When was a lie not a lie? Whenever it was necessary?

"It was an insulting question." She smiled at her husband and son as they came up. "Here's Captain Roger Haggard of the Twenty-ninth Foot. You remember Roger, Harry?"

"Aye."

"Roger and your father once put the bailiffs to flight," Emma told Tim. "It was a rare sight. Ten of them."

"We'd not have done it without the dog," Harry Bold said.

"That's true," Roger said. "Father had him put down."

Emma glanced at him again, then at her husband. "You'll come inside, Roger, and take a glass of cider."

"No," Harry Bold said. "I'll have no Haggard inside my house."

"He'll come inside," Emma said, her voice quiet. "I'd have him meet the rest of my family."

"She screamed, Mr. Haggard," Peter Wring said. "Kept shouting, 'Don't touch me.' Things like that."

"And what did you say to her?" Haggard asked.

"Well, sir, I don't rightly remember. I tried to calm her, sir."

"And the others? Toby Doon? Illing?"

"Same thing, sir. If they spoke at all."

Haggard leaned back in his chair, stroked his chin.

"Begging your pardon, sir," MacGuinness said. "You don't suppose . . ."

"I do not," Haggard said. "I just wanted to be sure no one had spoken carelessly. You've naught to concern yourselves with. Not after two years. And not so long as none of your lads are indiscreet, Peter."

"Not after two years, Mr. Haggard. You can rely on them. They know where their bread is buttered."

"Well, see that they don't forget it. I'm thinking of you, Wring. No one is going to bring me down for the rape of a peasant girl." He gave a grim smile. "But I'd not like to have to hang you."

Wring licked his lips. "I'd not like that either, Mr. Haggard."

Haggard nodded, waved his hand, and Wring left. MacGuinness remained. "A sad business, Mr. Haggard."

"Aye."

"Will you be sending for Master Johnnie?"

'Yes. But there's naught to fear there." He got up, and

MacGuinness held the door for him. Haggard climbed the stairs slowly. How damnably short was his breath nowadays. He opened the bedroom door, gestured the girl back to her seat, once again stood by the bed, and stared at his daughter. "Has she awakened?"

"Yes, sir, Mr. Haggard."

"Eh? Why was I not called?"

"It was only for a moment, sir. She opened her eyes, and looked at me, and gave a groan, and closed them again."

Certainly she looked peaceful enough at the moment. Perhaps she would die. Would that not be the best thing for them all? For her, certainly; she had hardly ever lived. For himself . . . But what a dreadful thought. She was Alice Haggard. She was his daughter. The only daughter he had ever had. And she was as beautiful as her mother, for all the twisted hate that seethed within her. Oh, Alice, he thought. If only you could have loved me. I would have loved you. I could love you now.

But she sought only to destroy him. As if he needed to fear a twisted young woman who was in any event out of her mind. As if he needed to fear anyone. Even Roger. Haggard had no need to fear.

But, oh, to be left alone. There was the dark pit lying at his feet. There was the pit over which he had hovered for the past fifteen years. He had never ever been close to Johnnie. He knew that now. He had never understood the boy. A poet. But it had been deeper than that. He had feared, all along, the weakness that Alison's child would have to possess, without knowing what it was. But cowardice. He hated even to see the boy, however well he concealed it. And however well he concealed it, Johnnie was undoubtedly aware of it. He snapped his fingers. The answer to Johnnie's problems, and to his immediate past, was Barbados. Of course. Send him out to manage the plantation. Ferguson would look after him, and *he* need never worry about the boy again.

But throughout these years, only Alice had stood between him and his emptiness. Alice, standing and staring at him, hating him with all of her being, had yet been there. Always there.

But now there was Roger. And if she would attempt to drive a wedge between Roger and himself, then she would have to . . . But she included Roger in her hate.

He turned his head as the door opened.

"How is she?" Roger asked.

"Sleeping. It is certainly best. How did Emma take the news?"

"I did not tell her the truth of it. I told her about the sprained ankle, that was all. Father . . ."

"She'll not visit here. I told you that. She'll not visit here."

"Aye, well . . . so long as she doesn't know. And so long as Alice recovers . . ."

"Of course she'll recover. Will you be returning to the Bolds'?"

Roger's head came up. "Will you forbid me?"

"I'll forbid you nothing. I told you that, boy. You'll do what you choose."

"Thank you, Father." Roger stood beside him to look down at his sister.

But you'll remember she's a witch, Haggard thought. Oh, aye, a witch who has affected my entire life, has haunted my children, and now sits on the borders of my property, waiting for me to die, waiting for the opportunity to take my eldest son. His lips twisted. It was Emma he should have destroyed. Not her daughter.

Roger Haggard dismounted, tethered his horse to the ring. The ring, no less than the journey from Derleth, had become so familiar in the last two days that he might have been doing it all of his life. He might indeed. But looking over his shoulder was a waste of time. He had realized that long ago, while still in the army. He was here now, and there was a lot of living left to do.

If it were possible to make the girl feel the same way. Truth to tell, he was unsure of his own feelings. He could not understand her, the way she sat so quietly, or even left the room when he was present. The way she would not meet his eye. The way she avoided physical contact, even with her father and brother, only reluctantly accepted it with her mother. And never with Roger Haggard. He was twice her age. There was a problem, one which perhaps meant too much to her. Or perhaps she was too steeped in the hatred felt by the Bolds for John Haggard. There was something else he could hardly understand. Because *they* seemed happy enough to see him. Because of course he had fought with them, against his father's own people, all those years ago. They counted him an ally.

Was he an ally?

The door was opened, and Emma stood there. " 'Tis

madness you're at, Roger Haggard," she said. "After all these years, deliberately to set your father at defiance. You'll never pretend he approves of these visits?"

"Are you not interested in Alice's health?"

A quick frown. "She'll be well?"

Roger smiled, kissed her on the forehead. "Improving every day. She'll be walking by tomorrow, and is impatient to do so, I promise you. She'll be over here by the end of next week."

Emma led him inside. "And then you'll be no longer coming."

"Try to keep me away." He looked around the neat little kitchen, inhaled the aroma of the stewing rabbit. "Harry not at home?"

She gave him an old-fashioned look. "No. And neither is Tim. You did not know that?" He flushed, and she laughed. "You'd never make a liar, Roger Haggard. 'Tis not a family characteristic."

"I wanted to see you."

"And now you do. There's no cider. Will water do?"

"Water will be splendid." Roger sat in one of the chairs beside the table. "And Meg?"

"Saw you coming and went out the back."

"She does not like me."

Emma handed him the wooden mug, her face serious as ever when she discussed her daughter.

"I am sure she likes you very well."

"But she cannot stand my company."

"She finds most company hard to stand, Roger."

"Is she crippled? Half-witted? Is there some blemish on her skin? I confess I do not understand the matter at all."

She gazed at him for several seconds. "There is no reason for you to understand," she said at last. "You went away, lived your own life. I have no doubt that during those years you experienced many things you would rather forget."

"And I have forgotten them, at least insofar as my daily life is concerned."

"Meg is not yet twenty. You must give her the time."

He frowned at her. "But you'll not give me the courtesy of an explanation."

"It is not your concern."

He leaned forward, elbows on the table. "I suspect it is, Emma. I think you are lying to me. I think the Haggards are indeed connected with Meg's experience."

She would not lower her gaze. "You may believe what you will, Roger. And if you intend to badger me, I should prefer if you'd not call again."

He threw himself back in his chair. "Have I your permission to go out the back and speak with her?"

"You have not. What are you pretending, to come a-courting?"

He felt his cheeks burn. "Would that be so impossible for you to understand?"

"It would be impossible for me to believe. What, Roger Haggard, heir to probably the greatest fortune in England, soldier, man of the world, suddenly seeking to court a peasant girl he has known less than a week? You must take me for a fool. As I mistook you for the boy I knew and loved. I had not suspected a man could change so."

Was she really angry? She certainly looked it. He could hardly remember Emma angry. She had not been an angry person.

He nodded. "You are right. I have moved too fast. I apologize."

"There is nothing for you to apologize to me for. Just remember that Meg is my daughter."

Roger shrugged. "Perhaps that is a part of it, Emma. I always loved you, I wish to love her as well."

"Then do so, with my blessing. As a sister."

"And if that is not possible?"

"Then do not visit us again. Meg is not for you, Roger. She is not for any man. She wishes to be left alone. If you are truly a gentleman, you will respect that decision."

Once again she would not look away.

"Does Alice know the truth of this matter?"

"What matter?"

"Be sure I shall ask her."

"You may do whatever you wish. And Alice will no doubt do whatever she wishes."

He gazed at her in impotent irritation, then got up. "I apologize again, for taking up your time."

Emma caught his hand. "Roger. Of all the people in the world, I'd want you as my friend. Don't quarrel with me. Believe me, Meg has very good reasons for wishing to be left alone. Please believe me."

"And you'll not tell me them? I may be able to help."

"You can do nothing for her, Roger."

"But you've no objection if I ask Alice?"

Again her face settled into that rigid composure. "You may do whatever you wish," she said again.

He mounted, walked his horse away from the cottage, drew rein as he saw the girl. She was standing by the trees, and as she saw him, she raised her arm, then lowered it again and stepped into shelter. Roger's heart pounded as he looked over his shoulder. He could not tell if Emma was watching him or not, but he doubted it. Hastily he turned his horse, walked it into the shelter of the trees, dismounted. Meg remained several feet away from him, face flushed and hair untidy. She was having trouble with her breathing.

"Is Alice really going to be all right?" The words came out in a rush.

"We think so."

"Did she really sprain her ankle, Captain?"

"That's what the doctor says."

"You don't think she was assaulted?"

Roger frowned at her. "Assaulted? Alice?"

Meg was chewing her lip. "I was assaulted, Captain." Once again the words seemed to tumble over each other; she was saying something she had kept bottled up for too long.

"You?" He stepped closer, and she stepped back.

"Here," she gasped. "In this wood. I was assaulted. By five men."

"My God," Roger said. "But . . ."

"Johnnie was with me, Captain. And he . . . he ran away. Papa said he'd kill him if he ever came here again. He ran away. You'd not run away, Captain?"

"No," Roger said absently. "I'd not run away. Who knows of this, Meg?"

"Well . . ." She flushed, "Nobody. Save Alice. And the men."

"Were they never caught?"

"No, Mr. Haggard."

"But you made charges."

"Me, Mr. Haggard? They wore masks."

"My God," he said again, and again approached her. This time she did not withdraw, leaned against a tree instead, watched him come closer. "But Johnnie . . ."

"He never come back, Captain. Never sent a message. He'd asked me to marry him, Captain. But he never came back."

"Oh, Meg," Roger said. "Oh, my poor, poor Meg."

She did not seem to hear him. "They said I was demented, Captain. Mama and Papa said that. But I'm not demented now. And I thought maybe Alice had been assaulted. She might have sprained her ankle, fighting them. I sprained my wrist fighting them, Captain."

Roger shook his head. "No. You've naught to worry about there. She was found by Father's gamekeepers almost the moment she fell from her horse."

"I'm so glad, Captain. So glad. I was so afraid that it might have happened to her, too."

"Aye. But it didn't. It happened to you. And I am so glad you told me, Meg. Meg . . ." He reached out and took her hand.

"I'd best be getting back," she said. "I don't like the woods. They frighten me, Captain." But she hesitated. "Will you come again, Captain?"

"Would you like me to?"

"I'd like you to come again, Captain. But not to the house. Here in the wood."

"I'll be here tomorrow after dinner. I'll look for you, Meg. Will you come?"

"You look for me, Captain."

Now, why had he said that? Did he want to see her again? A tinker's daughter, who had been raped, and by five men? A very lovely tinker's daughter, who had been raped by five men. And was therefore an easy lay? She hardly gave that impression. And if he was looking for an easy lay, were there not many girls in his own village who would willingly raise their skirts for the Haggard heir? And who were not almost related to him.

Because she was, almost related to him. And she had been raped, by five men. While his own half-brother stood by and watched, and ran away. John Haggard junior. Did Father know of it? Father could not possibly know of it. He would never have Johnnie in the house again. If he spoke of the boy with affectionate contempt, it was because of his ambitions to be a poet. A boy who had watched a girl who had placed her trust in him being raped by five men. Roger kicked his horse from a trot into a canter. He supposed he had never hated anyone so much in his life. Someone he had never seen.

And someone who was responsible for even more than that. For undoubtedly there was the truth about Alice. She would certainly know what had happened. If Johnnie had not

confessed it, then the Bolds would have told her. She knew
all about what had happened to her stepsister, and all about
the cowardice of her half-brother. It must have been lying
across her mind like a lead weight for all of these two years,
slowly eating into her sanity, mixing and confounding itself
with her hatred of her father, until, as Harrowby had suggested, the blow on her head had caused her brain to snap. All
caused by Johnnie Haggard.

He rode through the cut, down the drive to the hall. The
carriage was already at the door, and the inmates were still
disembarking. The *inmates*? Roger frowned as he watched
the tall, slight young man embracing his father. That had to
be Johnnie. Then who was the other, now shaking hands? A
shorter man, more heavily set, although not a great deal
older, with reddish-brown hair and a limp, and striking features, at once handsome and vaguely repellent because of
their expression of bored arrogance.

"Roger," Haggard said. "Back in good time, boy. This is
Johnnie. Now, isn't it a strange thing, my lord, to be intro-
ducing a man to his own brother."

"Quaint," Byron agreed.

Roger dismounted, shook hands. He'd not betray the boy
before Father. Not yet. But the fingers were limp, and as his
gaze ate into the pale blue eyes, Johnnie flushed.

"I've been looking forward to this moment," he murmured.
"For two years."

"As have I," Roger said, and turned to Byron.

"And Lord Byron," Haggard said. "Johnnie's best friend."

"My pleasure, Captain," Byron said.

"And mine, sir. Byron. I know the name."

"You do, by God," Byron remarked.

"Lord Byron is the toast of England," Johnnie said. "You'll
have read *Childe Harold*?"

"I'm afraid not."

"A fantasy I scribbled while upon my travels," Byron explained, looking a trifle embarrassed by Johnnie's obvious
adulation. "But what do you suppose? The public has taken
me up."

"Well, come inside, come inside. Nugent, some wine. Ned
will see to your things." Haggard ushered them to the door.
" 'Tis not often we have a famous personage at Derleth."

"I should like to see Alice," Johnnie said.

"Aye, you should. I'll take you up. You'll excuse us, my
lord."

Byron nodded. They had reached the top of the grand staircase, and Roger gestured him into the drawing room, where Nugent was already pouring wine.

"And are you also at Cambridge?"

"No longer, more's the pity," Byron said. "They were happy days. No, no. You have no idea, my dear Haggard, what the life of a literary giant is like. I have scarce a moment to call my own. And the ladies . . ." He paused to see what effect his words were having on his host, and sighed. "Well, I seized the opportunity to visit Johnnie, don't you know. We were at school together."

"Some wine." Haggard sat down, stretched out his legs.

"And so I was at Trinity when the news arrived about your sister. You'll appreciate how sorry I am to hear it."

"It is good of you to say so."

"But she'll be well again, eh?"

"We hope so."

Byron regarded him for a moment, sipped some wine, walked across to the great windows looking out at the deer park. "A choice spot, Derleth. You'll not have been to Newstead?"

"No."

"It needs work. And money. More money than I can discover." He gave a brief laugh. "What would you? I spend years cultivating the Haggard heir, only to discover he is not the heir after all. There is a turn-up."

It was difficult to decide whether he was bantering or being unhappily frank.

"Johnnie will never want," Roger said.

"Oh, indeed not. I should hope so, at the least. Ah . . ." He faced the doors as Haggard and Johnnie came in. The boy was pale. "Is she . . . ?"

"She is as she has been for the past two days, my lord," Haggard said. "We keep her under sedation. But I am encouraged. Encouraged, sir. She almost seemed to recognize Johnnie here. Almost. There is some prospect of a recovery. You'll wish to change for supper, my lord." He rang the bell.

"I would, Mr. Haggard. Are you coming up, Johnnie, lad?"

"Well, I . . ." Color flooded back into Johnnie Haggard's cheeks, and he glanced from his father to his brother.

"Stay for five minutes," Roger said. "I would like to get better acquainted."

"Quaint," Byron agreed. "Dashed quaint."

"This is my housekeeper, Mary Prince, my lord," Haggard said. "She'll show you to your room." He looked at Roger, raised his eyebrows. "I shall be in the study for a while," he said, and left the room. Nugent poured two fresh glasses, bowed, and also left.

Johnnie brought Roger's glass over. "I'll drink to Alice's recovery. But also to your homecoming. You must be very happy."

"And you?"

"Equally so." He gave a guilty smile, and a secretive one, Roger thought. "I never supposed I was cut out to be squire."

"No doubt there are squires and squires." Roger sat down, the glass dangled between two of his fingers, watched the liquid sparkle and threaten to slide over the edge. "Alice has told me a deal about you," he lied.

"Alice?" Johnnie flushed, sat opposite. "She *will* be all right?"

"Father thinks so. And Emma thinks he is right."

Johnnie's head came up, his flush deepening. But Roger would not spare him.

"Does Father know what happened?"

Johnnie licked his lips. "No. Of course not. He thinks I fell from my horse that day. But you don't understand . . ."

"I think I do," Roger said. "I've spent a long time in the army. With the best will in the world, some men just cannot face an enemy."

"No," Johnnie got up. "You *don't* understand. You weren't there."

"And they cannot be criticized for that," Roger said. "They're unlucky if it happens in battle, because then they are put against a wall and shot. But it is something to be sympathized with. I am trying to understand, you see."

"But you can't," Johnnie wailed, and checked himself. "You haven't talked with Father?"

"About that? Obviously not, or I wouldn't have asked you if he knew."

"Ah." Johnnie gave a sigh.

"What is unforgiveable," Roger said, "is your refusal ever to visit Meg again."

"I . . . I couldn't. The shame of it. The way she looked at me . . ."

"Aye," Roger agreed. "But you *will* visit her again, Johnnie. I will come with you."

Johnnie Haggard's shoulders slumped. "You don't understand," he said again. "I behaved badly. I know that. I confessed it to Alice. And she knew I had too. But she knew how to have me make it up. She said she'd find the men who were responsible. If it took her the rest of her life, she'd find who were responsible, and then I could avenge Meg. I could avenge myself. You'll see. When she finds out . . ."

"When she finds out?" Roger shouted in sudden anger. "Do you not suppose that is what has driven her from her mind? The burden of finding those men? The burden of concealing your cowardice? The burden of knowing what happened to her own sister? You are as guilty as anyone of her illness. And to what end? Do you really suppose that if Alice were to enter this room now, leading one of those rapists by the hand, you would be able to avenge Meg? Do you really suppose you have the stomach for it, you sniveling little coward?"

Johnnie Haggard stared at his brother for a moment; then he turned and left the room.

He ran up the stairs, brushed a maidservant aside. "Master Johnnie . . ." she said.

"Oh, leave me alone," he snapped. He wanted to weep. He knew he was about to weep. He had no doubt that Roger was right, that it was the weight of everything that had happened which had driven Alice insane. But he was even more concerned with his own position. Roger knew! How could he live with that hanging over him for the rest of his life? Whenever he chose, Roger could tell Father . . . Johnnie just could not consider that. And knowing that secret, what of the other? Byron should not have come. Oh, God, Byron should not have come, not to Derleth, not into Father's lair.

"But, Master Johnnie . . ." The girl was hurrying after him. " 'Tis Miss Alice."

"Eh?" He checked, looked down at her.

"She is asking for you, Master Johnnie."

Johnnie frowned. "She's asleep."

"No, Master Johnnie. She woke up, and when I went to give her the laudanum, she asked me to wait until after I'd seen you. 'Tis a whipping I'll get, Master Johnnie, if the master finds out."

"Then why . . .?"

She licked her lips. "Miss Alice said you'd see me right, Master Johnnie."

Johnnie gazed at her for a moment. Alice, asking to see

him? Alice, who was out of her mind? He chewed his lip in indecision, then nodded. "I'll see you right. We'd best return there before you are missed."

She scurried in front of him, up the next flight of stairs, and along the corridor, opened the door. Johnnie closed it behind himself, stood by the bed. Alice's eyes were open.

"Alice? But . . ."

"I had to pretend," she whispered. "Don't you see, I had to pretend. Father wants me to be mad. That way I can't cause any trouble."

He sat beside her. "But . . . your head?"

"It hurts. But not so much as before. When I saw you this afternoon, I near gave myself away. Listen . . ." Her fingers wrapped themselves about his wrist. "I have found the men."

"Eh?"

"I know who they are. They are Father's gamekeepers. Peter Wring and his people."

"Peter Wring? By God——"

"Ssssh, and listen. They don't matter. They were only doing what they were told. It is Father sent them."

"Father? That's impossible. Why——"

"Why is it impossible?" Alice's voice was suddenly fierce. "Do you suppose he would ever let a Haggard marry a Bold?"

"But . . . I was there. I might have been beaten up. I might have been killed."

"But you weren't," she said.

Johnnie gazed at her, his brain tumbling. They had tied him up instead of hitting him on the head. And when he had tried to escape, his wrists had been undone. So he had run away. They had known he would run away. My God, all of these years, with Peter Wring knowing he was a coward. He felt sick.

"You'll avenge Meg," Alice said. "You'll avenge me. You'll avenge yourself."

"Against Father? Oh, I . . ."

The nails were cutting into his flesh. "You must," she said. "You must. Or . . . or I'll tell him you ran away."

"No," Johnnie said. "No, you mustn't do that. Alice . . ."

"Then kill him," she said. "He's not worth keeping alive. He's a bully and a tyrant and a vicious monster."

"I . . ." Johnnie licked his lips. "I could take him to court."

"For God's sake." Alice's fingers relaxed, and she lay back.

"*You'll* take John Haggard to court? Who do you suppose is the magistrate around here? He is. Oh, you are even more of a coward than I supposed. I *will* tell him. I may as well."

"No." Once again Johnnie licked his lips. "No. I'll . . ."

"You'll kill him," Alice said. "Execute him. He deserves execution, for all of his crimes. For murdering Charlie. Because he did. For murdering Annie Kent. Because he did. For shooting Rufus. For throwing Mama out. For turning Meg into a cabbage. He deserves to die, Johnnie. Kill him. Kill him. Kill him."

"Talavera," Byron said. "My word, were you there, Captain? I was in Spain then too."

"Were you?" Roger inquired.

"There's a coincidence," Haggard agreed.

"Well, I was in Seville and then in Cádiz, on my travels, don't you know. A charming place, Spain."

"Except where the French happen to be," Roger said.

"Faults on every side," Byron pointed out.

Roger laid down his knife and fork. "Do you support Bonaparte, my lord?"

"Would you not agree he is the greatest man of his age?"

Haggard snapped his fingers, and Nugent hurried forward with more wine. The meal had been difficult from the beginning, with Johnnie just staring at his plate, Roger obviously in an aggressive mood, and Byron eager to accept any verbal challenge. "You are not eating, my lord. Is the meat not to your taste?"

"The meat is perfection itself, Mr. Haggard. Alas, I have an inclination to grow fat at the slightest opportunity. Why, would you believe it, I once tipped the scales at two hundred and forty pounds? When I was at Cambridge, Johnnie. *Would* you believe it?"

"No," Johnnie Haggard said.

"You certainly show no evidence of it now," Haggard agreed. "And you'll not find my beef fattening, my lord. 'Tis one of my own cattle. Anyway, here in Derleth there is sufficient to do to keep a figure trim. Tomorrow I'll show you over the mine and the factory."

"The factory?" Byron inquired.

"A cotton mill."

"Ah. I had no idea you indulged in such misguided ideas."

"Misguided ideas?" Haggard drank some wine. The young man was his guest.

"In my own country of Nottinghamshire the people burn such enormities."

"By God," Haggard commented. "And you support such criminals?"

"I, sir? I hardly would support crime. But equally I would hardly support this money-grasping Tory administration under which we have suffered too long. Why, they go from bad to worse. Suspending habeas corpus, and now this new law prescribing the death penalty for frame breaking, why, 'tis barbarous. And giving such powers to the local justices. Why, sir, that is equivalent to placing the entire Midlands under martial law. I spoke against it in the Lords. Caused quite a stir, as I am told. But what would you? The Commons passed the bill just the same. It lowers England to the level of Russia."

"And what penalty would you prescribe for the destruction of another man's property?" Haggard inquired, his voice dangerously low.

"Well . . . a fine . . ."

"Which none of them could possibly pay," Roger said.

"Or a brief term of imprisonment. But to take a man's life because he resents your taking his livelihood in the first place, why, 'tis barbarous, as I said."

"Aye, well, we have none of that here," Haggard said. "Derleth is a happy place. You've seen that, Roger?"

"It seems so, Father. And as my father says, my lord, there has certainly been no frame breaking here."

"You should congratulate yourselves." Byron leaned back to allow his plate to be removed. "It does not really alter the situation. The country is being badly run, and there is an end to it."

"And how would you change the system, my lord?" Haggard asked.

"Well . . . you've not met John Russell?"

"No," Haggard said. "He has Whiggish sentiments, I have heard."

"Oh, indeed, so have I. You'll not object to a Whig sitting at your table, Mr. Haggard?"

"Of course not. Tell me what your friend Russell would propose."

Byron leaned forward, his face suddenly animated. "A reform of Parliament."

"Eh?"

"Parliament, Mr. Haggard, is the most unrepresentative

body in this kingdom. You'll not deny that. Great cities like Manchester, with no representation at all, little villages like Derleth returning a member. Why, man, you are a living example of the system. How many electors have you here?"

"Why . . . twenty-odd."

"All of whom work for you or are tenants of yours. The seat is therefore yours, and your son's after you, for as long as you care to take it up. Now, sir, do you really represent these people?"

"I do indeed, whenever there is a matter of importance to Derleth."

"But do they have any choice?" Byron insisted.

"Why should they require a choice?"

"Why . . ." Byron leaned back again, looked first at Roger and then at Johnnie, who continued to stare at his plate. "With the best will in the world, Mr. Haggard, you cannot really claim to be one of these people."

Haggard was frowning. "And *you* would claim to be one, you mean?"

"By no means. I would never dream of standing for the Commons. I happen to have inherited a barony, and I will take my place in the Lords, to be sure. But in defense of the common man. The man who is being trodden underfoot year after year to pursue this senseless war against Bonaparte."

"The greatest man of our age," Roger said dryly.

"Quite." Byron did not appear to notice the sarcasm.

"And you consider that if more people had the vote," Haggard said, leaning forward, "a different spectrum of the nation might be elected to Parliament a spectrum which might well choose not to fight the French?"

"I would consider that a certainty," Byron said.

"And I, sir, think that a slander upon the good name of the British people. What, not fight the French? By God, my lord, was there ever an Englishman who did not wish to fight the French?" He pointed at Roger. "Tell him."

Roger considered the matter, remembered the men with whom he had worked and fought for so long, men who only wished to be allowed to go home. Would Corcoran really want to fight a Frenchman, were he not dragooned to it? Frenchman? Or anyone?

Byron was smiling. "I think perhaps Captain Haggard agrees with me."

"Roger?"

"I suspect Lord Byron may be right, Father," Roger said.

"The nation's policies might well undergo a considerable change were the basis of parliamentary election more widely spread. I would hesitate to say it would necessarily be for the better."

"Oh, come now, Captain Haggard. Could you honestly say it would be for the worse?"

"Stuff and nonsense," Haggard shouted. "This nation is the greatest on earth, and shall I tell you why, sir? It is because for the past thirty years the Tories have held power, undisputed. They have known what is best for the country, sir, and they have guided it to prosperity. The Whigs, sir, are the party of disgrace. I'll have none of it. I'll have no more of this subject."

Byron continued to smile, but now he bowed his head. "Of course, Mr. Haggard. My apologies for provoking an argument. Believe me, sir, I shall not mention the matter again."

A gentle tap on the door, and Johnnie Haggard's head jerked. He knew who it was, of course. Who it had to be. But would he dare come here, in the middle of the night?

Byron closed the door behind him. "Your father is every bit as fierce and as reactionary as you painted him."

"Byron . . . can you imagine what he would say should you be discovered in my room at midnight?"

"He should be grateful. I see you, sitting on the edge of your bed, your head in your hands, as you sat throughout dinner, with your head in your hands, at least metaphorically speaking. Whatever is the matter? Or do the ghosts of your ancestors rise up to strangle your desires whenever you enter your own home?"

"No jests, I beg."

Byron sat beside the boy, threw his arm around his shoulders, gave him a gentle hug. "I was not jesting. I offered to ride home with you, and you accepted with joy. Now you act as if I am a drag. I shall leave tomorrow."

"No." Johnnie turned violently.

"Aha." Byron kissed him on the nose. "Things are not so bad as I supposed. Yet shall I leave, anyway. You'd not have me quarrel with your father?"

"Father." Johnnie pulled away, paced the floor. "If you *knew*."

"Tell me. Else why am I here at all?"

Johnnie stopped, faced the bed. "That business I told you of."

Byron nodded.

"I spoke with Alice tonight. She's not as demented as they suppose. She has proof that it was Father commanded the attack on Meg Bold."

"I had never doubted it for a moment."

Johnnie Haggard frowned at him. "You never said so."

"Would you not have punched me in the eye?"

"Well . . ." Johnnie's shoulders slumped. "Father. I can hardly believe it. And yet . . ."

"It makes sense on every count. It is the sort of thing your father *would* do. Instinctively. Not that you didn't deserve *it*. Taking up with a serving girl. My dear Johnnie—"

"Don't start that again," Johnnie said. "I'm in no mood for it. It was a beastly thing to do. If it hadn't happened . . ."

"You might well have married the wench, and regretted it every minute of your life."

"Oh . . ." Johnnie's shoulders rose and fell. "Alice says I should kill him."

"Who?"

"Why, Father."

"Kill your own father? Patricide, amongst the English landed gentry? There would be a tale. Your trial will attract everyone in the land. Standing room only, for twenty miles each side of Derby. I promise you I shall write an elegy as will never have been heard before."

"Must you jest about everything?" Johnnie shouted.

"You'd best lower your voice, or I shall have to compose some more jests, and in haste. If I amuse myself, my darling Johnnie, it is because I never heard anything more silly in my life. You, kill your own father? You, kill John Haggard even if he were *not* your own father? Do you suppose, Johnnie, that if you held a loaded pistol and that redoubtable old man pointed at you and said, 'Drop it.' you would not obey him?"

"Oh, Christ." Johnnie Haggard sat on the bed, then slipped from it and knelt, his head on Byron's knees. "What am I to do? To live here, knowing what he has done, knowing . . . What am I to *do*?"

Byron stroked the boy's hair. "It's an unjust business, living. So let us see. Your dad has been an utter scoundrel. But you'll not bring him down by legitimate methods. Not while he backs the Tories and they control the country. Revolution? There would be fun, eh, Johnnie lad? Rape and pillage and murder. Your father hanged on his own porch. Oh, what *fantasies* it conjures up. The trouble with revolutions is that you never can tell where they will end, who will eventually be cut down. I'll wager Desmoulins never supposed he'd lay his head on the block. But still, the old monster should be punished. . . ." He snapped his fingers. "Hit him where it will hurt most."

"Eh?" Johnnie raised his head.

"Money. Your father worships only money, so you have told me, and so I have heard from other sources. Why, it is said he only reigns supreme in this valley because everyone is in his pay, in some form or other. So there is how you can hurt him, with no risk to yourself."

"How?" Johnnie was frowning with bewilderment.

"Smash his frames."

"Eh?"

"Oh, go the whole hog. Burn his mill."

"You're joking."

"I'm not. What could be better? He prides himself on having his people well in hand. Why, you yourself say he manages Derleth as if it were Haggard's Penn in Barbados. Believe me, to have his factory destroyed would shake him up. He'd never be the same again. *That* would be a punishment."

Johnnie Haggard slowly pushed himself to his feet. "Burn Father's mill? We'd be hanged. You heard him at supper."

"Oh, come now. He may be an old monster. He'd hardly hang his own son. Anyway, how could he possibly know it was you? Another case of Luddism."

"I'd need help," Johnnie said.

"You'll not lack for that, surely. What about these Bold people?"

"They hate me."

"They hate you because of what happened to the girl. But if you were now prepared to avenge her . . . You told me they were spinners themselves. They have a grudge on that score as well."

"He'd cut me off without a penny."

"Only if he catches you, Johnnie. Who's going to even *suppose* it could be you? It could be the Luddites from anywhere."

Johnnie Haggard sat on the bed, chewing his lip. "I suppose it *could* be done."

"It could and it shall. Listen. Strike while the iron is hot. You want to get over to Plowding first thing tomorrow morning, see these Bold fellows, and tell them what you plan. I'll wager they'll follow you."

"You'll come with us as well?"

Byron smiled at him. "I'd be no help to you, Johnnie boy. What, with my game leg? But I'll be here to make sure you have an alibi. It'll be as simple as falling off a horse." He threw his arm around Johnnie's shoulder. "It'll be great sport. And it'll make you a man again. And your father will never *know*, there's the beauty. He'll think it was a judgment from heaven. Damn, we'll *tell* him it was. Oh, it will be sport."

Chapter 5

The Magistrate

A twig snapped, and Johnnie Haggard shuddered. What dreadful memories that sound brought back to him, memories which had in any event been clouding his brain throughout this journey. But he made himself remain still in the saddle, although it was difficult not to shiver in the early-morning chill. His horse pricked up his ears inquiringly.

"By all that's holy," Harry Bold said.

"Maybe he's coming after Meg again," Tim remarked.

"Aye, like a dog after bitch's scent," Harry growled.

They carried cudgels as well as their fowling pieces, were spaced as usual, one to either side of the nervous horse.

"We'll not let him go, Pa?"

"Not till he's felt the weight of my stick," Harry said. "You'll get down, Mr. Haggard. And don't suppose we'd not drop you."

Johnnie dismounted. Sweat was pouring from his shoulders. But he kept his teeth gritted so that the men would not see his chin tremble.

"We'll treat you better than what you let happen to Meg," Tim said. "You may use your fists. Against me. You let me, Pa. I'll tan his hide for him."

"You can have first go," Harry agreed.

Johnnie licked his lips. "Please," he said. "I came here to see you. To speak with you." To his relief, his voice did not shake.

"Oh, aye?"

"What brought you, then?" Tim demanded.

"It's about Meg."

"Oh, aye?"

Once again his throat and lips were dry. He licked, and swallowed. "I know who attacked her."

They gazed at him.

"It's true," he said desperately. "Alice found out. She . . .

371

she and I have been hunting for them these past two years, and we've finally found out."

"Who are they, then?"

"They're not important," Johnnie said. "It's the man who paid them to attack Meg. To attack me. It's him you want."

"That makes sense. And your sister has found this out as well, has she?"

"Yes."

"Well?"

"It's . . . it's Father."

Once again Bold exchanged glances with his son. His fingers tightened on the stock of his gun. "If I really thought that . . ."

"It's true."

Harry Bold's brows drew together. "Haggard? Don't give me that. You're his son."

"But he knew I was courting Meg. He wanted to end it."

"You could have been killed."

"I could have. But they didn't harm me."

Bold looked at his son. Tim shrugged. "Could be."

"Proof," Bold said. "Where's your proof?"

"Would I accuse my own father if I didn't know for sure?"

"Who were the men did it?"

"Well, Peter Wring, and the gamekeepers."

"Wring," Harry Bold growled.

"But you don't want them," Johnnie insisted. "It's Father you want."

"Your own pa?" Tim inquired. "You want us to kill your own pa?"

"Kill him? I said nothing about killing him."

"Oh, aye," Bold remarked. "You'd not have him killed. What do we do, write him a letter of protest? Take squire Haggard before the magistrate? He is magistrate, boy."

"Listen," Johnnie found himself panting. "Don't you think I thought of killing him, too, when I first found out? Don't you think I hate him as much as you do? I know now that Alice was always right, that he is a horrible man. I want to hurt him. I want to avenge Meg as much as you do. But killing him isn't the answer. For one thing, you'd . . . we'd be caught. We'd be hanged. What kind of revenge would that be? Don't you see? We must do something which can't be traced back to us. We must smash his frames."

"Smash frames?"

"And burn the mill, as well."

Bold frowned at him. "Burn the mill?"

"That'll hit him where it most hurts."

"And you don't suppose arson is a hanging offense? So is frame breaking, nowadays."

"But he'll never suspect us," Johnnie said urgently. "It'll just be a case of frame breaking spreading to Derleth. He's sure it could never happen here. It'll really upset him when it does."

"Burn the mill," Tim said half to himself.

"There's watchmen," Harry Bold said.

"One man. And I'll tell you something else; the watchmen for the mill are Father's gamekeepers. So we'd be getting our own back on them as well."

Harry Bold pulled his beard. "You'll be riding with us, Mr. Haggard?"

"Of course I will be. I'll set the torch with my own hands. But there must be no guns. No bloodshed."

"Oh, aye?"

"Sticks. No one must ever suspect it wasn't just a case of frame breaking."

Harry Bold hesitated, then nodded. "All right, Mr. Haggard. We'll do it next time Peter Wring is watchman."

"I said there's to be no killing," Johnnie insisted.

"Who said anything about killing?" Harry demanded. "But you'll not stop me blacking his eye. You find out when he'll be there, and tell us."

Johnnie chewed his lip in indecision. But having taken them into his confidence, he *had* to trust them. "All right."

"Where'll we meet?"

"In the woods beyond the mill. At one in the morning."

"We'll be there, Mr. Haggard. Just name the day."

"I'll let you know." Johnnie Haggard mounted his horse, rode into the trees.

"There's a turn-up," Tim commented.

"Aye. Little bastard. I don't know what he's at, Tim, boy, but we're going to damn well make sure we gets what *we* want, eh? You leave it to me."

Roger Haggard sat his horse in the trees, used his telescope to watch the turnpike and the wood beyond, and the little cottage. Carrying out a military reconnaissance, he thought. Captain Haggard, on duty. His heart pounded more painfully than at any time in Spain.

And his arm was free of the sling today for the first time.

He could move the fingers; the severed tendons must be on their way to mending. It really was a quite miraculous cure, but it carried with it the concomitant that he must soon return to the army. Only a week ago he would have been happy to do so. Time enough to come home to Derleth for good when the war was over, when he had had a little more time to acclimatize himself to the prospect of spending the rest of his life here, of being squire. For the moment he felt like a fish out of water. His mind told him that everything Father did was right, that only by creating wealth and more wealth could England remain as strong as she needed to be; and he knew wealth could in the main only be created by wealth. But his heart told him there was something wrong with the way Father was doing it. There had always been something wrong. It was surely wrong to extract the wealth of sugar from the sweat of slaves, just as it was surely wrong to extract the wealth of cotton and the wealth of coal from the labors of people prevented from ever enjoying noonday sunlight, from playing cricket when the weather was fine, from enjoying life in proportion to the work they put into living. And the two were irreconcilable. Therefore it would be best to go away again and return when he had decided irrevocably on which side of the fence he wished to take up his position.

As if there could ever be any doubt on which side of the fence Roger Haggard would have to take up his stance.

But that had been last week. Now he wished to stay here forever. Now the thought of returning to the horror that was Spain lay across his happiness like a leaden bar.

His happiness. He had not supposed ever to use such a word again. But he was happy. He could laugh, and he could sing. And he could sit his horse here, for nearly an hour, waiting and watching, feeling the slow growth of pleasure as he watched her come out of the back door of the cottage, her chores completed, and walk, with apparent casualness, across the little vegetable garden, before stepping into the wood.

He touched his horse with his heels, and it obediently moved forward. No drumming of hooves to alarm Emma. He had been prepared to do that, had Meg decided against coming. But she was there.

Meg Bold. A small red-headed elf whom life and his own brother had treated abominably. How could he hope to put that right? And why, indeed, after his fine words, had he not forced Johnnie to accompany him to kneel before the girl and humbly beg her pardon? He had not really wanted to do that, had been relieved to learn that Johnnie had already left the hall this morning, saddled up and gone no man knew where. He had leaped to horse himself, supposing that the young scoundrel might have anticipated matters and ridden over to Plowding. But he had not possessed even that much courage.

He was a strange lad. Certainly quite lacking in spunk. He would sit at dinner, thinking to himself, for the most part ignoring everything that was said around him. Roger doubted they could ever be friends. Certainly not after last night's quarrel.

He had entered the same stand of trees as Margaret. Now he drew rein and waited. She was the country girl. She would find him when she was ready. If she wished. A fine sweat gathered on his brow.

"Good morning, Captain Haggard."

He dismounted, released the reins. Cavalier was too well trained a mount to wander far.

Meg came through the trees, pushing auburn hair from her forehead with her right hand, threadbare blue skirt held from the ground with her left. Her feet were bare, the toes dusty. He had a sudden agonized thought that no doubt she went barefoot in the rain and the snow as well. But they were beautiful feet.

"Thank you for coming," he said.

"It is a long ride from Derleth," she said seriously.

"A worthwhile one." She was close enough for him to take her hand. She looked down at it curiously, lying in his, but made no effort to withdraw it.

"You've news of Alice?"

"She will be well."

"I can't stay long," she said. "Ma will miss me."

"You'd not make me ride twelve miles just to turn round and go back again?"

She made no reply, and very gently he rested a hand on each shoulder.

"Johnnie hasn't been here? Has he?"

"Johnnie?" She stepped backward so suddenly and so violently he had no time to release her; his hands scraped across the bodice of her gown, and she gave a little shiver. But she did not move away, and his hands once again settled on her shoulders.

"He came home yesterday," Roger explained. "And went out again early this morning."

Her cheeks were pink. "He'd not come here, Captain Haggard. Pa would kill him."

"And what would you do in his defense?"

Her eyes flickered. "I don't want him to come here, Captain."

Still she had not moved, and Haggard's hands were on fire. He must either step away himself, or he must bring her into his arms. Her face was only inches away; he could feel her breath.

"What *do* you want, Meg?"

Her eyes came up, great blue-green pools.

"Suppose . . . suppose I were a wizard, Meg," Roger said, "and could grant you any three wishes. Now, there is something to think about." He attempted a smile, but the girl's face was entirely serious. Her lower lip sucked in beneath her teeth for a moment. "Tell me," he said.

"I . . . I'd have to think," she said.

"Has Emma never told you about the good things in life?"

Meg shrugged; her shoulders rose and fell in his hands. "What's good, Captain Haggard? Mama says she's happier now than she ever was at the hall."

He had made a mistake. He was losing her. She could envisage none of the things he would have chosen, or any lady would have chosen. She was afraid of them. Therefore she would be afraid of him.

But he could not contemplate losing her. It was time to launch all his reserves, in a do-or-die effort.

"Well, then . . . suppose I could put back the clock, Meg? Suppose I could make those men disappear from your life, make you as you were before that night." Oh, stupid Roger Haggard. He was truly grasping at straws. And he had lost. He watched her face close. Because suppose she said yes? Of course she would say, "Oh, can you?" And what would he say then? "Then you'd be back with Johnnie," he said, in another attempt at humor.

Her eyes gloomed at him. "He'd still be a coward, Captain Haggard."

Haggard found his jaw slipping, and hastily closed his mouth. But was she not absolutely right?

"But you . . ."

She stepped backward, and his hands fell to his side. She turned away from him again.

"Do you hate those men very much?"

He could hear her inhaling. "I would like to see them hang," she said, her voice quite different from anything he had heard before. "I would like to stand beneath them and watch them kick their last," she said. "I would like to drag on their feet." She fell to her knees, keeping her back to him. "And I'd like to . . ." Her voice died.

Haggard knelt beside her. "That's one dream I will make come true," he said. "I promise you that, Meg."

Her head turned, and she looked at him. Her tongue had appeared in her mouth for a moment; then her mouth was closed again. And Roger felt the pounding in his heart increase.

"But you'd not change what happened," he said.

Still the sidelong glance. "I want everything Ma had," she said. "I want it for me, and I want it for Ma. But I don't want it ever to end. I know Johnnie could never give me all those things. He asked me to marry him, Captain Haggard. And I said yes. Even if I knew it would never be. But he . . . he didn't want to touch me. And I didn't know if I wanted him to. Now . . ." Again the little shrug. "Now I can't marry anyone, Captain. I've had five men inside me. There's no man would take me to his bed as his wife. But that's how it should be, Captain. Isn't that so? Because no man who *would* marry me could give me what I want. Would you give me what I want, Captain?"

Haggard took her shoulders again, and very gently brought her toward him, half-expecting her to pull away. But she came, and her eyes stayed open, seeming to grow wider and wider. They had thought her no more stable than Alice. And all the while, for two years, she had been thinking and philosophizing to herself, making up her mind what she wanted and what she would have, if not from him, from some other man.

Did that thought disturb him? Her face was against his now. He could kiss her eyes and her forehead and her nose and each cheek, and only slowly allow himself the luxury of her mouth. His hands slid from her shoulders down to the small of her back and then sought the gentle curve of her buttocks. She shuddered against him and moved, freeing one leg; her knuckle brushed his stomach as she lifted her skirt.

Her mouth slid from his. "Don't hurt me, Captain Haggard," she said.

Very gently he eased her onto her back. But he wanted to

look as well as to touch, himself lifted the skirt of the gown above her knees, slowly uncovered the smoothly muscled flesh of her thighs. She lifted her body to allow him to raise the gown higher; she wore nothing underneath. Meg Bold, a tinker's daughter. His for the taking, really. So why did he tremble and find it difficult to breathe? Why did he gently lower his head to kiss her pulsing groin, to move the dress higher with his head?

Her hands touched his cheeks, pressing him closer, and her knees came up, hugging him tighter yet. "Love me, Captain Haggard," she said. "Oh, love me."

He had to release her, kneel away from her, to take off his breeches. He thought: What an absurdity, for Roger Haggard to lie upon a bed of fallen leaves, to listen to the buzzing of the bees and the calls of the birds, when there were so many beds at his command. But this was what she wanted. This was what she must have wanted from the moment the men had left her alone—someone to do what they had done, and in the same place, only with love and with gentleness. He realized it probably did not matter who, save that he had to be a gentleman. But it did not even make him angry.

Her eyes were closed. He knelt between her legs; they parted readily enough at his touch. She breathed evenly, keeping herself under control. He understood that he was sharing the supreme moment of her life, and the most dangerous as well. If he hurt her, or even disgusted her, her life as a woman would be finished. She'd never risk this again. He kept himself back, breached her with only his tip, heard her moan, and watched her head turn to and fro on the grass. Was she pretending? He knew nothing save whores, there was his trouble. And Alison had been the greatest whore of all. But Alison had not allowed him to enter.

Because if it was her greatest moment, he realized it was also the most important moment of his own life. They shared a mutual horror, arising out of the mutual desires that were their bodies. If he was exorcising her demons, she was doing no less to him.

He slipped in and in. She was warm, so warm he felt on fire, but perhaps that was his own passion. He surged to and fro, and her hands bit into his back, through his shirt. He felt the material rip and then the pain of the nails driving into his flesh. But now he was kissing her again, and her eyes were open, and her hands were sliding up his back to hold his head and bring it ever closer to her. And her body was thumping against his even as he came himself.

He slid half off her, to relieve her of his weight. Her mouth followed his round, although the passion had left her fingers. She kissed his ear. "Will you give me what I want, Captain Haggard?"

It was utterly unreasonable to be so happy. She was nothing more than a girl. A girl who had been savagely mistreated, who had withdrawn into herself and had worked out her own salvation. That it was he she had chosen was merely chance. She meant nothing to him, could mean nothing to him. He was Roger Haggard, heir to Derleth and to Haggard's Penn and to the Haggard millions; she was a tinker's daughter. He could certainly set her up as his mistress, the way Father had set up Emma. But would that not be to start another chain of events which might well be tragic?

And yet he was happy. He wanted to sing as he rode down the track from the trees, past the ever-humming mill and the clanking wheel of the mine pumps, was even pleased to see Byron sitting on the terrace reading a book.

"The best of the day to you, my lord."

"Indeed, Captain, it is a magnificent afternoon. I shall be sorry to leave Derleth." He smiled. "Although I suspect your father will not be sorry to have me go."

Roger dismounted, tossed his reins to a waiting groom, sat beside the poet. "He is unused to being argued with. It is a fault. I suppose equally of mine. I mean, for not arguing with him more often."

"Why should you?" Byron asked seriously enough. "Do you not agree with everything he stands for?"

"Not everything."

"You surprise me."

"And you forget I spent near twenty years as a common soldier."

"By God, so you did. There is an unusual situation for a future Tory landowner."

"A confusing one, to be sure. I was interested in your thoughts on a possible reform of Parliament."

"You opposed them."

"Instinctively. I have been thinking about them since. This John Russell fellow. Do you suppose I could meet him?"

Byron stared at him in surprise. "It would be my very great pleasure, Captain Haggard." He wagged his finger. "But you want to be careful. Should the Tories even suppose you are mingling with Whig principles . . ."

"The Tories can think what they like, Lord Byron. My principles are my own."

"Spoken like a man. I promise you I shall arrange an introduction. You have made my day. Why, here is Johnnie. And what have you been up to, my pretty boy?"

Johnnie was flushed, as usual. Roger had never met a man who blushed so readily. Or perhaps it is my presence, he thought, after our quarrel of last night. Well, he deserved it, to be sure.

"I've been for a walk," Johnnie said. "Down to the village." He gazed at his brother—uneasily, Roger decided.

"Walking," Byron said in disgust. "Captain Roger and I have been discussing politics. You'll not believe this, boy, but we have a possible convert to Whiggism here."

"I'd not believe it either," Roger said.

"I said possible. And did you have a successful walk, Johnnie, lad?"

Once again the deep flush. "I think so."

They were exchanging a message with their eyes, Roger noted. Johnnie and Byron. Two poets. The one with all the world at his feet, the other with all the world looming over him. But they were friends.

Roger got up. "I'm to change my clothes," he said, and left them.

Haggard stood by the bed, looked down on the sleeping girl. Was she really sleeping? Harrowby had suggested they reduce the laudanum dosage, and according to the maids, Alice was awake quite a lot of the time, without, apparently, being in great pain. But now her eyes were shut. I hate you, she had shouted. Just like Alison. Just like Emma, in the beginning. Just like Adelaide Bolton, all those myriad years ago. I hate you. His mouth twisted. Perhaps even Susan had thought, I hate you, Haggard, as she had died. But they were wrong. I am not a hateful man, he thought. I wish only to love. So I have made mistakes. There is no man can claim never to have done that. You cannot hate somebody for his mistakes.

And the odd thing was that he hated nobody. Why should he? He was Haggard.

She sighed and moved in her sleep. A strand of auburn hair fell across her face. Very gently Haggard lifted it, moved it onto the pillow. And watched her eyes flop open.

"Do you hurt?"

She stared at him, perhaps trying to focus.

"You'll soon be well," Haggard said. "Harrowby says your ankle is nearly mended." He smiled at her. " 'Tis only your head we must consider."

Still she stared at him.

He bent over her. "Get well, Alice," he said. "Get well girl. There is a lot of living you have to do. Get well."

He kissed her on the forehead, straightened.

"I hate you," she whispered. "I hate you. Leave me alone."

Haggard met her gaze for a moment, then turned away. He glanced at the girl sitting in the corner, pretending not to have heard. Then he stepped outside, closed the door behind him, walked slowly to his room. He never slept in the tower nowadays; it was too lonely, too remote from the rest of the house. He liked to hear the murmur of activity; even in the dead of night, he liked to hear the chiming of the clocks. The tower room was a place of memories.

"How is she?" Roger, standing at the head of the stairs.

Haggard shrugged. "Her ankle is mended."

"But not her mind."

Haggard glanced at him, made no reply.

Roger walked beside him. "She will be well, Father."

"Aye," Haggard agreed. "She will be well." He paused at the door to his room, and it was immediately opened by Simpson. "I'll bid you good night. Lord Byron leaves in the morning."

"Yes." Roger hesitated. He wants to say something, Haggard thought. "I shall have to be leaving soon, as well." He moved the fingers on his right hand. "I can grasp again."

"Stuff and nonsense, boy. You'll stay here until you are truly well. At least until Alice recovers. I need you, boy. Johnnie is no help in a crisis like this. He never visits her. Where is he now? Drinking with his poet friend?"

"I have no idea," Roger said. "I think he retired early. Lord Byron is in the library reading."

"Reading," Haggard said disgustedly. "No doubt that's where he gets so many of his absurd ideas."

"Are they absurd, Father?"

Haggard frowned. "You'd give the vote to every Tom, Dick, and Harry? You'd give the vote to Simpson here? That would be a fine way to run the country. Eh, Simpson? What would you do with the vote?"

"I don't rightly know, Mr. 'Aggard." Simpson was laying out the nightshirt and cap.

"See what I mean? People like Simpson would have to be *told* how to vote, and the next thing, you'd have a tyranny like Bonaparte's. Don't give me stuff and nonsense like that." He hesitated, wondering what it was Roger really wanted to discuss. But apparently he was not going to do it tonight. "I'm for my bed."

Roger nodded. "Aye. Good night, Father."

The door closed. Haggard allowed Simpson to undress him, drape the nightshirt over his shoulders. He lay in bed while the valet doused the candles.

"Good night, Mr. 'Aggard, sir."

"Good night, Simpson."

Once again the soft click of the door. He listened to the barking of a dog, drifting up the hill from the village, to the chiming of the clock. It was eleven. On a magnificent summer's night. He had to do no more than sleep.

And think of the future. Roger's future. That was all that mattered. It was criminal that the heir to a fortune like his had to go off to fight a senseless endless war in a remote part of Europe, to risk his life, in defense of what? No French soldier was ever going to march up Derleth High Street.

My God, he thought, I am thinking like that upstart Byron. But Roger seemed to like the fellow. Or at least he was willing to listen to him. Because he was Johnnie's friend? There was the true future, and if Roger and Johnnie could be friends, then was it secure. Why, he thought, with me dead, even Alice can be friends again.

But that was looking too far ahead. He was not going to die. Not for a good many years. And not until Roger was finished with fighting, certainly. Haggard, he thought, and found himself smiling. It was time to shake himself. Why, he realized, he had slipped back into the same even way of life at Derleth that he had had at Haggard's Penn. Haggard's Penn. What memories that brought back. The smell of grinding, the gentle soughing of the wind in the canefields, Emma running down the front stairs to tell him she was pregnant, with Alice.

And were there not other Emmas? He had but to look properly. As soon as Roger returned for good, he'd find himself another Emma, and then he'd pay a visit to Barbados. That would shake them up. Why, after all these years Ferguson must suppose *he* owned the place by now; he was in fact due to be retired.

He slept deeply, was awakened by a noise. He opened his eyes, discovered that it was already daylight, although very early. And someone was shouting outside his window, waking the whole house, from the buzz of sound.

Haggard got out of bed, strode to the window, looked down on Toby Doon. Toby had lost his hat, and his white hair was flopping as he ran down the drive. "Mr. Haggard," he shouted. "Mr. Haggard," he screamed. "The mill. The mill."

"Halt there, Toby Doon." This was Ned, emerging from his room over the stables, scratching his head. "You'll wake squire."

"The squire." Toby Doon fell to his knees at the foot of the steps. "You must fetch him."

"I am here, Doon," Haggard called from the window. "What's amiss?"

"The mill, Mr. Haggard. 'Tis burning. And, Mr. Haggard, Peter Wring is dead."

Haggard dismounted, pushed hair from his eyes. He had stuffed his nightshirt into his breeches, forgotten his hat. It was a warm morning in any event, but it was rendered hot by the gigantic glow coming from the burning building. His factory, built like a fort. Well, the walls still stood. But the door had fallen in and the dawn breeze continued to whip the flames within. The mill resembled a gigantic oven. It glowed.

"There." Roger pointed, and he saw the body of a man lying beside the stream. Peter Wring lay on his back, his shotgun beside him. Corcoran dismounted and ran across. Roger followed more slowly, as did MacGuinness. Byron, who had also tumbled out of bed, remained standing beside Haggard.

"Shot, sir," Corcoran said. "At close range."

"Blown in two, more like," MacGuinness said.

Haggard slowly walked down the slope. He suddenly felt very old and tired. When had he first met Peter Wring? On the night James Middlesex had absconded. And no man could have had a more faithful servant, ever since. The face itself was almost unrecognizable. But Wring's hands were tied behind his back.

"Bound, he was," Corcoran muttered.

"Cold-blooded murder," MacGuinness said.

"Cold-blooded execution, you mean," Roger said. "This was someone with a grudge."

"But his piece isn't fired," MacGuinness said. "Now there's a strange thing."

"He was surprised," Roger suggested.

"Surprised? Not Peter."

"What, then?"

MacGuinness shrugged. "I couldn't say, sir. Save that he knew who it was."

"And didn't know they had come to kill him," Roger mused.

Haggard gazed at the blazing factory. The flames were beginning to die down now. But they had spread to the mill wheel, and that was starting to disintegrate, with gigantic hisses.

"Horses," Corcoran said. "There were horses."

"Can you track them?" Haggard asked. He was amazed at the evenness of his voice.

"That I couldn't say, Mr. Haggard. I can try."

"Then do so. MacGuinness, you'll fetch the rest of the gamekeepers. I want those men. By God, I want those men." For the exhaustion was slowly being replaced by a burning anger. The greatest anger he had ever known. He was Haggard. He had spent far more money on this village than he had really got out of it. Because it was his village, just as these were his people. And now one of them had been shot to death. "You find them, MacGuinness. Don't fail me in this."

He walked back up the slope, gazed at Byron. "These are the people to whom you'd give the vote?"

"I'd like to say I'm sorry, Mr. Haggard," Byron said. "I don't condone murder."

"Ah," Haggard said, and mounted.

"But perhaps if they had the vote they'd have less cause for it," Byron said.

Haggard glanced at him, turned his horse. Roger also mounted, and Byron followed their example.

"You don't suppose they were local people, Father?"

Haggard shook his head. "Local people would never have killed Wring." He urged his horse toward the gap.

"And what are you going to do?"

"Do?" Haggard did not turn his head. "I'm going to hang them. Every last one of them."

"And then?"

"Rebuild. Do they really think they can bring down John Haggard?"

He drew rein as they came through the cut. The road was a mass of people, as the rumor had spread. Now they surged forward to surround their squire.

"Is it true, Mr. Haggard?"

"The mill's burned, Mr. Haggard?"

"What's happened, Mr. Haggard?"

Haggard held up his hands, and they fell silent.

"The mill has been burned," Haggard said. "It is destroyed." He waited, while a great "Oh" rippled through the crowd. "And Peter Wring is dead," Haggard said. "He was tied up and then shot. It was the most brutal murder I have ever heard of."

Once again the gasp. Then someone shouted, "We're with you, Mr. Haggard."

"Oh, aye," shouted another. "You tell us what to do, Mr. Haggard."

Haggard held up his arms again. "The factory will be rebuilt," he said. "As soon as it can be done. But you've no cause to worry. I'll pay your wages every week until it *is* rebuilt, just as if you were working. You've my word on that."

"Hooray for Mr. Haggard," someone shouted.

"Horray for Mr. Haggard," the cheers were taken up.

Haggard waited for them to finish.

"And who'll avenge Peter Wring?" asked Jemmy Lacey.

"I will, Jem," Haggard said. "I'll avenge him. By God, I will. I'll find those people, so help me God, and they'll hang for it. You've my word on that as well. They'll hang for it, so help me God."

Once again the cheers, and he touched his horse with his heels to walk it through the crowd.

"Do you really suppose they'd vote different, my lord?" Roger asked. "If they could?"

Byron glanced at him. "Your father knows how to sway a crowd, Captain, and good luck to him. My argument is merely that they should have the *opportunity* to vote differently. Not that they necessarily would."

Haggard walked his horse down the drive, dismounted slowly and stiffly. The servants were all there waiting for him, Ned to take his bridle, Nugent with a glass of port, Mary Prince fussing about him.

"Look at you, sir," she said. "Nothing warm, not even a coat. Mr. Haggard, you'll catch your death of cold."

"Be off with you, woman," he growled, and drained the glass. He went inside. He did not wish his anger to fade, not until Peter Wring's murderers stood before him. He wanted to boil and boil and boil inside, so that he could throw the full weight of his hate at them. He climbed the stairs slowly, aware that all the domestics had remained gathered at the foot, staring after him. And suddenly aware that Alice was standing at the head of the second flight, also staring at him.

And this Alice was not half-asleep. On the contrary, her eyes seemed to blaze at him.

"Is it true, then?" she asked.

"You should be in bed." He climbed toward her.

"Is it true?" she asked again. "That the mill is destroyed?"

"It's true."

"And Peter Wring is dead?"

Haggard nodded. "He was murdered."

"But you're alive," she hissed at him as he came closer.

Haggard frowned at her. "Is that such an unpleasant thought?"

"You'll always be alive," she said. "You're indestructible. You're Haggard."

Clearly she had not entirely recovered her wits. Haggard nodded. "I'll always be alive, Alice. I'm Haggard. Now, come on back to bed."

She stared at him for a moment, then turned and limped in front of him. She wore her nightdress. Nothing else. At her door she halted, seemed to be waiting.

"Shall I open it for you?"

He made to reach past her, and she turned suddenly, leaning her back against the panels, covering the handle. "Leave me alone," she said. "Go away. Leave me alone."

Haggard's frown deepened. If anything, she might have suffered a relapse. "I'll see you to bed," he said.

"No," she snapped. "I hate you. Go away. Leave me alone."

She gasped, and Haggard heard the sob coming from behind her. He seized her shoulder, jerked her forward and to one side, opened the door, gazed at Johnnie. The boy was on his knees by the bed, weeping.

"Get out." Alice pounded at his shoulders with her fists. "You've no right to enter my room. You've no right."

Haggard stared at his son, and Johnnie slowly raised his head. "I didn't want it," he whispered. "Oh God, please believe me. I didn't want anyone to die."

Haggard's heart seemed to slow, and yet there was no diminution in the blood pounding through his veins.

"Who didn't you want to die?" he asked, his voice curiously low.

Johnnie reached his feet, licked his lips. "I . . ."

"Peter Wring?"

Johnnie stepped backward, and his knees touched the bed. "Why can't you leave him alone?" Alice had stopped pounding and was speaking in a normal tone. "Haven't you tortured him enough?"

"Was it Peter Wring?" Haggard asked again.

"We were to burn the factory," Johnnie gabbled. "Nothing else. We were to burn the factory. But they wanted Wring. They didn't tell me that, Father. I swear it."

He stopped, and his jaw slowly sagged as he gazed at the expression on his father's face.

"We?"

"I . . . I . . . I . . ."

"You were *there*?"

Johnnie sat on the bed.

Alice closed the door. "And why shouldn't he be there?" she demanded. "Wring deserved to die. He raped Meg Bold. Don't trouble to deny it. As you deserve to die, Father. For having sent him. You all deserve to die. Only, Johnnie doesn't have the stomach for killing."

Haggard turned to her. "Your doing?"

"Can you deny it?" she spat at him.

He gazed at her. Was he afraid of her? Was he afraid of anything she could say or do? He decided he was not. Not even if she could prove it. And he didn't suppose she could do that. But it would be necessary to face her down.

He turned back to Johnnie. God, how he hated the boy. Alison's child. How could he do other than hate him? But he kept his voice quiet and even. "Get up, boy. Don't be a sniveling coward all of your life. You believed her?"

Johnnie licked his lips, pushed himself to his feet. "Isn't . . . isn't it true?"

"Do you really suppose I'd waste the time?" Haggard demanded. Did it matter? Why did he not tell the little lout, and watch *him* squirm with hatred. "And do you suppose the virginity of a tinker's daughter is worth the life of a man? Her mother was a whore. A whore, do you understand? She was my whore. Then, when I threw her out, she went whoring elsewhere. A whore's daughter, that's who you were pulling after."

"You'll not say that." Alice struck at him, but he caught her hand easily enough, turned her, and sat her on the bed. "You'll not," she gasped.

"I thought you were a stickler for the truth, miss? You." He pointed at Johnnie. "I want the names of the men who rode with you. I want the name of the man who shot Peter Wring."

Johnnie stared at him, mouth opening and shutting.

"So you can hang them all?" Alice snarled.

"That's right," Haggard said. "So I can hang them all. Quickly, boy, or you'll dangle beside them."

Johnnie Haggard licked his lips. "I was there, Father. I led them. I'll not betray them."

Haggard's hands opened and shut. But he could not control them. His arm shot out and the flat of his hand slashed across Johnnie's face. The boy tumbled backward, struck the end of the bed, and sat on the floor. The door opened, and Roger stepped in.

"Father?"

"He led them," Haggard said. "He's boasting of it. My own son, a Luddite and a murderer."

"Christ," Roger said. "Is it true?"

"He had cause," Alice gasped. "He had cause. He——"

"He's due for a hanging," Haggard said. "Because of her hate."

Alice's mouth closed slowly. She bit her lip instead. Roger glanced from one to the other in bewilderment.

"But I'll save you, boy. God knows why. I'll save you, if you'll give me the names of those at your back."

Johnnie held on to the bedpost to pull himself to his feet. He remained out of reach of his father's hands, and tears were rolling down his cheeks. But his face was set. "I'll not, Father. They rode with me, at my bidding."

"Who?"

Johnnie shook his head.

"Why?" Roger demanded. "In the name of God, why?"

"I didn't want Wring to die," Johnnie said. "But he deserved to. He raped Meg. And Father sent him to do it." He caught his breath, as if amazed that he should have spoken the words.

Roger stared at his father.

"Do you believe him, boy?"

"I . . . of course I don't."

"Aye, well, it was all a product of Alice's diseased brain."

"It was not. It was . . ." But again she checked herself.

"Alice?"

Her shoulders slumped. "I don't know. I . . . I was sure. I lay under the tree, and there were five men. Wring and the others. And I thought I . . . I don't know." She threw herself on her face across the bed, shoulders racked by great sobs. "I don't know. Oh, God. I don't know."

"Christ," Roger said again. "Oh, Christ. You believed her, Johnnie?"

"I . . . I . . ."

"The names, boy," Haggard said. "The names."

Johnnie shook his head again. "I won't. They trusted me. I won't."

"Trusted you," Haggard snorted. "And you'll hang for them?"

Slowly Johnnie's head came up. His lips were trembling.

"Oh, aye," Haggard said. "Don't suppose being a Haggard will save you from the noose. You'll hang, boy. You'll hang."

"Of course he means to frighten him," Roger said. He stood in the center of the Bolds' kitchen, gazed at the startled faces. Even Harry and Tim looked to be frightened. "And I wouldn't have supposed Johnnie had the courage of a louse. But he won't betray them."

"Perhaps he's afraid to," Emma said. She drove her hands into her hair. "Perhaps . . ." She gazed at her daughter.

"I'm sorry for it, Captain Haggard," she said. "Oh, I'm sorry for it."

"Perhaps if . . . There's nothing you remember about the men who attacked you?"

"Leave the girl be," Harry Bold growled. "You think she wants to remember? Leave her be. You've no cause coming here, anyways. You've got trouble in Derleth, that's your business. Haggard's business is Haggard's business. You're happy enough to say that when things are going well. Like you say, it'll serve the young puppy right. Beginning what he can't finish. Let him get frightened. Let him get frightened to death. You clear out of here and leave us be, Captain Haggard."

Roger looked from one to the other. "I'd like a word with Meg alone," he said.

"You'll not," Harry said. "You'll not speak with her. Who do you suppose has suffered worse than any? Worse than your stinking brother ever could. You'll not speak with her, Haggard."

"Emma?"

Emma sighed and raised her head. "She isn't well, Roger. You can see she isn't well. She hasn't been well since that night. Harry's right. You've no right to pry. You had no right to pry in the first place. Johnnie deserves a good thrashing."

"She's . . ." Haggard glanced at Meg. Her eyes were wide, beseeching him not to betray her. How like Alice she is, he thought. She had given him everything she had to give. Now she did not want him to allow her family to discover that. He shrugged. "If that's the way you feel, Mrs. Bold. I'll say good day." He went to the door, hesitated there, looked over his shoulder. "If you should want to see me again, you'll know where I am."

He sat his horse in the trees and watched the cottage through his glass. But without hope now. He had sat here for three hours, and she had not come. She had not even left the house to feed the chickens. He could not believe that she could have used him so coldly and dispassionately to regain her womanhood. Dispassionately? He could not believe she was that good an actress.

But she was not coming. And he was wasting time. Valuable time. There was so much to be done at the hall, where Johnnie was confined to his room. Father had used the emergency power granted the justices of the peace by the recent legislation to hasten the trial—summary justice in the case of frame breaking had in any event been one object of the law—and the neighboring magistrates who were required to make up the quorum were already sent for. If he was about to frighten his son, he was making a very good job of it.

She was not coming, and there was an end to it. For a last time he leveled the telescope. Slowly a frown gathered between his eyes. Meg had not come out to feed the chickens for the very simple reason that there were no chickens. Nor was there any smoke issuing from the chimney. Fool that he was for not noticing that immediately.

Would it have made any difference? He kicked his horse, cantered across the meadow, down the path. The front door was locked, but he could peer in through the windows. The stocking frames were still there, as was the empty range, the four chairs, the wooden table. Nothing else. He went round the back, stared into the bedroom. There were no blankets, no clothes. The Bolds had abandoned their home.

"But do *you* believe it?" Roger demanded.

Byron sat on the terrace gazing out across the deer park. "What I believe, my dear Haggard, is immaterial. Your brother certainly believed it, as he had been told so by his sister. It is she you wish to question."

Roger sighed and sat down. "And drive her a little further out of her mind? What advice did you give Johnnie?"

"Ah," Byron said. "I dissuaded him from doing anything foolish."

"You would not call murder foolish?"

"Now, you know that was not premeditated."

"Not by Johnnie, at any rate," Roger agreed. "I know that." But by accomplices? By Harry Bold and his son? If they knew, or if they even believed, that Peter Wring had raped Meg, there was motive enough. Motive enough for them to flee afterward, too. For fear Johnnie would betray them, while he, poor deluded fool, was now set on playing the hero. But, Roger wondered, did he really want them betrayed? Did he want Meg's brother and father to hang? Did he want Johnnie to hang? But that was nonsense. Father would never let it come to that.

He got up. "I had thought you were returning to town."

"I'll stay, if you don't mind," Byron said. "Johnnie is one of my closest friends. I'll not desert him."

"Good of you," Roger remarked dryly and went inside. He climbed the stairs to his father's office, but the room was empty. He went upstairs again, opened Alice's door. But she had asked for, and been given, some more laudanum, and was asleep. He seemed to be surrounded by gray clouds through which he could not push. But that was nonsense. He was Roger Haggard. He had pushed through thicker clouds than these in the past.

He ran downstairs, called for Corcoran. "I may need a couple of good arms."

"I'm with you, sir," Corcoran agreed.

They rode through the gap, gazed at the burned-out mill. Under MacGuinness' directions, men were already clearing the blackened timbers, dragging out the shattered frames, testing the walls for strength. Squire had said rebuilding would commence immediately, and it was doing just that. While Peter Wring still awaited burial. While John Haggard junior still awaited trial.

"MacGuinness," Roger called.

The big man raised his head, slapped his hands together, came toward the horse. His laborers stopped working and watched.

"I'd like a word with you, Mr. MacGuinness," Roger said. "In private."

"Oh, aye, Captain Haggard. In good time, sir. In good time."

"Now," Roger said.

MacGuinness shook his head. "Squire's orders are to have this site cleared by the time he returns from Derby. Can't stop for nothing, Captain Haggard."

"MacGuinness . . ." Roger hesitated. The other men had laid down their tools and drawn closer. Among them were the remainder of the gamekeepers. Wring's accomplices? Alice thought so. But Alice had as good as admitted her mistake. And in any event, they were closing their ranks against *him*. He was the outsider now. He'd been away too long.

MacGuinness smiled at him. "You ask squire, Captain Haggard. You ask him if I can stop work to speak with you, and I'll be willing. You ask squire."

Ask squire. Roger was in front of the house to greet his father.

"Father. We must—"

"What's he doing here?" Haggard's arm was outflung, the finger pointing at Byron.

"Well, he's Johnnie's friend . . ."

"Friend?" Haggard's voice rasped. "Lover, more like. They're a pair of damnable sodomites. You," he shouted, stamping onto the terrace. "You are no longer welcome here, sir. Get off my property."

Byron stood up. His face was cold, if his cheeks were bright. "Your manners do you little credit, Mr. Haggard. I am your son's friend."

"You, sir? Why—"

"His only friend, I would estimate," Byron continued. "Oh, I shall leave your miserable folly, sir, as you demand it. But I shall not go very far."

He went inside, and Roger scratched his head in sheer amazement. "Surely you've no right to make such an accusation?"

"No right?" Haggard snapped. "Johnnie as good as confessed it. My son . . . Christ, I can hardly believe it."

"Aye, well, it takes all sorts. I'd agree with you that his lordship was a bad influence. But now he's gone . . ."

"You talk as if there was nothing wrong," Haggard said. "As if it scarce matters whether a man loves a man or a woman. By God—"

" 'Tis Johnnie concerns me," Roger shouted. "Surely this farce has gone far enough. Only Johnnie matters now. I wish to know when you are going to drop the charges."

Haggard stared at him for several moments, then turned on his heel and went inside.

Surely this farce has gone on long enough. He sat at his desk and stared at the closed door. To know what to do. He was John Haggard. He could do anything he wished, within reason. But he was justice of the peace for Derleth. Over the years these people had grown to respect him and to trust him, and now one of their number had been killed in his service, and he had promised to bring the murderer to justice.

But the murderer was his own son. A sniveling coward who was also a sodomite. Did he wish such a son? Could a man execute his own son?

He was John Haggard. He could do anything he wished. Therefore he could drop the charges and release Johnnie. So perhaps the people of Derleth would then hate him as much as everyone else hated him. Would that be so very hard to bear?

And what of Johnnie? He had stumbled on the truth, even if he no longer believed it. Was he then confessing that he would execute his son to prevent his own crime being discovered? Then what of Alice?

Unworthy thoughts. All unworthy thoughts. He was overtired, and he was too emotionally disturbed. Where was the John Haggard who had ridden out to face Malcolm Bolton? Then it had been a simple matter. The cause of the duel had been puerile. But it had had to be fought. And if it had to be fought, it had to be won. Better to kill in a puerile cause than to be killed in one. He had made the decision without the slightest hesitation. That was Haggard law. Do what is right, and what is right for Haggard is right for the community at large. It had to be so. But for his wealth and his paternalistic attitude, Derleth would have declined into a vast slum. Haggard law.

And Johnnie was Alison's son. How had he hated her, while she had lived, just as he had hated her since her death. Could Johnnie really be any different? He had all of his mother's perversions, all of his mother's secret ambitions and desires which had so infuriated him. Johnnie should never have been born. He should have been the babe which had killed her, and he should have died with her. There was the truth of the matter.

But could a man kill his own son? It had been done before. There was even a biblical text about it, something about plucking out mine own eye, if it offends me. He found himself smiling in his despair. John Haggard, quoting the Bible.

"Gentlemen." He stood in the doorway of his study.

"Mr. Haggard." Squire Burton of Plowding took his hand. "We . . . well . . ." He glanced at Sergeant McCloud.

" 'Tis a devilish situation, Haggard," McCloud remarked. "A devilish situation."

Haggard closed the door, indicated chairs. He'd not anticipate.

"The fact is, Haggard . . ." Burton wiped his brow. "You'll not be sitting?"

"Why not?"

"For God's sake, man, you cannot try your own son."

"Why not?"

"Well . . ." He glanced at McCloud.

Who cleared his throat. "The fact is, Haggard, we are wondering if you'd like to withdraw the charge. Then we could enter a *nolle prosequi*, and the whole thing could be forgotten. There is not a shred of evidence that your son was involved."

"He confessed to it."

"Save his confession, I was going to say. Now, sir, if he were to withdraw that confession, I do not see how we could proceed. I don't suppose we could. Now, sir, there is yet time for you to convince the young man of his utter folly. I've no doubt some girl is involved, what?" He paused and gave a nervous laugh. "Or . . . something of that nature. He's protecting someone. Well, sir, it's absurd. So, sir . . ."

"He has confessed to murder and to arson and to frame breaking," Haggard said. "It is written down."

"It can be mislaid, easily enough."

"You are asking me to condone a miscarriage of justice."

"In the name of God, sir, is it not a miscarriage of justice to hang your own son? It will come to that, sir. Once we take our places and he takes his, why, sir . . ."

"You'll know he has refused counsel?" Burton asked.

"That is his prerogative," Haggard said. "It would be useless in any event."

There was a knock on the door, and MacGuinness pushed in his head. "Master John's been taken down, Mr. Haggard."

"Thank you, MacGuinness. We hold court in the school hall, gentlemen. Shall we go?"

"Haggard . . ."

"They are waiting for us, gentlemen." Haggard opened the door. "In the circumstances, McCloud, I'd be obliged if you'd act as chairman."

"What are we to do?" Burton whispered.

McCloud hesitated; then his face cleared. "He means to punish the boy. That's certain. But he'll never hang. The sentence will have to be commuted."

"To transportati...
McCloud sighed,
outside the door.
They are waiting, ge...
"State your full name,"
John Haggard drew a l...
gard," he said. Amazingly,
with weeping. He could look
to identify some of the pe...
spot; he had put on his u...
his face equally red,
simple to see, leanin... his
contempt as he s...
inn. But b...
packed ...

...n? Is that any better?"
...and shrugged. Haggard had remained just

...ntlemen."

...MacGuinness requested.

...ong breath. "John Simpson Hag-
...his eyes were dry. He was finished
... around the schoolroom, even try
...ople. Roger was easy enough to
...niform and was a blaze of crimson,
...features strained. Byron was equally
...g back, his face a picture of composed
...urveyed the court; he had taken rooms at the
...enind them the faces were a blur; the hall was
...uite literally to the door.

...John Haggard," MacGuinness said, "you are accused that
on the eighteenth of July last you did feloniously and unlawfully kill and murder one Peter Wring gamekeeper, and further, that on the said date you did feloniously and unlawfully
enter a mill the property of . . ." MacGuinness drew a long
breath. "Mr. John Haggard of Derleth Manor in the village
of Derleth in the county of Derbyshire and therein, did
destroy stocking frames and other equipment to the value of
two thousand pounds, and further, that on the said date you
did set fire to the said mill with a view to destroying it utterly. How plead you to these charges?"

"I plead guilty," Johnnie said.

There was a violent buzz, and Sergeant McCloud banged
his desk with his gavel.

"I will clear the court if I have to," he remarked. "Mr.
Haggard, you will face the bench."

Johnnie faced them, stared at McCloud. He would not
look at his father.

"You understand the gravity of these charges?" McCloud
asked.

"Yes, sir."

"You understand that the penalty is prescribed by law, that
we have no room to make exceptions?"

"Yes, sir."

"Well, then, do you persist in your plea?"

"Yes, sir."

McCloud sighed and glanced at Burton.

"Do you not suppose, Mr. Haggard, that it would be better
for you to consult with counsel before taking such an irrevo-

cable decision?" Burton asked. "I am sur[e] agree to an adjournment."

"I have no need for counsel, sir," John[nie]

"For God's sake, boy. 'Tis your life [we]

"I have pleaded guilty to murder, s[ir.]

Burton stared at him for a m[oment, threw up his] hands and leaned back in his seat[s.] [McCloud glanced at Hag-] gard, leaned toward him.

"Do you recommend transport[ation or some such punish-] ment, Mr. Haggard?" he said. "Be[sure we shall support you."]

"There is no possibility of trans[portation for any] three offenses the prisoner has comm[itted." Haggard did not] whisper, and his voice was clearly audi[ble.] [You have done] your best to irregularize these proceeedings a[s it is. Justice de-] mands that the proceedings be completed now. I de[mand it."]

McCloud turned back to the court.

"Prisoner at the bar, have you anything to say before I pass sentence?"

Johnnie Haggard's face was pale, but his lips were firmly pressed together. Just a trace of brightness showed at his eyes. "I have nothing to say, sir."

McCloud looked right and left. Burton raised his eyebrows and then closed his eyes. Haggard stared at his son.

McCloud sighed. "Prisoner at the bar, you have confessed to three grave and criminal offenses, each one of which carries with it the death penalty. This court can do nothing more for you. You are therefore sentenced to be taken from here back to your cell, and from thence to a place of execution, and there you shall be hanged by the neck until you are dead."

Once again the court surged into uproar. People were shouting from the back, "Murderer," at Haggard. Others were just shouting. Illing touched John Haggard on the arm. "There's a room for you at the inn, Mr. John," he said, "if you don't mind my company for the night."

"We'll have you out, Johnnie," Byron said. "They'll not hang Johnnie Haggard."

"You'd best stay inside awhile, Mr. Haggard," MacGuinness muttered. "The people are in an ugly mood."

"I have faced mobs before, MacGuinness." Haggard stood up, gazed at Roger, whose mingled anger and disbelief were easy to see. Haggard attempted to signal him with his eyes, but Roger turned away. Even Roger. He did not yet understand the responsibilities of being squire of Derleth, of being Haggard.

He went down the aisle, and after a brief hesitation Burton and McCloud followed him.

Roger remained seated, staring after them. He did not believe he was truly awake. But what had he expected to happen? Once the case came to court, it could have only one conclusion. Father was playing his savage game to the very end. He pushed himself up, found himself face to face with Byron.

"Well, Captain, your father has had his little joke," Byron said. "And in very poor taste it is, too. How far will you permit it to go?"

"No farther, you may be sure of that," Roger said.

"Aye, well, it will be a close-run thing. Sentence has been passed. You're talking of a reprieve now."

"I shall organize it."

"I wish you fortune. I am to Derby to obtain the lieutenant's intercession, whether Johnnie wishes it or not."

"On what grounds?"

Byron closed one eye. "On an irregularity. Surely it is an irregularity for Haggard to try his own son?"

"Even if he did not ask for clemency?"

"An irregularity is an irregularity, Haggard. I'll make him listen if I have to keep him up all night."

"There's not time. There is only one man can save Johnnie now, and that is Father. And by God, I will see to it that he does. You'll excuse me, my lord." He turned away, pushed his way through the crowd, stopped as a woman stepped in front of him, stared at Margaret Bold.

Emma stood behind her. Each woman wore a shawl thrown over her head and gathered under her chin, and would have been indistinguishable had they not removed them. But Meg and Emma in Derleth? And after having run away.

He seized the girl's hands. "Meg." It was outrageous of him to be happy. But never had he been so happy. "Oh, Meg."

"We must speak with you, Roger." Emma's voice was low.

"You shall. You shall. Come on." He escorted them toward the door, and checked. From outside they could still hear the chanting of the crowd. He did not know what might be happening out there; he did not suppose it would greatly worry his father. But Meg and Emma . . . "We'd best wait awhile," he said.

"They are cursing the squire," Emma said.

"Aye. Who'd have thought it, eh? After all these years." He found them seats; the hall was rapidly emptying, and they were almost alone in the corner of the room. "Oh, Meg, Meg . . ." Once again he took her hands. "To run off . . ."

"It was Pa's doing," she said. "Pa and Tim. They made us go."

"Because they were afraid?"

Meg licked her lips and glanced at Emma.

"They were afraid, Roger. Did you know?"

He shrugged. "I guessed."

"But you did not ride after them?"

"I was more concerned with Johnnie."

She nodded. "That's why we're here. Johnnie didn't shoot Peter Wring. It was Harry."

"Cold-blooded murder, Emma."

"Execution, Roger. He raped Meg."

"Now, Emma, you don't believe that? That was a concoction thrown up by Alice while she was confused by the bang on her head. Even she no longer believes it."

"But it's true," Emma insisted, her voice rising. She looked around herself, flushed. "Tell him, Meg."

"Well . . ." Meg licked her lips. "After you left us that morning, Pa said we must get out of here. Ma and me didn't know what he was talking about, but he was that determined. We couldn't argue with him, Captain. It weren't possible. He was like a madman. Tim, too. It was all haste, haste, haste."

"We left that night," Emma said. "Stole away in the darkness like criminals. Well, I suppose we were. Abandoned everything."

"I know," Roger said. "I visited you the next day."

"Did you?" Meg's eyes glowed. "Then you would have forgiven me, Captain?"

"Forgiven you, I—"

"Finish what you have to say." Emma insisted.

Meg licked her lips again. "Well next day we were into Leicestershire, and still hurrying. They wouldn't talk, Pa and Tim, but by now we knew something dreadful had happened. And at last it came out. Weren't murder, Pa kept insisting. It were justice. Peter Wring deserved to die, and so did Toby Doon and George Illing and all of them."

"But I told you—" Roger began.

"Listen to me," Meg said almost fiercely. "Toby Doon. It

was the first time I'd heard that name. And suddenly I knew that I'd heard it before. When Pa asked me if I could tell him about the men who . . . who attacked me. I couldn't think of a thing. I could only think of them holding me and holding me and holding me. But then I remembered they'd used his name. Someone had said, 'Your turn, Toby Doon.' And another had said, 'Hold your trap, you silly bastard.' "

Roger frowned at her. "You'll have heard the name, Meg. In conversation, in—"

"How?" Emma demanded. "Your father's gamekeepers don't come over Plowding way. They're not that popular."

"Plowding people work in Father's factory," Roger pointed out. "They'd know Toby. It's possible Meg may have heard the name."

The girl stared at him with her mouth open. "You don't believe me?"

"I want to believe you. God, how I want to believe you. But you're asking me to believe that Alice was right, that Father did engineer the whole thing. My God." He found himself staring at Emma.

"If he did, Roger Haggard," she said, "if he did, then he cannot go through with the execution of Johnnie."

"I doubt he means that anyway," Roger said. "It is just his way."

"His way?" Emma cried. "You don't know your father very well, Roger. His way? You weren't there when he turned his people out into the snow. You *were* there when he sent his men against Harry and me. Oh, there are so many things. I don't know them all. I can't tell you them all. But when John Haggard determines to do something, he does it. You must stop him, Roger, or that boy will hang. God knows I have no love for your brother, but you cannot stand by and see him hang."

Roger bit his lip. "You understand, Meg, and you, Emma, that if I threaten to make the whole thing public, and Father calls my bluff, there will be warrants sworn for the arrest of Harry and Tim? Murder warrants. They'll be taken and hanged."

"Aye, well," Emma said, " 'tis a large country."

"Are you serious?"

"Don't you understand?" she cried. "I'd not do it. Christ, I'd not do it. But we had to come back and see. If Johnnie had been sent to prison, if he'd been transported, why, we could have said nothing. But he's innocent of murder, Roger.

And he's played a better part in this, keeping his mouth shut, than he has ever done before."

Roger gazed at Meg. "Is that the only reason you came back?"

Her tongue stole out and then retreated again. "They'd not let me, Captain," she said. "They'd not let me."

"Are you going to sit there the day?" Emma demanded.

Roger got up. "No. If you're sure, we'll face Father down. Come on."

"Murderer," the crowd shouted.

"Jeffries," bawled someone else, more learned than the rest, and referring to the infamous Bloody Assizes of a hundred and thirty years before.

Haggard stood on the steps of the school hall and gazed at them. He was surprised more than angry. Certainly he was not afraid of them. He was their squire, they were his people. And he was avenging one of them. He felt like holding up his hands, making them a speech, explaining why he'd been so inflexible. But he'd not appeal to a mob. Not even his own mob. Not anymore.

"We'd best be away, Mr. Haggard." MacGuinness stood at his elbow, faithful as ever.

Or was he faithful? Haggard glanced at him. "And what would you call me, MacGuinness?"

"Me, sir?" But MacGuinness would not meet his gaze. Even he would condemn the squire, if he dared.

Haggard went down the steps; Ned had come across, as indeed had all the servants from the hall, and he held the bridle. But he said nothing. Haggard swung into the saddle, looked around him, and the crowd fell silent. But they were all there. He could make out Jemmy Lacey and his sister; Nugent, the butler; Toby Doon and Geroge Illing; Hatchard; Porlock, his face a study in consternation, Mrs. Porlock clinging to his arm. All there. His own people, in whose cause he had wasted more than twenty years of his life. And at the back, Squire Burton and Sergeant McCloud, sitting their horses. All gathered to condemn him for upholding the law.

He turned his horse, rode through them. They parted before him. From behind him some of the shouts started again, but those within reach of his gaze remained silent. Would not one of them shout, "God Bless you, squire?"

He rode up the drive to the hall. He had been a fool. He had been a fool to come to England at all. Every catastrophe he had known had arisen from that simple mistake. Well, that was not altogether true. He had been as unpopular in Barbados, and he had suffered even greater catastrophes. But there the sun had shone. There his people had been slaves, who dared not criticize, who dared not even hold any opinion contrary to their master's. There, with Emma, he had been happy.

And there, with another Emma, he could be happy again.

He dismounted, left the reins hanging; the horse peered after him inquiringly. He walked to the door, and it opened for him. Mary Prince. Of all the servants, only Mary Prince had remained.

"You look tired, Mr. Haggard," she said. "A glass of port will do you good."

Haggard glanced at her. Mary Prince. He could remember the coal dust dribbling down those slender legs. Mary Prince. He had taken her on the day his world had fallen apart. The day he had thrown Emma out. Mary Prince.

He climbed the stairs. "Mr. Haggard?" she called.

"Leave me," he said.

"But, Mr. Haggard—"

"Go away," he shouted. "Go and join your friends in the village. Go and chant 'Murderer' with them. Leave me alone."

He climbed the next flight, opened the bedroom door. Alice was sitting up; when she saw him, her face seemed to close.

"Where is your maid?"

"I sent her away. I sent her to the village."

"She is supposed to stay with you day and night."

"I am not a child, Father. Nor am I truly ill anymore. I asked her to bring me a report of the trial."

Haggard nodded, sat on the bed. She regarded him as if he were about to assault her, carefully eased herself away from him. How like Emma she looked. In many ways, how like Emma she was. And they knew each other so very well. He did not want sex from her, or from anyone. He was too tired. To dispirited, perhaps, at this moment, anyway. But he wanted her company. Even if she would not speak, he still wanted her company. Just to see her, that red stain on her shoulders, those small, composed features. Just to see her was to remember. Just to remember was to be John Haggard of Haggard's Penn once more.

"Well?" she asked.

"He was found guilty."

"And?"

Haggard shrugged. "The law is quite specific about each one of his crimes. Certainly about murder."

"He didn't kill Wring. Not Johnnie."

"He has never denied it."

Her frown began to gather. "And you allowed sentence to be passed? On your own son? You could stop it, Father." She seized his hand. "However much you hate Johnnie. However much you hate me. You cannot let him hang."

She had never taken his hand before. Her fingers were cool. "Hate you, Alice? I have never hated you."

She stared at him, and flushed. Her fingers relaxed, but they did not move. "You'll save him, Father. Please. Oh, God, please."

Haggard gazed at her. "We'll leave this place," he said. "You and I, Alice. We'll leave the hall. Roger will be back to live here soon enough. We'll leave it, you and I, and we'll return to Barbados. You remember Barbados?"

"I . . ." Her eyes were wide. "I remember Barbados."

"Will you come with me, Alice? Back to the Penn? Back to the sunlight and the sea and the trade wind?" He smiled. "Back to the hurricanes? Do you remember the hurricanes?" But even hurricanes would be better than English weather. Hurricanes were something for a man to match himself against. A man could not fight this deadly, endless rain. "I should have gone back years ago. I should never have left. But we'll go back now. Will you, Alice?"

"If . . . if you wish it, Father. If you'll save Johnnie."

"You'd bargain?"

Her chin came up. "If that's how it must be, Father. Me, for Johnnie."

He frowned at her. There was no love in her eyes. Not even a suggestion of affection. She was concluding a business deal. Why, Alison had looked like that when they had sat around the table in Brand's house discussing the marriage contract. Me, for Johnnie. She was set to be the martyr. She'd look after him for the rest of his life, sacrificing her own happiness, and never letting him forget it for an instant.

He moved her hand, got up.

"I will, Father," she said. "I'd never leave you. I swear it. Just let Johnnie live."

Haggard closed the door behind him. He walked along the corridor, climbed the stairs to the tower room. However empty it was kept nowadays, it remained ready for occupation. The bed was made, the room was carefully swept and dusted every day. The desk was neat, and there would be paper in the drawer.

He stood at the window, looked out at the deer park. This was the most attractive view in Derleth, away from the village and the cut to the mine and the factory. He was a fool to have abandoned it. He was a fool.

Hooves. He went to the other window, looked down on the road from the village, on the drive, watched Roger galloping up to the house. Behind him there was a pony and trap and some people, women. Come to beg for Johnnie's life. Everyone in the world begging for Johnnie's life. Loving Johnnie. Hating Haggard.

Haggard sat at the desk, took out a sheet of notepaper, and began to write.

Roger flung himself from the saddle, ran at the door. Mary Prince stood there. "Captain? Oh, Captain . . ."

"Where is my father?"

"He went upstairs. He seemed very upset, Captain."

Haggard took the stairs three at a time. At the top of the second flight he saw Alice, just leaving her bedroom. "Alice?"

"Father was here," she said. "He was in a very strange mood."

"Wouldn't you be, after sentencing your son to death? Where is he now?"

"I don't know. He said we were going back to Barbados, and when I agreed, he just turned and walked out of the room."

The sound of the shot was dull in the huge, empty house. For a moment they stared at each other; then Roger ran along the corridor, Alice limping behind. But she did not climb to the tower, remained in the withdrawing room below, turned to look at Emma and Meg as they came in, escorted by Mary Prince.

"What . . . ?"

"I don't know. There was a . . . Oh, God, I don't know."

Roger came slowly down the stairs, holding the sheet of paper in his hand.

"John?" Emma asked. "Mr. Haggard?" She ran for the stairs. Roger caught her arm. "You'll not wish to go up there, Emma."

She shrugged herself free. "I am as much wife as he ever had, Roger Haggard." She climbed the stairs.

"What did he write?" Alice asked.

Roger sighed. "Who'd have thought it? Father, the most self-contented man I ever knew." He held out the paper. "The most determined man I ever knew. He has written a recommendation that Johnnie be retried, because of prejudice on the part of one of the magistrates, himself. He wrote that, and then he shot himself."

Alice sat down. "Perhaps none of us knew him well enough," she said.

Meg just stood there, stared at her mother as she came back down the stairs. "You loved him, Ma. More'n you ever loved Pa."

"Aye," Emma said. "I loved him. God, how I loved him. If I'd not been proud two years ago . . ." She gazed at Roger. "What will you do? You are squire of Derleth now."

"Do?" Roger looked at the stairs. His father, a suicide. The world would not forget or forgive. But did the world matter? Father had been Haggard; that was sufficient. As he was now Haggard. He walked to the windows, looked out at the drive and the people gathered on the road beyond. They had come to hate the squire, just as only a few days before they had gathered to support him. But *he* was the squire now. They would depend on him for their livelihood and their guidance. It was his business to decide their future. By giving them more freedom, as Byron would have it? By thinking of it, at the least.

"You'll not let Johnnie hang," Alice said.

"No. But he'll not stay here. He'll not stay in England. He committed a crime, Alice."

"Transportation? He'd not stand that." Her voice rose. "You may as well hang him."

"Not transportation. I shall drop the charges against him. But he'll go to Barbados. And for the rest of his life."

"And Harry?" Emma asked.

Roger Haggard turned back from the window. "I said I'd drop all charges, Emma."

Emma hesitated, then dried her cheeks. "Aye, well . . ." She glanced at her daughter. "We'd best see if we can find them."

"Do you *want* to find them?" Roger asked.

Emma bit her lip.

"You'll stay here," Roger said. "For as long as you wish." He walked across, took Meg's hands. "Forever. Here is where you belong."

"But you'll stay as well?" Meg asked.

Haggard looked down at his uniform. "Aye. They'll give me a discharge." He squeezed her hand, kissed her on the forehead. "I must go and talk to those people. My people."

About the Author

Christopher Nicole, who currently lives in the Channel Islands, has traveled widely in Europe, the Orient, and the Americas. Other Christopher Nicole novels available in Signet are the best-selling CARIBEE, THE DEVIL'S OWN, MISTRESS OF DARKNESS, BLACK DAWN, and SUNSET, his five-book historical saga of the Caribbean.

Big Bestsellers from SIGNET

- [ ] **THE RAGING WINDS OF HEAVEN** by June Lund Shiplett.
  (#E9439—$2.50)
- [ ] **REAP THE BITTER WINDS** by June Lund Shiplett.
  (#E9517—$2.50)
- [ ] **THE WILD STORMS OF HEAVEN** by June Lund Shiplett.
  (#E9063—$2.50)*
- [ ] **DEFY THE SAVAGE WINDS** by June Lund Shiplett.
  (#E9337—$2.50)*
- [ ] **THE HOUSE OF KINGSLEY MERRICK** by Deborah Hill.
  (#E8918—$2.50)*
- [ ] **THIS IS THE HOUSE** by Deborah Hill. (#E8877—$2.50)
- [ ] **THE PASSIONATE SAVAGE** by Constance Gluyas.
  (#E9195—$2.50)*
- [ ] **MADAM TUDOR** by Constance Gluyas. (#J8953—$1.95)*
- [ ] **THE HOUSE ON TWYFORD STREET** by Constance Gluyas.
  (#E8924—$2.25)
- [ ] **FLAME OF THE SOUTH** by Constance Gluyas.
  (#E8648—$2.50)*
- [ ] **SAVAGE EDEN** by Constance Gluyas. (#E9285—$2.50)
- [ ] **ROGUE'S MISTRESS** by Constance Gluyas. (#E8339—$2.25)
- [ ] **WOMAN OF FURY** by Constance Gluyas. (#E8075—$2.25)*
- [ ] **WINE OF THE DREAMERS** by Susannah Leigh.
  (#E9157—$2.95)
- [ ] **GLYNDA** by Susannah Leigh. (#E8548—$2.50)*
- [ ] **SWEETWATER SAGA** by Roxanne Dent. (#E8850—$2.25)*

* Price slightly higher in Canada

Great Reading from SIGNET

☐ **LOVE IS NOT ENOUGH** by Ruth Lyons. (#E9196—$2.50)*
☐ **LET THE LION EAT STRAW** by Ellease Southerland.
(#J9201—$1.95)*
☐ **STARBRIAR** by Lee Wells. (#E9202—$2.25)*
☐ **LAND OF GOLDEN MOUNTAINS** by Gillian Stone.
(#E9344—$2.50)*
☐ **THE PURPLE AND THE GOLD** by Dorothy Daniels.
(#J9118—$1.95)*
☐ **THE MONEYMAN** by Judith Liederman. (#E9164—$2.75)*
☐ **SINS OF OMISSION** by Chelsea Quinn Yarbro.
(#E9165—$2.25)*
☐ **CALL THE DARKNESS LIGHT** by Nancy Zaroulis.
(#E9291—$2.95)
☐ **GOODBYE, BEVERLY HILLS** by Sandy Hutson.
(#E9300—$2.25)*
☐ **COVENT GARDEN** by Claire Rayner. (#E9301—$2.25)
☐ **ALEXA** by Maggie Osborne. (#E9244—$2.25)*
☐ **SELENA** by Ernest Brawley. (#E9242—$2.75)*
☐ **THE WORLD FROM ROUGH STONES** by Malcolm Macdonald.
(#E8601—$2.50)
☐ **THE RICH ARE WITH YOU ALWAYS** by Malcolm Macdonald.
(#E7682—$2.25)
☐ **SONS OF FORTUNE** by Malcolm Macdonald.
(#E8595—$2.75)*
☐ **ABIGAIL** by Malcolm Macdonald. (#E9404—$2.95)

Buy them at your local

bookstore or use coupon

on next page for ordering.